Who had opened the locked doors of the balcony?

The cold wind swept past me as I moved swiftly from my bed to the doors to fasten them. I stood close to the edge of the balcony, near the railing, and searched the dark. The scraping sound had stopped and it was still now—much too still, for the wind had mysteriously abated. The scent of roses surrounded me.

As I turned to reenter my room, thinking that perhaps I had been mistaken after all, that I had not locked the doors, I raised my head and saw that there was a light shining from the top of the tower. I moved to the center of the balcony and squinted my eyes. I was able to discern a human shape—a man's—that disappeared from view as it strode back and forth, back and forth, in front of the candle, obliterating the light for brief seconds at a time.

I stood on the balcony, watching the tormented person, whoever he was, battling his own private demons and then suddenly, without warning or notice, I felt a force at my back and I stumbled forward into the iron railing. My unslippered foot first touched, then pushed through, the low fence as one of the metal posts broke and gave way. I heard myself scream as I put my hands out in front of me and haphazardly reached out to take hold of something, anything, to steady myself. Just before I lapsed into an abyss of darkness, I smelled the heady odor of musty roses. I cried out once more, and then I felt my body crumple and fall onto the terrace.

DISCOVER THE MAGIC
OF ZEBRA'S REGENCY ROMANCES!

THE DUCHESS AND THE DEVIL   (2264, $2.95)
by Sydney Ann Clary
Though forced to wed Deveril St. John, the notorious "Devil Duke," lovely Byrony Balmaine swore never to be mastered by the irrepressible libertine. But she was soon to discover that the human heart — and Satan — move in very mysterious ways!

AN OFFICER'S ALLIANCE   (2239, $3.95)
by Violet Hamilton
Virginal Ariel Frazier's only comfort in marrying Captain Ian Montague was that it put her in a superb position to spy for the British. But the rakish officer was a proven master at melting a woman's reserve and breaking down her every defense!

BLUESTOCKING BRIDE   (2215, $2.95)
by Elizabeth Thornton
In the Marquis of Rutherson's narrow view, a woman's only place was in a man's bed. Well, beautiful Catherine Harland may have been just a sheltered country girl, but the astonished Marquis was about to discover that she was the equal of any man — and could give as good as she got!

BELOVED AVENGER   (2192, $3.95)
by Mary Brendan
Sir Clifford Moore could never forget what Emily's family had done to him. How ironic that the family that had stolen his inheritance now offered him the perfect means to exact his vengeance — by stealing the heart of their beloved daughter!

A NOBLE MISTRESS   (2169, $3.95)
by Janis Laden
When her father lost the family estate in a game of piquet, practical Moriah Lanson did not hesitate to pay a visit to the winner, the notorious Viscount Roane. Struck by her beauty, Roane suggested a scandalous way for Moriah to pay off her father's debt — by becoming the Viscount's mistress!

Available wherever paperbacks are sold, or order direct from the Publisher. Send cover price plus 50¢ per copy for mailing and handling to Zebra Books, Dept. 2712, 475 Park Avenue South, New York, N.Y. 10016. Residents of New York, New Jersey and Pennsylvania must include sales tax. DO NOT SEND CASH.

LOST ROSES
OF
GANYMEDE HOUSE
CONSTANCE WALKER

ZEBRA BOOKS
KENSINGTON PUBLISHING CORP.

ZEBRA BOOKS

are published by

Kensington Publishing Corp.
475 Park Avenue South
New York, NY 10016

First printing: July, 1989

Printed in the United States of America

For Ben and Ginger,
with love

Chapter 1

"There, Miss, that be Ganymede House in the distance." The driver pointed a bony finger beyond the turn of the road. "Ye can scarcely see the manor from here—there's a bit of mist this morning—but wait a while and you'll see it clear for yourself. Some say the estate is the most beautiful in the whole of Yorkshire."

The carriage turned from the country road onto a private lane lined on both sides by tall stately elms. Once we passed onto the narrow dirt road and were within the confines of the low stone walls that faced the public thoroughfare, I felt chilled; the mist seemed not yet to have dissipated here, as it had across the distance we had just travelled, where the sun had already warmed the cool grounds. The contrast between where I had already been and where I was going now was virtually the same as clear and clouded, or as light and darkness. I shivered in the unexpected coolness and the driver, seeing me draw my cloak around me, tried to make me feel comfortable.

"The sun just takes a bit longer to get here," he said, "but it's something you'll be grateful for when we're in the midst of a hot summer. Then you'll be glad for the respite from the heat." Nevertheless, the man urged the horses on as though he failed to believe his own words and wanted to waste as few moments as possible within the enclosure of the darkened woods.

I had always dreamed of having my own family and my own place in London society, but alas, it was not to be. As the only child of a kindly but inefficient solicitor and his equally kindly but inefficient wife, what should have been an inheritance sufficient to allow me to live in comfortable surroundings turned out, upon the reading of the wills of my parents, to be nonexistent. The inheritance I had heard about during the years I was growing up simply never materialized. Thus, at the age of nineteen, while my friends were preparing for an endless round of parties and balls, I had to consult with my father's partner about terms of employment that would allow me to live a respectable, but diminished, life.

"I'm afraid, my dear Miss Scott," my father's partner, Henry Clayton, said, staring down at my parents' last will and testament, "that your father did not provide for you as adequately as he had wished. He had hoped that the money would be forthcoming so that he could have left an estate for you, but . . ." Mr. Clayton's voice trailed off.

"I know," I said, "my father was not the most astute of men when it came to handling finances."

"But a warm soul," Mr. Clayton interrupted. "He was the noblest of people. His clients came to rely on him and his word."

"But they did not pay him, as you and I know." I took a deep breath and asked the question that I was dreading. "And now, Mr. Clayton, what is to become of me?"

Mr. Clayton shifted slightly in his chair. "I have taken the liberty of investigating some possibilities for you, Miss Scott, all on a confidential basis, to be sure, and have found a few excellent positions that you might find to your liking." He adjusted his glasses and then peered over them at me. "Of course, you don't have to choose immediately . . . you do have income enough to see you through the end of this year and possibly through the beginning months of next."

"Which isn't too much, since it is already September."

"Ah, well. Yes, that's true." He handed me a packet of foolscap on which the names of various people were inscribed. "I remember your father telling me of your accomplishments in the arts and in mathematics," he said. "'Mathematics?' I used to say to him. 'A girl and mathematics?' Well, well." He cleared his throat. "The names are of those who seek a governess for their children. I thought that since you are schooled in these subjects you might want to consider these positions. It is a noble and respectable calling, Miss Scott, and these names are of only the highest quality. I investigated them myself."

I turned the pages. "The Hunts and the Rowes. Are they not connected to Lady Phillips?"

"Yes, I believe they are—on the good lady's side."

"Then it would be impossible for me to accept either of those two positions. Before my parents' deaths I was entertained as a guest in their cousins' homes." I ruffled the papers. "No, that would not be very comfortable nor satisfactory for either of us."

Mr. Clayton pressed his lips together. "Ah, well," he said, "then I'm afraid that only leaves the position at

9

Ganymede House in Yorkshire."

"Indeed it seems that way." I sighed, weary of all the decisions I had made these past weeks.

"You don't need to choose immediately, Miss Scott. Today is Friday. Think about it during the next few days and perhaps we can discuss it further on Monday." He rose, eager to end the distasteful session. He had watched me grow; he and his wife had dined at our house; I had played with his children. Now that it was time for us to end our good acquaintance, it was just as difficult for him as it was for me.

I gathered my handbag and stuffed the sheets of paper into it. "I will let you know," I said and left quickly.

So it was with much trepidation and thought that I approached Ganymede House. It was a drive of about four miles along the private road until we approached the well-kept lawns of the estate and when the main house finally appeared, no longer shrouded in mist, I caught my breath. It was as Mr. Clayton had described it. Indeed, it was more than the driver had promised; Ganymede House was one of the most beautiful places I had ever seen and I marvelled that so few people in my former association had ever visited there or had ever spoken of it.

Once we emerged from the woods, I saw that the grounds were manicured low; the dark green colour of the grass was still vivid although it was already well into autumn. As we drove on the dirt road gave way to white crushed stone paths leading up to and around the manor, and to an intricate maze of boxwoods and evergreen shrubs off to one side.

The main house was three-storied and was without the elaborately carved ornamentation associated with houses nearer to London. The simplicity of the lines and arches of the dark brick and stone house served to show to full advantage the splendor of the intricately appointed leaded windows and gables that topped the structure, but the eyes of the viewer tended at first to ignore these features, for attached to the house, rising high above the manor, was a massive stone tower covered with ivy, much like a section of a medieval castle. That it was older than the main house was obvious, but the side-by-side proximity of the two structures shocked the eyes first with disbelief and then with beauty as the sun reflected off the limestone edifice.

Beyond the house, tower, and vast expanse of lawn, the mist still hung low, obscuring the view of the horizon. Almost as if in answer to an unasked question, the coachman spoke of it. "Where the fog is, Miss, there be the cliffs. A right beautiful sight, you'll see, and folks tell me that it's one of the best places to watch the sea. You be sure to go and view them, Miss."

Again I involuntarily shuddered, for I have never enjoyed watching the moving waters, but knowing the man expected me to answer I did so. "I shall certainly have time enough," I answered shortly.

The coachman pulled up at the entrance of the house and had already opened the door of the carriage when the huge wooden door of the manor house swung open and a man I judged to be in his late sixties came out to greet me. There was a puzzled look on his face as I stepped from the carriage and introduced myself.

"I'm Miss Scott. Miss Sarah Scott. I've been engaged as governess for the children," I explained.

The man still seemed perplexed. "We weren't expecting you until next week, Miss."

"But my letter to Mr. Grayson . . . Has it not arrived?"

"Ah, that explains it, Miss. Mr. Oliver is away—has been these past weeks and he hasn't seen to his mail. It's all still lying on the table in the Great Hall." He smiled now, a kindly fatherly expression that was meant to reassure me, "We'll never you mind, Miss, Mrs. Keanne and I will be welcoming you." He picked up two satchels. "If you'll follow me, Miss Scott, we'll get you inside. Have you eaten today?"

"Yes, thank you. We stopped for breakfast at daybreak when we changed horses."

The old man looked up at the sun in the sky. "Aye, but that's been more than five hours. Come along." He turned to the driver who was still unloading my trunks. "I'll send help and you can refresh your horses in the stable while you join the hands at lunch."

"I'd be obliged," the horseman said, touching his cap. "Good day, Miss."

Inside the large rectangular entry hall, Mrs. Keanne, the wife to the gentleman who greeted me, came forward.

"A mix-up in the times," her husband explained, introducing me. "I was telling her about the Master not being here."

The small angular woman looked me over. "Did you tell her that Mr. Oliver won't be home until tomorrow evening?"

"Haven't had a chance yet." He turned to me. "Bertie's right, the Master's not due until tomorrow."

"And the children?"

"With their father."

"I see." I followed Mr. Keanne up the stairs while his wife walked behind me.

"The Blue Room, Mr. Keanne, if you please. I've already opened the curtains and aired it out and I'm sure Miss Scott will be comfortable there." We turned left at the second floor landing. "The children's wing is at the end of the hall, next to your room. Master's chambers and the guest wings are to the right."

Mr. Keanne stopped at a doorway and turned the brass handle. "This is your room, Miss. I'm sure you'll find it to your liking."

His wife waited until I entered the room and looked around before following me. "The linen's fresh," she said, indicating the bed. "There is a goodly supply of candles," she continued, pulling out a drawer of a small bedtable to show me the tray of fat white tapers. "Mr. Keanne will build you a fire later to take the chill out of the room." She looked at her husband. "Of course, we won't be needing it until this evening." She pulled the bedspread taut, smoothing it although there had not been any discernible folds in it. "Luncheon is always at noon and supper at eight o'clock. Mr. Oliver prefers to take the evening meal with the children unless, of course, there are guests, and I expect he will ask you to join him. He breakfasts alone at half past seven while the children are served in their quarters at the same time. The Master prefers his morning and afternoon meals quiet. Breakfast, luncheon, and tea are served in the schoolroom and you'll be overseeing the children like the other governess, I expect. High tea is at four o'clock. As to your duties and obligations, Mr. Oliver will explain those when he meets you." She turned toward the door. "I'll leave you now and send up Tillie to help you unpack." She looked at my two cases. "If you need her."

"There are two other trunks on the stage," I

13

volunteered, lest she think that I came to Ganymede House without proper clothing and accessories. Orphan I was, but beggar I was not.

"Mr. Keanne will bring them along shortly. I will serve you luncheon in one hour in the small dining room, if that suits you *today*," she said, stressing the last word so that I knew I was allowed that special privilege only because of the oversight of my arrival time, but with the implication that I was not to expect it again.

"Thank you, Mrs. Keanne, that suits me very well." I waited until I heard the door click before I turned around to survey my new room. I was pleased to find that the paper on the walls was of a cheery blue floral design, intermingled with green leaves and golden butterflies. On the bed the counterpane was of a deeper blue, almost matching the braided rag rugs on the highly polished wooden floors. At the windows, crisp white sheer curtains fell from ceiling to floor and were held back at the center by brass circles. The cornices and draperies were fashioned from a heavy deep blue velvet, not quite matching, but in fact quite complementary to the colours of the rugs, and these, too, were fastened by matching brass circlets.

In front of one of the windows, facing outside, was a small wooden and brass appointed desk, its top completely outfitted with blotting paper, pen and ink, and sealing wax.

Between the two windows were curtained French doors that opened onto a small balcony, but they were locked. I decided that tomorrow would be soon enough to ask Mrs. Keanne for a key to open them. I felt my relationship with the housekeeper to be precarious, although I knew not why, and I did not want to do anything to upset the balance.

There were two small lady's chairs covered in green velvet flanking the fireplace on the side wall, and I saw that a great walnut armoire had been readied for my clothes. All the wood pieces, including the bedstead, smelled of lemon and cedar and tucked away in the various drawers were scented evergreen shavings.

The entire effect of the room was not unpleasant; indeed, it was rather cheerful considering the lack of a fire, and I was determined that with a few of my personal effects—a picture of my parents, a fan that I carried at my last cotillion, and several other trinkets from my former home—placed discreetly atop the tables and fireplace mantle, this room would serve me well as my residence.

I sat down on the bed, but jumped up quickly at the sound of knocking, fearful that Mrs. Keanne would find me in the act of resting when she thought I should be unpacking my clothes.

"Come in," I said and instead of the small woman I had already met, a young girl, fresh-faced and smiling, entered.

"I'm Tillie, Miss, the upstairs maid," she said curtsying. "I've come to help you settle in."

"Yes, well, thank you, Tillie," I answered. At least this young maiden, I thought, seemed pleasant enough and together we both carefully emptied out the valises and trunks into the drawers and closet, finishing just a few moments before I heard the clock strike twelve. By trial and error I found my way to the small dining room where I was to lunch.

The table was set for one, and when I sat down Mrs. Keanne entered the room, a silver serving dish in her

15

hand. "It's a simple meal," she said unapologetically. "We weren't expecting you." The statement sounded like a rebuke.

"I'm sorry I'm putting you to the trouble." Mrs. Keanne did not reply, instead waiting until I had taken the creamed vegetables on toast onto my own dish.

"I'll leave the service on the sideboard, Miss Scott," she said, "along with the fruit and tea." She indicated a large piece of carved oak furniture set against a far wall.

"Thank you," I said, once more knowing that there could be no other appropriate answer and Mrs. Keanne, having accomplished her required duties, left the room. Despite my confusion I was able to eat all that was upon my plate. I was indeed hungry and the lukewarm reception I had encountered, instead of causing me to lose my appetite, only served to make me hungrier and I ate not only the vegetables but two pieces of fruit from the crystal bowl.

When I finished the meal and the tea, I moved to an adjoining room, hoping to further investigate my new residence, but I got no further than a long narrow corridor—a picture gallery, I realized—and I walked slowly past the rows of portraits not recognizing any of the twenty or thirty oils that hung on the walls. They were mostly of gentlemen, all looking the same except for their costumes, and all having one thing in common: a shock of grey hair that seemed to grow counter to the rest of the black hair on their heads.

I stepped forward in order to examine the portraits more closely, but just then Mr. Keanne entered the room, and I did not want to seem too inquisitive on this, my first day at Ganymede House.

"Those are all Graysons," he said. "That one you're

looking at now—he's Mr. Oliver's great-grandfather and some around here say he was a harsh, but just, Master."

I wanted to ask him about the present lord of the manor but I hesitated for fear that he would think me a gossip and instead remarked on the picture in front of me. "Their hair . . ." I began and Mr. Keanne bowed slightly.

"Aye, that's the mark of a Grayson. People say all the males have had it. They're born with it. Leastways, all till now," he said shaking his head. "But, if you're through with lunch, Miss, perhaps you'd like to walk the grounds. It's a lovely day, clear and crisp. We won't be getting too many more of them now." He opened the doors to the hall and I meekly followed. I gathered that neither Mr. nor Mrs. Keanne were too happy about having their last day before the Master arrived home spoiled by the intrusion of a new governess, and I quickly retired to my own room to fetch a suitable cloak and bonnet to walk the grounds of Ganymede.

Chapter 2

Despite the fact that I was excited and apprehensive, I was able to fall asleep once I had eaten the supper provided by Mrs. Keanne. Again, the meal was solitary— Mr. and Mrs. Keanne remaining in the kitchen—and since the fires had not been lit in the dining room nor in the adjacent sitting room, I supposed that I was not expected to linger. I took this hint and withdrew early to my room.

I spent a few moments sorting out my clothes in the drawers and cupboards but I was more tired than I had expected and I fell asleep without even having time to think about my new home and my new charges. Whatever was to come would come and since I no longer was in a position to direct my own fortunes, I had resolved not to remonstrate with whatever the fates had intended for me and to accept what was to be.

I was awakened by the sound of activity outside my windows but I paid it little heed, after all I was a stranger to the house and the customs of it. I could distinguish the trotting of horses' hooves, and low muffled voices, and the closing and opening of doors, but to tell the truth, the journey had exhausted me and I fell asleep again. When I awoke once more it was quite dark and still. The fire in the grate had died down and only tiny glowing embers were left among the ashes. The room had become chilly. I reached for the candle on my bedstead and struck a match, holding it until it ignited the wick and when it was lit I held my fingers close to it, capturing the small amount of heat within my cupped hands.

I waited, remembering that the large wooden clock in the foyer struck every fifteen minutes and when at last it did, I was surprised to hear only two strikes. Because of my excitement I was now no longer sleepy and I knew that this, my first night at Ganymede, was to be a long night. Although I abhorred the extravagance of wasting a candle I felt more comfortable with the miniscule light flickering beside my bed.

I mused on all that I had seen so far—the lovely well-tended grounds, the numerous fading rose gardens, the kitchen garden still fragrant with the last unpicked leaves and flowers of herbs and spices, and for want of a better term, the many moods of the exterior of Ganymede House. Where care had been taken, as in the gardens and lawns, there seemed to be an air of contentment. I had watched several species of chirping birds flying over— no doubt on their annual winter journey—sometimes landing to pull a worm from the ground or pluck a seed from a flower. But where the woods began at the front of the estate and to the side of it, next to the tower, it was almost as if unhappiness hung like an unseen screen, forbidding anyone who approached the house or the huge old trees to find joy or cause to be happy.

Even I, a stranger, seemed repelled by the feeling and I

felt no urgency to investigate nor to walk near the woods. There would be other days, I reasoned, and I used the excuse to see only the immediate surroundings at first.

I had intended to inspect the outside of the tower, but by the time I had finished wandering through a small ornamental boxwood maze and gotten lost in it twice, it was growing dark. When I returned to the house I had barely time enough to refresh myself before the evening meal was placed on the table.

I sat up in bed and looked around hoping to find a book to read, but with the exception of the well-worn black Bible on the table, there was nothing else. I remembered that downstairs, in an area adjoining the Great Hall, was the library. I put on my wrapper, tying it tightly around me lest I should meet someone even at this late hour, and decided to make my way there in order to procure some reading material to pass away the hours. No one was in the darkened hall and despite my candlestick I had to grope my way, trailing my hand against the wainscotting of the carpeted passageway until it led me to the stairs where I was able to cling to the wooden bannister as I began silently to descend.

I had hardly stepped onto the stairs when I heard a noise coming from a room below me, off the foyer, as though someone had stumbled or a chair had overturned. I quickly turned back and up the steps to the hallway, but not before I heard the fumblings of a door handle as it was being pulled open. Without a second thought, I extinguished the candle, fearing that a member of the household would see me. As I had not calculated the number of steps to the landing nor the paces to my room, and because it was dark in the house, I had to retrace my way, slowly and deliberately, fearful that one misstep would betray me.

I heard heavy footsteps on the parquet floor of the foyer—hesitant, almost stumbling—and then dulled sounds as someone climbed the carpeted stairs. Evidently the nocturnal walker was much more accustomed to the house than I and was able to negotiate the steps much quicker. There was another stumbling sound as though someone had misjudged a step and just as I reached the hall I saw by the light of the quarter moon filtering through the Great Hall front windows a shadow of a man, and I pressed myself close to the wall, holding my breath so that whoever it was would not see or hear me. The person had no candle to light the way which made my presence undetectable.

Fortunately, whoever it was turned the other way, toward the guest wings, and I waited until I briefly saw the glow of a lamp within one of the chambers as a door was opened and closed. Then I continued my way back to my room. I heard another soft click from down below, and light footsteps, sure and steady, move off and away from the foyer to another part of the downstairs.

I stayed awake the rest of the night, thinking about the shadow I had seen, speculating about it, coming to no conclusions, and eventually reading some of my favorite verses from the Good Book. Thus it was that when I was awakened by a knock on the door by Tillie bringing me my morning tea, my arm felt numb and I realized that the big black Bible had rested across my forearm when I had once again fallen asleep.

"Good morning, Ma'am," Tillie said curtsying and putting the tea tray on the table. "Master has asked that you meet with him this morning at breakfast." Tillie curtsied again and turned to leave the room.

"I didn't know Mr. Grayson was home. Mr. Keanne said he would be returning this evening."

"I don't know about that, Ma'am. Mrs. Keanne just asked me to deliver the message to you." She curtsied once more and left.

I drank my tea hastily, not wanting to keep my new employer waiting, and when I had washed my face and put on my dark grey dress, I made my way to the dining room. As I passed the nursery I stopped briefly to hear any sounds that might be forthcoming from a room with two children, but hearing none, continued on my way down to meet my new Master.

Mr. Grayson was seated at the far end of the table, eating his breakfast and reading a journal of some sort, and when I entered the room I waited at the door so that he might have the honour of opening our conversation. I remained so a few seconds and when his attention was not forthcoming I descreetly coughed so that he would know I was there. He looked up and saw me and put down his knife and fork and half-rose from his chair.

"Miss Scott? Please join me," he said. I took a chair at the opposite end of the table but he shook his head. "No, not that seat, if you please," and indicated one closer to him. "Will you have some breakfast?"

"Yes, thank you," I answered as he rang for Mr. Keanne who came and served me.

"I am sorry I wasn't here to welcome you—a mix-up in schedules, I understand. Even my own plans changed abruptly yesterday." He picked up a letter I recognized to be on Mr. Clayton's stationery and briefly read it. "I understand you are schooled especially in mathematics and the arts."

"Yes."

23

"As you know I have two children, Miss Scott—a daughter, Antonia, who was six just last month, and a son, Virgil, who will celebrate his eighth birthday in the spring. I require that they be educated, Ma'am, Virgil to be able to make his way in the world, and my daughter to be able to understand the necessary art of running a manor home. Toward that end I would like them to know the basics of reading, writing, at least simple mathematics for Antonia, higher for Virgil, of course . . ." He stopped and looked at me. "You do know higher mathematics?" he asked.

"Yes, Sir, I have been schooled in Euclidean geometry and beyond that," I answered and Mr. Grayson raised his dark bushy eyebrows in disbelief.

"There aren't many women . . ." he began and then broke off, returning to the subject of his children and my duties. "I expect both my children to know the proper manners of the day, the correct forms of attire, some history of our country and our shire and, most certainly, of the Grayson family." At the mention of the last two I started to speak, but he silenced me by holding up his hand. "I realize, Miss Scott, that you are a stranger to our area and about my family you know nothing. Therefore I will send several books to your room, if I may, explaining the features of Yorkshire, which I may tell you, are fascinating for all readers of history. You will find the countryside and the customs quite lovely and perhaps, in your eagerness to learn and understand them, you may impart your knowledge and your discoveries to the children. Sometimes, through the eyes and view of an outsider one is presented with a better perspective for the familiar.

"About the Graysons, you are ignorant," he said and I

sat up straighter in my chair at his choice of word, dismayed that his presumption was wrong since he did not allow me to explain that I had indeed done some reading about the family. But he continued, unaware of my thoughts. "I also have reading material about my ancestors—journals, diaries, letters. It's an illustrious family, Ma'am, with its usual array of Kings' enemies and friends, blackguards, squires, etc. We are like most English families except that we lack, Miss Scott, a disproportionate amount of sacredness in dealing with our forebears," he said quite reasonably while I smiled slightly. "We recognize that there is good and evil, honor . . ." here he looked away for a brief second, "and dishonor, in all proper families," and again I started at his choice of words, "but we do strongly adhere to *noblesse oblige*, Ma'am, when dealing with the country-people and the workers on the estate."

He paused for just a moment. "About the children. I am sure you are better equipped to deal with them than myself, having probably been around small children more often than I." I did not contradict him, but if truth were known, my only contact with young people was through the association of my friends' nieces and nephews and of course, my own childhood. But I already felt that Mr. Grayson was accurate in this logic, I did seem to be more suited to dealing with young people than he.

"What I want for my children, Miss Scott," he said leaning forward slightly toward me, "is for them to discern and choose the correct things in this world; to have respect for themselves and others; to be able to converse in society; to have appreciation for the arts and cultures of the world; and, of course, to honor their family." He sat back and stared at me. "That is what I wish for my children," he said. "Do I make myself understood?"

"Yes, Sir, you do. It is what any father would normally wish for his children."

"I do not know what other parents normally wish or do not wish for their children, Miss Scott. I only know what I want—nay, what I demand—of my own." Mr. Grayson's countenance remained calm, unfurrowed, yet I could tell that this admonition came from a very impassioned man and I quickly changed my words to sooth the situation so that he not think me a dissenter to his guidelines.

"Of course. I will most certainly respect your wishes in the training of your children."

"About the background of the children, what you must know, Miss Scott, is that their mother, my wife, has been dead for a year. The children rarely speak of her now. In fact, I suppose they don't even recall her." He said it so evenly I wondered at the emotion that must have lain underneath the surface, but I had no time to ponder it, for he quickly continued. "Of their education, Virgil has always shown an aptitude for numbers which is why I specified that their new governess be knowledgeable in that subject. He has had formal schooling since the age of five. The governess preceding you taught him elementary numbers, grammar, history and some geography of the world. He is very eager to learn and, I'm told, very quick." He looked at me and then continued.

"Antonia has shown, so far, no special predisposition toward anything save her playthings although she has been in the schoolroom for a year. She has mastered simple numbers and the spelling of words appropriate to her age. Both the children have a passing knowledge of Italian. My wife was enamored of the language and was quite fluent in it and taught them simple phrases." He looked up. "Do you happen to know the language?"

"I am fluent in it, yes. And, of course, French."

"Good. I would prefer for them to speak the Gallic tongue and am not inclined to further their education in Italian. In fact, I would prefer them not to speak the language in my presence."

I nodded. Mr. Grayson, I was beginning to understand, had very definite opinions as to what constituted the education of a young person.

"Both children are quiet and obedient and I will put at your disposal, Miss Scott, the report I received from their previous governess. She, I might add, left our employ after three very satisfactory years in order to marry a widower." He glanced down once more to Mr. Clayton's letter. "I see you have recently lost your parents and your home. About your parents, I extend my condolences. Of your home, Ganymede House offers you comfortable rooms, the grounds, and food and warmth. On the days you are not charged with my children, you may have at your disposal a carriage and horses to go wherever you choose. Whatever luxuries we enjoy here we will gladly share with you." He looked up briefly, nodded curtly as though to reinforce his words, and continued, "I am obliged to be away several days a month while I attend to my properties and on those days Mr. and Mrs. Keanne will manage the household. They have been with me . . . with Ganymede . . . for many years and have done an excellent job and you will not be required to do anything except your specific duties. I reiterate, Ma'am, that I expect nothing more from you than for you to properly educate my daughter and son."

"I understand, Sir."

"Good. Do you have questions?"

"Yes, a few. If I run into problems," I began, but was again stopped in midsentence.

"I don't foresee any, but if you do, please either bring them to my attention, or deal with them yourself. I don't believe in corporal punishment, Miss Scott."

"Nor do I, Sir!" I answered, insulted that he even thought me capable of physically assaulting a child. "I believe there are much more decent and effective ways."

"Quite. I gather the wages are satisfactory."

"Yes, Sir, Mr. Clayton has already explained them to me."

He started to replace the letter into its envelope. "If there are no other—"

"Just one, Sir. Will you introduce me to the children?"

Mr. Grayson seemed surprised at the request. "No, it is not necessary that I be there when you meet them. Mrs. Keanne will take you up when you have done with breakfast." He looked at me. "Is there anything else?"

"I think not." He returned to his reading matter, never glancing my way again, and as I sat there, eating yet another solitary meal, I took the opportunity to appraise my new employer who neither expected nor wanted table talk.

He was not an unattractive man; indeed I imagine in his circle of intimates, both male and female, he would be considered handsome. He was a big man, neither ruddy not light complexioned, and I attributed the colour to his being active in the outdoors as befitting a gentleman. His eyes were dark, deep-set, and he had a straight nose above a determined mouth that had not, since I had met him this past hour, relaxed into a smile. In fact, if one were to remark of any lines or creases in his face, they were all of a downturn pattern, as though he was not inclined to laugh too much or too often. He was a man, I gauged, who was preoccupied with unhappiness.

He sat straight in his chair and held the paper to the side of him as he read. I could see the characteristic Grayson forelock of grey as it swirled counter to the rest of his black hair. It was by far his most endearing feature, for I could find no evidence of compassion in his manner. Ganymede may present me with all the creature comforts as he articulated, but I had noticed that he never mentioned the word *companionship* when describing my relations with either him or the children. But then I suppose, companionship was foreign to a man of Mr. Grayson's temperament. It was as though *noblesse oblige* filtered down to everyone on the estate, including me, but beyond that, simple courtesies such as welcoming me warmly to his home were not thought of, nor extended, although I took it as a compliment that he did not ask me about my own accomplishments in light of the fact that I was to teach them to his children.

I finished with my breakfast and waited for him to acknowledge the fact that I was ready to leave the table. Finally, as he was turning a page in his reading, he happened to glance up and saw me sitting there with my hands folded in my lap.

"Would you care for more tea?"

"No, thank you. I've had sufficient."

"Then," he said ringing for his housekeeper, "I shall ask Mrs. Keanne to show you the way to the nursery." I thanked him and took my leave. Mr. Grayson rose automatically, yet never fully acknowledged that I had left the room.

Chapter 3

Having met their father I had no idea how the children would treat me and when Mrs. Keanne showed me into the nursery I was quite surprised to see the two of them already seated at the school table, their hands folded in front of them, their eyes raised toward me. As I entered they both stood, in respectful silence, while the housekeeper made the introductions.

The young boy made a bow from the waist. "How do you do, Ma'am?"

"Very well, thank you, Virgil." I turned to the young girl who curtsied.

"Good morning, Ma'am," she said in a soft voice.

"Good morning to you, Antonia." I nodded to the housekeeper. "Thank you for introducing us, Mrs. Keanne. I'm sure we'll get along fine." The housekeeper understood that I was dismissing her and that the nursery was my domain.

"Very good, Ma'am. Now Master Virgil and Miss Antonia, mind Miss Scott and there'll be a treat for tea," she said as she left and I was struck by the gentleness in her voice.

"Well," I said, after the housekeeper left, "Please sit down." The young girl obeyed but Virgil remained standing and I looked around for a chair near the table. When I was seated, Virgil then sat, thereby letting me know that he already was quite skilled at proper manners. "Well," I repeated myself looking out toward the window, "since you and I don't know each other and since it is a lovely day outside, perhaps you would join me in a walk around the grounds so that we might share information about ourselves."

The children looked at me and then away, their hands again folded in front of them, neither of them displaying signs of the delight I had anticipated.

"Would you like that?" I asked while both looked straight ahead. "Or is it that you don't like an occasional half-holiday from the schoolroom?" I smiled but it seemed to be wasted as the children still did not react. I tried once more, hoping that they would respond to the idea and to me. "I do think some fresh air is quite in order as part of the schoolday, don't you?" Antonia nodded her golden head and the ringlets fell across her eyes so that she had to unclasp her hands to hastily brush them back.

"If you think so, Ma'am," Virgil said, "a walk would be quite nice this morning."

At last, a slight breakthrough. "Then why don't you show me where your wraps are kept and we will get ready."

To anyone observing us strolling around the grounds, we probably made a charming picture, two beautiful children and a young woman enjoying the weather, but as one of the participants the portrait was slightly askew. The children were quiet and respectful and answered the

32

general questions I put to them, but they added neither words nor thoughts, and when I would try to get them to elaborate on their comments on such small topics as the weather or the flowers, there were awkward silences. I did not know whether they did not know the answers to my questions or simply did not wish to talk. They were much like their father in this respect—they wasted no words and sadly, I noted, no emotions. What would gladden most people, a free hour among nature, did not seem to touch them, and I felt great disappointment.

We walked toward the woods, the white gravel of the pathway crunching beneath our feet. "Well," I said, "shall one of you tell me about yourself or shall I begin?"

Silence again.

"Alright then, perhaps I should start. First, my Christian name is Sarah and I come from London." I turned to Virgil. "Have you ever visited there?" and when there was no response I continued, explaining the London of my childhood and the way I remembered it. The combination of the crisp morning air, the recollections of an untroubled life, and my sudden uprooting made my voice waver for just the briefest of moments, and suddenly I had a wish that I were not here at Ganymede but in my own lovely part of London with my own friends.

But as I looked down at my two charges with their somber faces and their correct but stiff manner, I suddenly had a feeling of pity for them and all thoughts of my own small predicament fluttered away with the wind. Already I was intrigued by these two sober children.

"Tell me," I said to Virgil, "what you like to do at Ganymede on such fair days as this?" The young boy made no reply, yet I pursued. "Do you kite?" I suggested as a gust of wind ruffled my cape. "Or, perhaps you enjoy painting or drawing or music?"

Silence still, not disrespectful, but for want of a better clarifying word, a cautious silence. "Well, perhaps you will tell me what it is that you like best." I was careful to keep my voice soft as I did not want to upset the children, and we walked, the three of us, silent for a few moments. I had made up my mind not to press any other questions upon the children; clearly they were disconcerted by my probings, when suddenly Antonia looked at me, her ringlets peeping through the front of her bonnet.

"Virgil likes to go boating."

"What a lively pastime. I often enjoyed sailing on a lake in Scotland when I was in the country on vacations. Do you boat often?"

"Only when Cousin Edward is here." Virgil looked back at the house. "He's really our father's cousin," he amended. "He comes to see us sometimes when he's in the vicinity. He doesn't live in Yorkshire."

"Well, perhaps he will come once more before the cold weather sets in so that you may go boating," I suggested to the boy.

"Yes, Ma'am," he answered and that was the last he was to say about his cousin or his recreation.

We walked one turn around the front of the house in total silence except for my occasional comment about the day, and when I told the children that it was time to return to the classroom there was no remonstrating or pleading to remain just one more moment, and the three of us quietly climbed the stairs to the schoolrooms.

What a strange pair they were, I thought, as I watched them silently take off their cloaks and hang them on their pegs. I had expected giggling, furtive whisperings, or childish silliness, but none of these were forthcoming.

34

My position as governess seemed quite easy in this respect for I understood there would be no disobedience, but I did so wish for less reticence and more childlike qualities in these two young ones. Their quietness disturbed me and I vowed that I would not only try to teach them their school lessons but perhaps also some lessons in the art of being a child.

After luncheon and the short rest I thought would be best for my charges, we returned to the business of school and I was surprised and delighted to find that both children were rather quick learners. Though they offered me no help in ascertaining at what level they were in their studies, I had the guidelines set by their previous governess and it was but a simple step to resume the children's education. I encountered no resistance to the lessons and much to my delight I found that the children rather enjoyed their studies. Virgil, especially. I was able to detect a rare show of emotion when I spoke of poetry and at one point the boy even astounded me by reciting a line from one of Mr. Keats's odes.

"Ah, I see you know the poem," I said smiling at Virgil, who immediately became quiet and inward once again, and I secretly berated myself for going too fast in trying to gain his confidence. Young children, I knew, liked to take their time about forming friendships and allegiances and I had to restrain myself lest I appear either too dominant or too demanding.

"Virgil learned that from . . ." Antonia began but at a glance from Virgil put a small hand in front of her mouth.

"From . . .?" I asked.

"I forgot, Ma'am," the child said looking down at her hands. Thus I learned that Antonia was not only her brother's spokesman, but also his secret-keeper. Well, I thought, let them at least have that little game to themselves. If I were to intrude into what I felt was their last bastion of privacy I feared I should lose whatever respect I had from the children.

"So," I said, "now that I know you are familiar with the poem, perhaps you would enjoy trying your hand at writing one of your own." Neither responded. "Come, come, children, pick up your pencils and I shall help you. It need be only two lines. What shall we write about, Antonia? A pet, perhaps? Do you like dogs? Or horses?" Each time the little girl shook her head.

"She does, too." Virgil now answered for his sister. "She had a special pony."

"Thank you, Virgil," I said, "Then perhaps, Antonia, you can write about your pony." At that the child dropped her pencil and I could see tears glistening at the corners of her eyes. "My dear child, surely you aren't crying about the task. No, come," I said, walking close to her desk, "I shall help you. It's quite easy and it's fun," I said trying to cajole her. "Tell me your pony's name. Perhaps we can rhyme it."

The child brushed at her eyes, smearing the charcoal from the pencil across her cheek. "He's not my pony anymore. I'm not allowed to ride him. No even with Old Martin."

"But why not?"

"Father says I'm not to ride until I'm older." The young girl sniffed away her tears.

"Well," I answered, "perhaps we can do something about that. Perhaps if I tell him that I'm quite accomplished with horses, he will allow me to teach you and you will have your pony once again."

The child's eyes brightened and I could see that while

36

there was no outward show of acceptance, I had at least earned a measure of Virgil's respect by trying to placate his sister. Already I knew that these two children acted as one, each protective of the other, each feeling some unspoken sense of loss, and I wondered if Mr. Oliver might be wrong—that perhaps the children, even though they were indeed quite young, remembered and missed their mother.

After I had dismissed my charges from their studies and saw to it that both were washed and changed, Tillie brought in the tea and sandwiches, and, true to her word, Mrs. Keanne had sent up a generous portion of iced pound cake for a treat. I cut the slices and the three of us ate the sweet although not even polite conversation took place in the hot, stuffy room. I felt that I had already tried too hard to prove myself to the children and thought that the best course would be to wait until they had a chance to warm to me slowly and on their own terms.

When we were through I excused myself from their company, leaving both of them with the free time I knew all children needed. I retired to my room, read for a few moments, prepared for tomorrow's lessons in the classroom, and took a short rest before I dressed for my first supper with the Grayson family.

I was not apprehensive about it. I had already taken one meal with the children and while it was uncomfortable and silent, it was not unendurable. Surely, I thought, their father will teach them the art of dinner table conversation, and I prepared my dress, assuring myself that I would do my part in the social form of discourse.

Mr. Grayson was standing by the door as my charges

and I entered, and after the automatic courtesy of escorting me to my chair, the same one he had asked me to sit in in the morning, he summoned Mr. Keanne who began serving us.

Mr. Grayson spoke once to Antonia, asking the child about her lessons, and once to Virgil, reminding him of an incident that had happened the previous week. Both children responded in polite voices—the lack of affection apparent even to me, a stranger—but their father seemed not to notice.

While we waited for the second course, my employer looked toward me. "I hope you found everything in order and to your liking, Miss Scott."

"Yes, quite so, thank you. The children are very good in the schoolroom." Mr. Grayson merely nodded and although there were ample opportunities to speak or to ask questions throughout the course of the meal, the three Graysons—father and offspring—exchanged no more words. What manner of family was this, I wondered, that had nothing to say to each other? As I ate I was surprised to find that I, too, hesitated to speak. Whatever it was, I realized I also had already fallen under the spell of Ganymede.

After the meal was finished the children were excused and as was the custom that was explained to me, Mrs. Keanne took them to their rooms and saw to it that they were bedded. When I started to leave with the children, Mr. Grayson stayed his hand, indicating that I was to remain and I believed him about to converse with me.

I was wrong. Mr. Grayson poured himself a glass of port, offered me tea, and sat back in his chair studying the cutwork of the crystal goblet as it reflected the candlelight. For a full half-hour we remained thus, neither of us speaking, my employer hardly acknowledging my presence. When at last he had finished his wine, he rose, extended his arm and led me into the small adjoining sitting room. I sat close to the fire, for the house had begun to grow chilly, and when I was settled, Mr. Grayson bowed. "I wish you a good evening, Ma'am," he said and left me sitting there where I remained, confounded, for a few minutes until I heard Mr. Keanne approach.

"I shall retire," I told the elderly gentleman as I made my way to the stairs. "I trust that it will be right with your Master."

"Yes, Ma'am," he said extinguishing the candles and already beginning to stoke the fires and I knew not whether he had witnessed the puzzling action of his master.

I returned to my room and sat at my desk. This is indeed a strange family, I thought, that has no intercourse and, disturbingly, no laughter. I took up my pen to write in my day book, but I was apparently more tired than I had suspected and as I lay down in my bed in the dark I had barely begun to recount the events of the day before I fell asleep.

Chapter 4

By the time Tillie had knocked on my door to awaken me on this, my third day at Ganymede, I had already been up for close to an hour, eager to get to my charges. I had formulated a plan in my head, one that I thought might help the children and me to become, if not friends, then at least somewhat more than just governess and pupils. I proposed to speak to Mr. Grayson about Antonia resuming her riding and perhaps to ask him if he would take Virgil boating before the frost sets in. What better way, I thought in my own exuberance and with happy memories of my own dear mother and father to bolster me, for son and sire to become familiar. And the more I thought of my plan the more determined I was to broach it to Mr. Grayson as soon as possible, perhaps this evening at supper.

I entered the nursery and again the two children were sitting silently at the table, their hands folded. When I closed the door I saw that the breakfast dishes had been laid on the sideboard and were awaiting me. We bowed our heads in prayer for I understood this to be the custom, and when the children had uttered their "Amens" I inquired as to whether they had always eaten breakfast with their governess.

Antonia shook her head and Virgil spoke so quietly I had trouble hearing him. "No, Ma'am, we ate with our parents all the time," and when I raised my eyebrows questioning the statement, he finished. "Before our Mother died."

"I'm sorry," I said sympathetically, "I did not wish to remind you of unpleasant memories."

Virgil looked at me, his dark eyes defiant. "They were not unpleasant memories, Ma'am," he said in a spirited voice and once again I questioned whether Mr. Grayson's ideas about his children and their mother were correct. It was something else I decided to speak to him about, but I could hardly yet introduce the subject since I was still a stranger to the family. Perhaps in the coming months I might find a way to speak of the family sadness.

Our school lessons went well and I found Virgil quite bright and determined to achieve. Mr. Grayson's estimate of Antonia, however, was quite correct, for the young girl was much more interested in her dolls and toys, though she did try hard and never fussed at the work I gave her. She was rather young, I thought, to be kept at schoolbooks for so long a period and I was sure that some compromise could be worked that would allow her more time to entertain herself and exercise her own imagination.

In the afternoon, after tea, I asked the children if they would like to accompany me on another walk in the gardens but no sooner had we put on our apparel than the skies clouded and we heard the sound of heavy rain on the windows. "Well," I said taking off my bonnet, "it was a rather good idea but I'm afraid we shall have to postpone our outing." The children seemed neither disappointed nor pleased for they still were paying me odd deference. "Perhaps you would care to show me around Ganymede House?" I suggested. "I have been here for only a few days and I have yet to see the entire house. And what better way to see it than to have as my guides two who have lived here all their lives." I smiled at the children but we were back to solemnity as when we first met and they did not reply, so I thought it best not to pursue the idea. "But of course, we can always see it some other time or I can view it at my leisure. I am sure we all have other things to do," I said, fearing that I was still, in both Antonia's and Virgil's minds, not to be trusted.

I went to my room and stood at the window as the rain pelted onto the small balcony outside and I made a mental note to ask Mrs. Keanne for the key to unlock the French doors. Why the doors were secured I could not comprehend, for there was certainly no danger of intrusion. The balcony was a good thirty feet above ground and though there were tall rhododendron bushes close to the house, they could hardly support the weight of a fully grown person should an intruder settle on our manor. Perhaps, I thought, Mrs. Keanne had closed the doors against the drafty weather and in my hasty arrival she simply forgot to open them and leave me a key.

The rainclouds had greyed the sky even more and when the chimes heralded the five o'clock hour it was already dark enough outside to suggest midnight. As I watched through the rain-muddled windows I saw a coach swing onto the driveway and pass the house and although they gave minimal light I was glad to see the flickerings of the side coach lanterns as the horses made their way to the stable.

I felt the cool wet wind blow through the small gaps of the panes and I shivered and stepped back to the other side of the room, glad that Mr. Keanne had already set a small fire in the grate. I left the heavy draperies parted so that I was able to see flashes of lightning streak across the dark skies long before I heard the crash of thunder, for I thought that viewing nature's spectacle would make me less apprehensive. When a particularly harsh clap shook the ground nearby and rattled the pictures on my desk, I started, and then remembered that I had experienced great anxiety when I was young whenever there was a thunderstorm. I decided to return to the nursery to give whatever comfort was needed to my two charges.

The hallway was not yet lit with candles and as I opened the door from my room another flash of brilliance sent jagged lights through my bedroom windows and into the darkened corridor. I was glad that I was now past my own fearful childhood and had conquered my own irrational terror of thunder and lightning, for in truth, these sounds were of such intensity as to even cause me, at my age, to startle. I hurried to the nursery lest Antonia and Virgil be frightened and fully expected to find them hiding in a closet or a corner, huddled together, away from the sound and the fury of the heavens.

The children were neither; instead they were standing very close together in front of the small windows, their backs to the door so that they did not see me enter, watching as the shocks of light continued to hurtle downwards from the blackened skies. With each more violent thrust, the children nodded their heads slowly, as though confirming the force of the storm, and at one point, before I made my presence known to them, they actually moved closer to the window and put their hands on the panes of glass, drawing the zigzag shape of the thunderbolts on the moisture.

"Antonia . . . Virgil," I called, and they both tensed. "Come away from the windows so that you may be safe." The children stepped back but continued to watch the spiraling lights as if they enjoyed viewing them, saying nothing and hardly acknowledging me. "Children," I said again, "away from the windows," and at last they heeded me and moved slowly away.

"I was worried that you would be frightened," I began, but Virgil merely shook his head and it was my turn to be astounded as I, for the first time, realized that the young boy's hair was unlike his father's and all the previous Grayson males: there was no characteristic grey forelock in his dark hair. I stared at the place where the swirl should have been so that I was vaguely aware that Virgil had spoken and had to repeat his statment to me.

"I am sorry," I said to the boy, "but the sounds of the storm . . . I did not hear you." I was still amazed at my discovery.

Virgil looked back toward the window. "I said, Ma'am, that we like the rain. It doesn't frighten us. Not any more."

Antonia nodded her head and fingered a small golden locket around her neck. "Rain helps the flowers," she recited, quietly adding, "and it helps us to remember." Virgil stepped closer to his sister and took her hand and, as if in response to a secret signal, the young girl became silent and continued to stare out at the swirling rains.

I sat in the chair next to the fireplace and waited with them until the storm had passed and when all was quiet—

save for the steady tapping of the gentler raindrops on the windows—I heard the hall clock chimes indicating there was only fifteen minutes until supper. When I had taken care that the children were preparing for the meal I hastily dressed and the three us entered the dining room just as the last chime tolled the hour.

Mr. Grayson was not yet at the table when we took our seats. After a few moments, he entered and bowed formally to me. "Your pardon, Ma'am," he said, "but I was kept late in the stable by the storm. The horses were restive and we had to quiet them." He brushed at his head and I could see that droplets of water were still clinging to his hair and almost remarked on it, but wisely I curbed my voice. The set of Mr. Grayson's mouth and the narrowing of his eye repelled any levity, so instead I merely nodded to him and accepted his apology.

Again the dinner conversation consisted of one question put to each of the children and one sentence about the evening meal to me. The remaining time passed in silence. How terribly uncomfortable I felt sitting there, having much to say and yet having to be quiet, for it was certainly not my place to initiate conversation. Antonia and Virgil looked only at their food, even when Mr. Kenne served them, eating so quietly that only the scraping sound of a knife and fork as they touched a plate broke the silence and thus another meal was finished in unhappy quiet.

When once more their father excused them, the children bowed to me and to their sire and made off for their nursery with Mrs. Keanne. Again the port decanter was placed in front of him and again Mr. Grayson offered me tea and while I sipped my cup of the black Indian brew I became emboldened, perhaps by the turbulent weather, and I asked if I might speak to my employer.

At first he either did not, or pretended not, to hear me. "I would like permission to speak to you, Sir, about your children," I repeated, this time a bit louder.

Mr. Grayson set his goblet down. "Yes?"

I hesitated, not fully understanding why, but it was more than the distant look on his face; indeed, it was more in the manner and attitude on his part, an attitude of humouring me, yet mingled with the merest suggestion that I had still to learn the ways of my employer's table.

"About my children? You have encountered a problem?" Even though he asked me the question his tone conveyed that if there were something not quite in order he neither wanted to hear nor talk about it.

I shook my head. "Oh no, Sir, they're fine children. And very eager." I spoke quickly in order to dispel any thoughts that I did not enjoy his son and daughter. "In fact, it is because they are so quick that I should like permission to take Antonia riding with me," I said reevaluating my requests for both children. Clearly, Mr. Grayson was in no form to entertain both my suggestions. "I understand she once rode but no longer is allowed."

He answered immediately and firmly. "She is much too young."

"Young girls her age are already in training. I myself—"

Mr. Grayson appeared to look not at me, but beyond me, his dark eyes growing cold while dismissing me and the subject. "The matter is closed."

"But, Sir," I protested.

Mr. Grayson picked up his goblet and poured another

47

finger of port into it. "I don't care to discuss it, Miss Scott."

"As you wish," I answered, and having nothing further to say, "If you'll excuse me, then." I stood and he half-rose.

"Your servant, Ma'am. Goodnight." I could tell by the tone of his voice and the faraway look in his eyes that already he had lost interest in me and our conversation.

I lay awake that evening thinking that all my plans for inspiring filial love and devotion in the children were to no avail. I could tell from Mr. Grayson's manner that though he wished to educate his children he had no desire to establish a relationship built on anything other than the happenstance of contributing to the birth and existence of his offspring. I wondered sadly if there ever had been love in this family.

Chapter 5

My life at Ganymede House soon fell into place and in my first few weeks at the estate there were enough details concerning the children's lessons to occupy my time so that I had no opportunity to fully explore the house and gardens save for the rooms I used daily and the paths the three of us strolled on our airings. The pattern of my life remained constant and on those occasions when I had spare time I was engaged in mending my wardrobe, writing letters to two or three friends who had not abandoned me when I left their circle, and in reading the books I found in the library which afforded me the adult stimulation which was lacking in conversation.

My life was of a different weave now, and the Sarah Scott I fancied myself to be when I was in London was rapidly fading into a pleasant memory. When letters arrived from my old acquaintances it was difficult for me to envision them at their dances or dinners with little on their minds except the style of their gowns, their latest beau, and the current *bon mots*. They were neither interested in, nor able to comprehend my life as it was

49

now. I was the unfortunate one that fate chose not to smile on and although they were sad at the turn in my life, it did not affect them except that they no longer had one more female in their society of friends. That they continued to write amazed me, for I was already beginning to think that since I could not regale them with tales about my life or stories about my young charges and Master, for to do so would be to breach a code of respect, the minute details of my days here were of no consequence to them. I expect, as the seasons progressed, that by the time of the New Year, their exchanges of confidences to me would be limited and would dwindle to an occasional note and greeting-letter wishing me the best.

The children continued to progress in their studies and when I told Antonia of her father's obstinacy—although I did not use that word to her and couched it in softer tones—the child took it with gentle ease. She did not question me for a reason. I could tell she was unhappy at the outcome, but both she and Virgil thanked me politely for taking up the subject with their father. I could only reply that I would continue to pursue the matter at a later occasion.

Thus the days began to grow shorter and we entered into October and the air chilled. Mr. Grayson kept his distance from the children and never visited their rooms, yet he never denied me books or art supplies when I asked for them. Indeed, if anything, he seemed to delight—actually a word much too strong for his response—in providing the articles I requested. I suppose he was of the mind that as the children turned more and more to their studies he would be relieved more and more of his fatherly duties.

Mrs. Keanne and I kept our distance. She attended to the house and the kitchen and I to the children. She continued to send up special sweets for Virgil and Antonia and if for nothing more than that, I had good feelings toward her, for the children clearly need extra attention and I cared not where it came from just as long as the two were made to feel comfortable and loved. As I made no objection to the confections, I suppose, and because I did not keep the children at their books overly long, she did unbend a little and whenever the three of us passed her on our way for a walk the housekeeper would give me a half-smile and speak a few more words than was necessary. Ours still wasn't a comfortable relationship, but it was bearable, and her good husband, who was not of the same nature and disposition, always offered me a kindly smile and a few cheery words.

Our meals continued as they began: Mr. Grayson commenting once to each of us, listening politely to our replies, and then lapsing into silence. It was a tolerable but unhappy existence, more so for the children than for me. This was not what I envisioned for the rest of my life and were it not for the other hired help on the estate I would lack for adult speech.

Mr. Grayson and I continued our habit—actually his preference—of sitting at the table as he drank his port and I my tea. Every evening we repeated the same motions and said the same things—he offering me tea, my acceptance, and then his silence as he stared gloomily into his goblet. We passed the obligatory thirty minutes together before he would escort me to the small parlor and then would withdraw bidding me goodnight. It was a custom that for families enmeshed in daily preoccupations of country life might be welcomed as a respite from the day's problems, but how odd a way for Master and governess, who had little in common, to spend their evenings. And yet I had no power to change the pattern.

Thus my memories of the gay life in London faded rapidly and I was more and more drawn into the fabric of Ganymede.

Chapter 6

"Master'll be gone today, Ma'am," Tillie said as she brought me my morning beverage. "He's asked Mrs. Keanne to see to the house." The young girl put the tray on the table.

"Thank you. I was informed that Mr. Grayson's estate duties sometimes kept him away overnight." I sipped at the hot brew. "Have the children been told?"

"I'm not sure, Ma'am. Perhaps Mrs. Keanne will tell them." She curtsied and left the room and I sat at the table. How nice it would be, I thought, if their father had remembered to say goodbye to them. But now that I was wise to the ways of this house I knew that that was only fanciful thinking, and when I passed Mrs. Keanne outside the nursery I asked her if the children knew their father would be absent that day.

"I've just told them," the housekeeper replied. "But it makes no difference. It's just like any of the other days. It doesn't change their schedules. It's schooling as usual."

"I thought perhaps he might have spoken to the children," I persisted but was interrupted by Mrs. Keanne.

"Why should he, Miss Scott? Mr. Grayson's comings and goings don't affect their daily lives. Of course," she began and then hesitated, "he used to, but now he never . . ." Her voice became soft. "Ah, but he hasn't done that for a long time." She shook her head vigorously and passed on down the hall, her head still moving side to side as though she were speaking to herself. Poor children, I thought, and then because I could do nothing to rectify the matter, I entered the nursery, once more ready to begin the day.

When we had finished with the morning session and had eaten lunch I again gave the children a choice of walking the grounds with me or an hour's free time to do whatever they would. I had initiated this break in the daily routine due to the intensity that Virgil gave his books and the inattentiveness of Antonia who needed a respite from the daily schooling.

The children chose not to walk with me this afternoon although these past few days we had enjoyed the cool weather together. I know not why or how it happened but the children and I had come to a mutual respect, born not of a matter of course, and yet, not quite of mutual understanding. Whatever it was that made them trust me, even slightly, I dared not analyze or take it lightly, for in their eyes, I understood I was still an adult, and adults were not to be confided in until all traces of possible betrayal were nonexistent.

I saw to it that the children were settled in their chosen recreation—Virgil with a favorite book, Antonia surrounded by her dolls and Tillie to oversee them—before I began my own hour of free time. Unfortunately, it was not the best of days—the wind was quite blustery and the skies cloudy and as I felt the beginnings of a fall cold settling in my throat and chest I decided that today, much to my regret, would have to be spent indoors. Although I still had not yet viewed all the gardens of the estate since there were numerous individual sections devoted to special shrubs and flowers I had begun to enjoy the grounds of the house, especially as the leaves began their change into autumnal colors and gave quite another and more majestic look to Ganymede.

This was the season I enjoyed most for both its invigorating air and display of nature's jeweled-tone grandeur and even though it heralded the beginning of a bleak winter, convivial memories of past seasons spent in London during my youth continued to play in the far reaches of my mind. Although I had no reason even to contemplate it as truth, sometimes on my turns around the gardens I did spend a few moments in silly pursuit of a dream that someday I would be back in the city amongst my own friends. But usually, by the time I had again settled into the schoolroom, all those frivolous thoughts had vanished from my mind as I began to explain the basics of a mathematical problem or erased a board that had been used to teach sentence structure.

Today was a perfect sort of day to finally tour the interior of Ganymede and as I didn't want to disturb any of the downstairs help as they went about their daily duties, I decided to begin with the second level of the house. The third level, I knew, contained the rooms for the servants and although I was on friendly terms with most—no, with all save Mrs. Keanne—I felt it would not serve for me to walk the halls on that floor. I did not want any of the inside help to think me a snoop nor did I want them to think I was enlarging on my duties when Mr. Grayson was away.

The North Wing, the children's chambers, I was already acquainted with because I spent so many hours there. In addition to the schoolrooms, playrooms, and their individual bedrooms, there was a small bathing area and a double-sized dressing/cloak room containing two large armoires for clothing and floor-to-ceiling shelves piled high with extra-thick woolen blankets and sleeping accessories. Neither child used the room for dressing, instead merely storing their clothing there and laying out their next day's attire every evening in their own rooms. It was a ritual they had learned, they told me when I questioned them about it, when they were very small and I dared not inquire as to whether it was their mother or a governess who had taught them.

I walked down the long carpeted corridor beyond the staircase landing, toward the guest wings, quickly passing the closed doors of Mr. Grayson's quarters. These, I knew, were the first three rooms on the left, for I had seen Tillie deliver fresh linens to the chambers one afternoon and she explained that my employer occupied these rooms and that they each had connecting doors through which he could pass from one to another. When the maid had asked me if I would like to view the rooms I declined, for I had no reason to peer into Mr. Grayson's private chambers—they were of no consequence to me—and to do so merely for curiosity's sake would brand me forever as a gabber and one who wasted the maid's time in pursuit of idle prying.

I continued on toward the guest wings. In several of the books that Mr. Grayson had sent to me describing Ganymede House, there were detailed descriptions of the furnishings of these chambers that piqued my imagination and curiosity. Surely there could be no harm in looking at them—especially since my employer expected me to teach his children about the house.

I tried the first door I came to in the long hall beyond Mr. Grayson's quarters and found it unlocked and I pushed it open intending to leave it thusly so that anyone who passed would see me, and I entered into what seemed to be a lady's chamber. It was a fragile room, I could see that at first glance, one that had had much care in the selection and placement of furnishings. It was decorated entirely in white and gold and used simple silks and satins. Mirrors were used ingeniously to reflect light even into the room's dark corners where the sun's rays could not reach. The curtains were parted so that beyond the shut glass-paned doors there was an unobstructed view of the grounds and of the mist where the land gave way to the sea. It was one of the finest landscapes to be seen from the house and I marvelled that Mr. Grayson would be so much the hospitable host as to allow a guest to have such a magnificent view of the estate. I went to the French doors, for even though they were closed I was sure I could still hear the sounds of the waters through the glass, and I pressed my ear close to the panes listening to the dull roar of the sea lapping against the coast. I leaned even closer so that I might hear more accurately the din of the water slapping the seacoast and for a few seconds I was lulled by the faint rhythmic pounding of the waves against the rocks. Surely whoever slept in this room would be able to hear and fall asleep to the never-ending sea sounds in the night. As I turned my head it was then that I saw, hanging on the wall opposite the bed, a huge painting of an almost indescribably beautiful and delicate young woman, a woman whose physical beauty was so unparalleled that I found myself staring at her with open mouth.

The portrait, I now saw, dominated the room by both its size and subject. The woman, obviously in her early twenties, was standing by the edge of the sea, half-turned from it, dressed in a gossamer gown that billowed softly away from her body revealing the delicate curves of the upper half of her torso. She wore a large straw hat from which golden ringlets seemed to escape and curl about her face and one slender graceful hand was resting gently on the broad brim as though she was holding it against the wind. In her other hand she held a single long-stemmed white rose and she seemed to be extending her arm, raising it up and offering the flower to someone, perhaps to a person beyond the frame of the artist's eye. Her whole manner was that of invitation and promise and even the soft smile that played about her pale pink lips hinted at love and faithfulness. She was dressed entirely in white and although the portrait was indeed a pastel, the brilliant blue tint of her eyes seemed to be painted not of ordinary colours, for her eyes were undoubtedly her most extraordinary feature and the painter, whoever he was, seemed mesmerized by them, wanting to highlight them.

I approached the painting so that I could read the title.

"It's of Miss Rosamunda!" I startled, recognizing the voice of Mr. Keanne, and turned toward him and his voice softened. "I didn't mean to frighten you, Miss." He walked further into the room.

I pointed to the portrait. "She was beautiful."

"Aye." He nodded his head, agreeing with me. "She was the most beautiful woman in the whole of Yorkshire. Many a servant from another estate would tell me she was the loveliest woman they had ever seen. And I agreed with them." He approached even closer and looked up at the painting. "Those eyes were her true colour, Miss. They were most remarkable. They always looked like a perfect sky." He stepped back so that he could view the portrait completely again. "Aye, she was the most beautiful lady in the world."

"Antonia resembles her."

Mr. Keanne nodded his head once more. "She has her colouring, but not her spirit."

"She's young yet . . ."

Mr. Keanne remained looking at Rosamunda's picture. "When she first came here, Miss, after she married the Master, it was said that people would travel miles just to look at her." He sighed. "She didn't have an enemy in the world, she was kind and generous to friends and servants alike. Many a time I would be serving her and I would notice that young boys, much younger than even Master Virgil, would sit at her feet and just gaze at her." He smiled a gentle smile. "And her laughter, Miss, it was like the joyous sound of morning bells." He paused, as though still hearing the long-stilled laughter and then removed a handkerchief from his vest pocket and wiped at his eyes. "Aye, we all loved her. . . . We all loved her."

"Had she been ill long?"

"Ill, Miss?" He seemed surprised at my words and I asked my question again. I saw his eyes turn watery and he bit his lip and I could see he was truly pained. "She wasn't ill, Miss. I thought you knew."

"Knew what?"

"She died in a fall, Miss, a fall into the sea. It was a riding accident."

A cold tremor travelled through me and I folded my arms in front of me, rubbing the chill from them. "I'm sorry. I did not know. Then that is the reason Mr. Grayson does not want Antonia riding."

"That, and—" He looked around as though he remembered something and he broke off his answer. "How did you get in here, Miss?"

"I just opened the door. I was interested in seeing the guest wings. Apparently, I've wandered into the wrong rooms."

The old gentleman shook his head and spoke more to himself. "He's been at it again, has he?" he said as he closed the curtains darkening the room so that the picture was barely visible. "This room is supposed to be locked all the time, Miss." He nodded to me. "I think we should be going, Miss Scott. The Master doesn't like anyone to disturb this chamber," he said as he walked toward the doorway.

"Of course." I moved closer to the portrait for one last look at the woman and saw that just below it, on a small marble table, was a vase of faded white roses, their petals turning brown at the edges but their scent still noticeable . . . still permeating the air, and I looked at Mr. Keanne. "These flowers?"

Mr. Keanne merely stared at me and didn't answer the question and for some reason—perhaps embarrassment or a gentler sensibility on my part—I did not repeat my words and I walked past the stooped gentleman as he pulled the door shut and locked it with a key on a ring.

Chapter 7

I had other opportunities to explore the interior of Ganymede House for it now had begun to turn cold and blustering outside. While the children and I continued our walks about the grounds of the estate these outings were necessarily cut short by the chilly weather. I had already learned much about the exterior of the house and its acreage but on the fairly constant days I still spent much of my free time visiting the gardens. I had heard high praise of the hundreds of flowers and shrubs grown on the property from many of the estate workers and determined that one of my first priorities in learning about my new home should be the gardens before they were winter-prepared. Thus when it was cool but clear, much like this late afternoon, I looked forward to my singular explorations for I was entirely more cautious of the children's health that I was of mine.

This afternoon, after the school day and while the children were given free moments before dinner, I anticipated that my time would be spent exploring the grounds near the tower. I had avoided this spot—I knew not why—but lately had been directed to it by Old Martin, one of the gardeners I had met just this week, who told me of a surprise I would find within the maze of the shrubs. He would not tell me anymore—only explaining that most visitors were enchanted once they penetrated the middle of the "Tower Maze" and saw the "Greeks."

Though I was intrigued by Old Martin's words I still approached the area cautiously. Again I knew not why, but this section and the wooded parts of the estate seemed to depress me and although I told myself that I was foolish and was imagining too many things, up until now I still walked only those areas that were comfortable to me and the children.

There were no trees close by the tower, only the well-planned puzzle of tall boxwoods and bushes trimmed and shaped so densely that it was impossible to see through them. On one side of the plantings, facing the tower, was the beginning of the maze; between the double row of bushes I could see its entrance path set with paving stones of slate and mica so that the entire walkway glinted and gleamed enticingly in the late afternoon sun.

I walked around the outside of the bushes to the other side until I came to the exit of the maze by way of gauging fully the intricacies of the pattern. The egress opened to the long expanse of already stiffened and purple-browned lawn that led to the cliffs and the sea. Placed on either side of the exit path so that they framed the opening were large areas of tall wild grasses, yellowed now, but still able to sway gracefully with the wind that came off the water and rippled along the ground toward the bushes. It was a lovely sight, the tall graceful fronds seemed to sway and bow in majesty to the forces of nature.

I paced the length of the bushes again and hesitantly and defiantly entered the maze, at first following what seemed a simple straightforward pattern. I turned back several times to assure myself that the path was indeed straight and having done that became quite self-satisfied that I would have no uncertainty as to which way I would proceed when I was ready to return to the house.

I walked but a few minutes, stopping once or twice to read several brass markings identifying the more exotic flora, all barren now except for shriveled leaves, and resolved to revisit this garden again in the spring and summer when I could appreciate the blooms. All of the names were identifiable only in Greek—I recognized the language—and although they gave no clues as to their common floral names I could tell by the shapes of the leaves and the stems that most of these cuttings were foreign to England.

I came to the first puzzle. The glittering path branched in two directions and I had to make my initial decision then as to whether I should continue on a straight course or veer to the left. Both walks seemed equally inviting and again, being cautious, I followed my original straight line, but within a matter of minutes I found myself again faced with another choice. This time there were three paths—all set at exact angles—and still believing I could find my way out of the maze if I adhered to the most elementary route, I chose to continue following the straight line.

This proved to be a mistake for as I rounded a curve I was immediately forced to choose among another trio of ways. I still moved straight as I knew from experience that it was much easier to remember the simplest way when it came to retracing patterns. I followed the path and seemed to be rewarded for my choices, for up ahead I saw a bower of leafless heavy vines intertwined and stretched between two marble pillars which seemed to lead to a clearing of some kind. As I passed under the structure I realized why this was called the Greek Gardens.

In the middle of the area was a mini-maze, one created by white marble chips and low-lying plants that led to a large reflecting pool with a tall triple fountain in the middle. The water was no longer spilling over and I assumed that it had already been turned off for the winter, for the standing brackish water in the pool was now strewn with skeleton leaves and broken twigs that floated on the top. Beside the pool small marble benches were grouped so that, I imagine, several people could sit comfortably in the summer weather and watch while the streams of water from the fountain cascaded down into the shallow pond.

I pushed aside a few dried leaves from a bench and sat down, resting and enjoying the peacefulness of the garden, for even though it was quite chilly there was a calmness that seemed to permeate the area. It intimated that there was onetime a feeling of peace and gentleness in the maze and I reasoned that this must once have been the place where family members were able to withdraw from ordinary preoccupations in order to gain a few moments of perspective or to commune with nature and themselves.

Having rested and enjoyed the views for a few minutes, I looked round and saw that at various distances within the larger rectangular maze marble statues had been placed as if to stand guard and to protect the inhabitants and visitors. I did not recognize the statues for they appeared to be original carvings and not copies of those displayed in museums, and when I approached several of them I noticed that most of the nameplates of the figures were missing. I ran my hand over the arm of one of the unnamed goddesses noting that there was a minute crack in the wrist and made a mental note to speak about it to either Mr. Grayson or Mr. Keanne. Surely, I thought, they would not want this lovely area to decay, although I could not help but notice that the shrubs and bushes in this particular garden suffered greatly from neglect. This seemed unfortunate. To my way of thinking this should have been one of the loveliest and most cared-for gardens of Ganymede. Perhaps, I thought, the caretakers had not been able to see to this particular ground or perhaps they were already in the process of refurbishing the maze. At any way, though, a word to either my employer or the houseman would clear it up for me.

It was beginning to grow late, the sun had begun its descent, and it was time for me to return to the house. I looked carefully at the arrangement of the paths leading out of the maze and I determined that the correct way lay to the left where there were groups of small plants clustered in curves within curves, each delineated by the marble chips bordering the growth. I had remembered that I saw them as I entered the garden and as I walked past them I was particularly taken with the shape of one such serrated leaf. I bent low to read the name of the plant and I saw, underneath it, a chipmunk busily burying a small cache of nuts. Unfortunately I made too much noise and the little animal, now alerted to my presence, scampered beyond the withered growth. I followed it for a few moments trying to discover its tunnel so I could show Antonia and Virgil the burrow when we visited this garden together either before the advent of this winter's snows or the first blossomings of next spring.

The tiny rodent disappeared rather quickly and having lost it from view I decided to return to Ganymede, but it was then that I realized that although I had only taken a few steps from the remembered path I had turned myself around and the exact location of the walkway that I had followed was lost to me. I was now faced with the task of trying to find my way out of the maze in a rather haphazard fashion.

I was not unduly concerned for I used to enjoy and appreciate these problems when I lived in London and visited the botanical gardens. I had always prided myself on my ability to retain direction and while my friends were sometimes hopelessly lost in the mazes, I almost always was the first person to emerge from the convoluted patterns.

I followed a semi-circle design for a few yards but that proved wrong, for within minutes I was back to the pool. I decided to take the second of the three paths but after a few slight twists and turns I found myself approaching the fountain once again and I smiled, thinking that although it had taken me two false starts the maze would now be easy to solve.

I walked a few yards quite smugly and, to my annoyance, realized that I was once again approaching the fountain, this time from quite another direction. I was rapidly determining that finding my way back to Ganymede House might be harder than I realized, for the garden puzzle was deceptively intricate and well-thought out. But I have always enjoyed a challenge and I walked slowly to each crosspath, being only slightly apprehensive about the time and thinking that in a few moments I would find my way again although all the footpaths seemed to be familiar; the puzzle was more difficult than I had anticipated and I rebuked myself sternly for starting to explore this garden so late in the afternoon.

I sat once more on the marble bench, for I had grown tired, and contemplated my next steps. I was more vexed than worried, matters of inconsequence such as these never frightened me for I knew that eventually I would find the right path if I approached the problem logically and with patience. I looked up, hoping to see the house or the tower in order to get my bearing, but without success. In the dusk I could see nothing save leafless branches etched against the grey sky that was now filled with the diffused glow from the almost fully-set sun and suddenly, for no apparent reason, there was an abrupt change in the air. I felt a distinct coldness but it was more than a chill; rather it was as though an icy wind had blown quickly through the trees and shrubs and surrounded me, though when I looked at them not even the dark thin finger-like branches appeared to waver. And yet it was more than the cool wind that alerted me, for accompanying it was a faint scent of flowers—roses—and while my practical sense told me that it was impossible for any blooms to survive in this season still I looked for blossomed bushes near me. Of course there were none and I took a deep breath, sure that my nostrils were playing fancy with me by disguising the odor of the musty undergrowth.

I shivered and drew my cloak around me to ward off the cold and re-thought the maze, deciding that my first path might have ultimately led me to the exit if I had chosen a second turning more correctly.

I hurried now for it was rapidly getting dark and the walkways were not easily distinguishable. Several times I stumbled as my foot caught in dried tangles of stems and once I had to stop my fall with my hands, reaching out and scraping them against the trees along the walkway. As I righted myself from the near-accident I felt another wash of coldness penetrating through my cape to my skin and I shivered again and thrust my arms and hands deeper into the pockets of my cloak, pulling the material close to my body and in effect protecting it from the air and giving me a small sense of comfort.

The paths I was now choosing proved in error again and again, and when I realized it I had already recircled back to the fountain and found myself next to the marble statue with the small crack in it. I put my arm out to the goddess, pausing to catch my breath and trying to think of another plan or another way out. My hand rested on the deep cold smoothness of the statue's arm and as I looked up I realized that the chiseled face, now silhouetted in the half-light, was reminiscent of some-one. I involuntarily shuddered as I realized that the goddess was a depiction of the Lady Rosamunda. Whoever had carved the figure had deliberately used the face of the mistress of Ganymede as his inspiration. For some unknown and irrational reason, or perhaps because I was tired and a bit nervous, I stepped back and away from the glowing marble.

I was very cold now and I stamped my numbed feet to circulate the blood. Even this afternoon when it was sunny and I first began my ill-advised walk, the ground had been damp and now, as the darkest twilight approached, the earth was cooler and wetter and bits of dead twigs and leaves clung to the sides of my shoes as the moisture swelled the dirt.

The night was uncomfortably still and yet it was as

though waves of chilling winds continuously swept over and around me, sending my body into little spasms trying to keep itself warm. I could hear the sea clearly now for there were no day sounds to mask the crash of the waves as they broke on the rocks below the cliffs and in the dark, when all else was now quiet, it seemed as if the water was much closer than I remembered. It was as though my dulled mind had begun to play little tricks on me and I attributed it to the fact that I was cold and quite exhausted.

The light of the rising moon played flirtatiously with the Greek statues, making their marble bodies gleam cool and majestic in their abandoned loneliness, and I somehow—irrationally, I knew—felt that I was an interloper in this forbidding frozen tableau—a flesh and blood copy in this garden of chiseled stone and stilled fountains. For some reason I wanted to apologize for being there for I sensed that although this was a public garden by day, by night it was a very special private place that one had to be summoned, or invited to, to join with nature and the sculptures.

I would have gladly left the area but I had come to the conclusion that after all my trials I was not able to determine the pattern of the maze. Unless someone at the house missed me soon and came looking for me, this was surely to be a long, cold, and disturbing night, and I wondered if my garments were of sufficient weight to keep me warm. That I would be found I had no doubt, but the question of when was uppermost in my mind, for I worried not only about myself, but about the children and my duty to them.

My temples began to throb and I realized that despite the fact that I knew I would be released from this enclosed outdoor room either through my own sensibilities or someone else's leadership, I was beginning to grow anxious so that even the normal scratching sounds of nocturnal animals such as the chipmunk or field mouse that I heard seemed exaggerated and frightening. I was starting to feel extremely uncomfortable and each new sound—a snapping branch, a scraping leaf—seemed to take on more meaning and I began to have feelings and thoughts that I cannot quite describe. It was as though I was not alone there in the garden, it was as though someone were watching me, playing games with me, for whenever I relaxed and tried to think of a way out of the maze it seemed that another quickening sound or a breaking twig would impinge into my thoughts and I would lose track of my idea and have to begin again.

I was able to determine by the position of the moon and the early evening stars that more than two hours had passed since I had first ventured into the maze. I wondered how long it would be before I was rescued. My only consolation was that the children were not with me and were safely at home in their warm quarters.

"Thank goodness, the children are safe," I said aloud, at least congratulating myself on the fact that I had not taken them with me. I leaned against the statue again and suddenly the onslaught of cold air seemed to vanish and the sounds quieted and in the stillness I heard someone call my name.

"Miss Scott! Miss Scott! Be you in there?"

"Yes, here. I'm here," I said loudly. "Who is it?" I asked for I did not recognize the voice.

"It's Old Martin, Miss, don't you be afraid." The gardener's voice kept getting closer. "You just stay where you're at, Miss, and keep speaking and I'll get to you." I heard the stepping sounds of a person approaching me and I turned just as Old Martin emerged from the path behind me. "I reckon you're a mite worried, Miss," he said touching the rim of his cap to me.

"Yes," was all I could reply, for my teeth were chattering both from cold and fear.

"I didn't see you come out of the maze, Miss, and when Mr. Keanne asked if I had seen you, well, I figured you were still here." He came up close to me so that I could see his face. "This here's a bit more difficult than people think. Was planned that way by—" He broke off the words and took my arm. "Come on, Miss, it's this way. You just follow me." I followed the servant and he, sensing that I was still anxious about the time spent in the maze, continued to talk. "I know just about all the land here at Ganymede, Miss," he said as he expertly negotiated the curving paths. "Been here in service for nearly sixty years. But I was born on this estate, Miss, and me father he was gardener here before me. Head gardener he was . . . same as me. Know just about every plant on this entire land." He led me away from the sound of the sea and I understood that he was taking me out the maze entrance so that the first thing I would see would be the tower and not the cliffs. I marvelled at the man's compassion.

"Old Martin, they call me now, Ma'am, but when I was young I had me a head full of golden hairs although to look at me now," he said as he swept off his cap and displayed a bald head, "you would not know it." He continued to lead me through the puzzle and when we emerged from the maze he walked beside me toward the house and although I still had not said a word he continued to talk, dispelling my fears and apprehensions.

"Don't you be a fretting, Miss," he said, "lots of people get lost in the Greek Garden. Mistress used to laugh when she did. It were her favorite place on the whole estate, she used to say." He looked up. "Ah, we're back home now, Miss, safe and sound."

We approached the well-lit house just as Mr. Keanne opened the door. "Miss Scott, where . . . ? We have been looking for you."

Old Martin laughed, showing the gaps in his front teeth. "Miss got lost in the Greeks," he said, handing me into the door. "Reckon she needs something hot, Mr. Keanne." He turned toward me and tipped his cap. "You'll be alright now, Miss."

I thanked the kind man and went directly to my room and huddled under the blankets on the bed, pulling them around me, trying to warm my body. There was a knock on the door and Tillie came into the room carrying a pot of steaming tea.

"Mrs. Keanne said for you to take this and stay put in bed tonight, Miss Scott. She said she'll send a tray later and she'll tell the Master not to expect you for supper, if that's pleasing to you."

"Thank you, Tillie," I said and wrapped the quilt around me. Already the warmth was comforting me, lulling me into drowsiness. "Yes, that will be quite alright," I remembered saying as the parlor maid closed the door.

Chapter 8

The next morning I was recovered sufficiently enough to attend to my teaching duties and I managed to place no special significance on the episode when speaking to the children. They were polite and asked after me but showed no inclination to pursue the subject and I, now angry at myself because of my own foolishness, spoke no more of it. I thanked them for their initial inquiry as to my health and they took no more notice of the incident.

The servants and staff, however, were of another mind; they were all most kind to me and stopped in the course of their daily duties to exchange several words about my health. Even Mrs. Keanne acknowledged my fright of the past evening and sent what I knew was her special occasion poppyseed cake to the schoolroom for luncheon dessert. I appreciated it, and I made a mental note to thank the woman personally when later we met.

Only Mr. Grayson, whom I knew was informed of the incident since I did not appear for the last evening's supper, failed to speak of the fright when we were all assembled for dinner. I had grown accustomed to the rituals of the supper table and, like the children, tended to look down at my plate until each of us was asked one or two questions by the children's father. Dinner was still, for the most part, silent and sullen, but I had no way to change it and preferred to speak to Antonia and Virgil in the privacy of the schoolroom. I knew the children hurried their meal each evening, hoping to leave—nay, escape—the table as soon as possible and I wanted no part in delaying them; there was much more fun to be found upstairs in their rooms amongst their toys, games, and books.

But I could not escape from the heaviness of the evenings; I was expected to sit at table while Mr. Grayson finished his meal and enjoyed his wine. I had begun to use these times to silently daydream about my London days and if Mr. Grayson were to see a harmonious and sometimes smiling countenance, I doubt if he even questioned the reason.

This evening as I poured my tea I winced as the heavy pot put extra pressure on my scratched wrist and I put the vessel down quickly.

"I would hope you have attended to that bruise, Miss Scott." Mr. Grayson was looking at my wrist and I flushed as I realized that part of the angry red welt extended beyond my shirt cuff and was visible. I dropped my hands to my lap.

"Yes, thank you, I have."

"I understand you were lost in the Greek maze, Ma'am. I trust you are over your fright."

"Yes, I am, Sir. Thank you for asking."

"It is quite complicated and other novices, like yourself, have needed help in extricating themselves from the garden."

"Yes, that is what I have been told," I answered and because I was taken with his sudden expanse of speaking, continued the conversation. "I foolishly didn't allow myself enough daylight time to solve the puzzle."

"Not many people do the first time, Ma'am." He looked off into the room, staring into the blazing cavernous fireplace, and I expected this to be the end of the conversation, for already Mr. Grayson had spoken more personally to me in these few sentences than he had since my arrival. But this was not the case. "We hardly use the maze anymore," he said and it was the first time I had ever heard a gentling of his voice.

"That is the reason it is in such disrepair, then."

"Exactly. We have finer gardens on the estate now, and I trust you will investigate them. And, in fact, come next spring we will be replacing the Greeks. I find it no longer suits us at Ganymede to have that particular group of plantings."

"Oh, I disagree with you, Sir," I protested and then realizing that I had interjected myself into the affairs of the house I quickly added, "I beg your pardon, Sir. It was not for me to tell you about your estate matters."

Mr. Grayson became silent and poured himself a second glass of port. "The Greek Garden," he mused and I thought I saw a gentle look in his eye. He didn't speak again for a few minutes and I sat quietly, sipping my tea, thinking that this evening was one of the more pleasant times I had passed with Mr. Grayson. "The Greek Garden," he once more said and roused himself from his reverie and looked at me. "Yes, they will be gone in the spring. I fear that what happened to you will happen to others and it is a frightening experience."

"Perhaps, Sir, if there were instructions set by one of

the benches for others . . ."

"No." He shook his head. "No, the garden must go," and he closed the conversation.

"Of course," I said bowing to his reasoning. I started to rise to make my way to the sitting room.

"If you will do me the honor, Ma'am, of staying a few moments more . . ." I sat again at the table. "Tomorrow, Miss Scott, my Cousin Edward will be paying us a visit. You are not yet acquainted with him but the children find him to be good company and if they ask, they may be given extra time with him, if that is alright with you."

"I will see to your wishes, Sir."

"Good." Mr. Grayson drank the last of the wine, stood, and bowed. "By your leave, Ma'am," he said and left me—forgetting for the first time to escort me to the small parlor.

Chapter 9

"Begging your pardon, Ma'am," Tillie said knocking on the schoolroom door. "but Mrs. Keanne said to tell you that the children have a surprise guest waiting downstairs, if you would excuse them from their studies for a bit." I could see the children fidget in their seats for they evidently knew who their visitor was and I was glad to see them show emotion.

"Thank you, Tillie. Please tell their guest that Miss Antonia and Master Virgil will meet with him in a few moments."

"Very good, Ma'am." Tillie curtsied and winked at the children.

"If you'll just put away your lessons, please, and tidy up" I said to them, "then I think we shall declare this afternoon a holiday." I smiled at my charges and was rewarded by huge grins. My heart gladdened knowing that the children did indeed have a loving relationship with a family member. Whatever manner this gentleman had, I already knew I would be pleased with him—surely anyone who could inspire such trust and devotion from

Antonia and Virgil deserved to be accepted without condition.

I busied myself in the schoolroom while the children slipped away to their washroom and I heard, for the first time, chatter and spontaneous laughter as they washed their hands and faces. The sound so pleased me that I vowed to tell their cousin that his arrival had done much to restore my faith in family loyalty. Surely the gentleman in question should know how much the children loved and looked forward to his visits.

I erased the blackboard and put away the pencils we had been using and when I looked around the children were standing by the door, their hair combed, their faces clean and their eyes sparkling with anticipation.

"If you please, Ma'am, come and meet Cousin Edward. I am sure he would like to make your acquaintance." Virgil bowed slightly to me and already I could see the beginnings of an imitation of sorts of his father.

I brushed chalk from my dress. "I should like that very much, thank you," I said, flattered that the children would include me in their plans. I was further pleased when Antonia took my hand voluntarily and pulled me toward the door.

"You'll like Cousin Edward as much as we do." The children giggled and I smiled at the foreign sound; that their cousin could initiate such a response amazed me, for knowing my young charges these past several weeks I had feared all adults were forbidden to enter their child-realm.

"Indeed," I said as I finished smoothing my hair, "why do you love your cousin so?"

"Cousin Edward teaches us things . . ." Antonia began and then giggled again.

78

"Hush, Tonia," Virgil chided her, "they're secret."

"Ah, secrets," I said joining in their game. "What kind of secrets?"

"Nothing." Virgil kept his head down. "Cousin Edward said we weren't to tell them to anyone." Antonia shook her golden head, but finally giddiness overcame her and she started to laugh and the two of them covered their mouths with their hands.

"Indeed," I said trying not to overstep on this delicate scene, "your cousin is quite right—secrets are just that—something not to be told to anyone. I'm sure I shan't ask you to divulge them." Antonia took my hand again.

"Please, Miss Scott, come meet Cousin Edward," she once more entreated impatiently, "he's waiting downstairs for us." She tugged at my hand, pulling me gently toward the hall and staircase, urging me to hurry.

"My, this cousin of yours must be a wondrous person to have you act so. Tell me what else you like about him. What makes him so wonderful?" I closed the door behind me and we three started down the hall.

"He plays games with us." Virgil volunteered.

"And, he laughs and teases with us." Antonia joined in. "Oh, you'll see. You'll like Cousin Edward. Everyone does."

Virgil picked up his head and looked at his sister. "Not everyone."

Antonia nodded her head solemnly. "Oh, I forgot. Not everyone." I had not time to press the children as to who the "not everyone" was, for there, standing in the entry foyer next to the reception table, holding two large, gaily wrapped packages, was a tall gentleman of approximately six feet. A tan checked coat and dark suede hat were carelessly abandoned on the table, and lying atop this was a dark wooden walking cane. When the children got to the landing and saw the man, both squealed with delight.

"Cousin Edward, Cousin Edward," they repeated and ran the rest of the way down the flight of stairs. Antonia flung herself into her cousin's arms and the young gentleman hoisted her up and swung her around while the delighted girl shrieked with pleasure. When he had swung her several times, he set her back on the floor and turned to Virgil who was standing, waiting his turn.

"Well, Virgil, how are you?" he asked formally and the young boy bowed from the waist.

"Very well, Cousin Edward," he said in mock-serious tone and then they both burst out laughing and the man picked up the young boy, hugged him and playfully cuffed his ear.

"So, my fine lad, what have you been up to? Have you studied your mathematics?" he asked and the word must have recalled the children to their own manners.

"Cousin Edward," they said almost in unison and then Antonia looked to her older brother who turned to me and said, "May we introduce Miss Scott, our governess."

Mr. Edward Moore made his formal bow. "My pleasure, Ma'am," he said. "I trust the children have been good to you."

"Yes, thank you."

"And I trust my good cousin, their father, has also made you feel welcome in his home?"

"Again, yes, Sir. Mr. Grayson, the children and the staff at Ganymede House have made these past few weeks a pleasure," I answered, for there certainly was no reason to divulge to this gentleman my thoughts about a member of his family.

"I am most certainly glad to hear that, Ma'am, although it doesn't surprise me. These two moppets," he said mussing the children's hair, "can be quite a handful, but I'm sure you'll agree with me, Miss Scott, they're delightful children." He tugged at Virgil's hair. "Leastways, when they want to be. Isn't that so, my young friend?"

Virgil laughed and his sister stepped in front of him so that she too, could take her turn at having her hair pulled.

"You see, Miss Scott," Mr. Moore said to me, "they are absolutely incorrigible." And the children, hearing the new word started all over again to giggle and clung to their cousin who held them tightly to him as they both yelled with merriment.

"Well, Edward, how do you do?" The four of us turned at the sound of the deep voice. Mr. Grayson stood at the top of the stairs looking down at the scene.

Mr. Moore released Virgil's shoulder and looked up as his cousin made his way down the steps. "Very well, thank you, Oliver." He made a short bow. "And you?"

"Well also, thank you." Mr. Grayson returned the social gesture but neither made any attempt to shake hands. "Will you be honoring us this evening?"

"If I may, Sir. I was in the neighborhood—at Valencia, the home of the Judsons—and I missed these two little ones," he said, smiling down at Antonia and Virgil.

"Our home is yours, Edward, as you well know, for as long as you care to stay." The adult cousins stared at each other and coldness passed between them. Though they were polite their gestures and their words seemed to be wooden. They continued to stare at each other, Mr.

Grayson, stiff and reserved and Mr. Moore in detached observation until the senior cousin nodded. "I shall see you at dinner, then." He turned to me.

"You will join us Miss Scott?"

"Of course, Sir," I answered, but by that time he had already passed into another room.

"Well, I see that he still reacts the same way with everyone." Edward tousled Virgil's hair. "You must forgive my cousin, Miss Scott, he has not been the same since his wife died."

I nodded my head and looked quickly at the children, hoping that Mr. Moore would take my meaning. I preferred not to have anything negative said about their father in their presence, and certainly not to me at any time.

Mr. Moore understood immediately and changed the subject. "Well, Virgil, it looks like a good day out there," he said motioning toward the window. "Perhaps, if you work twice as hard at your books today, Miss Scott will give you leave to go boating after lunch." He smiled at me and even though the young boy said nothing, I could tell from the way he looked at his cousin that it was just the diversion he needed.

"There is no need to bribe me, Mr. Moore," I said. "As you may be aware, Virgil is an excellent student and one afternoon away from his studies will not hurt his education. Besides, in order to celebrate your arrival we have already decided that this afternoon will be a holiday."

"I say, children, you have an excellent and, I might add, understanding governess. You two are certainly in luck." He smiled at me. "That's not to say, Miss Scott, that your predecessor was not a kindly woman," he added.

"I understand she was a very fine tutor. She has done very well in teaching the children." I returned the smile and quite understood why the children were charmed by their favorite cousin.

Antonia, recovering from the chilling effect of her father's conversation with Edward, tugged at her cousin's cuff. "Swing me again, Cousin Edward. Swing me again."

Mr. Moore bent down and cupped the child's face in his hand and smoothed her curls away from her cheeks. "Well, I think that's enough, my beauty. And besides I believe, Tonia, there is a surprise here for you." He looked at the parcels on the table. "Now, my lovely young Miss, you must make a choice. Either a round-and-round swing or one of these packages." He held both the wrapped boxes high. "Which is it to be?"

The child stamped her foot in impatience. "Both." She reached up to take them.

"No, no, my little girl. One. Choose." He held the boxes higher and when Antonia pointed to one of them, he laughed. "You see, Miss Scott, my gifts are no match to a swing-around. Well," he turned to Antonia and handed her the larger package, "here you are my golden flirt. Come give your cousin a kiss." He bent down so that Antonia could kiss his cheek. "And you, noble Virgil," he said turning to the boy, "you also prefer the box?"

"Yes sir," the boy said with an all-too-rare grin.

"Well, then," Mr. Moore said, "come shake my hand and be done with it." He extended his hand and Virgil shook it and then Edward once more clasped the boy to his bosom. "Good boy, Virg, good boy." He stepped to the side of the children and watched as they tore the wrappings off the packages and I could see the look of delight in Antonia's eyes as she lifted a beautiful blue-silk dressed China doll from the box. It had golden hair, wrapped in ringlets and the painted eyes were of a blue much like the child's own. I remarked on the resemblance.

"Yes, Miss Scott, I saw that immediately when I was in the shop. It reminded me of Antonia and I could not resist it." He looked at the little girl who was already cradling the doll in her arms. "And," he asked, "does it suit you, my little charmer?"

Antonia touched the blue fabric of the doll's dress. "It's beautiful," she said. "It's like . . ." she began and I saw a look of understanding pass between the three of them. "I shall call her 'Josephine.'"

"Most fitting," her cousin said and smiled at me. "Don't you think, Miss Scott?"

"Yes," I answered and watched as Virgil, in silence, pulled a book from the tissue.

"It's of Greek mythology, Virgil," he said. "I thought it about time to indulge your fantasies. Besides, Miss Scott," he said turning to me, "he has been hoping for just such a book for the past few months." He smiled at me in the manner of a confederate and we both watched as Virgil opened the illustrated book and started reading the first page.

"Whoa, young man," Mr. Moore said, "not now. You'll have time to read it when I'm gone, but now," he glanced out the reception hall window, "what say we go boating before lunch since this is a holiday. Just in case there isn't another day for it before the winter sets."

Virgil looked at me. "May we be excused, Ma'am?"

"Yes, certainly," I replied. "Why don't you get your

84

greatcoat and hat?"

"I am sorry you cannot join us, Miss Scott, but there is only room enough for the two of us," Mr. Moore apologized.

"Say no more, Sir, for I am sure you and Virgil will do well without me. Besides, I do recognize the joy of two males at sport." Mr. Moore smiled and I found myself drawn to him and his good nature. It appeared that whatever his cousin, my employer, lacked in the way of warmth was to be found in his cousin's ways and manner.

"Will you be staying at Ganymede long?" I asked.

"Perhaps only three or four days, Ma'am. I have business in London at the end of the month." Mr. Moore must have seen a look upon my face when he mentioned my former home. "You miss the city, Ma'am?"

"Yes, sometimes," I answered honestly.

"Then perhaps," he suggested as Virgil came down the stairs, "after we return from our outing, we may discuss our mutual fondness for London, Miss Scott, for I too miss that city when I stay away too long."

I inclined my head toward Mr. Moore. "That would be most agreeable," I answered and suddenly my heart felt just a little lighter than it had for several weeks. Mr. Moore, whether he knew it or not, had managed to bring joy to Ganymede House, the children, and to me.

When we gathered for dinner that evening it was as if a transformation had taken place in the dining room; there was lively conversation and much amusement, for although Mr. Grayson followed his usual pattern of speaking for a few minutes, his cousin took upon himself the role of storyteller and conversationalist and talked almost constantly about his life, his friends, and his pastimes, much to the delight of the children who clearly enjoyed the changed atmosphere.

Mr. Moore's easy manner encouraged laughter; indeed he seemed to sense that the children needed it and he went out of his way to tell stories that would enchant them. He catered to their questions and on several occasions even included me in his circle, finding ways to bring into his narratives references of familiar landmarks in London. He spoke extensively of his travels on the Continent and regaled us with his tales of trips to foreign countries.

"Greece . . . Italy . . . the Aegean Sea . . . the Mediterranean . . . those are places, Virgil," he said speaking directly to the young boy, "those are places you must see, indeed you will see one day," and Virgil nodded, a wide grin on his face such as I had not seen before.

"Oh yes, Cousin Edward, oh yes! I have always loved to hear of those lands," he said caught up with the spirit of taletelling. "I remember when . . ." he began and at that recollection Mr. Grayson looked close to his son and an emotion I had not seen before flickered in his eyes. Were it from anyone else, I would have characterized that emotion as pain. But it was a pain mingled with anger and Virgil also saw the look and instantly averted his eyes, leaving his last sentence unfinished. There was an immediate dulling in the room.

Only a few seconds passed before Mr. Moore resumed his stories, and within moments the four of us were laughing at the foolish escapades of one of his hapless friends. Again, if for no other reason than the way he handled this awkward moment and made it less uncomfortable for the children, our guest earned my undying respect and admiration.

I could not help but observe Mr. Grayson's reaction to

his cousin. My employer was obviously not pleased with the frivolity of the evening nor with our easy acceptance of his cousin. He sat in silence, preferring not to join in when Mr. Moore began to tell tales of the two cousins' childhoods.

"Yes," he said to Virgil and Antonia, "your father and I shared many happy moments here at Ganymede when we were young. Surely you remember, Cousin," he said addressing my employer, "how we hid in the maze away from our tutors ..." Mr. Grayson nodded but said nothing and when the children begged their guest for more details, Mr. Grayson abruptly spoke out.

"I fail to see why tales of our youthful lives should be interesting to the children, Edward."

At once there was another silence and the children looked down at their plates.

"But Sir, our escapades would delight them" Edward answered. "Surely you remember our own fascination when Uncle told of our own fathers' games as children." Mr. Moore smiled again, cajoling his cousin to join in the merriment but Mr. Grayson would have none of it.

"No, I have no recollection," he replied and the curtness of the words chilled the rest of the evening as Mr. Moore gestured helplessly to me and the children and yielded to his cousin's wishes.

When the meal was over and the children excused from table, Mr. Grayson altered his usual routine; he had Mr. Keanne serve Mr. Moore a glass of port but waved off the decanter when it was placed in front of him.

"I have much work to do this evening, Edward," he said rising. "I trust you will excuse me." He turned to me. "Goodnight, Ma'am." I lowered my head, embarrassed that Mr. Grayson would leave me alone with Mr.

Moore. I knew not what my next words should be. But again, Mr. Moore came to the rescue and signaled Mr. Keanne who was standing at the back of the room.

"Would you take the port into the sitting room, Sir?" he asked. "I should appreciate it very much if you would honor me by discoursing with me, Ma'am. Although I care much for my two young relatives I fear my prattlings have tired you and I would very much like to talk of other things. Especially of our times in London, as we agreed this afternoon." Mr. Moore followed me into the small sitting room and when we had seated ourselves by the fire, Mr. Keanne placed both the wine and a silver teapot on a table before us. I saw there was a plate of biscuits on the tray.

"I think those are for me," Mr. Moore said, taking one of the wafers. "Mrs. Keanne knows these are a favorite of mine." He spoke to Mr. Keane. "Please convey my thanks to your good wife."

"I believe, Mr. Moore," I said sipping my tea, "you are a favorite of not only the children but of the staff, too."

"I assure you, Miss Scott, if I am it is because I also am pleased with them. As for my young cousins . . . well, you know them, Miss Scott; you educate them. Tell me, are they not fine youngsters?"

"Most certainly. They have impeccable manners for ones so young."

"That is because their mother taught them," Mr. Moore said and I marvelled at his ease in speaking of the late mistress of Ganymede House. I made no reply to this statement and he continued. "And their studies?"

"They are progressing well."

"Good."

How pleasant it was to have a chance to discuss my young charges! I readily welcomed their cousin's inquiries, explaining the course of study I was imparting to them.

Mr. Moore listened attentively, asking appropriate questions whenever I paused for breath. "Forgive me, Miss Scott," he said at one such juncture, "I should not be asking these things for I am not the children's guardian, but I am sure you have observed there is a breach between my cousin and myself. I am loath to ask questions about his children for fear he think me prying."

"Oh no, Sir," I said, "I welcome your queries and the chance to speak of the children."

Mr. Moore smiled at me. "Good," he said. "Tell me, do they still play hide and seek in the nursery?"

I shook my head. "I'm afraid, Mr. Moore, that all those childish games and occupations no longer figure in their lives. I—" I began but thought better of telling this stranger of my thoughts about the lost childhood of his cousins.

Mr. Moore was silent while I reflected on my words.

"And," he asked quietly, "do the children speak much of their mother?"

I was startled at the question but Mr. Moore's kind countenance moved me to speak honestly.

"No, in fact, never."

"I suspected that." He sipped his port. "I suspect it is still too painful."

"No, Sir, I disagree. Please," I said staring directly at him, "I believe it would be a blessing for the children to talk of their mother. In fact I suspect they have a longing to do so."

Mr. Moore sat up. "Indeed. Why do you say that?"

"I believe it to be because of their reactions and the way they respond. I believe they have many secrets between them," I said as Mr. Moore watched my face.

"What kind of secrets?"

"That I do not know, Sir. Perhaps, in time, you may ask them. For now I am not privy to that portion of their lives."

Mr. Moore slapped his thigh. "Well done, Miss Scott, well done. How lucky for Virg and Tonia to have such an understanding tutor. And now, Ma'am, let us talk no more of the children. Let us speak of our mutual attraction to London." Mr. Moore bent his head to me and I noticed that he, too, did not have the Grayson forelock; instead his hair was dark blond and wavy so that the ends of it sometimes formed ringlets that tapered across his forehead. When, in the telling of an especially amusing story, one curl fell over his eye I found myself thinking about his fair good looks and easy manner and I was distressed to find that, lost in this reverie, I had missed several sentences of the tale. I was glad that I was sitting in shadow for I did not want Mr. Moore to see me blush nor speculate as to the reason for my discomfort. The moment passed quickly and we resumed speaking. We spoke at length about my former home and my friends and past life, and I enjoyed the chance to tell another adult of the happy times I had had when I was younger.

Mr. Moore listened and when I recounted a most happy event in my life he laughed with me and I realized fully how much I had missed the warmth of another's friendship. Thus, when we heard the hall clock strike eleven we were both surprised at the late hour. Mr. Moore summoned Mr. Keanne to attend to the candles and fire while he escorted me to my room. After he bade me goodnight and made his way in the darkened hall toward the guest wings, I could not help but notice a small shaft of light under Mr. Grayson's door. Evidently his work had kept him up.

Chapter 10

Throughout Mr. Moore's stay, Mr. Grayson continued to absent himself from all family events save the dinner table. Even at breakfast, I learned, by the time Mr. Moore had appeared at table, his cousin had already eaten and had left for his duties about the estate. I continued to teach Virgil and Antonia their lessons, but it was in a lighter mode, for the children were much more receptive to their breaks during the day and I, trying not to interfere on their times with their guest, often chose not to escort the three of them on their adventures. That Mr. Moore was inventive was beginning to become apparent to me; he found games and excuses to delight the children. He recalled long-forgotten childhood games to enchant them and, because it was still good weather, even proposed taking Virgil out boating again.

"This will probably be the very last day, Virg," he had said as the two of them journeyed forth, "for the weather is definitely turning cold." He wrapped a scarf around his throat. "We shall be back shortly, Ma'am, and then if it is agreeable, the four of us shall have a go at one of Mrs.

Keanne's excellent cakes."

He said this more to Mr. Keanne, who was standing next to the door, than to me, and I saw that gentleman smile. "I'm sure there will be a sweet treat for you, Sir. Mrs. Keanne, I believe already has something baking in the oven."

I watched as they left for the boathouse and when they were gone the good gentleman stood at the window and observed.

"The children are certainly enjoying their cousin, aren't they, Mr. Keanne?"

"Aye. They always did. A great favorite he is with the young ones . . . a great favorite."

"And of yours and Mrs. Keanne's too, I suspect."

"Aye," he answered again. "Mr. Moore was always a bit of an easy-mannered gentlemen. Always knowing what to say and obliging all. When he and Master were young they used to spend many a night carousing. Many times I would have to shake them awake and hurry them upstairs before their tutors would find them." He began to laugh and then mindful of my presence, stopped. "Begging your pardon, Ma'am, I didn't mean to be telling—"

"No, no, it is most interesting. I did not know they were so close when they were boys. They are not that way now." The old man shook his head deliberately and I continued, "Not since Mistress Rosamunda's death . . . ?"

"That I can't say, Ma'am." Mr. Keanne rearranged a bowl of flowers on the table. "If you'll excuse me, Ma'am," he said leaving the room and again I was thwarted in my quest to find some answers as to why Ganymede House was so gloomy.

After the two had been gone almost an hour, Antonia became restless and I proposed that we surprise her brother and cousin and meet them at the shoreline of the lake. This met with eagerness, and together we walked slowly down to a clearing where we were sure to be seen from the boat. I carried several small sweets for the two sportsmen and Antonia hugged Josephine close, who, since her cousin gave the doll to her, had become her instant favorite.

"Look, Miss Scott," Antonia said pointing out to the lake, "Can you see them? Virgil! Cousin Edward!" she called but of course we were much too far from the middle of the water where the boat seemed to be anchored and I was not sure that we were seen.

We stood by a large oak tree, waving our arms, but to no avail; the cousins were not looking in our direction and finally we decided to wait quietly until the boat came closer to shore. Antonia scampered away, behind the tree, searching for acorns, and I had no more than settled myself upon a blanket on the ground when I glanced out to the lake and saw Virgil and Mr. Moore beginning to exchange places. Virgil was standing up, in a most dangerous position, when the boat began rocking and I saw Mr. Moore reach out to the young boy but it was too late; the boat shifted suddenly and Virgil toppled backwards into the water. I could see him floundering close to the small craft.

"Virgil! Virgil! Help him, Mr. Moore!" I screamed and ran closer to the water's edge. At the sound of my voice, Mr. Moore looked toward me and then quickly dove into the water and put his arm around the flailing youngster, rescuing him from a fate I do not even want to contemplate.

Mr. Moore put Virgil into the boat, then climbed in himself and propelled the craft toward where I stood, horrified at the scene I had just witnessed. I quickly sent Antonia to the house to get help and to warn Mrs. Keanne to be prepared to have pots of hot water ready to take the chill off Virgil and Mr. Moore.

"You have saved him, Mr. Moore," I shouted when the boat came closer to the shore line. "Thank heavens you are a strong swimmer." I put my cloak around the shivering boy and led him quickly back to Ganymede where both Mr. and Mrs. Keanne stood waiting frantically in the hall.

"Please inform Mr. Grayson of the accident," I said to the servants. "He will want to know immediately."

"I'm sorry, Ma'am," Mr. Keanne replied, "but he doesn't seem to be in the house. I've sent one of the other men to locate him."

"Very well," I said hurrying Virgil up the stairs ahead of Mrs. Keanne who herself carried a steaming pot of water. "Had it not been for Mr. Moore," I said as I continued down the hall, "I shudder to think of what may have been. Truly, he has saved the boy."

Later, when all was quiet and the children abed— Virgil with an extra heating brick in his—Mr. Grayson, Mr. Moore and I had a late dinner. My employer had finally been found, completing chores on the estate, and when told of the accident had come quickly to verify Virgil's safety. He was most solicitous of his son's comfort, asking questions of him as to his physical requirements, and when he finally saw that the boy was exhausted and needed his sleep he joined Mr. Moore and myself in the dining hall.

"I am in your debt, Edward," he said as he took his

place at the head of the table.

"Nonsense," Mr. Moore replied modestly. "I am sorry that the accident occurred. I should have been more vigilant."

"Why was the boy not wearing a life jacket?" Mr. Grayson put down his fork and knife and I found his querying tone to be a bit sharp to one who had just performed such an heroic deed.

"I could not find any in the boat, Sir. And, when we started out the wind was calm and I saw no need to take extra precautions. I know the boy can swim some." He took a sip of his wine. "Of course, now I know better and it won't happen again. I shall better equip us the next time."

"The next time," Mr. Grayson mused and thereafter lapsed into silence until Mr. Keanne cleared away the dishes and placed the wine decanter upon the table. "Please serve yourself, Edward," he said and, hardly looking at me, added, "I trust you will once again excuse me, Ma'am, for I have duties to finish."

We watched him leave the room and neither Mr. Moore nor I spoke but by mutual silent consent we made our way to the small sitting room.

"I feel I must apologize for my cousin, Miss Scott. His manners are sometimes lacking."

My heart went out to this kind person and my admiration for him increased tenfold as he stepped forward to excuse his cousin's rudeness.

"My concern, Sir, is that you have not been properly thanked for your courageous deed. If I am troubled it is not for you to apologize, Mr. Moore. I fear your cousin—"

"I pray you will not judge him too harshly, Ma'am. He

has been a most melancholy man since the death of his young wife. In fact—" Mr. Moore began and then stopped.

"Please, Sir, I ask you to continue this subject for to do so sheds light on the situation. I have heard from those who have lived here for a long time that this gloominess was not always so."

"That is quite true, Miss Scott. Ganymede House used to ring with the laughter of the children and my cousin and his lovely lady. It was indeed a pleasure to be a visitor here during those times."

"Then, the accident changed everything?"

"You know about the accident?"

"Not really. I have only heard snatches—that she tragically fell into the sea."

Mr. Moore sighed. "I doubt if anyone will ever know the truth of that terrible evening. How could the accident occur when Rosamunda was a skilled horsewoman? I sometimes think, Miss Scott, that the uncertainty of that night's events occasionally overwhelms my Cousin's mind and leads him to . . ." Mr. Moore delicately stopped speaking.

"Pray, continue, Mr. Moore. Let us speak frankly. Leads him to what?" And lest Mr. Moore think me too bold or too prying I added, "I can understand how my employer feels, for I too have suffered losses—my mother and father—but there are times when we must succumb to life's terms. Mr. Grayson, for his children's sake, should try to overcome his gloom, for surely Virgil and Antonia miss their mother, also. Of that I have no doubt."

Mr. Moore was concerned. "You spoke of that before, Ma'am. Have you told their father?"

"No, Sir," I said shaking my head. "I'm afraid my employer will hear none of it. I once tried to broach a similar subject with him, but he cut me off and I have not tried to speak so intimately since."

"Yes, that is what I mean," Mr. Moore said, returning to his original thought. "I sometimes wonder if my good cousin has not fallen into deep dejection and if it now colors his perception about all things: the estate, the family, himself, and even, I hesitate to say this, Miss Scott, and even the children."

I put my hand to my mouth and dared not think of the direction in which Mr. Moore was turning. "Surely, Sir, you don't mean that there are moments of black despair? Surely you are not suggesting that Mr. Grayson suffers from a form of . . ." I could not bring myself to complete the sentence and Mr. Moore saw my horror and stepped forward and took one of my hands.

"No, dear lady, please be assured that I don't think that it is possible that my cousin's dejection will drive him mad or hinder him from performing his parental duties." Mr. Moore released my hand but I could see that although he did his best to reassure me about his cousin's state of mind, he, too was worried. "Now," he added, feigning amusement, "we will speak no more of this and shall turn our attention to other matters."

But I would have none of it. "Come, Sir, we must speak of this," I said. "Were it not for the children I would not be interested, for it is surely none of my affair," I explained. "But they are my charges and I have pledged to do my best for them."

Mr. Moore smiled in that flattering way that I had come to know so often these past days. "How lucky they are to have you, Ma'am," he said, and then seeing that I would not surrender the line of conversation, he continued. "No, Miss Scott, I certainly do not think any harm will befall them here at their own home. I am sure my cousin's melancholia will not affect them." He poured himself a second small glass of wine. "I am afraid because I care so much about them that I allow my mind to wander far afield of reality." He forced a smile. "And surely, one cannot blame my cousin for the boating accident this afternoon for as you and I both know, he was not in the boat with us." A clouded look appeared on his face.

"Forgive me, Sir, but you appear distressed?"

"I was just wondering about the life jackets," he said. "They most always are in the boat. And most certainly Oliver knew that I was to take the boy out this afternoon." He ran a hand through his hair. "But that is stuff and nonsense, Ma'am, when we both know that my cousin had, by his own account, ridden far afield early this morning."

I nodded but as I did so I remembered that I saw Mr. Grayson's favorite steed in the stable as we passed it on our way to the lake. I almost spoke of it but decided it would be better for all if I did not voice my thoughts and accuse unjustly. But I vowed to myself to keep a more watchful eye on the children.

"Well," Mr. Moore said, recalling me to my sensibilities, "I see you are tired and I have kept you much too long after the excitement of the day. And I myself must rest, for I rise before dawn to continue my journey. And before I sleep I have notes to pen to the children." He extended an arm. "Come, Ma'am, let me escort you to your room."

There was suddenly a very heavy weight on my heart

and a look of sadness must have passed my countenance.

"There is something wrong, Miss Scott?" he queried gently.

"It is just that I did not know you were leaving tomorrow, Sir. I am distressed for I feel that both the children and myself are losing a friend." I wanted Mr. Moore to know he had brought great joy to all of us and that his departure would cause Virgil and Antonia unhappiness. But, I did not want to appear bold and tempered my comments.

"I shall miss the children," he said and then bowed to me, "and your wit and wisdom, Ma'am. I had not expected to spend such a delightful time at Ganymede."

His words caused me confusion and I stumbled on my reply. "You honor me, Sir," I said and felt my cheeks flame. "It was, in truth, your visit that caused us to shine. I—the children," I amended, "will be sorry that you are gone."

"I, too. Perhaps I may call on my way home from London in a fortnight. But am I too presumptuous" he asked, "in inviting myself for another stay?"

"Of course we should like that, Sir. The children will be happy to hear of your second visit and you yourself heard Mr. Grayson express that the comforts of Ganymede House are always at your disposal." I rose and took his arm.

"And you, Ma'am, what do you say of it?"

"I?" How I wished that the candles were not so bright for I cared not for him to see the smile upon my lips. "I, of course, would be glad to welcome you, too."

Later that evening as I prepared myself for sleep I was quite fatigued with the events of the day and when I lay down in my bed my body and senses played little tricks on me for I distinctly smelled the scent of summer roses. But since all the roses had faded at least two months ago I knew there could be no fresh flowers in the house. Perhaps, I thought, as I closed my eyes, Tillie had come upon some scentwater and had oversprinkled herself with it. And by the morning, when I awoke, the air contained no traces of the flowers and I put the imagined incident aside.

Chapter 11

We returned to the formality of Ganymede House after Mr. Moore left and I, if truth be known, joined the children in missing their cousin. For two days Virgil and Antonia sat glum in the schoolroom, trying but failing to show attention to their studies. I, myself, also wished that the days of the month would pass quickly so that we would once again welcome Mr. Moore on his way from London. In his notes to the children he had written that he would probably travel through the area some- time near the holidays and that bit of information, for the three of us, was the only bright spot to be found for the upcoming season.

How different from this my life in London had been! There, the Holidays meant a round of parties and glad tidings but here at Ganymede House there were no festivities planned and Mr. Grayson did not mention that any were forthcoming. I did resolve, however, to give the schoolroom a festive air when the time came. The dreary month of November was still upon us, however, so I did not trouble to think of Christmas just yet.

Mr. Grayson continued to absent himself from the children, save for the dinner table and our nightly questions, and I had lost all hope that things would change. The dinner pattern had already established itself many months before I joined the household and I knew that I could not alter it.

Aside from the schoolroom and the children's talk my only other conversation was with the staff, for Mr. Grayson seemed to lapse more and more into silence when we sat after dinner. He still kept up the pretense of sitting with me, but there was no discourse between us. As it grew darker earlier, my employer now excused himself sooner and withdrew from the room and I was left to my own devices.

This evening, though, perhaps because I had been kept indoors all afternoon by cold rain, I was restless and did not feel the need to retire early. After I walked about the small sitting room several times to look at the paintings, I decided to walk the length of the ground floor of Ganymede. I had already grown accustomed to the various halls and rooms and corridors and now knew my way about my new home.

I hurried quickly past the Great Hall, for as I neared the door I felt the cold wind pushing at it and heard the heavy oak frame strain with the force. I shivered and moved into the library where already the fire had reduced itself to insignificant embers and the candles were but stubs ready to snuff themselves out. I looked in the dim light at the walls of books, hoping to find something that would allay my restlessness, but no book title appealed to me. As I made my way to the next room I heard the screeching noise of a tree branch as it scratched across a window and I glanced up in time to see the limb quiver again against the glass.

The rain, I saw, had finally stopped. The wind, though, had much increased and was blowing forcefully through and against the trees, bending them low so that the few dried leaves that had clung tenaciously to the branches through the autumn months were now being pulled savagely from their connecting stems. The leaves whirled and fluttered about randomly and, because of the velocity of the wind, the brittle foliage appeared as if suspended in air, dancing one last time before being allowed to fall to the ground.

I watched the leaves as the blowing wind spun them round and round, tossing them high into the blackened sky. It was then, when I raised my eyes to follow them, that I saw a faint light in the topmost window of the tower. I blinked my eyes quickly, for I was perplexed. I had not realized that the tower was still in use, nor could I understand which members of the household would possibly be there so late on such a cold and gloomy evening. I watched in puzzlement for several minutes until I saw the light flicker and pull away from the small window, as though a candlestick had been moved. Soon there was total darkness in the tower.

I waited a few moments longer but saw no one emerge. By then my eyes were strained from peering into the blackness and though still puzzled, I made my way to my room. Perhaps, I told myself, it was only the moon's reflection that played tricks on me, but I knew my excuse was weak for there was no moon this night. And yet I had no other explanation for the illumination. Mayhaps one of the servants would put forth an accounting if I asked them in the morning.

Nearly all the candles in the downstairs had been

extinguished and I saw that the sitting room had already been closed for the evening. I walked slowly and quietly up the stairs, thinking about the odd light in the tower, and when I reached the second landing I noticed the door to Rosamunda's room open and close quickly. In the half-light I saw Mr. Keanne emerge. He made his way softly toward where I was standing, pausing to listen at Mr. Grayson's door, and I debated as to whether to make my presence known. Finally, because there was no way to avoid our meeting, I spoke.

"It is only I, Mr. Keanne."

The servant turned toward me, accustoming his eyes to the half-light, and seemed startled. "Miss Scott. I thought you had gone abed before this time." His voice seemed hesitant. "You were not in the sitting room."

"No," I answered feeling compelled to explain, "I wandered about. I could not sleep." I kept my voice low for I did not want to disturb anyone else in the household and in particular, Mr. Grayson.

Mr. Keanne came close to me. "Do you require anything, Miss?" His voice was now gentle and solicitous.

"No, thank you," I began but at that moment there was a muffled sound from beyond the master bedroom and we both turned to look at the door. Mr. Keanne stiffened. "Perhaps your master needs your assistance," I suggested although I could not distinguish the bidding.

The old gentleman nodded his head. "Aye, if you'll excuse me, Miss," he said hurrying to the bedroom. As he entered it, I distinctly heard a voice that could only be Mr. Grayson's cry out a single word, a word that I could not discern. I waited but a few seconds to see if my help was needed but as Mr. Keanne remained beyond the door for that time, I felt that all was in control.

The next afternoon, after luncheon and while the children were resting, I purposely sought out Mr. Keanne, hoping to get some explanation from him about the light in the tower. I found him in the library straightening the shelves, and this was the ploy I needed to begin my conversation. Mr. Keanne listened politely, continuing to work on the books, and when I had finished my narrative he shook his head.

"You must have been mistaken, Miss. No one uses the tower anymore. It's been closed."

"But," I persisted, "I am sure . . ."

"No, Miss, it was probably the moon and stars."

"Mr. Keanne, it was a black night," I insisted.

"Then," the old gentleman said staring me straight in the eye, "may I suggest that it was just a trick of—"

"Of my imagination?" I was annoyed that he was not taking me seriously. "Perhaps, Sir, but I rather doubt it." I turned away. "I am sure . . ." I began but I did not finish. I knew Mr. Keanne had closed the subject.

That evening, after supper, I resolved to wait again until all was quiet so that I could once more watch the tower. No matter what Mr. Keanne suggested, I knew that there was someone there and I was determined at least to vindicate my own observations.

I had not long to wait, for Mr. Grayson excused himself even earlier than usual and I hastened to the library windows to keep my watch. It was not a moonless night and there were stars in the skies, but I knew that neither of these natural phenomena were responsible for what I had witnessed the prior evening.

Shortly after I heard the clock chime nine, my vigil was rewarded, for a soft glow suddenly appeared and

107

shone from one of the small windows at the top of the tower. As I watched, the solitary figure of a large person, silhouetted by the candle's light, stepped into view and stood at the window. I could not determine who it was. I watched, bewitched, for now I felt that Mr. Keanne surely could not refute what my eyes had seen for a second time. I vowed that I would ask more questions in order to solve this riddle.

I stayed by the window, hoping to recognize the figure, but upon hearing the Hall clock chime the half hour I grew weary. With a measure of disappointment I decided that I should retire to my room. But it was at that moment I heard a downstairs door close and soft footsteps echo in the Great Hall. Not wanting to be discovered nor appear to be spying, I snuffed my own candle and waited, in the dark, until whoever it was passed the library. I stood alongside the window, within the folds of a tapestry so that I could not be seen in case someone looked into the room. Thankfully I had the good sense to take that precaution, for Mr. Keanne peered into the room and, not seeing me, departed.

I breathed a sigh of relief, for although I had every right to be in the room, I knew that the servant would not look kindly upon my being found there after our talk this afternoon. I waited until I heard no more sounds in the antechambers and took one last look at the tower. To my chagrin, the window had gone dark. Whoever was there had, in the moment just past, abandoned his watch.

Again I went to my room in total darkness, feeling an unhealthy disquietude. Why had Mr. Keanne denied what I saw, and who was it that inhabited the tower and at so late an hour? If I were to remain at Ganymede House, I knew I would have to have these answers.

I lay awake long into the night, not only because of my puzzlement but because I heard constant unaccountable noises throughout the house. I told myself that it was merely the inclement weather and all its attendant sounds that kept me awake, yet somewhere in the back of my mind I recalled hearing another kind of timbre—I thought it to be a human voice and one that appeared to be in trouble and misery—but I dismissed that theory as one of those late-night figments of imagination that possess one's mind when one is too tired yet too exhilarated to sleep.

I had just begun to enter that twilight time when sleep is almost assured when I heard the scamperings of quick-paced steps near my room and, seconds later, a door closing hard. I instantly reached for my wrapper, fearing that there existed an emergency in the nursery. I opened my bedroom door only to find the hallway in total darkness, and when I looked toward the children's wing I could see that all was quiet. Whatever or whoever had passed my door was not in the vicinity of the children's rooms.

I looked the other way, towards the master and guest wings, and saw a thin shaft of light below the door to Rosamunda's room. I debated as to whether I should investigate or return to my bed. This was the second time in two days that someone inhabited Rosamunda's room and now I could not dismiss it as a matter of coincidence. Whoever was there now, I realized, had had access to it constantly, and who it was at this late hour I could not imagine.

I thought once more about investigating and while I hesitated but a few seconds I heard another sound—a deep voice, although it seemed to be too guttural, too frenzied to be human.

"Rosamunda!"

The intensity was not unlike that of a wounded beast crying out in pain and misery and I shuddered at the pure animalistic sound as I recognized from whose throat it came.

"Rosamunda," Mr. Grayson yelled once more and for the first time since I had come to Ganymede House, my heart went out to the master of this estate. For to hear the cry of Mr. Grayson was to hear the sound of lingering and intransient hopelessness.

I heard footsteps approaching the wing from the servants' quarters and I knew the faithful Mr. Keanne was once more about to serve his Master in the middle of the night, so I quietly shut my door and returned to bed. But there was to be no sleeping. Somehow I knew that the light in the tower and the figure of a man and the cries of Mr. Grayson were all connected and I vowed that come the morning I would ask either Mr. or Mrs. Keanne for an explanation.

I pulled the bed quilts closer to me, yet despite their bulk and their warmth I was cold. I could not decipher whether it was the late hour chill of the room or fear or apprehension that caused my body to shiver. I heard someone pass close to my door and I lay still, holding my breath—foolishly believing that someone was listening for movement from my room. I remained rigid and tense until I saw the first rays of a winter dawn penetrate the dark in my room, and with this comforting half-light I gave myself up to Morpheus for a short time.

Chapter 12

After the school day was over and while the children were resting in their rooms I decided to walk the grounds outside the tower. I had not yet investigated that part of the estate; it still held some terror for me since the episode of the maze. But now, since I had seen the candlelight at the top of the structure for these past two evenings, I knew I had to confirm my suspicions that someone was visiting the tower nightly.

It was a cold afternoon but it was clear and I saw that most of the outdoorsmen—the gardeners, the farmers and stablehands—were busy attending to their late autumn tasks. The days were shortening and the weather was increasingly turbulent and I suspected that the snows would soon descend upon us, trapping us inside for the next four or five months until the spring. I have been warned that the winters in this northern part of England were quite severe and paralyzing and that there was not much visiting amongst friends during the cold months. It was a time, frankly, that I did not look forward to—the cold climes had never appealed to me and the thought of

111

no walks around the estate or occasional chats with the workers about mundane but pleasant topics made me sad. I had been told that even the regularly passing mailruns with their out-of-town news would only occasionally make the trip for the next several months. The thought of such isolation filled me with dread. Oh, how I yearned to be back in London, anticipating joyful holiday parties and spectacular Boxing Day extravaganzas, instead of being in my present situation—that of attempting to solve mysteries of the estate. There were secrets hidden deep in this house, secrets that affected all who lived here including me, and more and more it seemed that I was becoming completely enmeshed in the gloom of Ganymede!

There were so many strange customs in this house: sitting silently with my employer after dinner; the relationship between Mr. Grayson and his children; the reverence and irreverence for Rosamunda; the light coming from the late Mistress's room. How would I ever learn to distinguish all the nuances and vague replies that I met with daily: I kept my own counsel and waited to see if all this curious behavior would straighten itself out in its own fashion.

For today, though, I was more concerned with what I believed to be another concealment and since late last evening when I watched the solitary candle flicker in the tower window I promised myself that I would at least try to puzzle the mystery of the evening lights. It intrigued me and I knew that I had to investigate alone for Mr. Keanne was doing his utmost to keep me from discovering the truth.

It was a calm day, the wind had not been blustery, and I walked toward the massive tower with anxiety while still marveling at the beauty of the stone construction. The building appeared to sparkle and shimmer in dozens of intricate patterns as if hundreds of tiny points of light—golden-red now from the setting sun—reflected off the mica so that it served as a cold, but beautiful, beacon to those who worked on the estate.

I walked slowly around the structure—observing it, investigating it—and eventually came upon a small wooden door facing away from the sea that was built into it. It had a huge wrought-iron keyhole and a black oversized handle, and I wondered if perhaps the door was unlocked. I summoned my courage, not quite knowing if my stern resolve would allow me to enter the tower and explore it should it be open. My lost hours in the Greek maze had etched a fearful memory in my mind, and I needed time to dispel certain apprehensions.

I pulled at the heavy door but it was locked. The huge wrought iron keyhole held fast. Whoever dwelled in the tower at night must surely have the key.

"Master be here . . . Master be there." The sing-song voice at my back startled me and I turned and saw a young man of about eighteen or nineteen years of age standing away from the deep purple-grey grass, close to the tower, watching me and smiling. "Master be there . . . Master be here," he sang in a voice that deviated neither up nor down in tone but when he had repeated the refrain for a third time he began to laugh. I stepped away from the door.

"Who are you?" I asked for I had not seen this person in the gardens or fields before.

The man continued to laugh and chant and I looked around, unsure of what my next actions were to be. I could see that he did not understand me and would pay no attention to my questions.

"Willie!" Old Martin came running toward the tower. "Willie!," he shouted. "You be leaving Miss Scott alone." The older man went up to the still laughing young man, took his arm, and pointed to the stables. "Now, Willie, you go on home and finish up the chores. The horses need tending."

The man called Willie stopped laughing and nodded somberly. "Aye . . . the horses . . . the horses." He turned and looked at me. "I take care of the horses everyday. Everday . . . and everynight." He stopped and frowned and turned to Old Martin. "I took care of the horses that night, too, didn't I?" he asked. "Took care of them good, too, didn't I?" He looked away toward the sea and wrinkled his brow in remembrance. "Only the brown one came home alone, didn't she? All alone without Miss Rosamunda. And I took care of her, didn't I?" He paused, recollecting the scene from somewhere deep within his memory. "It were raining and I got all wet . . . all wet . . . my hair and my breeches and my face, but I still took care of the horses." He trembled and touched the stone building and abruptly changed the focus of his questions. "No one lives here, huh, Mr. Old Martin. No one except . . ." Willie's vacant eyes became big. "Except . . ."

Old Martin took the man by his arm once again. "It's all right, Willie," he said soothingly. "That's right—you took good care of the horses. You always do. Run along now, Willie, go take care of them again."

"Aye." Willie looked at Martin and then at me. He smiled and looked up at the tower. "Master be there . . . Master be here . . ." he sang as he ran toward the stables.

Old Martin doffed his hat. "He wouldn't have hurt you, Miss. He's just Willie—a harmless soul."

I smiled. "Thank you, Martin. You seem to be rescuing me all the time."

He laughed and I could see the spaces in his mouth where some of his teeth had been. "You'll find out all the ways of Ganymede, Miss. Just takes a while, that's all." He wiped his brow with an earth-soiled cloth and glanced up at the tower window. "Now why don't ye just go back to the house, Miss? The wind's coming up and it won't do for you to take a chill."

"Martin, what Willie was saying . . . about the horse?"

"Aye, Miss. I suspect you know about the accident."

I shook my head. "Not too much."

He nodded. "Aye, best that you don't know it all. It wasn't a pleasant thing."

"The tower . . .?"

Martin walked beside me, puffing his pipe so that the smoke of the tobacco whirled around his head. He chewed on the stem of it several times and I could see he was thinking of his answer. "Some people say it's haunted, Ma'am. Been haunted since that evening when Mistress's horse came home alone."

I shuddered and looked away toward the sea just as a sharp breeze swept over the land, ruffling my skirt, and I clutched at the fabric lest it swirl immodestly about my legs. I shivered again and in truth I did not know whether I did so because of the wind or Martin's words.

"But . . .?"

Martin took another puff on his pipe. "One of the estate hands saw a light in the tower one evening, Miss, about a month or two after the accident and when we went to investigate it there was no one in the tower. We opened the door since it was locked, and no one came out of it. And we climbed all the way to the top and . . ." His voice trailed off so that I had to wait until he finished his sentence.

"And . . .?"

"And, Miss, 'tweren't nothing there. Only the fragrance of white summer roses." He got quiet again and I could tell he was remembering the evening. He looked at me. "And, Miss, there weren't any roses. It was too late in the season. I wasn't the only one who smelled them, Miss . . . other people . . . that's why they say the tower is haunted, Miss. We—me and the other men—saw the light once or twice more and when we went to have a look about there was never anything there but the smell of roses . . ."

I did not tell Martin that I, too, had smelled the peculiar scent of roses on several occasions and had also seen the lights in the tower. It was just another piece of a puzzle that I thought best to keep to myself.

Tillie was in the room, preparing it for sleep, when I entered my chamber that night, and I watched while she turned down the bedcovers. She was a pleasant young woman, a complacent worker who needed instructions to carry out her duties but once told, was able to accomplish most of them without difficulties.

"It's a right fair evening out there, Miss," she said as she paused in her work. "One of those rare nights when we have a respite from the wind." She shook her head. "Long as I've been here, Miss, and that'll be going on near four years, for I came in service when I was

116

thirteen—started as a scullery maid in the kitchen, I did, Miss—the beginnings of winter have always been drafty in this house until we find the cracks. We've had the workers here this season already trying to plug up the holes but sometimes that wind still whistles through. Not that you'll notice it much here, for this room was always snug, Miss, but it used to be that even the flames in the fireplace would dance in some of the other rooms." She looked at my fireplace and the steady burning blaze from the huge split oak logs. "Especially in the guest wings, Miss, but Mr. Keanne saw to the workers fixing them." She shook out the pillow and then smoothed it. "Mr. Keanne says that Ganymede House is tighter than most manors in the countryside," she added proudly.

I stepped close to the French doors on the far side of the wall and rattled them to make sure they were closed tight against the cold air. Then I remembered they had not been opened since my arrival. I turned to Tillie.

"Do you know anything about the key to these doors?" I shook them again. "Why have they been locked and the key not left here in the room?"

The young maid shook her head vigorously. "I don't know, Miss," she said quickly but just the way she said it gave me cause to think otherwise. I fixed my eye upon her. Tillie looked away and I persisted.

"Is there something . . . ?" I began but she kept shaking her head. "Tillie, surely the Reverend Benjamin would object to you not speaking the truth." At the mention of the rector's name, the young girl stopped moving her head and paused. I could see that she was frightened.

"Please, Miss, don't ask me. It's none of my business, they said. They said to ignore it."

117

I sat at my desk. "Who said?" I inquired gently lest I dismay the poor girl more.

She continued to smooth down the sheets and I could see that she was thinking whether she should reveal the answer to my question. "Mr. and Mrs. Keanne, Miss. They said it was all foolishness and we, the servants, weren't to repeat such meanderings to anyone."

"Tell me, " I urged. "What foolishness with the door? Is there a reason why it is kept locked?"

Tillie nodded her head. "Yes, Miss. It's just that several of us . . . Moira . . . Cleo . . . the undermaids who sometimes work upstairs in training . . . well, we heard things, Miss. Especially at night. Mrs. Keanne says it's just the wind making strange sounds but many of us, especially the ones who have heard it, are not so sure, Miss." The girl shook her head very slowly. "We're not so sure, Miss."

"And the sounds, Tillie? What are they like?"

"God-awful sounds, Miss Scott. Like someone or something was moaning. And it weren't in any other rooms except those that face the sea. When we first heard it, Mrs. Keanne said it was probably an animal from the barn lowing and that the sound were carried by the winds as they swirled about, but," Tillie said, her eyes widening so that they were great pools of deep brown, "somedays there weren't any winds to speak of and still we heard it." She tugged at the corner of the sheet. "You can ask the others and they'll tell you the same. About the moans. Our Moira's never been known to lie, Miss, her being so religious and attending Catholic Mass and all. But one day she came down the steps to the kitchen and she was shaking and she even crossed herself, Miss, like the Catholics do, and Mrs. Keanne had to give her a cup of tea to calm her. She said she heard them, Miss, the sounds . . . and she said it was more like a lady's crying. Like a lady's crying her heart out but poor Moira didn't know what to do and she came downstairs and without her finishing her chores even—she was that scared. Mrs. Keanne made her sit in a chair and drink the tea although she couldn't even hold her cup, Miss, she was shaking so hard. And Mrs. Keanne didn't even scold her until later the next day, until Moira had taken hold of her senses."

I listened, fascinated by the maid's retelling of the story, not knowing whether to believe any part of it or to put it down to the vivid imagination peculiar to young girls' minds. "And the key, Tillie?" I asked, bringing the servant back to my original question. "What does this have to do with the key?"

Tillie looked at me as though I hadn't understood anything she had told me. "About two or three days later that's when Mrs. Keanne had us lock all the doors to the outside, Miss. She said Master wanted them sealed up just in case there were prowlers in the area. That's what they said, Miss . . . that the moanings probably came from thieves off the road and that they were trying to frighten us." Tillie stared at me. "You do believe me, don't you, Miss?" she asked and I was hard pressed to answer her.

"I do believe that Mrs. Keanne asked for the keys, yes, Tillie, and that Mr. Grayson wanted the doors locked," I answered truthfully, not adding that I did not accept the excuse given the household help. I looked at the French doors. Surely no one would climb the bushes, I thought, to invade the house. It would be physically risky and besides there were too many estate workers in the area. No matter what Mr. and Mrs. Keanne told the servants, that certainly wasn't the real excuse for the locking of the doors.

There was something wrong. It was as if there was almost an inherent *undercurrent of evil* here at Ganymede House. I knew not what prompted me to feel that way, and yet I knew it was bound up with the Lady Rosamunda's death. But even so—I could not accept the chatterings of fearful maids and half-witted stableboys of hauntings and cries in the night. No, all the tales *must* have a logical explanation.

I stood at the doors after Tillie left me and I watched the moon cast shadows on the bushes below. Surely the rustlings of the shrubs could not be mistaken for the wail of a woman, not even by foolish superstitious workers. But then, how to explain my own sighting of a person in the tower and the definite perfume of roses? Most positively I had seen the silhouette with my own eyes and smelled the aroma with my own nose.

I gazed out to as far as I could see in the dark, trying to determine where the edge of the land met the sea, out beyond the lawns, to the cliffs where Rosamunda met her death. What secrets did she take to her watery grave, I wondered. Was there no answer to the question?

Chapter 13

The next day when I saw her in the hall I asked Mrs. Keanne for the key to the terrace doors in my room, and after much hesitation on her part she produced it.

"You'll not need those doors open in the winter," she said and folded her hands in front of her, trying to tip the balance of the exchange in her favor.

"Perhaps there will be a warm day before the frost takes hold," I answered more for her benefit than mine, for in truth she was probably right. But I wanted that key to see what was out on the terrace and to hear for myself if there were any sounds of women wailing or thieves' trickery.

Mrs. Keanne was correct—there were no such times when I wanted to unlock the doors to the outside because of the continuous inclement weather. It remained cold and bleak throughout the next few days, and the children and I were of a mind to study and work as though industry and a quest for knowledge would hasten the season.

It was exactly the sort of climate that seemed

especially conducive to learning, and one afternoon, in an attempt to keep the children warm and to change the pattern of the schoolroom, Tillie and I shifted the work table so that it was closer to the now-constantly lit fires. The new arangement, though it impinged somewhat on the space in the room, fostered a more cozy atmosphere—one that more cheerily expressed the joy of learning—and the children and I profited much from the closeness of the heat. Antonia and Virgil seemed to apply extra pressure to themselves to study and I, challenged by their industriousness, spent many after-hours preparing lessons for them.

It was not an unpleasant time for me, although I did wish that Mr. Moore would return to Ganymede. Gone was the laughter and the teasing—the openness during dinner was once again replaced by our quieter and sterner times at table. But with the prospect of Mr. Moore returning to Ganymede in the near future both the children and I suffered more easily the nightly formal discourses with their father—moreover, the legacy of their Cousin Edward's light-heartedness served to allow the young people to answer their father in kinder tones.

Even Mr. Grayson seemed to change as the weather became more dreary, as though he knew that without his children and me at table there would be no other humans on the estate who would speak to him through the impending cold months. It was as though he understood that a continuance of his and his ancestors' life blood would not occur unless he cultivated the minds and emotions of his begotten children. I suspect that is the only reason for Mr. Grayson's moments of lapsed brevity, for as master of Ganymede he knew the value of progeny and the continuation of Graysons as heirs and keepers of the estate. Thus while there was no discernable enlightenment at dinner, there was a gradual blunting of the questions and their phraseology.

It was at these times, when the dinner table atmosphere was not so rigid, that I was able to watch my employer interact with his offspring. On one or two occasions I did detect a . . . what shall I call it? . . . a note of gentleness creep into the man's tone. The use of a word . . . the easing of a gesture . . . were sufficient to allow a limited relaxation of the strict dinner hour guidelines we had all learned to obey.

Even the children recognized the slackened tension and it was at these moments that I could see that their own reserve melted as they answered their father in quiet, yet spirited, manner. There were even episodes when the children would watch their father as he ate— waiting for him to speak, to ask a question, to acknowledge them—and on the times when he did so, I could see that their eyes would light up with happiness.

But these occasions were too few. Mostly we sat, the four of us, quietly eating our dinner, waiting for the time to pass before the two youngest members could be excused. It was a perplexing time, these meals, and I have often reflected on what caused the irrational and instant changes in Mr. Grayson's mood. But it was a bewilderment that I could not answer.

I sat back this evening and watched my two charges speak of their lessons. Oh, how I had grown so quickly to love them, to want to protect them, and had I any influence, I would have spoken to their father about his demeanor toward them. Surely, I thought in my meditation, someone should speak up for them. I hesitated to discuss the matter, for my employer paid

123

little mind to what I said and it would stand me in no good stead should I reproach him about his conduct with his brood. No, it was much better that I hold my tongue and work in my own small way to assure the children that there was love in the house.

There was something quite charming and yet forbidding about the children. Although they now accepted me, I found that the less I intruded into their quiet moments, the more I was allowed into their lives. It was a paradox, and I learned it well. The more I held my questions, the more the children called for me. Thus I spoke of nothing but school subjects by day but, in the evening, before I retired to my own room, I had now begun to bid the children a good-night although usually they were fast asleep.

This evening when I looked in on them I saw that the two children were slumbering despite the sounds of the wind at their shutters. Antonia tossed and turned and I rearranged the bedcovers over her, though I was sure that she would kick them off again during the night. By her side, as it had been since she was given it, was Josephine. Antonia's small fingers clutched the doll, pulling it close to her, and when she moved I saw that the doll also moved, so tight was the child's grasp on it.

Virgil was sleeping calmly in his room as though there were no secrets nor worries in his young life. I reached out and brushed his hair back and saw that where the Grayson forelock should be it was dark and straight, and I wondered what he would look like if he had the Grayson swirl like his father and grandfather. I examined his handsome face in the half-light and determined that with the peculiar characteristic he would certainly resemble more his father, but even without the distinctive family trait he bore strong resemblance to the long line of Grayson males portrayed on the gallery wall. Perhaps, I thought, this straight lock was the one wayward birthmark of his mother's family that he had inherited.

I thought of the children's names and how fitting they were for them—Antonia, the romantic and Virgil, a name of wisdom to live up to and admire. Oh how difficult it must be, I imagined, for such a young man to have to carry on the tradition of the Graysons and to be expected also to possess the wisdom of a Greek scholar. Such a heavy burden for such a sad little boy!

I concluded that Antonia must be her father's pride although I did not see too much extra favoritism accorded to her. At table I sometimes winced inwardly at each occasion when Mr. Grayson would look favorably on his daughter and slight his son. I did not know if this rejection was deliberate, yet I could not help think that the mere act hurt both of the males. Why anyone would want to intentionally reject the boy was far beyond my ken, for the lad was a joy, and my heart ached for him. But even sadder, I thought, was the laughter of his child that Mr. Grayson was missing. My pity was directed toward the father, yet I knew I would do everything to love the child even more, to make up for his parent's rejection. Watching Virgil sleep in his bed I knew that this would not be difficult.

Chapter 14

It was a strange day at Ganymede House. We had become accustomed to the seasonably cold weather and yet today it turned suddenly warm, and when I returned to my room after luncheon I found it to be much too heated. What better time, I thought, to open the French doors.

I turned the key inside the small lock and pulled at the doors just as Tillie knocked and entered my room to refill the water pitcher on my wash table. The young maid was horrified, for to go against Mr. Keanne's orders was unthinkable for any of the staff.

"Oh, Miss," she kept saying, watching as I opened the doors. "Mr. Keanne . . . Mr. Keanne forbade it."

"Never mind Mr. Keanne, Tillie," I said as I swung the doors wide and stepped onto the balcony. "My room needs an airing and what a glorious day to do it." I turned to the maid. "Is it not a beautiful day, Tillie?"

I looked around me and saw that the view from my terrace showed the back of the estate to full advantage. I could see one side of the Greek maze, some of the tower, and the long expanse of wind-swept lawn that led to the cliffs. I listened—thinking that I might hear the sea, but it was of no use—the water was much too far away for me to detect the sounds of the waves against the cliffs. This did not dismay me, my fondness for the water had not increased since I arrived at Ganymede House.

I moved closer to the iron railing surrounding the balcony. "Surely, Tillie, you can not be afraid of such a glorious day as this." Tillie watched me from inside the room and I could see that she was frightened even to come close to the doors. "Listen," I said as a slight breeze swept past me and into the room, playfully spinning the hems of the curtains. "You must agree, Tillie, you can only hear the rustle of the wind. Come," I held out my hand, "come listen and smell the air," I urged but the maid stepped back still further from the doors.

"If you please, Miss, I'd rather not . . ." she said and I could see the apprehension in her eyes. Certainly all the foolish talk about women moaning and robbers preying on the household had frightened her and I did not press her to join me on the balcony.

I stepped back into the room, much to Tillie's relief, and left the door ajar. The maid, now quite dismayed lest Mr. Keanne find out about the unsealing of the portals, continued to fill my pitcher, but I could see that her hand shook and when she had finished she glanced once more toward the balcony.

"Will that be all, Miss?" she asked and when I answered in the affirmative the young woman's face relaxed in relief and she curtsied and left me.

I sat at my desk, watching the curtains sway in the breeze—enjoying the fresh air as it penetrated into my room—and the combination of a heavy luncheon and the unaccustomed warm zephyrs soothed me and lulled me into a gentle rest. I put my head down on the desk thinking that a few moments thus would refresh me and I closed my eyes as the gentle breezes washed over me. I knew that Tillie would come for me when it was time for the second half of the day's schooling.

I was able to resume my tower virgil early that evening—Mr. Grayson told me at dinner that he would be at a late meeting with his estate managers in his private study at the far south end of the house. This suited me very well and I took my position at the library window and watched the dark tower—waiting while I heard the hall clock chime nine times and then the quarter hour, yet no light appeared at the top of the structure.

So much for mysteries, I mused, and made straight for my room, passing close to the study where I heard gentlemen's voices speaking in a jumble of camaraderie and seriousness. I was not able to discern their conversations, nor did I want to, and moved swiftly past the room and up the stairs lest someone see me and think I was listening.

I took up my poetry book, once again reading the words of the Romantics, delighting in their pastoral descriptions and feeling pleasantly eased. The abrupt changes in the weather had made me drowsy and though it was not yet my usual bedtime my eyelids felt heavy and I quickly prepared for bed.

It was not a peaceful sleep, however, for my mind drifted in many directions. I dreamt of the tower's lights and the unknown persons who met there at night. I remembered Mr. Keanne's negative replies to my questions about Ganymede House. Poor befuddled Willie's sing-song rhyme, "Master be here, Master be there," echoed throughout my disturbed sleep and I turned in my bed, unable to arouse myself from the slumber, yet knowing deep within my unconsciousness that I should. "Master be here, Master be there" became louder and suddenly I sat bolt upright as I felt cold streams of air sweep over me. I reached to draw my blanket around me.

But it was not the lack of coverlets that chilled me. I saw that across from my bed pale moonlight flooded into my room through the wide-open French doors. I stared at the open space in bewilderment for I had a strong recollection that I had locked the doors in the afternoon—most definitely remembering that I had pulled them twice to verify their closings before I went back to the schoolroom.

I reached toward the foot of the bed to retrieve my wrapper, but as I did so I heard the sound of metal scraping against metal and I saw the heavy velvet draperies undulate and the sheer curtains beneath them lift up and down, side to side, flapping noiselessly against the open doors. The diaphanous fabric swayed eerily in the dappled half-light—at times appearing to be a chimerical yet shapeless human form. I watched the flowing movement—fascinated as segments of the curtains raised up and billowed out like beckoning arms that bid me to follow . . . follow . . .

I took up my candle and struck a match to it, but the small flame flickered for only a few seconds before another sweep of wind invaded my room and extinguished it. I lit another match, but even before I was able to set fire to the candlewick the flame was snuffed out and while I groped for yet a third strike I smelled the overpowering and now too-familiar scent of roses permeate my chambers. I turned quickly in all directions yet saw nothing, and when once more the cold winds swept past me I moved swiftly from my bed to the doors to fasten them. Again I heard the scratching of metal coming from somewhere on my terrace and without thinking of my own safety, for my mind was addled and confused, I rushed toward the sound to investigate.

I stood close to the edge of the balcony, near the railing, and searched the dark. The scraping had stopped and it was still now, much too still, for the wind had mysteriously abated. While I was able to see several feet ahead of me it was entirely too dark, and I was not able to determine who . . . or what . . . lurked near my terrace. I took a deep breath. The scent of roses now surrounded me, and I felt my heart beating quickly, I remained motionless, listening to determine any little sound, straining to hear and see. I could not detect any form, and managed to convince myself that I had heard no sound and smelled no roses except perhaps in my dreams.

As I turned to reenter my room, I raised my head and saw that there was a light shining from the top of the tower. I moved to the center of the balcony and squinted my eyes and was able to discern a human shape—again, a man's—that disappeared from view as it strode back and forth . . . back and forth . . . in front of the candle, obliterating the light for brief seconds at a time.

I stood on the balcony, watching the tormented person—whoever he was—battle his own private demons and then suddenly, without warning, or notice, I felt a slight force at my back and I stumbled forward into the iron railing. My unslippered foot first touched, and then pushed though the low fence as one of the metal posts broke and gave way. I feared that the entire railing was loosened and I heard myself scream as I put my hands out in front of me and haphazardly reached out to take hold of something, anything, to steady myself. Just before I lapsed into an abyss of darkness, I smelled the heady odor of musty roses swirl about me. I cried out once more and then I felt my entire body crumple and fall onto the terrace.

I know not how long I lay there, for when I awoke I was in my own bed surrounded by Mr. and Mrs. Keanne and Tillie. I was told that the butler had heard my cries and found me slumped on the balcony, where I had fainted. He had carried me into my room where I was quickly put to bed. The three had stayed with me until I regained consciousness and now Tillie hovered near me—a brandy glass in her hand, proffering it to me but I refused it. I had more need for answers than spirits.

"The doors . . . they were open," I explained.

Mr. Keanne nodded his head. "Aye, Tillie told us you had unsealed them today." We both looked at the maid who put her head down.

"But I closed them . . ." I protested.

"You probably didn't test them, Miss," he said gently. "The wind came up sudden-like."

I shook my head for I could see that there was no sense denying his words. "Perhaps," I said weakly.

"No 'perhaps' to it, Miss Scott." Mrs. Keanne's barbed voice cut into the conversation. "It was foolish of you to open them. The warm day was only a cruel trick of the season—we're into the winter months now." She stared at me and I averted my eyes from her admonishing glare. "You should have listened to us, Miss Scott. There are reasons for everything."

"The railing . . .?"

"One of the reasons the doors were sealed," Mrs. Keanne answered quickly. "They need attending. They've rusted. Next spring."

"And the roses . . .?" I persisted.

The old woman looked at me and spoke sharply. "There are no roses, Miss Scott. There are no flowers. Everything's gone, everything's dead!"

I closed my eyes. It would be to everyone's betterment if I spoke no more of this evening's accident nor of the contemplation of ghostly apparitions and unexplained sounds in the night. I shook my head once more and thought it best to say nothing of the man in the tower. It was best to keep my own counsel now. I knew for certain that Ganymede House had strange secrets. Perhaps I would be able to uncover them sometime in the future.

Chapter 15

I spoke no more of the incident and when I met Mr. Keanne in the hall the next morning he said that the workmen would begin fixing the broken rail when the weather turned warm. I understood that it was his way of informing me that the French doors would remain closed until he or Mr. Grayson wanted them opened, and I simply nodded my head in acceptance.

Oh, how I yearned to have a confidant! I was now beginning to think that the mysteries of this place would best be solved if I could speak of my theories to someone else. But I was afraid, because I knew that Mr. and Mrs. Keanne had a closed mind on such subjects. It would do me no good to suggest that all was not right in the manor, for I was still considered a newcomer.

I had very briefly entertained the idea that I would speak of my fears to Mr. Grayson, but my employer had been preoccupied in the last weeks with estate business. On my walks around the grounds I had heard talk—whisperings, really—from stablehands and undergardeners about fences being mysteriously broken and prize horses getting loose and found in pastures far away from their stables.

When I asked Old Martin about it, he told me that animals had indeed been found wandering on the grasslands near the moors several mornings.

"One time it was Mr. Grayson's own prize stallion, Sabre, that went far afield, grazing in land that he had never been in. That horse requires special handling, Miss, and Master is just about the only one who can properly handle him. That were strange—Sabre being free like that. And another morning it were the mare—Venus, we call her—that's no longer ridden. She's a right pretty thing, she is, Miss, all light-brown colored with a flowing dark brown mane." He took out his pipe from his coat pocket and tapped it against the sole of his boot. "And that be very curious, too, Miss," he continued. "That mare, she's never rambled. Kind of shy, she is. Always very gentle-like . . . always wanting to snuggle up to you and put her nose against your arm and nudge you, that's why the Mistress loved her so. Why, she would feed her sugar and carrots. She loved that horse." The gardener seemed to forget that he was speaking to me and he looked off toward the moors—flooded, for once, in bright sunshine. "Aye, Venus, she were always a gentle animal," he said and puffed on his crooked stem pipe.

"And even Euripides—they tell me he's been seen roaming the grounds more than usual. Yea, but that's nothing different with that animal. He's been that way since . . ." He puffed heavily on the cold pipe, tamping the tobacco at the same time.

"Euripides?" I questioned for I had not heard that name mentioned before on the estate.

Old Martin looked at me. "The Mistress' dog. You

know, Ma'am, that big old black shaggy dog that roves about here."

"I've never seen him."

"No, probably you haven't, Miss. He stays with me now—he doesn't like to stay in the manor house anymore. Not since the accident. He's turned a little mean, you see, growling at stranger and family alike. Not at the children, though, not at the children—but if someone approaches them too quickly or touches them . . . well, Euripides can turn on you." Old Martin kept tamping the pipe. "Some say he should be put out of his misery—that he's fevered at times when he hears the winds and rains—but other than that he's a right faithful animal, Miss. I keep him in the cottage with me whenever he has a mind to stay inside. Euripides and me, we get along just fine." He looked at the hollow bowl of his still unlit pipe and then struck a match to it, sucking at it so that the tobacco finally caught.

"About the horses, Ma'am, I don't know how they got out. Except that there was a break in the fence. Perhaps it rotted out. Sometimes one of the workers will forget to get around to fixing things—you know how it be, Miss, . . ." he said looking at me. "I know there's been some foolish talk 'round here about something not quite right . . . not explainable . . . that the animals know something before we humans do, but that be all foolishness, Miss. Sometimes the men say things just to cover up their mistakes." He coughed. "But no harm was done about the animals—it was easy enough to send Willie over to the meads to get the horses and lead them back home. The creatures take kindly to him, Ma'am, and he takes good care of them." He tipped his hat to me and I knew he wanted to return to his gardens.

"Afternoon, Ma'am."

So even the fieldhands had their superstitions! Or perhaps it was only their way to relieve the monotony of the lonely isolated winters here in the North—this telling of tales. This year it was to be suspicious stories about the horses. I wondered that so many exaggerations could be tolerated! The thought dismayed me, and again I yearned for a trusted companion, one whom I could take into my confidence if for no other reason than to help me explain the mysterious events that occurred here.

Still more days passed and I had no rationale as to who, or what, had been on my balcony that fateful evening, or who inhabited the tower at night. I continued to see the light shining occasionally, though not as often as before.

As to the French doors to my room, there would have been no need to open them even if they were not sealed tight. The weather was most unpleasant and I oft preferred to pull the draperies shut. I found much comfort in my warm chambers despite my accident and I spent many evenings beside my own blazing fireplace surrounded by my own treasured trinkets.

The metal soundings I heard on that strange night continued for several days after my fright, but I determined that the broken column moved in the wind and scraped against the iron guard rail. It was something I wanted to discuss with Mr. Keanne, to perhaps have it repaired before it caused me any more discomfort.

About the slight blow to my back that caused me to lose my footing on the balcony, I still could not say. I tried to reason out Mrs. Keanne's argument that I merely stumbled, but that seemed too exaggerated for me to even consider. I would certainly have felt an object beneath my bare foot. Perhaps, if I allowed myself to recall that extraordinary event in depth in quieter moments, I would come to a more plausible explanation.

The one thing that continued to distress me was the scent of roses. Mrs. Keanne's chastisement rings true: there are no flowers in bloom here in November. Yet on several occasions—far too many now to recount—I have smelled the sweet traces of the blossoms. It was the one positive and most disturbing fact that I must certainly keep secret, for I had already made myself suspect in the staff's eyes.

I rejected the idea of speaking to Mr. Grayson. His mind was employed in other directions, and to tell the truth, I did not expect that he would take me seriously. He was a most practical man, and any suggestion to him that all was not right at Ganymede House would not sit well with him. He would think me tattling on his staff or, even worse, that I deem his management of his estate and affairs to be derelict. Rather than risk his coolness, I said nothing. It was a difficult and troublesome choice I made and one that kept me at arm's distance from the staff.

So it was with great and pleasurable anticipation that I had begun to look forward to seeing Mr. Moore on his return to Ganymede House. Already he had proven himself a friend and confederate. Perhaps I might feel comfortable revealing my inner thoughts to him.

Chapter 16

It was almost as if another celebration had occurred at Ganymede House when Mr. Moore returned to visit. The children seemed to pay more attention to their studies, and to laugh more. I considered myself fortunate indeed that I once again had adult companionship in the house.

The first evening, when we had all gathered for our dinner, Mr. Moore amused us all—save for Mr. Grayson who sat in silence throughout the entire meal—by recreating his recent adventures in London. Mr. Moore had the gift of authoring descriptions of the sights and sounds of the city that produced awe in the children's voices and in my imagination.

"And," he said as his young cousins listened with wonder to his account of an evening's display of fireworks, "there was a marvelous time when the Royals passed by in their coach. Virgil, you would have enjoyed the pagentry . . . the pomp. Scarlet uniformed guards . . . crossed swords. And when the golden carriages stopped . . . the roar that went up . . ." Mr. Moore sat back in his chair. "All of London was there paying its respects. It was a beautiful spectacle, Miss Scott. One that I'm sure you were familiar with in the days when you resided in the city."

I nodded my head slightly and was glad that the children did not look at me, for I felt my eyes mist at the recollection of past days.

Mr. Moore looked at Antonia who was staring at him with wide blue eyes—eyes almost, but not quite, the colour of her mother's—from across the table. "Were they beautiful, Edward? Were the ladies beautiful?"

Mr. Moore smiled at his cousin. "Not half as beautiful as you, my beauty. Not by a half." Antonia grinned and put her elbow on the table. Realizing what she had done, she looked at her father and removed it quickly. Although he did not speak to anyone, Mr. Grayson's presence did quiet the children's exuberance and Mr. Moore, seeing the child's gesture, diverted her attention back to him.

"There are so many things to tell you. I have stories enough to amuse you for days." He glanced at me. "But, Ma'am, we will speak more of London later for I have spoken much too long about myself. Tell me, pray do tell me, what your days have been like these past weeks."

The brother and sister began to speak in unison, though they said different things, and when the babble became too loud their cousin teased them into quiet. "One at a time . . . one at a time, if you please." He started to laugh and the children joined in. It was a happy noise, one that had often been missing in the house, and I looked at Mr. Grayson, sure that he would be amused also by the children's antics.

I was wrong, of course. Mr. Grayson sat at the head of the table with something akin to a scowl on his face. And

142

unfortunately my glance to him was interpreted as a warning to the children who immediately quieted and looked at their cousin as if to seek a lead as to their next actions.

Mr. Moore, seeing the frown cross his cousin's features again deftly turned the talk to the mundane matters of the dinner table and when Mr. Keanne appeared with the special cake sent up by Mrs. Keanne, the five us ate the sweet in silence, although I did see a blinking of the eye pass between the children and their cousin. Thank Heavens for Mr. Moore! He was most definitely the one bright spot in the children's lives at that moment. Did not their father understand that he, too, could have their love and affection if he but joined in their merriment?

When we had finished with our meal the children exacted a promise from Mr. Moore that he would tell them more stories the following day and I invited the gentleman to join us at lunch in the schoolroom.

Mr. Moore shook his head and looked at his two young cousins. "No, that would not do, Ma'am. I never enter the classroom, for to do so would be for me to step out of my character as their relation. I'm afraid," he said and then pulled the children to him for a kiss, "that I would begin questioning them about learning and I would become a tutor and then I should be stern and demanding." He made a harsh face and then smiled at me and I could not help but feel happy, for Mr. Moore had found a charming way to suggest that in the schoolroom the children were mine and he didn't wish to usurp my authority.

The children bade their father goodnight and were taken upstairs by Mrs. Keanne. We three adults then adjourned to the small parlor, but again Mr. Grayson pled estate duties and excused himself, indicating the wine decanter for his cousin. "For your pleasure, Edward," he said in measured tones, and the two of us waited silently until Mr. Grayson was safely out of earshot before we continued our conversation.

Mr. Moore quickly resumed the pace of our dinner talk and regaled me with stories of the parties he had attended, telling me the latest news of the London crowd that I used to know and enjoy. At one point, in the midst of his lavish accounts, he stopped abruptly and looked at me.

"Oh, I do beg your pardon, Miss Scott. Do I make you sad, Ma'am? I did not mean to make you yearn for those things that are no longer available to you. I am most sorry. I did not mean . . . I do ask your pardon."

I shook my head, most anxious to lessen his fears. "I can only reassure you, Mr. Moore, that I am not unhappy, for in candor, I am beginning to forget about the past. Now, please, do go on. I enjoy hearing your tales." I looked at him and smiled. "Please, continue. You are indeed an excellent story teller."

We proceeded thus for several more minutes and when there was a break in the conversation Mr. Moore walked about the room slowly, stopping at a display of ferns on the small table, stroking the rounded leaves inattentively while looking at me from the corner of his eye so that I could not see his full expression as he spoke. "I am comforted, Ma'am, to see that you and the children are well."

I looked up from my needlework at the gentleman's curious statement wondering at his meaning. Had Mr. Moore heard anything about the balcony accident or about my jumbled words immediately following it? I watched his face for some show of skepticism, but there was none. I continued my end of the conversation in a light vein.

"Of course, we are all well, Sir. Except for the times that we spend inside because of the inclement weather, the children and I are able to enjoy walks about the grounds and take in the air. They are robust, Mr. Moore, and their minds are alert and eager to learn. They are most healthy, Sir."

"And you, Ma'am?" He made a slight bow to me. "Are you well?"

I held my needle tighter and wondered if Mr. Moore suspected that something was amiss. Did he know of matters that had taken place in the past weeks? Had he heard gossip from the staff? I knew now that his questions were not idle probes into the family life at Ganymede House and I longed to speak of my puzzling thoughts. But as the governess to the family I knew that it would be improvident of me to cast groundless aspersions on anyone or to talk of irrational and incomprehensible acts or of fragrances that have no reason to be in the house. No, it was best that I said nothing, for although I was sure of my own suspicions, I dared not tell anyone of my conjectures that there was some unexplained danger lurking in the house. I could not repeat my thoughts to anyone—not even to Mr. Moore. It was better simply to answer his question with certainty.

"I, too, am well, Sir," I said and continued my sewing and since the good gentleman did not press me any more I took it that servants' accounts of my strange mishaps had not reached his ears.

Mr. Moore inclined his head toward me. "I am glad to hear that, Ma'am." His voice dropped lower. "Very glad to hear that." He did not explain the sentence yet I could hear an intimation of solicitude that seemed to go far beyond the usual polite inquiries of health and for a few moments we were both silent.

"And my cousin, Miss Scott—what of him?" This question and the strength of the gentleman's voice startled me so that I was unable to answer quickly, choosing instead, to think of an appropriate response. Mr. Moore stood by the open fire, waiting—rubbing his hands—his back to me so that he could not see my face. "Come, come, Miss Scott," he spoke forcefully, and when I still hesitated the gentleman chided me. "It is a simple question, Ma'am, and should have a simple answer." I still paused and Mr. Moore sighed. "I understand, Miss Scott . . . all too well, I am afraid." He poured a small glass of claret for himself. "I respect your loyalty, Ma'am, but shall we speak plain?" He sipped the wine and I kept my head to my cross-stitching, hoping that my own countenance displayed no trace of my concern. "I feared that something would be out of joint . . . that something might happen" and the way he spoke of his worry distressed me for it seemed to echo my own apprehensions. "Frankly, Ma'am, that is one of the reasons I returned to Ganymede so soon."

My hand involuntarily went to my mouth, suppressing my words. "Mr. Moore . . ." I began, but he shook his head so that I fell silent.

"I am sorry, Ma'am, for I do not mean to make you anxious but . . . and this is difficult, Miss Scott, for me to acknowledge," he said and I could see the trouble in his eyes. "But, Ma'am, I have seen the darkening moods of

Oliver and I thought it best to cut short my own holiday in London. In case I am needed."

His words alarmed me. I had not suspected that Mr. Moore was able to detect any change in my employer's demeanor and told him so—asking him also to explain his last sentence.

Mr. Moore twirled his glass so that the dark liquid streaked his goblet. "You must understand, Ma'am, my cousin and I were once on the most friendly terms—in fact, we were inseparable when we were younger. But then . . ." he shook his head. "But then came the accident and . . ." He took another sip of his wine and there was only the hissing of the burning wood as sap oozed from it and met the flames. "If you ask anyone— Mr. or Mrs. Keanne—or anyone else on the estate, they will all tell you what I am about to say. They will all confirm my words, Ma'am." He sighed again. "My cousin was once a loving and devoted father . . . husband . . . friend . . . and cousin. There was no one better than he, Miss Scott. You must take my word for that. A finer and more generous person you would never have encountered. It was said of him on more than one occasion . . . on more than one occasion . . .," he repeated, more to himself than to me.

I felt I must stop him from saying more. "Sir, please, do not trouble yourself. I do not wish for you to be afflicted with unhappiness."

He held up his hand. "Please, Ma'am, hear me out. I must speak . . . and I do trust you, Ma'am, not to divulge my words to anyone else."

I could only nod my acquiescense, pleased that the good gentleman would confide in me. He sat down across from me—a troubled look on his face—and I took up my yarn, silenced by his words, waiting for him to continue.

"You must not think too harshly of my cousin as he is now. He has had a terrible shock. His beloved Rosamunda . . ." He shook his head again and I could see the gentlemen's eyes glisten as he recalled the tragedy that befell Ganymede.

"Pray, Mr. Moore. I beg you not to agitate yourself. We will resume this conversation tomorrow. Come, let us speak of other things."

Mr. Moore looked at the fire. "No, Ma'am. I feel I must speak to you, so that you may have some compassion for Mr. Grayson." He stood up and came to me and took my hands in his and held them. "Before . . . when his wife, the beautiful Rosamunda, was alive he was a most kind man, Miss Scott. Charitable to all. No man in the North of England could compete with him, such was his renown in the area."

He looked down at my fingers and realized he was holding them. He dropped my hands and stepped back—an anguished look on his face. "I do apologize, Miss Scott." He glanced at the door as footsteps approached. "I mean no disrespect, Ma'am. I would never compromise your reputation."

I took up my yarn again. "Please, do not trouble yourself, Mr. Moore. I understand that no dishonour was intended," I said, knowing that it was only in the heat of the moment—the heat of his passionate defense of his cousin—that caused him to bridge the gap of manners.

Mr. Moore finished his glass of wine and I put away my embroidery hoop as we both heard the footsteps pause at the door to the sitting room. I glanced quickly to the entrance and lowered my eyes.

"It is late, Sir. Perhaps tomorrow we may finish our

talk—if you so desire," I said as Mr. Keanne entered the room. Mr. Moore stood to escort me to my chambers—indicating to the man servant that we had finished with the room.

It was a most anxious time I spent that evening and the next day, for all manner of fears and frights accosted both my dreams and my waking hours. The exact reason for Mr. Moore's anxiety about our health—the children's and mine—still eluded me yet I could not help but feel that both he and I were of the same mind: something at Ganymede House was amiss.

The next evening I eagerly awaited the end of the meal for the time when Mr. Moore and I could again sit by the fire and talk.

After Mr. Grayson had left us in the small sitting room, Mr. Moore, having taken his place across from me, merely smiled. "I am afraid, Miss Scott, that I worried you needlessly last evening. Please, do not pay it any mind. It was only that I was apprehensive . . ." He picked up his glass of wine. "No," he said resolutely, "we will not talk of such foolishness again. For that must indeed be what it is—absolute folly. I am in a much better frame of mind this evening. The children and I have played frivolous games today and I see that they are indeed very well. How could I ever think . . .?" He nodded toward me. "My cousin, Mr. Grayson, must be infinitely obliged to you, Ma'am, for your care of his children."

I did not want to press Mr. Moore for more details about our previous conversation. Perhaps, I thought, he had a change of mind about his own trepidations. I would wait both for his explanation and for a more appropriate time to express my views.

Mr. Moore's mood had definitely taken an upturn this

evening and he tried to amuse me even though I suspect he knew I had questions. "We must do something different tonight, Ma'am. Perhaps a walk? Let us take a turn around the portrait gallery, Miss Scott." Mr. Moore held out his arm to me and I took it. "Let me be your guide, Ma'am. Let me tell you about all these former Lords of Ganymede House."

Mr. Moore was an excellent chronicler as he explained some of the history of the Grayson clan. He told me about the past owners of the estate, amusing me with anecdotes of their lives and their families. He was well versed on the lineage and revealed several secrets about the menfolk— admitting that some of the gentlemen, as he said, were best suited to be painted in dark somber colors "befitting their outlook on God's life." He felt me stiffen as he touched near our previous conversation and he turned to me and explained. "I only mean, Ma'am, that they were not the merriest of men."

We came upon the portrait of Mr. Grayson's father and I looked at Mr. Moore. There was but a slight resemblance of the two and I saw that he, too, like Virgil, did not have the characteristic swirl in his forelock. He saw me look at him, at his hair and he touched his head.

"You are wondering why I do not have the distinguishing features of the Graysons?" He smiled at me. "There is a very simple reason, Ma'am. I am not a true Grayson." He pointed to the painting of the late owner of the estate. "My mother was James Grayson's half-sister. Our grandfather had two wives and my mother was the daughter of his second wife. Hence . . . Moore. My father was not related to the Graysons at all and in fact, did not come from these parts. We have a small house in Surrey, Ma'am." He looked around the gallery. "Nothing as

150

grand as this. In fact, compared to Ganymede House, it is quite small . . . quite small." Mr. Moore looked at the portrait of James Grayson. "Uncle James was quite benevolent to my mother after my father passed away and, indeed, Oliver, too, has seen to our necessities through the years." He continued to stare at the portrait. "You see, Miss Scott, my father had only a small accounting and when that was passed on to me the majority of the inheritance had already been used up in taxes." He arched his hand. "No, Miss Scott, our estate is not to be spoken of in the same majesty of Ganymede. We are no rivals."

"I am sure your home serves you well, though, Sir." I did not mention to Mr. Moore that the only reason that I was here, as governess to the children, was that I, too, had found myself in reduced circumstances and had to adjust to another standard of living.

"Come," I said, taking his arm once again. "Tell me more about the former masters of Ganymede, if you please. No one else has volunteered to tell me about them." I smiled at him and lowered my eyes. "Please, Mr. Moore, I find the accounts fascinating."

I had an agreeable time with Mr. Moore as my guide. Not even the ominous feeling I had about the house invaded my consciousness while we conversed about the lives of the Graysons. We spoke for another hour or so, and when we returned to the sitting room for the last of our refreshment before we retired, I could not but help feel that the children and I were indeed fortunate. Mr. Moore was a loving and kind mentor to them and a good friend to me. The winter days at Ganymede were at last taking on some cheer.

Chapter 17

I knew that the plan for today would be that my employer would attend a horse auction at a neighbouring estate and Mr. Moore, in an attempt to effect a reconciliation with his cousin, offered to accompany Mr. Grayson. The suggestion was accepted with little emotion but Mr. Moore pressed on and that afternoon the two of them rode out together.

As for us—Antonia, Virgil and myself—the three of us ate alone that night and when Mrs. Keanne took the children upstairs I followed my usual pattern and went to the sitting room. Mr. Keanne had laid a fire, and I found it pleasant to sit there. I had grown accustomed to being by myself in the evenings, for except when Mr. Moore accompanied me, the evening hours afforded me the luxury of thinking my own thoughts and putting my life here in Yorkshire into perspective.

I sat watching the fire, likening the deep blue blaze to my new life. No longer was it brilliant-colored, with fancy balls and the latest gowns. Now I had settled into a quiet country life and, like the flames, continued on a steady course, neither overly colourful or particularly animated. Mine was a contented life—and if I had once hoped for something more, I had been able to lay aside those expectations and accept what I had been given.

I continued my daydreams thinking of the children that I now loved very much—planning lessons that were both educational and pleasant. I had taken a fondness for tutoring. I was always surprised when something I taught my pupils was learned and enjoyed. It was some measure of satisfaction for me and one that made my days and nights at Ganymede productive. No, I conceded that it was not a harsh life I had now!

My reverie was interrupted by the sound of tapping at the window and although I did not hear the wind come up I supposed that in this season all manners of changes of climate were to be expected. I continued at my sewing and gave the noise no more consideration. Mr. Keanne appeared at the doorway and asked if I required anything, but I told the good man that I requested nothing and that I would linger a while longer if that did not inconvenience him.

"No, Miss Scott. I still have to close the other part of the house. I will return later."

Again I heard the tapping—this time more rhythmic and insistent. Perhaps it was a twig that moved across the window. I tried to pay no mind to it, but the continuous sound caused me to lose my concentration and misplace a stitch and I had to rip the thread. I looked over to the window—still heavily curtained—and wondered if the night had indeed turned wild.

I ignored the sound for a few more moments but the emphatic rapping continued and I thought that when Mr. Keanne returned I would tell him about it. But as the disturbance persisted and Mr. Keanne did not make an appearance, it fell to me to remove the entangled twig.

I parted the heavy curtains and shutters and examined the framework of the sealed windows but I could not see anything amiss. I closed the curtains once more, assured that whatever had been the cause had now been liberated and would no longer jolt the pane.

I had taken a slight chill when I stood by the window and I poked at the fireplace grate so that the logs tumbled against themselves and the fire caught once more. The flames flared briefly and then resumed burning low and as I warmed myself I was surprised to hear the same tap . . . tap . . . tapping at the window. Now, exasperated that I had not looked in the right place, I pulled the draperies and shutters apart with a mixture of annoyance and anger and when I did so I instantly fell back and screamed. There, standing away from the window but looking directly into it, was a large cloaked figure. Although I could not make out the features—for the figure stood in dimness and was dressed in dark clothes— I took it to be that of a man.

He moved slowly toward me, still in shadow, and I stepped back once more—afraid that whoever it was would come through the window toward me, but that did not happen. Instead the figure stopped just a few yards from the house, raised his arm, and beckoned to me . . . bowing low once . . . and then moved off— shuffling toward the trees, and vanished into the night. It all transpired so quickly that I questioned my own eyes as to whether what I had just witnessed had actually happened or whether the shadows had played tricks with my vision.

I stood there shaking, and then shuddered once again

for I realized that all around me—enveloping me—was the familiar scent of the roses. I put my hands to my head to fan the odor away from me, meanwhile looking toward the door, hoping that Mr. Keanne had heard my cry and would come to help me. But all remained quiet in the hall outside the room.

I went to the window and peered out again, but there was no sign of anyone or anything. After checking the fastness of the windows and shutters, I closed the curtains and waited a few minutes until I felt more calm. I did not want the servants to see me in this condition and it would be best, I thought, for me to speak of this happening in a strong and steady voice in order to convince them of my sighting.

I sat in my chair, gathering my thoughts, waiting while the beating of my heart returned to normal. But within a few moments I again heard the soft knock . . . knock . . . knocking at the glass. This time I did not respond. I watched the curtains but they did not move and soon the tapping at the window diminished. As I calmed, the intensity of the sweet perfume diffused until there was only a trace that lingered in the room.

A few moments later I heard the sound of fast footsteps come toward the sitting room. Whoever was approaching was in a most definite hurry and I moved closer to the fireplace, still frightened, but waiting to see who entered the room.

I sighed, grateful that it was Mr. Moore who seemed both rushed and preoccupied as he came through the door and spied me. "Are you all right, Ma'am?" he asked and I could hear the concern in his voice.

"Mr. Moore! Thank Goodness! I am most relieved to see you. I have had a severe fright. I am glad you are here,

Sir." I noted that he still wore his riding cape and boots for he seemed to have hurried to me without shedding them, such was his concern.

Mr. Moore looked at me. "I saw the lights in this room," he offered in explanation. "My cousin . . .?"

I shook my head. "Mr. Grayson? I do not understand, Sir. He went away with you."

Mr. Moore brusquely turned his head. "He is not here then?" he asked and when I confirmed his words, his taut face relaxed and he explained quickly.

"We came back separately . . ." he began but then looked carefully at me. "Miss Scott, my dear lady, what is wrong? You are pale." He purposely took my trembling hands. "Are you all right, Ma'am?" he asked and when I nodded he continued, "and the children? Where are they?" for I am sure he had by now seen the look of terror in my eyes. My hands began to tremble for his questions only served to make me more anxious. "I ask you again, Ma'am, are you all right?"

I nodded, but I knew that it would not be enough of an explanation for the good gentleman. "It was the noise and the figure that frightened me," I said and he listened carefully as I told him of the strange sounds that penetrated through the windows and the hulk of a person who lingered on the grounds.

Mr. Moore was most solicitous—offering me my cup of tea and imploring me to sit down and calm myself. He spent several moments waiting while I did. When I had full control of my voice he pressed me with more questions.

"And did you call for Mr. Keanne, Ma'am?" The patient man held my still shaking hands tight.

I shook my head. "I cannot, Sir," I said and then

recounted to him the strange conversations with the Keannes on the night of the accident. I explained that I dare not disturb the rest of the staff with what they call my "imaginings" for already I had been told that the entire episode was but a fixation of my mind.

"I shall speak to them immediately," Mr. Moore said angrily but I held out my hand.

"Please, Mr. Moore, do not do so. It is not for—"

Mr. Moore stiffened. "Of course you are correct, Miss Scott. This is not my house. I am not master of Ganymede. To say or do anything would be well beyond my domain." He paced around the room. "Perhaps if I spoke to Oliver," he said in a low voice and then his face tightened. "No, I cannot. That I know." He looked at me and the mention of his cousin recalled him to his original questions. "I am afraid Miss Scott, that I must add to your anxiety." He looked down at the floor and then up at me. "Do you not wonder why I am here alone? Why Mr. Grayson is not with me?"

I nodded for it was a question that crossed my mind when first I saw Mr. Moore on his return.

"I am afraid, Miss Scott . . . No, let me begin once more." The deep emotion in his voice and the pain in his eyes caused him to be silent for a moment before he began again. "Oh, Ma'am, I am fearful for you and the children," he lamented. "I am most apprehensive for your safety." I put my hand to my throat for his words caused a sense of doom to reverberate through me and I could not contain my horror as I felt my pulse quicken for the second time this evening. "Please, Ma'am," he took my arm and let me to another chair closer to the fire, "please come and sit here where it is warm and listen and tell me that you also think I am foolish and irrational. That what I think is false, that it is only because I do so love the children and respect you, Ma'am, that I worry needlessly."

He took a deep breath. "It is not enough to say that I came home alone, Ma'am. In truth, I followed my cousin home. There was a row—a shameful scene—at the auction and my cousin became angry." He looked away at the fire, the logs crackled, and I shuddered. I was becoming afraid. Surely, I thought, he will turn it aside—he will tell me that it is all a clumsy mistake—that he was worried for naught. But he did not, for he continued,

"It was a very simple thing that started it, Ma'am. Oliver wanted a horse—a very special young horse, he said—and when we looked at the animal it was indeed handsome. The owner of the foal spoke his asking price and my cousin began to bargain with him as we are all wont to do, and when the gentleman would not reduce his price much . . . well . . . Oliver was thwarted in acquiring what he wanted and began arguing and causing a scene that was painful to watch. Most of the men there had once been friends of my cousin, Ma'am, and they had often made excuses about his conduct since the tragedy—but this went beyond the bounds. The animal's owner then refused to sell the horse to Oliver at any price, and my cousin . . ." Mr. Moore's voice faltered, "My cousin, Ma'am has a raging temper, that is now unfortunately commonplace gossip, when he fails to get his own way. He spoke a few words not fit for your ears, Ma'am, left the horse ring, and then disappeared."

Mr. Moore poured himself a small glass of wine. "I tried to mollify him, Miss Scott, while he was arguing, but he would have none of it. He has been so used to getting his own way, even as a young lad," he said and then shrugged his shoulders. "Ah well, best not to remember those old days. They are better left to the past."

I felt a shiver run through my body, noticing that in his zeal to tell me about his cousin's actions today the good gentleman had dropped the charade of two innocent young cousins and had at last begun to reveal the true nature of their relationship.

So Mr. Grayson had always been dark of spirit and mind! Poor Mr. Moore, having to accept his cousin's moods and having to defend them so vigorously to the world! What a kind and wonderful man he must be to accept such a terrible burden and not to protest. Could any man not envy Mr. Grayson for the loyalty of his cousin?

"But what has that to do with the children or me, Mr. Moore?" I rubbed my arms to ward away the cold despite my being warm from the fireplace. Mr. Moore was silent and hesitated to speak and as I contemplated what caused him to ride home so swiftly I felt another stronger shiver run through my body.

"Surely, you do not—"

"I cannot say, Ma'am, what prompted me to come home so soon for there were more sights to see."

I did not believe him yet I did not challenge him. I am sure he knew what thoughts were in his mind when he rode so swiftly, yet I knew he would rather not speak of them. So many times before, in both actions and deeds, the gentleman had told me of his love for Antonia and Virgil. I knew that their cousin wanted to protect them from harm. But it was something, even I, was loath to articulate.

"Let me set your mind at ease, Ma'am, on one small point. My cousin's rage has always been known to subside rather quickly but to satisfy myself that all is well I have asked for permission to stay a few days more before I continue on my own estate matters."

Mr. Moore must have seen my look of consternation and he managed a small smile. "You do understand, Ma'am," he said trying to inject a note of levity into the conversation, "that even modest houses must be attended." He held up his hand. "But, Miss Scott, even then I will not be away long. I have been invited to stay with friends at Valencia for the holidays and since I will be in the area I will return within a month. I do hope that it will be right with my young cousins and you." He made a small bow and I was comforted in knowing that we would not be totally isolated from outsiders during the winter snows.

We both fell quiet, and a heaviness overtook my body—the evening's event had finally fatigued me. I put my fan to my mouth to conceal a small yawn, but Mr. Moore saw me.

"You are tired, Ma'am, and if you'll wait just a moment I will escort you to your chambers," he said and then went to the windows of the small room and opened the heavy draperies and looked out into the dark night. At last satisfied that all was well, he closed the curtains once more.

"You will be all right now, Ma'am. I have checked and there is nothing there." He took one step forward to me and I saw his eyes were earnest. "Let me assure you once

161

again, Miss Scott, that despite what some in this house have told you—I do truly believe you."

Only later did I realize that in my haste to tell him of all my mishaps I had forgotten to include the repeated scent of roses. As I began to sleep the mere recollection of the aroma seemed to trigger my mind and I had the distinct notion that the fragrance had again permeated my room.

Chapter 18

True to his word, Mr. Moore stayed a few extra days with us but when his visit had finally come to an end neither the children nor I were happy about his leaving. Only his promise to return just before the holidays made his leave-taking endurable, and quieted my fears about the safety of his young relatives. Mr. Grayson still continued to avoid his cousin and Mr. Moore told me, only when I questioned him for he knew that the subject frightened me, that neither of the two men referred to the violent scene at the horse ring. It was best, Mr. Moore said, "for both of us to put it behind us in the interest of harmony and better relations" and he had said nothing more to his cousin about the incident.

Mr. Moore and I had explored all the possibilities as to the identity of the strange person I had seen at the window but everytime we discussed it we came to no true answers. At one time Mr. Moore had suggested that it might be Willie, the stableboy, acting out a game, but I declined to accept such a simple explanation. The tapping and the bow were deliberate and calculated to frighten me. Whoever it had been had seemed a bit too sure of himself and had purposely wanted to terrorize, if not me, then someone else in the house. I was sure that poor Willie did not have by half the wits to instigate such a scheme. Besides, as I recollected, the figure's bow seemed vaguely familiar, but I was not able to locate it in my memory.

On the day before he was to leave, while the children were resting, Mr. Moore and I took one last turn about the estate. It was a cold but pleasant day with a high pale sun and grey clouds in the horizon but, as the gentleman had said, it afforded us the privacy of speaking our minds without being overheard by the children or the household staff. We had decided to be circumspect in our conversations, thinking that it would be best for all concerned not to reveal any of our suspicions to anyone, for while my thoughts were known to a few since the days of the balcony accident, allegations by me would only be dismissed as foolishness by the servants.

"The few people who already know, Miss Scott, will think that you have already forgotten the incident. It will be much easier for all of us—and for you to keep a lookout—without arousing any other skepticisms." It was good reasoning and one that I concurred with quickly. Now that I had Mr. Moore's understanding and loyalty, I no longer felt isolated or foolhardy.

We strolled the immediate grounds close to the house and when we passed close to the Greek maze I shuddered slightly and recalled to Mr. Moore my frightening experience within the complicated garden. Mr. Moore listened to my story and smiled ruefully.

"It used to be, Ma'am, that the maze afforded us much pleasure. Did you know that it was the Lady Rosamunda who redesigned it? She took great delight in specifying the placement of the bushes and shrubs and used to laugh whenever she, herself, would get lost in the configurations. Many afternoons and early evenings we would all gather in the middle of it, by the statues, and watch the fountain and sometimes, on an especially hot day, the children would play in the waters." Mr. Moore sighed. "It was a pleasure to be a guest here then, Ma'am. It was a lovely time for all of us."

I wrinkled my brow for despite what Mr. Moore had said, I could not envision Mr. Grayson as a family gentleman attuned to the lighter side of life and domesticity.

Mr. Moore must have seen the look of incredulity on my face. "I see that you do not believe me, Ma'am."

I shook my head vigorously for I did not want to give the impression that I thought that the gentleman told falsehoods.

"It is not that I doubt your words, Sir. It is only because I have not ever seen Mr. Grayson in such a light."

Mr. Moore laughed at me. "My dear Miss Scott, perhaps, at an appropriate moment, you will be able to ask Mr. Keanne to tell you of those times. You will see, he will confirm my words."

I put my head down—ashamed that Mr. Moore believed me to question his honesty. "Come, come, Miss Scott. I do not take offense at your thoughts." He looked around. "No, it would be difficult, in hindsight, for even me to believe that such times ever did exist here at Ganymede."

We walked even closer to the edge of the maze and I told him of Mr. Grayson's plan to disassemble it in the spring. He touched one of the evergreen hedges as though the feel of it would recall those pleasurable times he had just spoken of to me.

"So Oliver will wipe out yet another recollection of his beautiful wife!" He turned to me. "Miss Scott, I fear that what my cousin wants to do is erase all traces of Rosamunda. He wishes even to take away the children's memory of her. Is that not unfair, Miss Scott? Do not the children have the right to know of their mother?"

Mr. Moore's impassioned speech disturbed me, for I knew he had only the children's welfare at heart. Oh how I wished that I could reassure him that his young cousins would never forget their mother. All I could offer were truisms that no child forgets a parent and that a mother's love can never be erased.

"If you could have met her, Miss Scott, you would know why they must never forget her, why her memory must be kept. If there is any merriment in their lives then you must know, Ma'am, she was the reason." He parted the bushes slightly as though doing so would afford him a glimpse of the maze. "The lovely times . . . the lovely times . . ." he said and for a few moments I thought that he could see, in his mind's eye, the tableau of Grayson family life as it once had been.

I remained quiet and Mr. Moore soon roused himself from his musings. "Ah, but we cannot spend all our days living in the past."

We heard footsteps coming through the maze and as we watched Old Martin came toward us, holding a basket of gardening tools with one hand and tipping his cap to us with his other.

"Mr. Moore, Miss Scott." He looked up at the fading sun. "Won't be many more hours like this." He pointed to a dark cloud in the distance. "I can smell the snow." The gardner readjusted his cap. "Tomorrow, sometime, I reckon."

"Then I suppose I should be riding fast," Mr. Moore said. "I will have a long way to ride in the morning before I reach Valencia."

The gardner nodded his head. "Aye, that's a good three hours journey, Sir. Best you make an early start." He picked up a fagot that was near the entrance to the maze. "Willie," he yelled and the stableboy came running from inside the garden pushing a wheelbarrow in front of him, spilling dirt as he rushed. He approached us and when he saw I was with Mr. Moore he made a small clumsy bow. "Master be here . . . Master be there," he began and Old Martin stopped him.

"Now, Willie, that be enough. This here is Mr. Moore. He is not the Master here, he is not Mr. Grayson." Old Martin smiled at us and spoke directly. "Times he be a bit befuddled, Ma'am." He spoke slowly to the boy. "This be Mr. Moore. Master's cousin."

Willie smiled his slow-witted smile. "I know . . . I know," he said and for a few quick seconds his eyes sparkled and it seemed as though there was a wisdom that poked through to his mind. But then I saw the dull look return to his gaze and he bowed awkwardly again.

"I remember. I remember . . ." he said and Mr. Moore stepped close to him in a comforting way.

"What is it you remember, Willie?"

Old Martin turned to me. "Mr. Moore—he was always good to the boy even when we first knew he was senseless. He always took care to speak to him. And then, after the accident, when Willie would have ravings, Mr. Moore was the only one who would speak quiet to him

167

and not upset him."

Willie stepped closer to Mr. Moore and put his hand up to his mouth, hiding it, as he spoke into the gentleman's ear in what he thought was a whisper but was actually loud enough for us to hear. "I saw her . . . I saw her," and the way he said it in a breathless voice iced my fingers. I knew he was speaking of Rosamunda and of that disastrous night she died. "I saw her . . . and you . . . on the cliffs. Ye be the Master . . . ye be the Master."

Mr. Moore took the stableboy's hands. "No, no, Willie, I am not the Master of Ganymede House. I am not Mr. Grayson. You remember me, Willie. Mr. Moore? Remember the time when we fed the horses together?"

Willie shifted on his foot. "Ye be there . . . ye be there. It were raining. And lightning fearful. I was hiding in the maze. I saw. Ye be there . . . ye be there."

Mr. Moore was patient with the young boy so that I could only marvel at his gentleness. "No, Willie, you did not see me that night. I was not there." He turned to us. "The boy must be confused. Perhaps he saw me later, when they brought her up. I had returned that morning. It was . . ." Here his voice faltered, but he turned back to Willie. "It's alright now. It's all over now."

Willie shook his head and I could see his rotted front teeth as he smiled.

"Aye, Sir, that's what ye said—it's all over now. I heard ye over the roaring of the waters . . . over her voice. Ye said you would be the last . . . the last. Ye be there . . . ye be there. I saw you. I saw the Lady and her long hair—all flying about every which way. She were beautiful."

Old Martin stepped in then and took Willie by the hand, shaking him as though it would recall some sense to him.

"Don't pay him too much attention, Miss. He sometimes confuses the times—no telling which is the past or the present in his way of thinking. We just let him ramble on and then he'll stop." He picked up the bunch of broken twigs and then gave the young man a gentle cuff on his shoulders. "Come on, boy, let's be getting that tree into the ground."

Willie bobbed his head and then glanced once more to us. "I saw you . . . I saw you," he said as he darted away from us leaving the wheelbarrow behind.

"What did you see, Willie?" I called after him for he seemed to be agitated as if he wanted someone with whom to share his information.

"Leave him be, Miss Scott." Mr. Moore picked up a twig that had fallen from Old Martin's pile as the gardener hurried after the boy. "Poor Willie's been known to make up stories but no one here pays him any attention." He looked at me and I could see the kindness in his eyes. "Besides, if you make much to do about it it might reach my cousin's ears and then . . ." Here the good man shrugged his shoulders and I knew that he was trying to forestall a confrontation with Mr. Grayson over the possible dismissal of the stablehand.

"Once again you are right, Sir," I said slightly bowing to him and his wisdom. "It is best to ignore the poor man."

We continued walking about the estate—the cold wind hitting us in the back—but still enjoying the outing. Mr. Moore resumed telling me about the estate and the times he and his cousin had played on the grounds and even though there was a break in their relationship now I could tell that Mr. Moore savored the memory of all the times spent here when he was a child.

That evening, after dinner, I bid Mr. Moore a safe and pleasant journey and conveyed the hope that he would return to Ganymede soon. Mr. Moore took my meaning and held my hand for only a fraction of a second lest the servants see and gossip falsely about us. Then he bowed very formally to me.

"I will return to Ganymede shortly, Ma'am, though if you need me for whatever reason," and here he looked me straight in the eye so that I did not mistake his words, "you may send a message to Valencia. Old Martin knows the estate. I promise, Miss Scott, I will return immediately at your bidding."

I put my head down for I did not want him to see the confusion in my eyes. Instead I said softly, "I am sure there will be no reason to communicate with you before you return, Sir."

Mr. Moore bowed once again. "I pray that that will be so, Ma'am. Please, Miss Scott," he said and I saw the worry in his eyes, "please look after Antonia and Virgil. I fear they need a protector."

Later that evening, as I sat quietly at my desk, writing in my journal, I allowed myself the luxury of ruminating on his words and warning. I understood what Mr. Moore was speaking about but I knew that no harm would come to the children as long as I carefully watched them.

There were so many things I had wanted to say to Mr. Moore but because of his haste in leaving I had forgotten to express my opinions. I became annoyed with myself— why did I not tell him of the two or three times when the children had cryptically suggested that the memory of Rosamunda still lingered in their hearts? It would have reassured the gentleman, I know and I vowed that I would tell him of those incidents whence next I saw him. And why did I forget to ask him about the statue in the maze—of the goddess who resembled Rosamunda?

So many bewildering thoughts flooded my intellect and I tried to sort among suppositions, suspicions, and fact. I remembered Willie's words and his confusion about who was the master of Ganymede House and some of his ramblings returned to my mind *"Ye said—it's all over now. I heard ye over the roarings of the waters . . . over her voice."* Poor Willie—the tragedy had affected even his addled brain.

I recalled the way Willie had bowed inexpertly to both Mr. Moore and myself and determined that it was not the stableboy who had stood at the window. No, somewhere in the back of my mind, I could see the outline of another person bowing to me who seemed more like the frightening figure of that evening.

I fell asleep late that night and once again, just as the fire was dying in the fireplace, I smelled the familiar faint scent of roses and I vowed that I would be ever vigilant, that I would not allow the children to stray too long or too far from my sight. I would watch them as carefully as if they were my own for I now knew positively that evil dwelled here. I no longer could ascribe all the alien sights and sounds in this house to the "foolishness" to which the housekeeper and her husband would have me attribute it.

Chapter 19

Neither Antonia nor Virgil were in attendance in the nursery when I appeared for breakfast the next morning and when I inquired as to their whereabouts Tillie shook her head and looked troubled.

"It's the little Mistress's doll, Miss. She's lost. Miss Antonia and Master Virgil and I have been searching for her ever since they awakened." The maid wrung her hands. "We've looked everywhere, Ma'am . . . everywhere."

I knew how much Antonia valued her gift. It would be unlike her to just leave it lying about carelessly. I instinctively looked at the chair next to the table where the doll usually was seated for breakfast. "But that's quite impossible. Miss Antonia never lets Josephine out of her sight."

"Yes, Miss, that's why it's so strange. Young Mistress says she had it when she went to sleep last night. She says she remembers holding it next to her, but when she awoke this morning it wasn't in its usual place beside her in bed."

I smiled as I remembered how Antonia clutched the doll tightly even as she slept but I still saw no cause for alarm at its disappearance. There were several reasonable explanations as to where the cherished possession could be and I offered them to Tillie. "Perhaps it dropped to the floor or became entangled in the bed clothes," I suggested but the servant shook her head vigorously, standing firm in her convictions.

"Oh no, Ma'am, we searched all about the room. Moira and I completely took apart the bed. We looked everywhere, even in the cupboards thinking that it was mistakenly put away with the clothes or the newly-ironed linens but Josephine wasn't there. Master Virgil has been helping his sister, looking in all those secret places that only the young ones know about, but they can't seem to find the doll either." Tillie poured me a cup of tea. "It's quite upsetting for all of us, Miss. It's gone. And sure it's a pity—what with Mistress loving it so." She shifted a chair, scraping it along the bare floor, so that it fitted next to the table and she looked thoughtful. "Begging your pardon, Miss Scott," she apologized for the scratching sound, "but some of the furniture this morning was different when I awoke. It was all a bit off— out of sorts—like it wasn't quite right in its places." She moved a candlestick from the end of a table and placed it on a shelf and shook her head. "Like someone was unfamiliar with the nursery and all. Such as I used to be when I first come up here and kept putting everything in all its wrong spots. It's almost like someone was misplacing it—not knowing any better."

"Perhaps the children had already begun to search for Josephine," I said absently, "and in their haste they did not correctly replace—"

174

Tillie nodded. "Yes, Ma'am. That's probably it."

The maid's apparent distress and the fact that they had been searching for the doll for almost an hour seemed to be most curious. "Please go and find Master Virgil and Miss Antonia and bring them to the nursery, Tillie, and then after breakfast we all shall make a thorough search. I'm sure with everyone rummaging throughout the chambers we shall find it in a short time and quite probably in a most conspicuous place." I spoke to the maid in bantering tones, still convinced that the doll was somehow overlooked in the room and we would find it tucked away in a cupboard or a drawer.

"Yes Ma'am," Tillie curtsied automatically. "I'll see to where they are and tell them of your wishes." She spoke in an efficient and respectful manner although I could hear the doubtful tone in her voice.

The children came to breakfast quickly and I could immediately see the unhappiness in Antonia's face and the concern in Virgil's. They took their places quietly and I told the little girl that I was sure that Josephine's disappearance was probably due to some form of accidental carelessness and we would find her soon. Antonia brightened for just a moment and when I explained that we would delay our school lessons for an hour or so while we looked for her companion, both of them ate their porridge quickly—obviously not wanting to postpone the investigation further. Had it been any other child that this had happened to I am sure that there would have been moaning and wailing throughout the meal but Antonia, ever the brave little soul, managed not to cry, instead accepting the inevitable conclusion that Josephine had mysteriously disappeared and the only recourse was to seek the doll—even more diligently—

throughout the house.

After the breakfast dishes were cleared the child, aided by her brother, Moira, Tillie, and I, continued to search for the missing Josephine. That it was given to her by her beloved Cousin Edward and had already become one of her very favorite gifts prompted all of us who knew of the loss to search harder and in more impossible places. Yet the doll remained lost and mid-way through the morning we had no other alternative but to return to the classroom for our daily lessons. I promised again that once they were finished, we would resume the search and while I wrote out a summary of a text I watched the two of them at study.

Antonia sat at the desk-table writing her letters, every once in a while looking sadly at the empty place on the nearby chair where she had placed Josephine all those days since she had received the golden-haired doll. Even during his own lessons I saw her brother glance up several times—first looking at his sister and then at the vacant place and then out the window—as if he were waiting for something or some idea to occur to him. He would stare off for a few seconds and them put his head down so that the black forelock fell in front of his eyes. He would sweep a small hand through the errant hair in a defiant gesture and then he would write, pushing the stub of the pencil hard into the paper and the wooden desk. Theirs was an allegiance that I admired and as I came to know them I saw the unbreakable bond that existed between them.

There was silent communication betwixt them—something unaccountable—and I had slowly come to the conclusion that the two were secretly bound up in some unexplainable linkage that seemed to transcend the

176

confines and relationship of family. There were times that I had felt, but for no real reason I must admit, that there was a third . . . presence? . . . spirit? . . . force? I knew not what to call it, but it was as if there was another entity present in the room with us. And it was as though the children, in matters of great importance to them, seemed to defer to this unseen power.

Several times I had caught an unusual expression on the faces of the children when they were silent and attending to their studies and I was puzzled by it. It was a thoughtful quixotic appearance and yet when I looked closer I could see that there was also a hint of the unknown deep within their eyes. They did not appear uncomfortable with their surroundings or their tasks—rather it was the fact that they were so contented that first called my attention to them. It would show itself at odd moments and when I first noticed it I attributed it to many things. At first I fancied that there was a hidden joke between the children; another time I thought that they remembered something amusing. But I never asked for explanation nor did I allow them to know that I had noticed the look for I believed that the children had a right to their private thoughts.

Once or twice as Virgil sat quietly in the evenings reading the book his cousin had brought him, I saw that he looked up and away and I could witness a small, beautiful smile play around his mouth. The first time I detected it, it startled me—in my few weeks at Ganymede House I had not seen that look before nor had I detected a hidden sense of adult humour in the boy's character. Virgil did not strike me as a child who had fanciful flights of imagination; rather, he seemed to be grounded most heavily—like his father—in the practical values of the world. And yet that sweet, enigmatic smile caused me to stop several times and watch him surreptitiously, never letting him know that I observed him.

Once, on a rainy afternoon after classes, I came upon him as he held an illustrated geography volume talking to himself, but in so low a voice that I was unable to hear specific words or phrases. I suspected at first that he was merely reading aloud from the book but at one point he laid aside the print and continued the gentle conversation almost as though he were explaining something to someone. I was mystified at the boy's behaviour but did not query him about it for my feelings at the time were such that I heartily encouraged fantasy and impish conjuring of imaginary playmates for the children and any behaviour most closely resembling normal child's play.

This unfamiliar attutude was not just Virgil's, for Antonia, too, could be unpredictable. Less inhibited than her brother because of her still tender years, she also had the odd habit of smiling at unexplained delights. Just this week when she had finished a particularly difficult lesson in arithmetic and I had lauded her on her ability with her numbers she looked out of the unshuttered window in the classroom and smiled as though she was waiting for someone or something to acknowledge her achievement. And when I remarked much too quickly on her far-away look, for I startled her, she shook her head and offered the excuse that she was only happy with herself for learning. I accepted the simple explanation but I saw her glance at her brother who nodded his head and resumed his own studies.

I knew the children were having difficulty studying while the entire housestaff continued to look for

Josephine throughout the day and to no avail. The doll was not in any of the chambers.

Even Mrs. Keanne joined in the pursuit and had the scullery maids remove the stores from her kitchen cabinets, promising to box anyone's ears if she found that they were playing a joke on the "young Mistress." But of course Josephine was not found there, either.

Antonia remained quiet in the nursery with her brother, writing on her slate and waiting expectantly, while each time Tillie came back and reported that the doll still had not been located. In the early afternoon I asked that Mrs. Keanne send up a pot of tea for the children for I feared that the anxiety of the day would sicken Antonia and I was surprised to see that the elderly woman herself brought the refreshment and several pieces of seed cake in hopes of rousing the girl.

But it was all for naught. Antonia still remained by her brother's side, asking only that he not leave her. I signaled to Mrs. Keanne to meet me in the outer hall. When I had closed the door behind me I told the woman that I was worried about the young child. She and the doll had become inseparable. We—all of us—must surely have not searched in the right places. There had to be a reasonable explanation why we were not able to find it.

"I'll take my revenge on anyone who has set out to hurt the young miss," the housekeeper said angrily. Like me, she also thought that the disappearance of the doll was done more in callous sport than mere forgetfulness. "'Tis a cruel joke to play on the little girl."

I agreed once more with the elderly woman and the two of us—forgetting our antipathy—suggested places where Josephine might be found. But, alas, one or the other of us or Tillie or another maid, had already explored and

179

found nothing.

I returned to the classroom with a promise from Mrs. Keanne that the house would be searched carefully once more before the evening meal, but by the time we sat at the dinner table no one had reported seeing the missing doll.

Mr. Grayson asked his usual questions this evening and by dessert time when he failed to notice the children's lack of enthusiasm for food or their obvious melancholia I volunteered a statement hoping that it would stimulate his curiosity and perhaps his concern.

"We have had a strange happening in the nursery, Sir. Antonia's doll is missing and we've not been able to find it all day."

My employer looked at the child and then at me before he spoke and I could detect a hint of boredom in his voice at our worry about such trivial things. "Have you searched the nursery?"

"Yes, Sir, but the doll is not there. It is nowhere in the children's chambers."

Mr. Grayson's eyes grew dark and pensive and he gazed at his daughter but said no more—neither offering her consolation nor encouragement—and I was both surprised and full of quiet anger that he would treat his child in such a callous manner.

Later when just the two of us sat in the small room Mr. Grayson continued to brood, leaving his wine untouched in its glass, and on the few times I lifted my head from my needlework I saw him staring off into the fire. Several times I thought I detected a word or two from him but when I looked up to answer him I saw that he neither was speaking to me nor expecting a reply. Finally, once, before he took his leave of me, he poked at the burning wood in the fireplace and succeeded in igniting the flames even brighter and I wondered why he would disturb the already set fire.

"The missing doll . . . Antonia's doll," he said with his back to me as though he were still examining the flames. "Is that not the one she received from her Cousin Edward? The China doll she calls Josephine?"

I was surprised that he even knew the name that Antonia had given her toy. "Yes," I answered hoping that he would speak again but he said no more. A few moments later he bowed politely and excused himself.

I laid my work aside and retired early. The events of the day weighed heavily on my mind and I had hoped to fall asleep early this evening. But it was not to be—I kept recalling all the places where we might find Josephine—waking to remind myself that the rooms had already been examined. I finally fell into a deep sleep dreaming about how happy I would be if we could find the doll and resume our lessons without the sad shadow of the lost Josephine hanging over the schoolroom.

Chapter 20

When it finally became obvious that the doll would not be found we offered alternative solutions to Antonia. I promised another toy to be ordered from London; Mrs. Keanne offered to sew a rag doll; even Old Martin pledged to fashion a wooden babe if it would please the child. The young girl accepted all offers with a wan acknowledgment but I knew that nothing could take the place of Josephine in the small girl's heart. Thus, we three settled back into the routine of the schoolroom and though I knew the children thought about the missing doll they went about their studies in a creditable fashion.

One afternoon, while we were at our lessons, Tillie burst into the room and frantically signaled me.

"Please Miss, may I speak to you privately?" she said softly as she looked at Virgil who had raised his head briefly at her entrance. I nodded and set the children to their tasks of reading in their story books and walked to the far end of the room, away from where they could hear us.

"Yes, Tillie. What is wrong?" I asked yet already

knowing that only an emergency would have tempted her to interrupt the schoolwork.

The maid's eyes were big. "If you please, Miss Scott," she began and I saw the bewildered pleading look on her face. "Please, Miss," she began again, "Mr. Keanne asks that you come downstairs right away in your cloak. He said that I was to stay in the nursery with the children." Tillie looked around the room and eyed the children. "He was most certain about that, Ma'am . . . most certain. I was to stay with them here in the schoolroom until you returned."

Her words and manner frightened me. "In my cloak? Why? What is it?"

The young woman did not answer me, instead she put her hands on my arms and pushed at me. "Please, Miss, go now. I'll stay with Master Virgil and Miss Antonia. I won't let them be alone," she said and I could see that there were glistenings in her eyes and my mind thought ahead of what terrible tragedy could have befallen Ganymede House.

I rubbed my chalked hands on the apron of my dress. "I'll go immediately," I said and I could see the girl relax a bit.

Downstairs Mr. and Mrs. Keanne were waiting for me in the Great Hall, their coats thrown over their arm. They were standing there talking quietly with Old Martin, and I saw in their eyes the same look as appeared in Tillie's.

"Mr. Keanne? You sent for me?"

The butler moved forward and took my arm. "Miss Scott, Old Martin has news. You'll want to hear him out," he began and then deferred to the gardener who took a step toward me.

"Well, you see it's like this, Ma'am. We—Willie and

184

me—were cleaning up some scraggly bushes around the side of the estate and Willie—well, he found her, Miss.'' I did not quite understand his words and the gardener must have seen my blank look. "Josephine, Ma'am. Willie found her. She were alaying in the earth."

I still did not comprehend his meaning. "Where is she?" I questioned and then turned to Mr. Keanne who looked numb. "Why did you not bring the doll to me, or to Miss Antonia?" I asked.

"Take her to it, Thomas." Mrs. Keanne's sharp voice crackled throughout the hall and I was amazed that the woman used her husband's Christian name in front of Martin and me.

Mr. Keanne nodded his head and buttoned on his coat. "Aye, Bertie . . . aye. Seems to me that that be the best way." He turned to me. "If you'll come with us, Miss . . ." he said and walked to the door and held it open indicating that I was to follow him and Old Martin. "It's cold and wet out there, Miss, but . . ." He shrugged.

Mrs. Keanne wrapped her shawl over her head and joined us and the four of us walked around to the side of the house making our way carefully past the leafless bushes and stiffened grass, taking pains not to step into the shallow puddles of dark muddy water that had formed in sections of the garden where the earth had sunk.

"Be careful, Miss Scott," Old Martin warned me as he led the group of us onto the soggy ground and when we had come to an area beneath the windows of the children's wing, he stopped and then pointed toward a low-lying bush.

"Underside there, Miss." He pointed at the mud with a gnarled cane. "That there be the doll Josephine."

I looked close and could see the dark mud that had

been stirred up and I saw mixed in with the wet clumps of dirt tiny pieces of pink and ivory plaster. Old Martin used the tip of his walking stick to move aside the lower branches so I could have a better view of the earth.

"There, Miss, ye can see it all now," he said and I shuddered as I recognized the ripped and matted blue velvet of the doll's clothing. My hands began to tremble and as I bent closer to pick up the fragments I gasped, for now I saw why Old Martin had not brought Josephine to us.

The doll had been viciously destroyed—savagely torn apart. Its beautiful painted China head was smashed in several places and what little remained of it was pulled and twisted grotesquely off its body so that it hung together by one jagged piece of porcelain which was not enough to stop the bran and sawdust from spilling out of its body onto the wet dank sod. I was horrified by the grisly attack on the doll. When I looked closer I saw the doll's crazed bright blue glass eyes continued to stare vacantly up at us through the mud. "Good God," I said and turned to the others. "Who . . . *why?*"

"Aye," Mr. Keanne said. "Our very same words when we first saw it." His wife leaned over the mutilated figurine and gently picked it up. The remainder of the body stuffing streamed out of it, trailing a line of golden-brown dust on the ground, until finally the muslin form collapsed, unrecognizable.

Mrs. Keanne cradled the wet cloth remains of the doll in her hands. "Best Miss Antonia doesn't see this," she said and pushed the tiny bits and pieces of crushed China and tattered blue cloth deep into the wet ground with her shoe. "Best we say nothing to her, I suspect."

I looked up to a window above us, to the children's

186

wing. "No, we'll not say anything to her." I held my shaking hands close to my sides. "I will speak of this to Mr. Grayson when he returns this evening."

Mr. Keanne rubbed his chin. "Do ye think it might have been the dog . . . Euripides? Many a time I've seen him pick up a ball or a twig and shake it until it falls all to pieces." He waited for confirmation from us but I said nothing and I heard Old Martin clear his throat. I did not know whether the butler was looking for excuses not to believe the cruel attack on the doll or whether he honestly believed that it was all done by the animal in a playful mood. "Could it not have been an accident? Or perhaps a joke that has gone sour? The young mistress could have left the doll somewhere . . . forgotten it like."

Mrs. Keanne folded the material into her pocket. "Aye, Thomas," she agreed with her husband, "it could have been Mistress' dog. He's acted strange since . . ."

Old Martin bent down and picked up a small remaining bit of glass and put it into his pocket. "This weren't no accident," he said firmly. He voiced my unspoken words. "This were deliberate. Deliberate. If ever I find . . ." he said enraged. The deadly intensity and meaning of his words frightened me.

I wrapped my cloak tighter around me, positive that someone or something evil was lurking about Ganymede House. I was terrified that some injury would come to the children. Whoever had destroyed Josephine was of a sick mind. I looked once again at the blue glass eye staring up at me before I stepped on it and buried it deep under the bush. This surely was no cruel joke that had gone beyond mischief. I understood the meaning of the message that he . . . or she . . . was sending us—that what happened to the doll was a warning—that harm might easily come

187

to Antonia or Virgil.

I took a deep breath and hurried to my room before returning to the nursery to settle myself. I knew that faithful Tillie was overseeing the schoolroom and I needed a few moments to calm myself before I continued the day's lessons and before I could sit and think about what I was to do to protect the children.

We kept the finding of the doll to ourselves and were careful to say nothing about it in the presence of the children but that evening, after dinner, when Mr. Grayson had poured himself his wine, I told him about Josephine and the way we had found her. I spared him nothing—not even my fears for the children—for I now knew that the situation could be grave. The lines around Mr. Grayson's jaw tightened. He closed his eyes briefly and then looked away and I thought I detected a momentary flash of anger flicker in his eyes. He took a sip of his port and I could see that the words had had an effect on him. He continued to sit, not saying anything, until finally he asked me to again recite the events of the day, and I did so, keeping my voice even so that I not be thought of as an hysterical woman.

At the end of the recitation he sat very still, asked me no more questions, then thanked me and bowed once more to me and excused himself. He did not say whether he was shocked or whether he believed me. I did not know what was in my employer's mind for as usual he had not chosen to confide in me. Yet I wondered what manner of man he was not to remark on the events of the day. What kind of father does not question for the safety of his children? What might any other parent have done or said in the same circumstances?

I sat for a few minutes, not bothering to pretend to

sew. There was surely evil here. I remember the words and warnings of my dear friend, Mr. Moore. He was right—I had to be twice on my guard for both the children and myself. Oh how I wished for his return to Ganymede! He surely would offer me some solution to this mystery.

I was awakened in the middle of the night by something I could not identify. It was but a vague stirring within me—a feeling of unease and disquiet. The events of the past days had been disturbing and I was unsettled at the fact that some of the servants had swiftly taken the excuse of the Keannes and were already blaming Euripides for the damage—choosing to believe it was playful mischief and not malicious intent. It was bandied about—below stairs—as the Keannes had suggested, that the dog had somehow found the doll and ripped it apart—jostling it in play—but as I recalled the scene under the bush I did not remember that there were any canine teethmarks on the fabric or on the porcelain.

I did not refute the butler's explanation with this evidence for to press my point I knew I would again be considered a foolhardy woman. Once more I decided it was best to hold my reasonings. But I rejected both the idea that it was Euripides who caused the mayhem or that Antonia was to blame for losing the doll.

When Josephine first became missing, all manner of thoughts and doubts went through my mind. I considered that Virgil was playing a trick, albeit a cruel trick, on his sister, but I quickly discounted that for the boy has never shown anything but the best regard and love for his younger sister; indeed as I have said before, he is

Antonia's best ally.

I paid no attention to another of Mr. Keanne's explanations—that someone from the staff had accidentally picked up the doll and carried it outside. No one—save the Keannes, Tillie and I ever entered the nursery and schoolroom.

No, I agreed with Old Martin; the viciousness of the doll's destruction was not an accident and I was beginning to more and more remember Mr. Moore's admonition to me about calling for his help should I think it necessary. Surely he would understand that no one outside of Bedlam would have done this contemptible thing purposely so as to hurt the little girl. Even as I thought those words I had become terrified—for I believed I had right off stumbled onto the reason that Josephine was stolen and mutilated. Whoever did such a terrible act of vandalism was warning us. Good God! Whoever was in such a black mind, I knew, was telling us that the same thing would happen to Antonia. I trembled and pulled the coverlets around me.

"Never," I said to the empty room so that the mere sound of my voice would fortify my resolution. "Never. I will not allow anything to happen to the children," and as I spoke the words aloud there was suddenly a rush of cold air into my room even through the doors and windows remained shut and despite my blankets I felt icy to the bone. I remained still, waiting and intuitively knowing what was about to happen, for intermingled with the cold air there was a strong scent of roses so as to daze my mind and flood my senses. It filled the room with an aura that could only be from another time. And even though my intellect denied it, my being accepted the only answer possible: the fragrance could only signal the arrival of the children's mother . . . could only herald the coming of Rosamunda.

I threw off the bedclothes and stood in the middle of my room, slowly turning round and round, searching the darkness yet knowing that I would not find any outward sign of another person or spirit. I was not afraid, rather I was quite calm, and as I stood there in the silent chamber and breathed the bouquet of the flowers I knew that something or someone was watching me. I could only hope that it would make itself known to me.

Everything was still. I only heard the sounds of the last embers of the fire hissing in the grate and yet I knew I was not alone. For several minutes, I remained—waiting for a harbinger or a direction and when none came I finally whispered into the almost-black room.

"Rosamunda." There was no motion in the room. I softly called the name again. "Rosamunda." How simply I accepted the premise that she was there in my chambers with me for despite all my intellect and curiosity and schooling never was I one to accept something I could not see or explain save for the Lord God! Yet, I knew that the children's mother . . . Mr. Grayson's wife . . . the beautiful Rosamunda was near . . . ready to reclaim her rightful place and duties as Mistress of Ganymede House. And yet I was not afraid.

"Rosamunda," I said into the quiet room and when I did not get an answer I continued in a whisper for fear someone would pass my room and hear me. "Why are you here?" and even though I asked the question, I knew the answer. Rosamunda had come from a long way to protect her children.

A soft current of perfumed air passed near my desk, fluttering the papers on it and then the curtains rippled at the windows as if a breeze had waved them and I marked in calm disbelief the path something, or someone, was taking toward me. I stood watching and waiting. And as the invisible presence passed close to the fireplace the dying ashes sputtered and hissed as though they had been summoned to blaze again and I held constant lest whoever or whatever was in the room with me should misinterpret any of my actions and flee. But I knew that that was not to happen for the fragrance of the blossoms moved nearer and nearer to me in rippling waves and I remained motionless, neither moving nor caring to, for I had no fear, at this moment of the unknown. Of *this* particular unknown!

"Rosamunda," I repeated once more, "I must know now why you've come. Is it your children? Do you want to protect your children?" Again there was a gentle zephyr and though I felt chilled I did not shiver and I continued to hold my ground. "I think I understand. You are their mother, but I, too, am worried about them. There is someone in this household who wishes to do them harm, isn't there?" I asked the question although I knew there could be no response. "Is that what you want from me, Rosamunda? For me to take care of your children?" I queried as I slowly turned a complete circle in the room as though I was expecting to see something—a shadow or a faintness or a brief moment of light. But there was nothing.

"I am afraid for them, also, yet I know not who to turn to to discuss these fears." And as I spoke I tried to piece out the complex puzzle. "There is much melancholia here, Rosamunda, and much maliciousness and although I know not why, I know that the children need to be protected." I spoke the words rationally and though I received no response I knew that the presence had stopped moving and was yet in the room.

"Do not worry," I said quietly and honestly addressing the deep darkness of the room. "I vow to you that no harm shall come to your children." I held up my hand in a show of oath. "I make you that promise. I shall protect your young," I said again although I knew not from whom the threats would come. "Do not worry," I said speaking as I slowly turned another complete circle of the room, "no harm shall come to Virgil or Antonia as long as I live. I make you that solemn promise."

The curtains fluttered briefly once more as the cold air currents passed adjacent to me. I reached out tentatively into the empty space as though I could touch something but of course I could not and I withdrew my hand.

There seemed to be a retreating from me and the chilliness dissipated as the dying ashes momentarily flared up and sprung to life. The room was suddenly filled with a brief moment of intense heat and light that illuminated everything in my chambers and then just as quickly vanished as if the unseen spirit had withdrawn from the area. The embers glowed brightly once more—a vivid golden blue—reminding me that it was winter and yet I still smelled the fragile scent of summer roses.

Chapter 21

I stayed awake nearly all night thinking about the extraordinary events of the evening—puzzling out the pieces and yet coming to no firm conclusions. Why Rosamunda had chosen to come to me and not to someone else in the household, I knew not, but throughout my midnight and early morning contemplations I did not retract the promise that I made to her: Virgil and Antonia would be safe within my care.

My easy acceptance of the phenomenon amazed even me. I had often heard of people who spoke of such things, but when I was in London with my friends we scoffed at the daft interpretations of the unexplained.

I was curious now as to whether anyone else at the estate had ever smelled the scent of roses or had ever suspected that Rosamunda still lingered in Ganymede House. It was not a subject I wanted to speak about openly—already I had been made to feel foolish since the balcony episode and this would only allow those here to continue that opinion of me. If I were to question I would have to do it carefully so that I did not arouse anyone's suspicion.

After breakfast and before the schoolday began I returned to my room and saw that Tillie was already about her chores. I instantly decided that I would query her yet speak in such a gentle fashion so as not to upset her.

I paused as I watched the maid straighten the bed linen and fortuitously it was she who opened the conversation.

"Mistress seems a bit more settled this morning, Ma'am." She plumped the pillows. "Not that she knows anything about Josephine, the way it was found and all . . ." She looked up—acknowledging my silent question. "None of the servants will say anything, Ma'am. It's just natural that we all know things. It don't mean anything, Miss Scott. What's below stairs . . . well, it stays there. No need to worry about the young Mistress learning about the doll. But whoever done it . . . that's cruel." She put her hands on her slim hips for a moment. "I don't know, though. Mrs. Keanne says that Euripides did it in a game." She continued at her task. "Still, it seems such a shame. Maybe Mr. Moore will bring her another."

I waited while the domestic spoke her piece—neither agreeing nor disagreeing with her—and then when the break came I spoke.

"It most surely was sad. And as you said Miss Antonia did so love the doll." I shook my head for effect. "There seem to be many things that are strange here at Ganymede House." I paused, waiting to see if she was listening.

"What kind of things would that be, Ma'am?"

I was careful not to hurry my voice. "Oh, just little things, Tillie. Like last night. It was almost as if I smelled something akin to a summer scent, if you will—a scent of roses here in the room." I watched carefully as Tillie heard my words and my vigilance was rewarded. The servant stopped smoothing the pillow slip and looked away—out the window. "Have you smelled it, too?" I questioned.

"No. Never." Tillie held her hands to the linen yet I saw a slight tremor. "Never," she repeated more positively and I knew that again she was lying yet this time I did not press her. Her actions confirmed much and I knew that I had to speak to Mr. Keanne about it.

"Ah," I said to Tillie, making my voice sound light-hearted. "I was much too alert and much too tired yesterday to sleep after finding Josephine. I am sure it was only my imagination playing tricks on me."

"Yes, Ma'am," Tillie answered and I could see that she was relieved that I would not question her further.

The opportunity to speak to Mr. Keanne came about quite unexpectedly. I had made my way along the upstairs hall, during the morning break, when I saw the butler standing in front of Rosamunda's room about to enter it. When he noticed that I was watching him he put his head down quickly, and muttered his 'good morning' so that I could hardly hear him. He closed the door behind him but emboldened by last night's episode I pushed on the door and confronted him as he pulled the curtains and drapes aside so that the sunshine streamed into the room. When he saw me, he paused, and I took the lead, hoping that my unexpected appearance would somehow throw him off-guard.

It was not to be. The gentleman had lived too many years and spoken to too many people to allow me to know his true thoughts.

"Miss Scott. There is nothing here in this room for you."

I nodded my head only slightly. "I think that is not so, Sir. I would like to talk to you." Here I paused and looked up at the portrait of his late Mistress. "I would like to talk to you about her."

I saw the stooped gentleman hesitate for just a moment and then he approached the painting.

"Aye. And what is it about the Lady Rosamunda?"

I did not waste time on preliminary speeches and told him of the strange scent of the flowers that appeared during times of stress and danger to her children. I did not elaborate on my thoughts or convictions concerning last night, merely speaking of the aroma.

Mr. Keanne just watched me, listening carefully. At one point he interrupted. "Is it not possible, Ma'am, that it is only your imagination—it is well past the season."

"I know, Sir. That is why I question. Tell me, have either you or Mrs. Keanne ever smelled the fragrance? Ever noticed the perfume in any of the rooms?"

He did not bother to deny or confirm the conversation or the question and I knew he was hesitating—trying to decide whether he should speak directly to me.

"Could it not be your imagination, Miss? As though you are hoping that the bitter cold season passes us quickly?"

I shook my head. "No, Mr. Keanne. It is not my fancy that plays tricks on me."

"Then perhaps it was your scentwater that over-turned . . . spilled. Perhaps Tillie . . ." I listened as the butler cited several excuses but for each one I shook my head—letting him know that I did not accept the evasions. "I can only then suggest, Miss, that it was—"

"No, Mr. Keanne. Please do not blame the mysterious odor on my vagaries. It will not do." I waited but a few seconds until I made my suggestion. I pointed to the likeness of Rosamunda. "Please, Mr. Keanne, I would like to know how the children's mother died."

The servant looked at the painting and then at me and I knew that somehow he understood that I also suspected the secret of the scent.

"How much do you know about that night, Miss Scott?"

"Only that the Lady Rosamunda died in an accident—that it was a terrible death—and that the misfortunes of Ganymede House have preyed on every inhabitant since."

"Of that you are right, Miss. None of us . . . not one person who was there will ever forget." He motioned to a chair next to the bed and I sat and I knew that at last I would have some answers. "I suppose you should know something about it." He looked away—out the clear window—before he took a deep breath. Then he looked at me. "It was a summer's day, Miss Scott, all warm and still-like—and little Mistress had been begging her mother to take her riding. Mrs. Grayson could never resist giving in to her children and so after their classes the two of them set out, Mistress on her horse, Venus, and Antonia on a small pony that was given to her. Willie, the stable-boy, went with them. Miss Rosamunda always had Willie accompany them—she took a liking to the half-witted boy, Ma'am, feeling sorry for him and all—and they rode off, Willie leading the young Mistress. Euripides followed them and Old Martin told me he heard them laughing as they went past the rose gardens.

"It was a pleasant day, Miss, bright but with just a hint

of a coming storm in the far clouds. Mistress said that she would be home in plenty of time should the weather change. Said they would be gone for just a little while and told Old Martin not to worry. And then they rode off toward the maze—the Greek maze." He shook his head, remembering.

"Well, once they got there the Lady dismounted saying she was going to go into it. Now, Miss Scott, some of this may be unreliable because this part comes from Willie and you know the lad—his ramblings. But Willie said that the Mistress said she wanted to sit in the maze for a while—that it would be cool there and for Willie to take Mistress Antonia back home. And that's what he did. He said he left the Good Lady and her horse and the dog by the side of the maze and that just before they turned back Miss Rosamunda called out to her daughter—telling her she loved her very much." Mr. Keanne paused and swallowed hard and I knew that retelling was most trying for him but he roused himself and continued.

"Well, it got to be late—first four o'clock and then five and then the clouds started scooting over the sun and soon it was going to be dinnertime and none of us paid it a never-you-mind, Miss, for we all thought that the Mistress had returned. But then Tillie came downstairs and told us that she hadn't seen her Lady and we questioned for a moment Mrs. Grayson's whereabouts. It is not up to us, though, to be privy to all that goes on in the house, so none of us fretted about it.

"Mr. Grayson had been away that afternoon tending to estate business, and Mr. Moore wasn't about. Although he had been staying at Ganymede House, he had gone to visit his friends at Valencia. He was expected back sometime that evening, though.

200

"Well, Master asked after his wife and when we couldn't find her in her rooms or anywhere about the grounds we asked Willie and he told us about her stopping by the maze. But still, Ma'am, we weren't too worried. Mistress loved the solving of the puzzle and we thought she might be sitting there losing track of time and all since it was still summer-light. Willie did mention that he thought he saw a man or someone on the far side of the maze, but you know Willie, Ma'am. His poor befuddled mind does tend to invent things. There wasn't anyone else we found out later. Just Willie making up his stories . . . that's all it was. But we did go down and have a look-around. And by that time the weather had turned and there was a storm brewing—coming in from the east it was—and we decided to search inside the maze. We did notice that neither Venus nor Euripides was about, but we didn't pay it too much mind and we even joked, Ma'am, that while we were out there the Mistress had probably returned and we would be the ones to miss our supper and get wet." He looked down at his clasped hands. "It seems so mean now to have laughed. After it was all over, we faulted ourselves for our not looking too fast and in all the parts of the estate.

"It had begun to rain then, Ma'am—one of those all-of-a-sudden-like storms that come up and beat at you. Pretty soon, although it was only about six o'clock on a summer's evening, it had already grown pitch-black. And then we got word, Ma'am, that the Lady still had not returned and we all began to be uneasy for it wasn't like her to worry us. We organized a search then, Miss Scott, at the direction of the Master and began looking very carefully. Had every man and boy from the estate out looking.

"The rain kept coming down hard-like and it was a rain that many in the shire said was the worst in history. All big sheets . . . like walls . . . coming down on us so that nothing—not even our hats and capes—could protect us. It was the kind of drencher that gets into your hair and falls down in drops into your eyes and almost takes the sight away." Mr. Keanne wiped at imaginary drops of water in his eyes. "It were a big'un, Ma'am, and then the lightning and thunder started. Huge streaks of it—balls of fire igniting the sky with sounds that shook the very earth we were standing on. Like the entire world was being shaken. But we kept on, Miss . . . kept looking . . . kept calling out Lady Rosamunda's name in between the noise of the thunder." He hesitated just a moment and I saw him silently form the words he had called out that evening. *Lady Rosamunda . . . Mistress Rosamunda . . .*" and then he shook his head.

"Must have been an hour or two later, Ma'am—the time gets mixed up while you're desperate—when both Venus and Euripides finally came home. The mare was trotting slowly—her mane flattened against her hide by the water and the dog—well, the dog was barking and circling the horse. And when we reined Venus in Euripides kept nipping at us—never did it before, Ma'am—kept nipping at us like he wanted us to do something and we followed him thinking that the animal knew something but it didn't. He kept shifting back and forth . . . back and forth. He was just acting crazy-like.

"We searched all night throughout the grounds and the gardens. Every man from the stables, the house, and the estate. We walked every inch of the land that evening. We even went to the edge of the cliffs although it was a danger to us all what with the slipperyness of the wet ground but it was all for naught—there was no trace of the Lady. Mr. Oliver was distraught and commanded Miss Padgett, the governess, to keep the children in the nursery—away from the searchers—and not to tell them anything, but we didn't know that they had already heard enough to make out that something was amiss.

"Mr. Edward arrived later that evening, like I said, and he joined one of the groups of men as they walked the moors over there on the other side of the estate but that was to no avail also. He never said anything—all grim-like was his face—for he, too, loved the Lady. They were all of such a happy family, Miss. Such a happy family," Mr. Keanne said, and I could again see the pain in his eyes. Still, though, I urged him to continue and after another brief pause he picked up the threads of the story.

"It was truly raining mightily that night, Miss; I've never seen the wind so strong nor heard the sound of the sea so angry since. Even on the moors, land that was known to all of us, some of the men were tricked into taking wrong turns and we had to redouble our tracks and rescue them—the fog and rain was so thick. The leaders finally had to resort to tying a rope around their waists so that if one of them got lost or trapped in one of the bogs, we could get to him quickly. And all the time the wind was blustering and between the wetness and the gales it had turned bone-chilling cold even though it was still only mid-August.

"Euripides kept running back and forth across the grounds, so agitated was he, and finally we had to put him on a chain in the pen to keep him quiet and out of our way. But with each bolt of lightning we could hear him—the crazed dog would set up a howling that matched the sound and fury of the wind. I don't know which was the most terrible, Miss, the heavens yelling at us or the dog's crying. And finally it was no use, we were all driven back to the main house by the storm where we waited until morning to continue our search.

"Many of us tried to sleep but all that night Mr. Grayson and Mr. Moore continued their vigil; there was no stopping the Master, in fact. While some of us were in the warm kitchen drying ourselves and fortifying our innards with food and something strong to ward off the chills Mr. Oliver kept going outside and walking up and down—unmindful of the rains. There he was, poor Mr. Oliver, getting more and more frantic and more and more silent at the same time." He looked at me explaining. "That's his disposition, Miss, he gets quieter and quieter as he gets more and more anxious. He's always done that since he was a little tyke. You've probably noticed the same thing with the young ones. No emotion, no surrendering to the hurt."

"Yes. I had marked it," I answered remembering Antonia's submissive acceptance of Josephine's disappearance. I was glad to know the reason why the two children react the same in times of stress, why they cling silently and stoically together. I understood finally that that was probably the only way they knew to express and share their pain. It was, indeed, an unfortunate family trait.

Mr. Keanne noticed my inattentiveness as I thought on this. "Would you want me to continue?" he asked.

I did not wish to be cruel and yet the horrifying story that the servant was telling me served to shed some light on the behaviour of the children. "Yes, please go on. I think it vital that I finally learn all the facts."

Mr. Keanne nodded his head. "Might as well be in for a pound as for a ha'f pence," he said and I took it to mean that I would be told the honest truth of that terrible night. "Well, the children were left alone for only a few moments, Ma'am—when Miss Padgett went to fetch some hot tea—and when she returned to the schoolroom they had disappeared. She came and told Mrs. Keanne and the two women set right away to finding them because they were afraid that in the midst of all this turmoil something might happen to them, too. They looked upstairs first but they couldn't locate them and then they thought that maybe they had heard the commotion downstairs and you know how children are, Miss Scott—always wanting to know everything, but they weren't anywhere on the main floor either.

"Well finally my Bertie found them in their mother's chamber. The two little ones knew something was amiss and had gone there to wait. Mrs. Keanne said they were sitting on the bed watching the sky light up—just sitting and watching and waiting. And that was another worry, Ma'am. Here we thought Master Virgil and Mistress Antonia were safe in their own rooms with the Governess—not suspecting anything wrong. But then we come to find out that they knew—we never learned how—that their mother was missing. We never did tell Mr. Grayson that bit of news because he had enough on his mind. The children told Mrs. Keanne they wanted to go out and search, too. But Mrs. Keanne calmed them and she and Miss Padgett allowed them to stay a bit more time in the Mistress' bedroom before they were taken back to their nursery."

I glanced briefly at the bed, trying to picture the two children as they sat there waiting for their mother. I felt a heavy pain in my chest at the thought of them watching for the mother who would never return.

"I'm telling you, Miss, it was a fearful night—a fearful time of waiting. Mrs. Keanne kept lighted candles in all the rooms—even those facing the cliffs. Mr. Grayson had ordered us to do so so that if the Mistress returned she would be greeted by the light. And the Master thought that if she had been hurt then perhaps if she saw the big house lighted up—even from a distance and through all that heavy downpour—then she would take courage and know we were searching for her and wait for her rescuers. We offered all kinds of thoughts about how she had lost her way or had maybe gotten a slight hurt and that all would be fine again when we found her." He stared at the picture of Rosamunda. "It was what we wanted to believe, Ma'am. We all wanted desperately to believe it," he said and I could hear the ache that remained in his heart from that time. And then he shook his head very slowly.

"But it wasn't to be. The next morning, at daybreak, when all was calm and summery again and the storm had gone out to sea, Euripides broke his chain and ran toward the cliffs and stopped just at the edge, howling, and when the men caught up to him they couldn't persuade him to leave the spot. Mr. Grayson and Mr. Moore were first in the group and when they approached the dog together the animal began growling, baring his teeth, and we had to put a muzzle on him and fairly drag him away from the scene. It was the first time he had ever done that, Ma'am, the very first time.

"It was then that Mr. Grayson looked over the edge and saw her . . . the Lady Rosamunda . . . God rest her soul. I don't think any of us who were there will ever in all our lifetime forget his expression or his wail. It went right though us, Ma'am, right through us. *'Rosamunda!'* he cried out to the waters below and there's a slight echo there at that part of the cliffs, Miss Scott, and it seemed like we could hear his voice over and over again, crying out her name.

"Mr. Moore took hold of his cousin then and we looked down and that's when we saw her, too. It was such a terrible sight! She was floating face up in a small cove— her golden hair fanned out from her face drifting in the water. She had probably lost her way in the storm and plunged over the edge into the sea. There was nothing anyone could do for her, of course. It's a good hundred feet there to the waters and the rocks." Mr. Keanne closed his eyes as though to push away the memory of that sorrowful morning.

"They went down right away to fetch her and when they brought her back up to the house it was as if she was sleeping. There were no marks—not a one—on her face. Mr. Grayson, himself, carried her in his arms the whole way back to Ganymede. It was such a sad sight, Miss Scott . . . such a sad sight." Mr. Keanne moved closer to the portrait. "She had on a pale blue riding habit, Miss— and it was all blood-spotted, and not even the rain nor the salt-sea took out the stains as she lay there that whole terrible night." Mr. Keanne lowered his head but not before I saw the tears that welled in the corners of his eyes. He wiped them dry with the back of his hand and I looked away—pretending not to see. "Ah well," he said finally, "That was last year and the Master still hasn't gotten over the death. That's why he's like he is, Ma'am—he still misses his Lady."

I remained quiet—speechless—while my heart went

out to that poor beautiful creature in the portrait and to her children, and yes, in spite of his coolness—Mr. Grayson. The loss of a loved one is most difficult to reconcile and especially the loss of a beautiful, young, beloved wife and mother.

"Where is she now?"

"We buried her in the Rose Garden, Ma'am. Beyond where all the bushes are, in a quiet place with a simple stone." Mr. Keanne had recovered his composure and was now closing the curtains. "It seemed the most fitting place to bury her . . . in her own garden among her blossoms. I see to it, personally, Miss Scott, that there are flowers on her grave throughout the year. Even on winter days such as now," he said and the mention of the word had drawn me back to the present.

"Winter . . ."

"Even winter, Miss. We spread dried rose petals for her."

Ah, the scent. Maybe another explanation for the past evening. Perhaps my eagerness to embrace the spirit last night was really nothing more than an indication of overtiredness. "And do you have the rose scent in the house?" I asked.

Mr. Keanne shook his head. "Oh, no, Miss Scott. Never in the house. Mr. Grayson would not approve. The rose petals are only on her grave." He straightened up. "Is there anything else?"

I was satisfied at his answer and knew I did not have to ask any more questions, for the servant already knew of what I spoke. "No, Mr. Keanne, not now. Thank you for telling me about the tragic accident. I am sorry I reminded you of such unhappiness. But knowing will help me to understand the children . . . and Mr. Grayson." Mr. Keanne barely nodded his head as I continued. "I will just stay and study the portrait a few more moments if you don't mind."

He looked up once more at Rosamunda's picture. "She was a lovely lady, Ma'am . . . a lovely lady. There wasn't anything we wouldn't have done for her. We all loved her so."

Chapter 22

It has been three days now that we have been locked inside because of the weather. Again, it is not a good day to be outdoors—it is still quite raw. Dark clouds loom on the horizon, but there is no sign of the first snowfall of the season. Today, the Sabbath, afforded us the only deviation in our monotony. After the household staff and the family attended chapel services and had lunch we returned to our usual plan for a Sunday, both Virgil and Antonia preferring to stay in the nursery so that they could read and play with their toys. It was an arrangement that the children themselves put forward and I had no reason to dissent.

I wandered the rooms downstairs—agitated with myself for failing to want to do anything special. I had already viewed the picture gallery several times; I wanted to read no books from the library; and I did not want to spend the day in my room writing letters or sewing or rearranging my cabinets. It was not a feeling that I am accustomed to—for in truth, most of my former London contemporaries much admired the way I used to welcome life and happiness. My acquaintances used to depend on me to challenge their minds but—perhaps because of the gloomy weather or the closeness of my bounds—I did not feel like creating inventive games to capture my own imagination or for my own amusement. Perhaps it had been the events of the past week—the mutilation of Antonia's doll; the appearance of what I believed to be Rosamunda; my accident; and yes, even the incident so long ago at the Greek maze that prompted the unrest. Even as I thought of it the knowledge that Rosamunda had spent her last moments in the maze seemed to send cold chills throughout my body.

Since my conversation with Mr. Keanne I was no longer comfortable in Ganymede House, yet my devotion to the two children would not allow me to entertain the notion that I should write to Mr. Clayton and ask his help in securing another position. No, I would stay—I wanted to stay—for I had already made Rosamunda a promise to protect her children and it was one I meant to keep. To that end I kept a careful vigilance of Antonia and Virgil—always taking care to know where they were and with whom and while I tried to be circumspect I knew that sometimes the children wondered why I frequently made appearances in the nursery when I was not required to do so.

I paced the distance between the sitting room and the kitchen, yet I did not intrude on the domain of Mrs. Keanne. We maintained an uneasy truce and while we extended ourselves to speak civilly to each other I still did not feel that the woman accepted me.

When I had walked the length of the downstairs of Ganymede three times, I sighed. This was a foolish preoccupation and I told myself that there were far better things to do with my time; I would go to my room and take up my journal—perhaps writing down the mysteries in my mind would relieve the disquieting feelings I had within me. And, also, I could more easily attend to the children's whereabouts without appearing too interested.

All was quiet upstairs and I hesitated to disturb the brother and sister at their playtime. I knew it would serve me no good to constantly watch them. I looked in the direction of the children's wing, ascertained that nothing suspicious was nearby, and closed the door to my own room.

The journal did not occupy enough of my own mind, I had become bored with my own jottings. I went to the French doors—they were now sealed in accordance with Mr. Grayson's orders—and looked out onto the winter landscape of the estate. Small patches of hoarfrost lay on the winter-dried grass and in the rays of the setting sun I could see bits and slivers of color where the rime reflected the orange glows. I watched the gleamings for a few moments but even those few spots of cold beauty failed to hold my interest and I walked the room, stopping frequently to arrange and rearrange my bibelots atop the mantle and my tables. It was an occupation I had done happily before but one that now afforded me no pleasure; in candor, it made me sad, for to see the pictures of my parents and all they represented in my life only reminded me of all that I have since missed. I replaced the tiny framed portraits in their spaces very gently but firmly, for sadness was a luxury I could no longer afford.

I glanced once more out the window and broke my own resolve—I would visit the nursery and see to the children. Perhaps they, too, were bored, and the three of us could devise a game that would please all of us.

The hall was quiet and when I approached the school room I could hear nothing—not an unusual phenomenon at Ganymede House for everyone in the household—domestic and family alike—tended to work or entertain themselves in silence.

I pushed open the door, expecting to see both Antonia and Virgil in the room but when I entered it, it was empty. Neither child was there, nor was Tillie, who had been charged to sit with the children while she sewed. I called for the maid but she didn't answer. Most probably Tillie and the children were together in the house—more likely the kitchen—for I knew the youngsters enjoyed sitting at the servants' table while Mrs. Keanne gave them huge cups of hot milk-tea and slices of her special cakes. It was an innocent treat and one that I heartily approved of—for although Mrs. Keanne did not take kindly to me she was more than generous with her love and devotion to the children.

I closed the door thinking that I would go back to my room when Tillie turned a corner and came into the hall. In her hand she held a plate of cookies and I stared at it.

"For the children, Miss," she said offering me an excuse and moved past me toward the nursery.

"But are they not with you?"

Tillie looked at me and shook her head. "No, Miss. I left them for a moment to fetch a sweet." She turned toward the schoolroom.

"They are not there," I said and a clutch of apprehension began in my stomach.

Tillie, however, did not share my concern. "They're probably just playing, Miss. Master Virgil loves to explore the house. We—the servants—all know that.

Many's the time we found them just walking through the rooms. There's no harm, Miss. Just silly child-like games in the middle of an afternoon." She glanced toward the Great Hall downstairs. "It's a right miserable day out there, Miss. One of those days when you just have to find things to occupy your head and hands so that you don't sit and dwell on the weather." She curtsied once more and took the plates into the nursery. "I expect they'll be back here for these in a short time."

I was not normally an anxious person. I was able to see the practical in most cases and did not frighten easily. But in light of the events of these last days, my good sense was replaced with caution. I surreptitiously began searching for the children—being careful not to share my alarm with the rest of the staff. If the children were playing games of hide and seek then I would have to think on a child's level as to where they would find the most exciting hiding places.

I walked slowly past my room intending to explore the guest wings; they were usually unoccupied and I knew there were many rooms that would suit a child's fancy for concealment. I had already gone beyond Mr. Grayson's quarters and was passing Rosamunda's room when I heard a sound—was it a lock that had clicked?—coming from within. For the second time within a week I entered. I saw the two young children, sitting close together on a love seat at the far end of the room, conversing softly. Neither of the youngsters saw me for they were preoccupied and seemed most content. I waited for a moment, watching them. I did not mean to intrude on these peaceful times and therefore I stood there, not wanting to disturb their tranquility, and as I did so, Antonia laid her head on her brother's shoulder. I saw

215

Virgil pick up a book by his side and begin to softly read to his sister.

I knew not what else to do and thus I knocked on the open door, wanting the children to know that I was there, yet also wanting them to know I had no reason or wish to spy upon them.

Antonia moved quickly to sit straight and I could see, even from where I stood, that Virgil stared at me—angry fire coming from his young, sad eyes.

"I was looking for you," I offered as a way to excuse my entering into their private world. "I did not know where you were."

Virgil's face remained tight—still letting nothing but the anger radiate from his eyes.

"Tillie told me you often hid from the servants in a game . . ." I continued, feeling that I owed the children an explanation for my intrusion. I closed the door behind me and looked around and to Rosamunda's picture and smiled. I felt that even to two so young I did not have to explain anything more and despite their tender ages both children relaxed and Virgil's face once again became, not calm, but resolute.

"It is a tranquil place to be," the young boy said. "It's most quiet," he said in a formal voice. He purposely did not look at his sister and I guessed he did not want to encourage her participation in the conversation.

"Yes . . . yes, it is," I answered and moved toward them.

"We often come here." Virgil was now pledged to continue. "We often come here . . ." he said stammering on the words.

Antonia jerked up her head. "We read here, and tell stories." She looked at her brother and then to me.

216

"And listen."

"Listen?"

"She means to me, Miss Scott," Virgil said holding up the book. "I read to her sometimes. She likes to listen to the stories."

I was prepared to believe the explanation until I saw the dark blue bound book that he held in his hands. "It is in Italian," I said.

Virgil put his head down knowing that he had been caught by his own explanation. Antonia looked at him and then bowed her head. It was a picture I cared not to see, for in the slight movement I could determine that the children were suffering from the pain of losing their mother.

"Do you remember the words?" I asked both of them softly for I wanted to convey my own true feelings to them. Both the children nodded for to tell me a lie was both unthinkable and not in their own code—the Grayson code—that had already been taught them. "Would you like me to teach you more of the language?"

Virgil shook his head and I understood: the language was the special bond that the children had with their mother, and no one—neither their father nor their beloved cousin nor I, their governess—could or should interfere. I looked at their mother's portrait.

"She was a very beautiful woman."

Again the two children nodded.

"And I'm sure you loved her very much." I waited a few seconds. "I'm sure you miss her very much."

That was the sentence that allowed me to enter their world, for Virgil began talking to me about how he had a key to Rosamunda's chambers—that when he saw one in the lock one day he had simply taken it and no one had

217

ever asked about it. It was, he said, a way to get into his mother's room.

I stood there and it was a strange reversal, for when we first met it was Virgil who stood while I sat. Now, I knew, it was for me to wait until the young children invited me to sit on their mother's possessions. It was a gesture they did not remember immediately and I stood there, holding onto the back of the white and gold chair for a few seconds until Virgil jumped to his feet and then asked me to sit and stay with them.

It was as if we had come to some unspoken agreement—that I was now allowed to enter their world and it seemed as if the floodgates to their memories opened up before me. I listened quietly, not wanting to insinuate myself too much without a specific invitation, and my patience was rewarded. They spoke first hesitantly, then without carefully choosing their words, and I knew I had been quietly judged these past weeks and had finally been deemed a friend. It was a touching moment for me yet I dared not speak.

The children told me of remembering Italian phrases when their mother was teaching them the language and although their pronunciation had suffered from the lack of use, I still was able to understand a few words that they spoke.

I replied in the language using very fundamental words, words that I knew Rosamunda must have used and at several points in the conversation—merely phrases about the weather and asking their names and where they lived—the children laughed. It was a sound that I savored and I silently thanked Rosamunda for allowing this lovely time with her children.

We stayed in the room for almost an hour as the

children told tale after tale of their life with their parents. They seemed to know the stories too well, as though they had recited them to each other often. How could anyone ever have suspected that these two—young as they were—could have possibly forgotten their mother! It was not only foolish to think thus, but I found it cruel. Clearly the children wanted to speak about Rosamunda, wanted to perpetuate her memory, wanted to retain all the happiness she had given them. Why, then, would the entire household act as though she had never existed? It was a question that most certainly needed answering and I knew that the only person who would tell me the truth about this matter would be Mr. Moore. Again I longed for his return.

I went to the shuttered window and pushed it slightly apart and saw that it was nearly completely dark. Dusk had fallen as we spoke. I explained to the children that we had to leave the room now. I did not have to tell them that I would not reveal their secret hiding place and, in matters that make my heart light, they did not ask me to swear my silence. The precious thread that these children had held for their mother was much too sacred for me to damage and somehow—as children are wont to do—they guessed my feelings.

I saw that the room was darkened. The shutters gave away no detail that it had been occupied. We went to the door. Virgil took out his key from a jacket pocket and I pretended not to notice as he locked the door and we walked toward the children's wing.

"And what would ye be a-doing there?" Mrs. Keanne's sharp voice could be heard throughout the Great Hall. We three froze as the housekeeper made her way up the curving staircase toward us. "Tillie has been looking for you." She glared at me and I could tell she was angry . . . ready to seize on any explanation that I had and use it against us—against me.

I decided that I would take the blame for our disappearance and I put my hands on the children's heads lightly.

"We have been for a tour of the house, Mrs. Keanne. In all these days I have yet to see the entire manor."

The older woman stared at me and I saw that in one quick glance she saw me holding the children—my arms around their shoulders—and I thought for just a second that her wizened green eyes shone soft.

"There's nothing to be seen in those quarters, just extra chambers for the guests." She sniffed. "If you want to see the insides of the rooms . . . ask me. I will have Moira or one of the housemaids show them to you." She looked at the children who remained still. "And as for you two . . . Tillie has been searching for you for almost an hour. There is some cake to tide you over until dinnertime." She glanced at Rosamunda's room and I knew that she had seen us come from it. "I think Tillie should be told that you've been found."

I saw as the children went toward their nursery the woman stared after them and her manner seemed softer yet still controlled. She watched them for a few seconds and then turned back—once more going back to the stairs.

"See that the children don't eat too many sweets before their meal," she said angrily and yet I could tell that once more, I had broken through her reserve.

What was in this house that caused people to not say what they were thinking? I watched the retreating back of the housekeeper. The puzzle still did not fit together.

Chapter 23

The days continued at Ganymede House, each moving into the next without any variety or change. The one bright spot in my life was that the children and I were now fast becoming friends ever since the episode when we three lingered in Rosamunda's room. Though we had not revisited their mother's chamber I could tell by the way they acted toward me, that I had been invited to stay permanently in their confidence. I still had many queries to put to them, but I dared not ask them yet, for I did not want to upset the delicate balance we had achieved. Patience . . . patience . . . I kept reminding myself, for I knew all my answers would come eventually.

If the days were much alike, the evenings, after dinner, were always the same. I spent my time, after Mr. Grayson left me, alone in the small sitting room. It took me a long time to become accustomed to the solitude but ever since my talks with Mr. Moore in the room, I enjoyed working by myself, in my chair next to the fire, thinking my own thoughts. It was not an unhappy time for me any longer—I acknowledged to myself that Mr. Grayson offered no companionship, and I made peace with that position, since I could not possibly change it.

But this evening was very different and very surprising. I was escorted into the parlor by my employer and instead of him excusing himself as was his custom, he took a seat at the far end of the room—neither offering explanation for his deviation from his usual behaviour, nor, I suspect, considering that I needed one. He instructed Mr. Keanne to set up both the tea service and the wine decanter in the room. I was puzzled that he would change his routine after so many evenings, but once more, it was not for me to question. I knew if Mr. Grayson deemed it necessary that I know the reason for his change of habit I would be told in due course. Again I learned to accept things as they were.

Mr. Grayson's presence disconcerted me as I worked at my petit-point. I was frustrated because I wished to sit alone this evening and continue thinking about Rosamunda. I still had not come to an understanding of why the late mistress of Ganymede House chose to reveal herself to me, and furthermore I did not know how I could protect her children from the unknown persons or evil that abounded in this house. It was a subject I wanted to pursue this evening but with Mr. Grayson in attendance in the room I was not able to focus my thoughts on the puzzle.

Thus the two of us, master of the estate and governess to the children, passed a quiet thirty minutes, each absorbed in our own thoughts—I, trying to decide a course of action for myself and the children and Mr. Grayson—well, I simply knew not what his contemplations were. He watched me in an offhand manner that did not seem to be concentrated nor intended. He held a full glass of wine, neither sipping it nor refreshing it from the decanter yet also not really paying it any attention except to keep it upright lest it spill to the floor. I determined by his expression that his thoughts were on nothing particular, yet his half-gaze in my direction made me most uneasy for I could not understand what passed in his mind. I continued with my needlework—counting my crossings—and shortly I heard the sound of the clock chiming the hour. I knew not whether my employer expected me to speak, or whether I should simply keep to my own affairs—the course I chose—and so we remained, in respectful silence, listening to the occasional popping sound of the burning wood, until once again, on the quarter hour, the room echoed with the reverberation of the struck pendulums.

Mr. Grayson set his full glass onto the serving tray and I was startled to hear his voice addressing me.

"Your stitches are most precise, Ma'am." I looked up for I was astonished at his words. I knew I was expected to answer.

"I shall take that as a compliment, Sir, for I have on many occasions admired the needlework in this house." I touched the intricate embroidery design on the pillow lying beside me on the chair.

"That particular cushion was fashioned by my mother, Ma'am," he said with more warmth in his voice than I had ever heard previously. "In fact I remember her weaving it in this very room." He half-closed his eyes for a moment and then continued. "All the women in my family were skilled in home arts, Miss Scott. It was a trait much admired by their husbands and their own circle of friends."

I kept my eyes down, continuing to work the green flax

into a leaf motif. "Miss Antonia, though quite young, shows an inclination toward that skill, also," I said, sure that he would be pleased to learn that his daughter would follow in the Grayson tradition.

He bent his head briefly in acknowledgment. "I am sure, with you instructing her, Ma'am, she will be a credit to our family."

I was quite perplexed at this small exchange of affable conversation, for this was the first time since my arrival at Ganymede that Mr. Grayson had engaged in any form of amenable discourse with me. I hoped that my confusion would not show in my countenance.

"Both my children seem to have taken to you with much ease, Ma'am." I raised my head from my stitches as Mr. Grayson spoke. "I have noticed there is lately a difference in their manner. They seem more . . . more . . . " He groped for a word and I supplied two.

"Animated? Child-like?" I could not help but smile as I learned that he, too, saw a minor reshaping in Virgil and Antonia; it warmed my heart to know that I had already effected a change in their somber disposition.

"Animated?" He leaned back against his own chair and surprisingly he accepted the word. "Yes, that is it. They are more animated, more childlike . . . as they were before . . . far more so since . . ." He did not finish his sentence yet I knew his meaning and I continued knotting my thread. I had not expected my employer to have noticed the change in the children and I had hoped that he would not question me as to the cause, for I would have no reasonable justification to give him except that they now had me as a friend in whom they could confide. Fortunately he did not question!

"They are lovely children, Sir. I thoroughly enjoy

224

educating them. Nay, I will go even further. I truly enjoy their company." I looked up and smiled. "They are bright, quick children. They are a joy, Sir . . . a joy," I said truthfully.

Mr. Grayson set his glass down on the table and turned to look into the fire. "Their mother also enjoyed teaching them," he said and I wondered if he suspected that I knew that the children still spent many hours in their mother's room. I pondered also if Mrs. Keanne had spoken to him of the time she saw us coming from Rosamunda's chambers and if Mr. Grayson was somehow entrapping me into revealing and affirming the fact. I remained silent again and felt foolish for his next words "They used to laugh much, Miss Scott," confirmed that obviously, the gentleman knew nothing of the children's and my escapade.

After that exchange Mr. Grayson was quiet for a few moments preferring, I assumed, not to divulge any other history of their family life. Finally I heard him stand as a prelude to his leaving the room. It was a signal that I had heard on every other evening, but this time I was fooled again for, instead, he took a chair closer to me and watched while I plunged the needle into the cloth.

"Do you enjoy your stay here, Ma'am?" The question stunned me for I did not expect that my employer ever thought of my feelings. I smiled slightly and I fear I answered his query too quickly and too abruptly.

"It is hardly a stay, Sir. Were it not for your kind employment I would not be here."

Mr. Grayson pressed his lips together. "Of course. I am sorry I did not think . . ." he replied and I heard the apology also reflected in his voice.

I was mortified. My sharp answer had come much

too swiftly and decisively and it was now my turn to apologize.

"Forgive me, Sir, I did not mean to make light of your welcome employment of me or protest your household's generous beneficence toward me. I much appreciate your kindness, as you well know. It was only that you spoke to me as you would a guest." I looked away. "And that I am not, Sir. It is only your generosity that allows me to continue teaching your children. And for that, Sir, I am most grateful. And," I continued in hopes of allaying my own doubts as to whether my position pleased Mr. Grayson, "I hope that you are pleased with my work."

"Very much so, Ma'am. Although I do not often visit the nursery there are other ways to gauge a child's education, as you well know." He sat straight in his chair, watching me as I rethreaded my needle. When it was done I put my head down for I did not want my employer to see the heat of my face.

"When I was much younger, Mr. Grayson," I said by way of explanation of my biting retort, "I had a reputation as a woman who sometimes spoke too quickly and too abruptly. I do beg your pardon."

Mr. Grayson was most gracious in receiving my apology. "Indeed. But, Miss Scott, you have not answered my question. I hope you find Ganymede House to your liking."

"Yes, Sir, very much. It is far beyond what I had ever expected."

Mr. Grayson did not say anything more and yet he did not make an action to leave. He instead continued to gaze into the fire, standing up once or twice and then finally moving close to the fireplace to stoke the logs so that they burned brighter.

"Are you chilly, Ma'am?" he asked and I shook my head.

"No, Sir. Mr. Keanne does a most able job of igniting the fires for me." Mr. Grayson poked at the raging flames once more and then sat down again and stared at the blaze.

What a strange man he is, I thought as I watched him from the corner of my eyes. His actions were so different this evening and it was as though I was dealing with another side of my employer, a side I had never seen before. He was most solicitous of my comfort and because he was not a man who wasted words I was amazed that he would sit and discourse with me about something as trivial as stitches and whether I, the governess, was pleased with my arrangements. Still, though, it was a pleasant hour we spent together.

"The fire warms the room very well. It is most enjoyable to sit here in the evening." I smiled at my employer who seemed not to hear me and I sighed— perhaps he had taken my words as a rebuke for his absences. Perhaps it was best, after all, that I did not speak again and I quietly sorted my thread for the next design in my pattern. I glanced quickly at Mr. Grayson who did not seem troubled by my words but he also remained silent and leaned on his elbow and gazed at the fire.

"I suppose Ganymede House is much different than the times you spent in London, Miss Scott. Do you still miss them?"

"I beg your pardon, Sir?" The question was most distracting and I put a small unwanted knot in my thread as I contemplated my answer for I did not know which way the conversation was turning. I had not expected questions about me to be part of our dialogue. "In truth, Sir, I have found memories of my past life fading quickly. I . . . I adjust very well to whatever vicissitudes befall me. I learned long ago, Sir, the nature of acceptance." I wondered if I spoke too much. I did not continue for I did not want my employer to think that I was so unhappy with my position that I yearned constantly for my forgotten city life and friends. He looked at me and I saw a small frown on his face. I quickly put my head down and worked at the small tangle with my needle and hoped it was dark enough so that Mr. Grayson could not notice the embarrassment that betrayed my calm exterior.

"Now it is my turn to apologize, Ma'am. I did not mean to make you uncomfortable." His apology took me by surprise and my discomfiture was complete so that I knew it was my duty to turn the tide of the conversation.

"Please, Sir . . . I did not take it as an offense. And, yes, I am quite happy here at Ganymede. My former life in London only serves to sharpen my skills in teaching your children for I can pass on to them the ways and mores of the city. That is, Sir, if you wish me to do so."

"When the time comes, Miss Scott, I expect that it will be only fitting that they learn those ways . . . as you call them . . . so that they can be well-versed in them. My wife . . ." he began and instead of finishing the remark took a sip of his wine and replaced the glass on the silver tray next to him. He stood then and made his customary courtly bow to me. "If you will excuse me, Ma'am . . ." I nodded my acceptance and Mr. Grayson turned and left the room.

I was puzzled, for this was the first time that my employer had ever felt the need to converse with me on any subject save the rudimentary questions regarding the children's education. The fact the he chose to ask me intimate questions about my own life seemed highly curious and suspect. I enjoyed his speaking of his family—I enjoyed the fact that he allowed me into his own thoughts, even if it was only for a moment. It served to remind me that there was a capacity in everyone to have many redeeming features if one would only look for them. I was ashamed that I had not thought of Mr. Grayson in this light before, and I was now quite confused, for although I could not understand the motives for his strange behavior, I found him to be, on this one occasion, most pleasant. Had I not known him and his ways with his own progeny I would have even called him a hospitable and loving employer and father.

How many times things are not what they seem! I wondered if it occurred to Mr. Grayson that his presence this evening puzzled me, that his change in our routine called for at least a rudimentary explanation. What a difficult man he was to unravel, I thought as I reknotted my string. No matter, I thought, he is the master of Ganymede House and I was only a little more than a servant, a governess hired to oversee his children. I sighed again as I heard the clock chime another hour and I rubbed my arms, for the fire had burned down. Tomorrow I would think about the troubles that inhabit this house.

As I gathered up my reticule, I smelled just a trace of the scent of roses.

Chapter 24

The next evening after dinner Mr. Grayson and I went back to our usual routine. I sat alone by the fire in the sitting room able to think my own thoughts in solitude. But it was most vexing. Everytime I seemed to come to some conclusions something or someone in the house turned itself about and I was forced to change my bent and direct it another way. Last evening's time spent with Mr. Grayson did not force me to make another assessment of my employer, but I did come to some judgments about the way the gentleman's mind worked. I know that Mr. Grayson suffered from black moods. Even last night, when we spoke, I could see the small traces of his dark disposition filter through his words. His many fits and starts of sentences, his lingering gaze at the fire where there was nothing but flames to occupy his mind, and of course, his sudden departure all served to remind me that despite his singular attempt the night before at some form of conversation the gentleman was still not focused on the present. It was an affliction that earned my pity but one that did not blind me to the peril that surrounded the children. I did not rashly judge Mr. Grayson as the author of that evil, yet I did not take chances with anyone in the household. The children's safety was of prime importance to me and I knew I must be on guard lest something befall them.

How sad and frightening it was to be both a party and a spectator to the happenings at the manor. The pieces were slowly filling in now on the puzzle of Ganeymede House and when Mr. Moore returned I might have a complete understanding of the household. Were it not for the fact that we had received word today that the children's cousin would be in the neighborhood in a fortnight and would pay us another of his short visits, I still would feel lonely and outside the established order of this house. I would certainly welcome the gentleman most enthusiastically when he arrived.

How easy it was to blur gratitude and companionship with affection! Whenever I envisioned the young man I found that I wished to tell him everything I had discovered in his absence and to share my opinions with him. I found it easy to speak to him and hence, I looked forward to seeing him. Were I still in London I knew my circle of friends would most assuredly tease me about the way I anticipated those visits, saying that I certainly had a *tendre* for the young man. I could not assuage the fact that I did, indeed, have a warm spot in my bosom for him.

I sat in my favorite chair in the parlor trying to sort out fiction from fact about the household, thinking that it would be more difficult than I imagined to find the real source of harm to the children. I trusted no one and I watched each person carefully. Nobody—neither inside nor outside the staff—was excused from my suspicions.

My mind rambled that evening for these had surely

been curious times for me. In my days in London the only mysteries I encountered were of a frivolous nature—the acceptance of an unsigned card within a nosegay of flowers . . . a fatuous consideration of which young man would be a dinner or dancing partner. All trivial matters indeed and highly insignificant when compared to the matter of the destruction of Antonia's doll and the inhabitant of the tower.

My fingers became cold and numb working with the tiny stitches in my design and I folded the cloth in preparation to leave the room. The fire had begun to die and the air had a chill to it and I decided that a long night's sleep would be most advantageous for my mind and body.

But it was not to be! As I turned to reach for my shawl the door of the parlor was flung open and a disheveled Mr. Grayson entered the room and stood in the middle of it, hands folded behind him, staring at me. His waistcoat was unbuttoned at the top and his ascot askew and I could see that he had had more than his share of wine, for the dark brilliance of his eyes flashed at me.

"Good evening, Ma'am," he said in a slurred voice. "I trust the evening finds you well."

I continued to fold my cloth and thought that it would be kinder and more courteous to carry through on my resolve to quit the room and leave him to his privacy. Still, his question deserved an answer.

"Yes, Sir, but I am tired, and if you will excuse me, Sir, I will leave the room to you." I stood up but Mr. Grayson shook his head vigorously and the swirl of grey in his forelock fell across his forehead. I remembered Mr. Moore's references to his cousin's quick anger and I did not know whether I should be afraid of Mr. Grayson while he was in this humour although I could detect no signs of hostility in the gentleman.

"Please stay but a few minutes, Miss Scott. I enjoy watching you at your needle work. My Rosamunda . . ." he began and then lapsed into quiet. "If you will stay but a few moments I would most certainly appreciate . . ." he said again and I could not refuse the request even though I suppressed a yawn. I sat down again and took out my needle. There was no reason to disobey the demand and a few minutes more in my employer's presence would not hurt me. "Of course, Sir, if that is your wish."

Mr. Grayson moved his head slightly. "Only if it suits you, Ma'am." He took a seat opposite me watching as I stitched, offering no words and yet holding me prisoner by the mere fact that he was still there. Perhaps prisoner was too strong a word, perhaps the word should have been captive . . . for he was still the master of Ganymede and I was still the governess, and my duty was first to the children I was hired to instruct and then to my employer.

We stayed thus, the fire slowly burning down and I attending to my work while Mr. Grayson watched through half-closed eyes. I stopped my sewing for my mind was now too clouded with lack of sleep and sudden confusion and, as a consequence, I had to rip three stitches which I had done incorrectly. I kept the cloth in my lap as a pretense but I did not even have to do that, Mr. Grayson's eyes began to flutter almost immediately after he sat. Finally, the combination of the flames in the fireplace and the quantity of wine he had consumed throughout the evening served to make him first hazy, then sleepy and soon I saw his head slump to his chest.

I waited but a moment or so before I again stuffed my cloth into its case, for I knew that my presence was now

234

no longer needed.

"Rosamunda . . . Rosamunda." I turned toward Mr. Grayson and saw his mouth working, his face contorting, and I could see, by the light of the fire, a look of anguish pass over his sleeping features. "Why? Why?" he cried out. No matter that I was tired, I could not leave the gentleman now. I drew my shawl around me and waited, hoping that Mr. Keanne would come into the room and escort his master to his chambers so that he could awaken from his nightmare.

"Rosamunda . . ." Mr. Grayson cried out again. I kept my silence for fear of waking him and yet fearing to hear the thoughts he was about to reveal. Once more he shouted out, "Rosamunda" and with the sound of his own distressed voice his eyes opened briefly and he looked at me and held out his hand. All thoughts for my own safety were quickly dispelled. "Why did you betray me, Rosamunda? I do not understand. I loved you . . . I loved you." He closed his eyes once more and now my heart went out to the gentleman for I suddenly knew what had disturbed him all these months: he believed his lady to have been unfaithful. Poor Mr. Grayson . . . what a terrible tragedy to have to carry around with him! It was something I had never suspected of the beautiful woman in the portrait. I nodded my head slightly—another section of the mystery of Ganymede seemed to be moving into place!

I looked up and saw Mr. Grayson staring at me. "Why . . . why, Rosamunda? Did you not know I loved you? Did I not tell you? Rosamunda? Rosamunda? You were . . . you are my life . . . my world." I held my hand to my mouth in surprise at the statement and yet I turned my face for fear that my own heart would signal its

235

compassion and give me away, although I could only suppose the extent of the pain and anguish I knew the gentleman felt and was continuing to feel.

I shifted my body in the chair and Mr. Grayson misinterpreted the sign. "Stay," he pleaded, "stay with me, do not leave me just yet." He opened his eyes full and even so I did not know whether he saw me sitting there or assumed, because he wanted it to be, that I was his late wife, his Rosamunda. In either case I remained with him until the room grew chilly and Mr. Keanne finally came to close the dampers. The butler looked first at me and then at Mr. Grayson and again we said nothing to each other except the courteous and polite "Good evening." There was nothing more to say or add and I left Mr. Keanne to attend to his master.

Chapter 25

It had been a tiring day; the children had been restless. The events of the previous evening left me fatigued; I had little sleep for I spent a great portion of the late hours reviewing the plight of Mr. Grayson. And even though I remained in bed a full half-hour beyond my usual rising time this morning I was still exhausted and I looked forward to escaping early this evening to the warmth of my bed.

The dinner proceeded as usual and after the children were excused and Mr. Grayson sat at the table with his drink, I rose and asked permission to retire to my chambers. I had thought that my employer would welcome my leaving, but instead he sat back in his chair and continued to stare—at nothing in particular except for one of the oil paintings on a side wall—seeming not to hear me . . . or not choosing to answer. I knew not which supposition was correct.

I did not know whether or not Mr. Grayson remembered what had transpired between us last night but I did not want to bring the matter to his attention merely for conversation's sake or for somber discussion. The secret he had revealed to me in an unguarded moment was much too private and much too tormenting and I did not want to inflict more pain upon him. Thus I neither hinted at, nor intimated that I was party to his drunken words and so thought it best to take my leave as quickly as possible. My practical sense told me it would be best to be out of sight so that I would not remind him of his ill behaviour.

I again asked his pardon to leave, and this time Mr. Grayson turned toward me and I saw a momentary closing of his eyes, a barely noticeable expression of dolor, before he finally acknowledged me and stood absently and I took the motion as a note of dismissal. I bade him a pleasant goodnight and started to leave the room but he startled and surprised me with his next words. I knew then that no matter how much he had drunk and no matter how much he was distressed, he did remember last evening.

"Miss Scott, will you do me the honour and stay with me this evening? At least until I have finished my port? I have something most urgent to discuss with you . . . to ask you."

I stopped at the door. Surely, I thought, Mr. Grayson had had time enough, while we sat at the table, to speak, but mindful of my position in the household I acceded to his wishes.

"Of course, Sir," I answered and made my way to the sitting room sitting at my usual place on the divan. I took up my needlepoint and waited patiently until he decided to speak, for he had fallen back to his own ways and remained silent. I secretly hoped that he would not extend the conversation too long and I wondered if I should deny that I suspected he had been the worse for drink last night or that I had heard him and his accusation of Rosamunda. It was a most difficult situation to be placed in and if I spoke the truth it would be most embarrassing for the two of us. It was not my place to do so, and I could not condemn the man for what he did in his own home for it was most definitely not of my concern nor my position to rebuke him.

When Mr. Keanne placed the wine decanter and the silver pot of tea on the table Mr. Grayson poured a cup of the brew and handed it to me—a diversion in our routine and again another lapse in his manners, for he had not asked me to pour. He then refilled his own glass with wine and sipped it slowly as though to remind himself of his excesses of the night before.

I still had no clue as to what he wished to say to me, and in fact, I had to stifle a yawn, such was the intensity of my fatigue. My employer sat across from me—still silent and I assumed still watching me—and as he did so I did not look up—for I knew that in due time whatever he had cause to say would be spoken.

Mr. Grayson set down his glass and began to pace back and forth in the room, stopping once or twice to stoke the already brightly burning fireplace, then resuming his gait. "Miss Scott," he said, finally, and the resonance of his voice seemed overly loud for the room. His next words were pitched lower. "Ma'am," he said bowing slightly to me, "I owe you an apology for my behaviour last evening." I started to protest but Mr. Grayson held up a hand to quiet me. "No, Ma'am, please do not protest. If I had wisdom and the power to withdraw my actions I would most humbly do so. But I am neither wise nor almighty and so what happened must stand and it is for me to apologize for my own clumsy actions." He looked at me and bowed again. "I do beg your pardon, Ma'am. I can only promise you that it shall not happen again."

I was most surprised at the apology. I did believe that only on rare occasions had Mr. Grayson ever allowed his behaviour to run amok and I did also believe that rarely had he ever tendered an atonement.

I smiled. "Your apology is very welcome, Sir, and accepted with all good grace."

Mr. Grayson acknowledged my acceptance. "I do thank you, Ma'am," he said and then resumed pacing the room.

I did not know what else could or should be said of the matter. "If that is all, Sir, I would like to be excused. I have some letters that must be answered."

Mr. Grayson shook his head. "Please stay but a few more moments, Ma'am. There is one other matter . . ." I acquiesced and sat back against the feather pillows of the sofa and Mr. Grayson spoke with a deliberateness I had not heard before. "Miss Scott, I have a proposition to make to you."

I remained quiet, waiting for him to continue. He cleared his throat and began. "I do know, Ma'am, that you are quite fond of my children. You told me so yourself this past week." I nodded and still continued to stitch, wondering whether he was speaking softly as a prelude to sacking me or to asking me not to speak of his lapse in front of the children. He did neither, but continued on his train of thought. "And my children's welfare—despite what you have observed or heard—is still quite important to me. Quite important. My children are most precious to me," he said and the timbre of his voice as he spoke the words indicated nothing that could be faulted. He paused but a second. "I do not make excuses for my conduct, Ma'am, and I do see sometimes

240

at table that you try to smooth the way of the children towards me."

So Mr. Grayson has known my intentions.

"So . . . to resume," he said nodding his head. "My son and daughter, I tell you again, are very important to me no matter that they might not . . ." Here he left the phrase unfinished and it struck me odd but I was in no position to question. Whatever Mr. Grayson was to say to me . . . no matter what the proposition—and here my mind spun for what a strange word to be employed—I would have to wait quietly for clarification.

"Ganymede House has been my family's home for several centuries as you know, Ma'am. There has always been a Grayson in residence." At this he looked toward the gallery of ancestral portraits. "And, of course, I expect that Virgil will someday replace me as Master of Ganymede, Miss Scott."

I wondered why Mr. Grayson would speak of such unhappy ultimate events now, when all seemed to be going smoothly. I wondered if he, too, knew of the threatening circumstances. But as he did not speak of this, I held my words and instead offered a platitude though I did mean it sincerely.

"Surely, the times of which you speak will be a long day away," I suggested but Mr. Grayson merely shook his head.

"It is not for us to know that, Ma'am," he said roughly and I felt a rebuke and bent my head once more to the task of stitching. "I did not mean that to be as callous as it sounded, Ma'am," Mr. Grayson said. "It is a simple, yet correct, statement."

"Then I pray it will be merely that for many a year, Sir."

Mr. Grayson bowed an acknowledgment. "Thank you,

241

Ma'am. But in the matters of the estate . . . of Ganymede House . . . I must be practical." He again sipped from his glass and strode about the room. "Therefore I have something to propose . . . indeed, it is rather more in the nature of a proposition than a proposal I make to you, Ma'am."

"And what is that, Sir?"

Mr. Grayson did not hesitate. "I ask that you consider my proposal of marriage, Ma'am. I am asking you to be my wife and I am making a formal offer for you."

I gasped for I did not know what to say! I leaned back in my chair, my needle still halfway into the fabric, and looked down at my trembling hands. Surely I had not heard correctly. To offer for me! To propose a marriage to me! There had never been any intimation nor intent on Mr. Grayson's part. Indeed, there was never a suggestion, never even a single moment that indicated that he thought of me as anything more than a paid governess to his children. How could it be then, that I had heard him offer for my hand?

"I beg your pardon, Sir, I—I . . ." I could not even finish my sentence without my voice defeating me. I raised my head and Mr. Grayson looked me in my eye.

"I see that you are surprised, Ma'am, and well you may be. It is a question for which I had not prepared you."

I shook my head. "It is more than that, Sir. It is a subject you had not indicated . . ."

Mr. Grayson sat opposite me. "I had only thought of it, to be truthful, Ma'am, these past two weeks. But I have given it much consideration and I deem that it has much merit to it." He held the wine glass but did not drink from it. "I said to you, Miss Scott, that it was a proposition and not a proposal that I offer you. And that is just what it is.

I make no other pretenses and if you please, Ma'am, hear me out." He stood up again and walked the room while I, embarrassed and confused, kept my head to the task of needlepoint although I already knew that I would later have to rip out many, many stitches that had in the past few minutes become too large and too ragged.

"What I propose, Miss Scott, if it suits you, is that you and I contract for a marriage of convenience. Both for your sake and my family." He stopped and sipped his port and I was glad he did not look at me directly, for my face flamed and I am sure bewilderment showed on my features. "This is what I propose and these are some of my reasons, Ma'am, if you will do me the courtesy of staying and listening."

I plunged my needle into the cloth but so addled was my mind that I pricked my finger. I quickly withdrew my hand lest a drop of blood stain the fabric. Mr. Grayson did not see my mishap and instead continued.

"I know I have not seemed to be the most attentive of people at the dining table . . . nor in the house, Ma'am, yet I have seen your care and love for my children and I appreciate your devotion to them. He stopped briefly, then continued. "They, too, are happy with you. They listen to you. They are pleased that you are here. You are of an age that can still enjoy the antics of children . . ." Again my face flamed. This time I put my hand to my cheeks, but my employer still paid no heed to my gestures. "And," he persevered, "my children need a mother."

I listened, but I could not concentrate on the meaning of this strange proposal. Surely the gentleman had other women in his circle who would welcome the chance to mother his children, to be his wife and mistress of

Ganymede House. But I did not say anything and instead, at his request, listened to the rest of my employer's proposal.

"Of course there are other considerations, Miss Scott. Some of the justifications you are not privy to at this moment but I hope in time that they will make themselves clear. Ma'am, I have my reasons to ask that you love and take care of my children. That is of my prime concern." He walked back and forth and did not say anything more and I sat there, hearing the clock chime, but not knowing the hour, while I tried to sort out my feelings. I had been taken by surprise and I did not know how to respond. Surely I would need time to consider.

"You do not expect an answer this evening?"

Mr. Grayson shook his head slowly and I could see the earnestness in his eyes. "No, Ma'am. I understand it has come as a shock—a surprise, if you will—and that you will need time."

"Is there not anything more to speak of, then?" Surely more should be considered, but Mr. Grayson still said nothing so I asked the prevailing question concerning my part in this marriage.

"What do you expect from me, Sir? And what is to be my role if I accept this . . . this . . . proposition?"

Mr. Grayson frowned and I could see that the question had occurred to him also.

"I do not expect anything more than an arrangement. Of course, for the servants' sake and for your own reputation, Ma'am, I would expect you to move into quarters nearer mine, so as to give the illusion that we have contracted a full and civil marriage."

Now I could feel the flaming heat on my cheeks and I

244

knew that the intense warmth rivaled even that of the glowing coals in the fireplace. I pressed on immediately, eager to turn the direction of the conversation. "And what of your children, Sir? Will I still be allowed to tutor them? Will I still be their governess?"

"Of course. That should not change." He sat down once more, opposite me, and compelled me to look at him as he spoke. "As for your part in this bargain, Miss Scott," and here I raised my own eyebrows for the discussion had now taken the bent of a business dealing. "I have but two simple requests. I only ask that you raise and love my children and cherish them as your own . . ."

This first request was simple and I did not wait to confirm the petition, instead responding to it immediately. "Of course, that I already do. As you well know."

"Yes."

"Thank you. And your second request, Sir?"

Mr. Grayson took a deep breath. "And the other, Miss Scott, is that you honour me by not dishonouring me." How strange and plaintive were the words! Were it not for last night, I would not have understood. Again I answered quickly.

"Of your request not to disgrace you, Sir, I would most gladly promise, for it is not in my nature to do harm."

Mr. Grayson looked away. "I do believe that, Miss Scott, but sometimes, Ma'am, what we intend with all our heart sometimes . . . goes astray."

"Once I promise, Sir, I do not amend," I said forcefully. I could not answer any other way.

Mr. Grayson sat back in his chair as though he had completed an uneasy and unwelcome chore. I looked at him and saw no emotion in his face, no passion, no love.

It was up to me, then, to complete the conversation. "And what else do you expect of me . . . of such a liaison?"

Mr. Grayson turned toward the window, at the bleak North England landscape that I had already come to love. "Nothing else. I want nothing else, Ma'am."

I waited until he turned to face me again before I answered. "I see."

"But in return, Miss Scott, I offer you my name . . . my children . . ."

I raised my eyebrows again and Mr. Grayson saw my perplexity. "My *two* children," he stressed and I blushed that he was so accurately able to read and discern my thoughts. "I promise you, Ma'am, that I will make no demands on you, neither physically nor emotionally," he explained in a very abstracted voice and then continued as though he were reciting a legal brief. "For you, Miss Scott, you gain a family, a good and respected name and position, and a future that you do not now have at the moment. It is no small compliment I offer you, Ma'am, though I do not think those words adequate for the occasion." He swirled the liquid in his glass. "Though if you choose not to accept my contract, Ma'am, be assured that you will continue to be part of the staff . . . and will receive all the benefits due you. Should you decide against it, Ma'am, we will speak no more of it and it will be but part of our past. But," he looked at the still moving liquid, "I do hope you will consider my business proposition, Ma'am, for it has much merit for both of us . . . and my children."

So, I thought, I am to be negotiated for, much like a property or a workhorse. I was amazed that Mr. Grayson wasn't able to read those thoughts. But, instead, he continued—oblivious to my thinking. "There are other concerns, Ma'am, for you to consider—monetary remuneration. For if you accept my offer, then I, in turn and as a token of my thanks, will deposit into a separate account two hundred and fifty pounds every year for you to do with as you please. I will neither ask for, nor expect, an accounting. I will do that, Ma'am, as a token of my gratitude." He saw me move slightly and held out his hand to me, thinking that I was about to leave. "Do stay a while longer, Miss Scott, and give me the pleasure of your company and attention for just a few more moments. Surely that is not too much to ask while we are talking about such a weighty subject."

"No," I agreed and folded my hands in my lap while he poured himself another glass of wine, forgetting the simple courtesy of replenishing my cup of tea. "If you will do me the honor of considering my proposal—both marriage and business—I will ask Mr. Largo, my solicitor, to draw up a document that will validate and safeguard the provisions. You, of course, will be able to take it to a barrister of your choice. Surely Mr. Clayton, your late father's partner, would be careful in providing for your interests, should you choose him." He sipped his wine. "If you will consider it well, I am sure you will find the contract to your benefit and satisfaction."

I sighed once more, for although I was tired, this new and strange petition caused my mind to speed and work at twice its rhythm and sense. "I would like time to think about what you suggest."

"Yes, by all means." He drained his glass. "We shall speak no more of it this evening. Perhaps, if it suits you, you could give me your answer by the Holidays. By then you will know more of us—the Graysons and Ganymede

House—and you will be better positioned to answer."

I nodded. "That time will be quite adequate, Sir. And now," I stood up on very shaky limbs, "if you will excuse me."

Mr. Grayson merely suggested half-rising from his chair, inclined his head toward me, and resumed looking at the fire.

In the quiet of my room I thought of this incredible proposal. Although it was more in the order of an arrangement, I knew it could be a chance for me finally to have a place I could permanently call my home. I lay down on my bed, purposely not pulling the shutters closed, and watched through the panes of window the bright pale moon as it passed behind scudding clouds, casting all manner of leafy shadows on the bedroom walls and on the counterpane of my bed. I reached out to trace the moon-lit artwork but the shapes disappeared. I wondered, if I accepted Mr. Grayson's proposal, would true love—that I had always envisioned as part of my life—be as elusive as the shadows that danced and played a peeping game here in my room? I could only wonder, for I did not know.

So for the second time in only three months I was asked and gently forced to make a decision about my future. I lay awake a long time and when finally I fell asleep I still had not resolved any of my feelings—instead giving in to the prospect of thinking how I could reconcile my life as I had known it in London and the one I would be attaching myself to here in Yorkshire.

The next morning, neither Mr. Grayson nor I, according to the conditions set down by him, spoke of the conversation.

Chapter 26

I did not tell the staff of Mr. Grayson's proposal. I was not sure whether Mr. and Mrs. Keanne knew, for the old gentleman made it a practice to tread lightly when he entered the rooms where his Master was and so I did not know whether he overheard our conversation or not. But so far, neither he nor Mrs. Keanne demonstrated any knowledge of what transpired last evening.

I was still befogged because of Mr. Grayson's strange proposal of marriage; that it was a loveless proposition was obvious and I did accept all his reasons but I suspect that there was something more that made the gentleman ask for my hand. But what it was I had not the vaguest idea, and that was one of the things I vowed to learn before I tendered my answer to him.

Mr. Keanne looked out the leaded glass windows at the dull sky. "It seems as though it's to be a harsh winter, Miss Scott. They say that snow will be coming before the week is up." He polished a large silver tureen and when he spoke to me I searched his face for hidden words and meanings.

"Yes. Old Martin said to expect a heavy fall. I met him on my walk this afternoon."

Mr. Keanne continued rubbing the silver. "Best you don't go out during the snow. A person can get lost," he said, and I blushed as he remembered my ill-fated evening in the Greek maze.

"No, I shan't." I picked up a heavy carved silver candlestick and sat down at the end of the table, next to where the gentleman stood, and when I did he seemed to stiffen.

"Is there something wrong?" I asked him and when he did not reply I probed further, noticing that he looked at the chair that I occupied. "Is there something wrong with this seat?" I bent around and examined the back thinking that perhaps there was a flaw in it.

Mr. Keanne said nothing.

"Tell me, Sir, what is it about this chair? I remember that when I first came to Ganymede I sat in this very chair and Mr. Grayson asked me to take another." I waited for a reply but still Mr. Keanne said nothing and continued to rub the tureen harder. "There are so many unexplained things in this house, Mr. Keanne. Surely you have noticed that. There are far too many things. I am sure you know of what I speak." I traced the edge of the candlestick. "Can you not explain things to me? Surely you must trust me, Sir. I have told you before that I ask only for explanations that contribute to the children's welfare."

"Aye, that's so," he finally answered and then I saw his mouth working, and I knew he was deciding whether to speak of more Ganymede matters. "We—Mrs. Keanne and myself, Ma'am—can probably tell you about the house." He shook his head. "You remember, Ma'am, I told you that at one time this was a happy house though I know you can't quite believe the truth of that statement. If I were in your place I would question that, too." He paused and continued. "But it was a fine house to work in and Mrs. Keanne and I thought ourselves lucky to serve the Master and Mistress. Aye . . . lucky, indeed."

I dared not interrupt; there were too few opportunties for me to learn the history of Ganymede and its inhabitants and I wanted Mr. Keanne to continue.

He pointed to my chair. "No one has sat in that chair since the Mistress died," he said and I jumped up, eager to vacate it, lest he had overheard last night's conversation and should think me too willing and eager to take his Mistress's place. "That chair belonged to Miss Rosamunda," Mr. Keanne said, putting down the polishing cloth. "And the Master would sit at table in the morning with her and the children and, hard as it may seem, Miss, he would laugh and be delighted with his wife's talk."

He sighed and I could tell there was pain in the memory. "Sometimes it would be mindless prattle, to tell the truth, Miss Scott, but the Master, he didn't mind. Just the way he looked at Miss Rosamunda you could tell he was devoted to her. This may be gossip, Ma'am, but I once overheard him introduce her to some gentry at a dinner party as his 'rose of the world' he was that caught up with her. And the children! Aye, she was special to them, too. They would tease and laugh and she always had time for their words."

"But Mr. Grayson tells me the children have forgotten her," I said for I did not want Mr. Keanne to know that the children had already told me about their mother and their memories of the lady.

251

"That may be what he says, Miss, but Mrs. Keanne and I, we know better. They talk to us—Mrs. Keanne especially—about her. Don't you be fooled, Ma'am, they remember their mother well. We all do."

So that, I thought, was why no one ever spoke of Virgil having a key to Rosamunda's room—Mr. and Mrs. Keanne had banded together to act out a hidden conspiracy that allowed the children to visit their mother's chambers. It was an expression I did not expect from the old woman, yet one that I should have suspected. Again my heart went out to Virgil and Antonia and to their pain. No child should be denied the solace of a mother's surroundings—or her portrait—when all else has gone. Perhaps, I vowed, there would be some way to broach this subject to their father so that he could replace the painting in the formal sitting room. I thought it was something that all the Graysons needed to speak of and to see.

But it seemed Mr. Keanne read my thoughts.

"Don't you be telling the Master, though, Ma'am, for he doesn't like the children to talk of her."

"But why?" Again I asked the question for I wanted to find out just how much the gentleman knew and how much he was willing to make known to me.

Mr. Keanne shook his head. "I don't know," he said softly turning his head so that I could not see his eyes and I knew that I had yet to be taken into his complete confidence.

"Don't know, Mr. Keanne, or won't tell about it?"

Mr. Keanne just kept shaking his head so that the ring of white fringe on his head swayed. "You best be leaving it alone, Miss. Mister Oliver would prefer it that way."

"That is another thing, Mr. Keanne. Why does Mr.

Grayson reject the children? Especially Virgil? It is most obvious."

Mr. Keanne turned and looked toward the portrait gallery. "I don't know, Miss . . . perhaps the boy's hair?"

"Surely he doesn't suspect Virgil not to be his son—to be a false heir."

The old gentleman shook his head. " 'Tis not for me to say what he thinks."

"That is quite foolish, Mr. Keanne. Why the boy is the image of his father, except for the Grayson lock. Surely Mister Oliver sees that. He must surely have been told many times of the striking resemblance by many people."

Mr. Keanne turned away. " 'Tis a pity . . . 'tis a pity . . ." was his only answer and I shuddered that his master should be so blinded by superstition so as to suppose Virgil not to be his son. What a cruel joke fate had played on the boy, I thought, not giving him the swirl of grey hair. And crueler yet was the way the boy's father treated him because of this trick of nature.

"Has he always felt that way . . . always rejected Master Virgil? Surely his mother . . ." Just speaking of it chilled me for it was incomprehensible that a father would reject his own child.

Mr. Keanne looked down at the silver he was polishing. "No, Miss, not while Mistress Rosamunda was alive, not until her death. They were the finest family one could expect to work for." Again he shook his head. "What a happy time it was before. I remember it well. Mr. Oliver was the best of fathers, always laughing and playing with the children and telling stories to them even before they could understand the words." He put the polishing cloth aside as he replaced the bowl on the table. "Ah well, those days are gone forever." He bowed his head. "No use thinking back to them. It only serves to hurt everyone."

"The hurt is more in not remembering, Mr. Keanne. Surely Mr. Grayson wouldn't begrudge the children their mother's memory."

"He would and he does!" The voice behind me was angry and I turned to see Mrs. Keanne, a stack of newly ironed linen in her arms. She turned to her husband. "How many times must I tell you, Mr. Keanne, that we shouldn't gossip? Master wants it that way." She gave me a withering look signifying that I was not welcome in this room while Mr. Keanne was doing his work.

"But surely—" I began.

"There is no surely, Miss, begging your pardon. I have my orders. Once a household succumbs to foolish and idle talk there's no one in charge." Mrs. Keanne stood at the doorway to the dining room, obviously waiting for me to make my exit. "We all have our work, Ma'am. I'm sure the children are waiting for you, too." She glared at me and there was nothing more for me to say. I walked out of the room hearing whispered angry words passing between husband and wife.

"She was only asking, Bertie," Mr. Keanne began.

"Asking's snooping, Mr. Keanne. You know Master's orders. Would you prefer for us to be asked to leave?"

"She was only asking for the children's sake."

"Leave it, Mr. Keanne. I'll take care of the children and their mother's memory, God rest her, poor soul."

I knew not the intricacies of manor life nor the way information seemed to be passed to the domestics and although my conversation with Mr. Grayson was in strictest confidence, I felt sure that within a few days Mrs. Keanne was privy to it. Her manner, which had softened toward me in the last few weeks, once more hardened. When we were forced to speak we maintained civility, but I could feel the resentment directed toward me whenever we happened to be in the same room. I tried to speak with her about whatever was uppermost in her sentiments but the older woman rebuffed me several times and I felt it best to heed the caution of my mind and ignore the situation. It was just one more thing I had to consider when I thought about the position I would undertake should I accept the proposition tendered me.

A few days after Mr. Grayson's proposal I found myself in the kitchen, for my throat was dry and I wanted a cup of hot tea. The children were at rest in the nursery and I did not want to bother Tillie or any of the other servants and thought it best to get my own refreshment. The kitchen was deserted—for it was just after the luncheon was served and before the preparation for dinner was begun—and not even the scullery maids were at work. I was unfamiliar with the room and its many cupboards and set about searching for a cup and saucer to use for the tea. Finally, after several attempts, I located two sets of especially fine porcelain—two cups and saucers decorated in pale pastel flowers—and removed one for my use.

I had never seen this particular pattern in the house and determined that it must be the odds and ends of a set that had long ago been broken. I wondered why there had never been replacements for the pattern, for it was both unusual and beautiful. There were dainty pink and blue raised roses on the face of the ivory cup, as though they were scattered haphazardly across the surface. The flowers were delicately painted in the pale tints and outlined in deeper matching colors and were tied, one to the other, with a slim thread of gold that wove round and round the outside of the cup in a never ending circlet.

"You've no right to be in my kitchen!" Mrs. Keanne's words reverberated throughout the room. "We have abided by the rules, Miss Scott, you in the classroom and I here. You've no right . . ."

I jumped up, spilling the tea on the table and we both watched as the cup precariously teetered on the table, as though it were trying to make up its mind whether it should fall or not. Mrs. Keanne stared at the China.

"The cup! Miss Rosamunda's cup." Mrs. Keanne rushed by me and grabbed the China just as it was about to topple. "You've taken everything," she shouted at me. "First her children and then her husband. And now . . . all the last possessions." She hugged the cup to her bosom. "You have tried to destroy the last memories of that poor dear soul." Mrs. Keanne's eyes enlarged and misted over. For a moment, I thought she had finished, but instead, her sharp voice became even more strident as she raged at me. Were it not for her diminutiveness I would have been afraid of her, such was the force of her anger.

"You will not take the memory of their mother away from those bairns."

I stepped back, more in confusion than terror. "You do not understand, Mrs. Keanne," I said but it was of no consequence to the old woman. Her voice lowered and she hissed the phrase once more. "You will not take the memory of their mother away from them. I shall see to that."

I shook my head. I had no idea what the woman was referring to, nor was she of a frame of mind to explain and I moved toward the kitchen door. "You do not understand Mrs. Keanne," I said. "I have no wish to—"

"I do not trust you," she said coldly and it was the voice of a person who would defend whatever ideals she had established to be right. "The poor babes," she kept repeating over and over again. "The poor babes . . . never knowing their mother again . . . never speaking of her . . . never knowing the love of a good mother again." She looked at me. "You will never replace her!"

I have no idea how the sound of our voices travelled throughout the downstairs so that our disagreement could be heard by the help, but it was at that moment that Mr. Keanne came into the room and upon seeing his wife in such an agitated state, walked to her and put his hand upon her arm. "What is it, Bertie? What is it?"

Mrs. Keanne pointed to me. "Miss Rosamunda's cup. She was going to break it."

I tried to explain my innocence, but Mr. Keanne merely held up his hand to me.

"Please, Miss Scott," he said, turning back once more to his wife.

"Her and her snooping ways." The woman had recovered her equilibrium now and looked at me with hate and suspicion. "I'll tolerate you, Miss Scott. I will serve you because you will be Mr. Oliver's wife," she said and it was a shock to learn that my suspicions were confirmed. "But," she continued, "I will never allow you to be the children's mother. Never! You will always be an outsider to us here at Ganymede House," she said and the tenor of her voice caused me to shiver.

Mr. Keanne glanced at me. "Ah, Miss," he said gently and I could see the sorrow in his eyes. "You'd best be going. Mrs. Keanne. . . ." he patted his wife's freckled hand, "Mrs. Keanne and I have some talking to do. You understand. If you'll excuse us?"

"Of course . . . of course," I answered none too sorry to be able to leave the room. "I will speak with you later," I said and felt a surge of pity for the good man who had much too heavy a job to comfort his disturbed wife.

Later when I saw Mr. Keanne in the dining hall I inquired as to the woman and was told that she was much calmer now. "You'll have to excuse her, Miss. She and Miss Rosamunda . . ." he began but stopped instantly when he saw that Mr. Grayson had passed close to the hall.

"Some other time, perhaps," I suggested to the servant but he neither confirmed nor denied the suggestion and I went back upstairs to my room to change for dinner.

Chapter 27

It was another raw day—not fit for outdoor activities—and after lessons, I told the children that they were free to do whatever they pleased that afternoon. They seemed eager for the respite yet uneasy about their recreation. I offered to teach them another game or to sit with them and read to them but both suggestions were met with indifference and so I searched for another sport for them.

"We could go to the tower," Antonia said.

"Yes, we can show you the tower, Miss Scott." Virgil appeared beside me, seconding his sister's suggestion.

"But it is too cold and too damp to be outside," I said. "It is not the weather to walk in." I did not tell them that another reason for my hesitation was that my only encounter with the tower had not been pleasant.

"We don't go that way," Antonia giggled and then stopped as she must have seen me stare at her. She turned to her brother and they both looked sheepish, finally realizing that I had not before been entrusted with this bit of knowledge into their lives.

259

"It's alright, Antonia," Virgil said to his sister and then I understood that I had finally passed their criteria—whatever that may be—and I was being allowed into their world. "We could show you the tower, Ma'am, if you'd like. But," he said looking around and lowering his voice to a whisper so that Tillie, who was in the cloak room, could not hear, "you must not speak of it to any others."

I had been caught in a dilemma: should I accept the children's offer and keep silent about what they were so eager to show me, or did my duty and responsibility lie with Mr. Grayson? I looked into the two small innocent faces before me and saw that they were quite serious.

"If you ask me to keep it a secret, then of course, I shall." The children seemed relieved that I agreed to their terms and having told Tillie that we were just going to walk the halls of the house for recreation, the three of us left the nursery. Although I still had lingering doubts about my loyalty, I had to honor their request.

The children led me through the halls, past their father's chambers, close to the guest wings and stopped in front of an ordinary door—identical to all the others on the floor. Then—looking around to make sure that no one else was in the vicinity—Virgil took a small key from his tunic and turned the lock and pushed and I could see as it swung inward that the open door led to a small false room that gave way immediately to another sealed passageway. Virgil unlocked this entrance, too, and we went through to another area. Here, there was a small carpeted landing right inside the door and beyond it there was a wooden staircase and bannister that led downward and as I held my candle low—for Virgil had cautioned me to carry one—I saw that there seemed to be a gallery below. Virgil ran down the steps and I could tell by the quickness of his movements that he was all too familiar with this hidden part of the house.

The young boy looked back at me and smiled the sweet smile that I had come to love. "Don't be afraid, Miss Scott, we've been here before. Haven't we, Antonia?"

His younger sister nodded her head so that the golden curls tumbled onto her face and even at such an extraordinary moment I could not help but think of her as a painted angel—a seraphim from the portraits of Michelangelo or Botticelli.

I held on to the railing as I made my way downward and I saw that an artisan had once upon a time taken great care with this concealed way. The staircase, like the landing, was carpeted and thus soundless and the walls on either side had been painted in pale colors—perhaps to better reflect the candle flames and to throw more light for those who used this mysterious passage.

The staircase appeared to have been recently swept clean for it was without any particles of dust or dirt. In one or two tiny spots there were small drippings of candlewax on the covered treads but that was the only sign of unkemptness that I could detect.

Virgil and Antonia hurried down the steps—entreating me to follow the two of them and I saw that the entire staircase was decorated with now unlit sconces and candleholders so as to make it easy for people unfamiliar with the dark to walk safely to their destination.

"This used to be the way we would go to the tower," Virgil said. "Our parents would take us there when we were younger. It was a special playroom of ours." Antonia walked along next to me and for the first time since I had met her the girl showed a sense of free-spiritness, almost skipping down the steps, not needing to

261

hold to the railing as she made her way. "We would go there—especially when it rained," she said and I could see that she still remembered many occasions that both her father and cousin supposed had long been forgotten.

We had gotten to the bottom of the staircase and now a long carpeted hall lay before us and Antonia took my hand.

"Don't be afraid, Miss Scott, we've been here many times. You'll see." We walked a few more paces and Virgil stopped in front of a huge mural of the sea strangely hung on a wall here in the dark and when I remarked on the beauty and the familiarity of it Virgil nodded his head.

"It's of the cliffs, Ma'am, near the Greek maze. Our mother was quite taken with them—she loved the sea, Ma'am, and my father had it commissioned as a surprise for her." Virgil stepped close to it and raised his candle so that he could see it better. "It used to hang on the wall in the dining room—she said she loved seeing it when she ate—but then, after the accident, Mr. Keanne took it down and put it away. We only discovered it by accident when Antonia and I found the key to the door."

Antonia nodded and again her golden curls fell in front of her face and she smiled but neither of the children volunteered how they came by the key nor where they found it. I thought it best not to ask such questions. There would be other times for those answers.

The children continued on, urging me to follow them, and at the other end of the narrow passage we came upon a second staircase that led upwards and when I hesitated the two of them hastened me on.

"This is it, Miss Scott. Wait until you see it." Virgil scampered ahead, climbing the stairs with ease, and in a few moments he stopped at another door and pressed it so that it, too, swung open.

I realized I was on the bottom floor of the tower and yet I knew not how I had gotten here. Obviously, someone long ago had built the secret tunnel, perhaps for visiting clerics who were being persecuted or perhaps for an unobstructed escape route for men and women who needed a fast and unseen course away from the house. Whoever once upon a time used it—or whatever use was made of it—I knew not and the children could not tell me.

"Come." Virgil held out his hand to me and pointed to the wrought iron circular staircase so familiar to all towers and lighthouses. "To the top."

We climbed to the uppermost part of the round building—I more carefully than the children for they were much more surefooted than I—and when we stood at the top of the steps I saw that it was sparsely furnished. There was a small table in the middle of the room and a brass candleholder and a well-burnt candle stub on it next to a box of long matches. Near to these items was a small painted miniature cameo. Without even looking at it I knew that the delicate comely features were that of Rosamunda and when I picked it up to confirm it Virgil saw me and smiled.

"That was my mother's present to my father just before she had the accident," he said. "Was she not beautiful?"

I nodded and put the small picture down. "Yes . . . yes, she was. Mr. Keanne told me of her reputation for being one of the fairest in these parts."

The inside of the building was chilly and damp and I smelled mildew that had seeped onto the faintly moist stone walls. It was a cold room—both in reality and atmosphere—and it was not a place in which I would linger. I would most certainly much prefer it if my two charges did not spend too long a time here on many occasions.

There were two small windows cut out of the solid stone walls—from one I could see the side and back of the estate house and from the other I was able to see the limits of the lawns and the mist that rose thereafter from the edge of the cold waters of the seas. Even from this distance and this height I persuaded myself that I could hear the roar of the waves as they crashed on the rocks and I shivered recalling the scene that had been described to me of that terrible night.

But it was evident that the children had no such thoughts this afternoon. They pushed a chair to one of the windows and climbed on to it so that they, too, could see the view and I could not help but wonder what memories flooded into their minds. But they did not seem annoyed or frightened and I knew that they, like all other children, considered this time spent in the tower to be that of a secret nature—to be their own especial mystery.

"Does no one ever come when you are here?"

"No." Antonia turned and looked at me with her bright blue eyes. "No one knows we come here. We're careful." She touched Virgil's hand. "You're the only one who knows." The innocent blue eyes seemed to bore into me and for a brief second I thought I saw an older look inhabit her eyes. "You're the only one who knows."

"So be it," I said and smiled at her, making sure that she understood that their secret remained safe with me. She climbed down and moved the chair to the other side of the room—to the window facing the house.

"Look, Miss Scott, you can see the barns and the stable and someone walking toward the house. Look." I peered out the small opening.

"I think that's Old Martin," I said and both of the children laughed . . . willing participants in that age-old childhood game of seeing but not being seen by an adult. "He doesn't know we can watch him," I said as the old man disappeared into the stable.

The children continued to look down at the estate, shouting at me to look at the landmarks they were spotting—a familiar oak tree, a stablehand leading a horse, or a feature of the main house they recognized.

"Look, Miss Scott, you can barely see our nursery— there on the side . . . where the bushes are large. Right above them, Ma'am, that's where we are." Virgil pointed out the children's wing and when he mentioned the shrubbery I recalled in a flash the doll, Josephine, and I remembered her sapphire glass eyes staring up at me from beneath the branches. I shuddered. Antonia briefly turned her innocent blue eyes to me and the juxtaposition of Josephine's crazed-glass stare and the little girl's guileless gaze frightened me. I silently sighed. Were all the children's moments with me to be marked with some sort of reminder of terror? I tried to put the thought out of my mind. Here, with me, I knew that both of them would be safe.

I glanced at the other small window in the tower—the one facing the seas—and saw the brink of the cliffs and as I did so I knew finally who had occupied the tower room all those times I had seen the light from it: poor Mr. Grayson! I suspected that in extreme moments of his long-held grief he came up here to this room to watch and wait for his beloved Rosamunda although he knew full

265

well that she would never return. It was he who sat here or paced the length of the room thinking thoughts I could not suspect. I looked round the room once more, searching for hidden clues to my employer's thoughts but saw none.

I looked at the small painted likeness of Rosamunda's laughing face once more, and then placed the small portrait back on the table, carefully positioning it so that Mr. Grayson would not suspect that anyone had disturbed his memories.

"I think that this has been adventure enough for today," I said to the children. "I believe that it's time for us to return to the house. We will all be missed shortly." Both Virgil and Antonia nodded.

"But isn't it a wonderful room, Miss Scott?" Virgil touched the uneven and protruding blocks of stone that created the walls of the tower. "Isn't this wonderful?" He stood atop the chair that he had pushed to the window and looked out once more. "Can you not hear the ocean? Our mother used to hold us up so that we could look at it. She would tell us stories about it . . . about men sailing away upon the open waters and about women who waited for them to return from the seas in their ships." Virgil scanned the grey horizons and then jumped down. "But, we must go now."

I replaced the chair in its original place and the three of us moved toward the stairs. Just before we descended the staircase I took one more look about the room and remembered what the boy had said about the tales his mother told him and I thought of Mr. Grayson. There was to be no joyful conclusion to that love story.

Chapter 28

That evening, after the dinner meal, when I sat at the fire in the small sitting room, Mr. Grayson stayed with me once more, first reading from one of his journals and then initiating a period of small talk. We spoke of general things. I was touched by the fact that my employer did try to converse with me and show a bit more courtesy. The dialogue was originally of no import but presently, after sipping his wine, he cleared his throat and asked me if I would hear him out and listen to an important conversation.

"This will apply to our marriage, Ma'am, and I would like to speak to you now about it so that we have no secrets between us . . . even though . . . even though our marriage will not be a conventional one." He looked at me. "I have promised you that should you consent to be my wife I will do all in my power to deal honestly with you, and what I have to say, Miss Scott, is by way of an effort to do just that."

I continued my handwork, saying nothing yet giving Mr. Grayson the chance to expound on whatever he felt important enough to forego his early leave of me. I looked downward—purposely intent upon my crewel work—awaiting his explanation.

"I expect you should know all of the facts concerning my first marriage, Miss Scott. At least those that are pertinent to our alliance, should there be one." Mr. Grayson's mouth worked and I could see that this was indeed a struggle of his conscience—whether he should divulge secrets of his past marriage or whether he should withhold the truth and facts from someone who could possibly be his prospective wife. "I have not spoken of them before since they are of a personal nature and are not to be shared with everyone."

"Of course," I replied for I could see the wisdom of the words. What passes between a husband and wife need only concern them.

"But I do realize, Ma'am, that it is unfair of me to ask anyone . . . you," he amended and seemed not to notice the slight, ". . . to honour me in a marriage without telling you of some of the events that have passed here in Ganymede House." He bowed slightly to me. "And with your permission I will begin to tell you briefly of the times I spent with the children's mother, my wife, throughout the few years we had together." He paused and I saw a flicker of pain cross his features. "I will tell you that I was happy for all of the years of my marriage. My devotion soured, Ma'am, the day after my wife died and perhaps, if you will listen more to me, Miss Scott, I will tell you about the circumstances of that day—for it bears telling."

I waited as Mr. Grayson formed his next words. How strange I felt to be sitting here discussing the consideration of my marriage to my employer. It was of such an extraordinary circumstance that I found that my mind wandered a bit as I pondered the future as this gentleman's wife but I was called back to reality when Mr. Grayson rose from his chair and crossed to the shuttered window. There he turned his back to me so that I could not see his face yet I heard his voice very distinctly as though he purposely intended for it to remain steady.

"I was betrayed by my wife, Ma'am," he said without emotion and which revealed the extent of his anguish. "I was betrayed, Ma'am," he reiterated and I held my breath for those words confirmed what Mr. Grayson had said— had cried out—in his stupor the evening before he proposed to me.

"I am truly sorry, Sir."

He turned to me and his face was immobile, as though it were carved of granite. "There is nothing to be sorry about, Ma'am. It happened, I know not when exactly, Miss Scott—perhaps years before or only a few months before the accident—but it did transpire and I only tell you of it now so that you know all the true facts about my marriage. It is sufficient to say to you, Miss Scott, that my late wife, Rosamunda, has nothing to do with my life now."

"I can hardly believe that, Sir. No matter what the circumstances of her life, or her death, Lady Rosamunda has left her mark on this house. Surely you once loved her . . . that can not be erased so swiftly."

Mr. Grayson's eyes flashed in momentary anger. "It can be . . . and is, Ma'am." He looked at the flames in the fireplace. "I do not wish to discuss it any further. I spoke of it only because I wanted you to know that the memory of my late wife will not impinge on our relationship, or any relationship in this house." He sat down again and

269

picked up his journal and opened it to signal the end of the conversation. However I would have none of it.

"But the children—" I protested.

Mr. Grayson spoke with finality. "They have nothing to do with their mother. I see to it that her name is hardly mentioned in this home."

"I know that, Sir, but do you think that they forget their own parent? Would you expect them to forget you, should some tragedy befall you?"

"What I expect, Miss Scott, is that they, in time, will forget their mother so that they never learn the truth of her dishonouring the Grayson name."

"Can you be so sure of your words, Sir?"

Mr. Grayson nodded his head. "Sadly I must answer in the affirmative."

I countered no more. I had no facts upon which to base any presumption of Rosamunda's innocence or guilt and therefore felt there was no expected answer from me. Mr. Grayson returned to his reading and I continued with my needlework until the candle beside me flickered and the stitches were difficult to see. I then took my leave of Mr. Grayson, leaving him sitting beside the fire. Whatever hurt Rosamunda had given him I could see was, unknowingly, passed on to his children. I resolved to try harder to give them some measure of security and happiness.

Later that evening I sat at my desk in my room and watched as the stars twinkled merrily in the firmament. The evening sky was clear and there was a quarter moon that seemed the colour of pale wheat.

I stepped to the window and looked out upon that dark spot where I knew the cold water and coast met. Although I could not hear the waves crashing against the shoreline, I could imagine them. I was both uneasy and honoured that Mr. Grayson would speak so frankly to me. But then, I remembered that his confession was more of a practical matter—he had said that he thought it his duty to make his conscience known to his prospective bride.

Bride! What a curious word for me! Never in all the days I spent in London or the few months that I have been living here at Ganymede House, did I think that my life would be bound up in confusion at the word "bride." Bridal arrangements were something all young women in my status dreamed about. I, however, lacked a dowry and a trunk full of new clothes, yet my singular character also longed for the sound of joyously pealing church bells announcing my marriage.

No—never had I even thought that my chance at matrimony would come here in a bleak house in the north of England. I had not anticipated it but, because it was still a new idea to me, I had not yet fully rejected it or its implications.

I watched as the wind tousled the branches of a tree near my window and in some unexplainable fashion my room seemed once again to be flooded with the scent of roses. This was too much of a coincidence for me and I vowed to ask Tillie whether in her haste to prepare my bed for the evening she had overindulged with the fragrance. Yet, something deep inside me, my soul, far from my intellect, told me that the aroma of the flowers could possibly be Rosamunda come to remind me of my promise to protect her family.

"Rosamunda," I said into the chilled air. "You know what is happening here. You know that your husband . . . Mr. Grayson . . . has asked me to marry him." I turned around. If I were right, if this scent was indeed a heralding of Rosamunda—how I wished that she could advise me! But there were no signs about what I was to do. I sat down at my desk again to write in my journal, thinking that whatever I wrote would help me in my decision about Mr. Grayson's marriage proposal.

The next morning we received word that Mr. Moore was in the vicinity and would be with us that evening. It was something I looked forward to for I had much to tell him. As my only dear and concerned friend here I knew I could rely on his wisdom and that his answers would help me make my decisions.

During the first hour or so after their cousin arrived he was with the children—telling them stories and playing silly games and they naturally were delighted to see him and took up all his time. With the few moments we did spend together I was able to convey to him that I had matters of great importance and urgency to discuss with him. Mr. Moore assured me that we would have our discussion later when the children were asleep and we were not in the company of others.

I wondered if Mr. Grayson would stay with us after dinner but again, as he had done everytime his cousin had called upon us, he made his excuses. Later that evening, when Mr. Moore and I were alone, the two of us sat at table longer than usual. I poured him a cup of tea and put it in front of him and he toyed with the spoon, putting in more than his usual quantity of sugar and cream.

"You have seemed much disconcerted, Ma'am. Throughout the meal I wondered greatly about you. When I glanced your way several times this evening I saw something in your eyes . . . something that dimmed your usual cheerful self. Is there something that has

272

frightened you or hurt you, Ma'am?"

I nodded my head for I suspected that someone had already spoken to him about the finding of the doll, Josephine, but it was not that to which he referred for he continued, "There is still much unhappiness here, Miss Scott . . . it is as though I can feel it as soon as I enter estate grounds. Is that what concerns you, Ma'am?"

"Yes. That and more." I took a deep breath and told him about the smashing of Antonia's doll—how the staff wanted to blame it on Euripides but how I suspected that it was a deliberate act of vandalism. Mr. Moore listened with ever-increasing anger and I knew that he took my meaning—that he was also afraid of the warning that had been sent to us.

"But who, Ma'am? Who here at Ganymede would do such a thing? I have known most of the workers since I have been no older than Virgil. I cannot think who among them would hurt such a tender innocent child. Surely it must be an aberration? Perhaps a passing itinerant? For only a madman would conjure up such frenzy." He shook his head. "A madman . . . only a madman." He peered at me. "Is there someone? Who do you suspect, Ma'am?"

"I do not know, Sir. And because of that I keep an extra vigilance of the children. I have no other recourse."

"That's truth, Ma'am. My young cousins are lucky indeed to have you here in the house with them."

"They do not know I watch them carefully." I bent my head. "Of course, there are times when I am watching one child and cannot look after the other . . . when one is kept in the schoolroom and the other plays about the house." I looked at Mr. Moore. "It is a frightening thing,

Sir, when one is away from my attention, but I cannot trust anyone else to watch for I dare not confess my suspicions to others. I do not know who can be trusted."

Mr. Moore stirred his tea once more. "I am glad you confided in me, Ma'am. While I am here the children will have two defenders though I truly suspect that the violence has ended and that it was an isolated act of a wayward thief set out to alarm you before he robs you."

I breathed just a little easier. "You have given me reason to sleep sounder this night, Sir. I thank you."

Mr. Moore brushed away my gratitude. "The children are important to me, too, Ma'am. They are my own relations. We are of the same flesh."

"I do understand your concern, Sir." We spoke once more of Josephine and the way she was found and then I grew silent, relieved that I was able to speak of my dread.

"But," Mr. Moore said, "you alluded to several other unexplained events. Tell me of them, too, Ma'am."

I hesitated to ask the next question of him for it seemed, even to me, irrational and silly but Mr. Moore looked quite earnest and while I paused the good gentleman put all my doubts aside.

"Trust me, Ma'am. I want to know what alarms you. Is it about the children . . . and you?"

I did not know how to broach the subject. I looked at the gentleman and his kind countenance as he waited for me to speak.

"Tell me, Sir. . . ." I stopped, sure that my words would seem foolish to such a man as he. "Mr. Moore, do you believe in ghosts?"

Mr. Moore seemed stunned. He blinked as I asked the question and were it not so serious to me I felt he would have shown a smile.

"My dear Miss Scott, what an extraordinary question." He took one of my hands in his. "No, of course I do not believe. Apparitions are only figments of the mind. They are not of science. Come, Ma'am, you are not speaking seriously." He looked at me. "Ma'am . . . you are not jesting?"

I shook my head. "No, Sir. It is a serious question. There is a reason I ask."

"Pray, Ma'am, tell me your cause for asking such an unusual question."

I felt foolish as I told him of the scent of roses that constantly came to me and of the time that the air became chilled and the curtains fluttered though there was no discernible breeze. With each example I put forward Mr. Moore shook his head, and when I finally stopped speaking he pushed back his cup.

"About the roses, Ma'am. Someone is obviously using too much scent water or scattering too many dried petals. That is all."

"But they said the rose petals were for Rosamunda's grave."

Mr. Moore looked at me curiously. "Who said such a thing, Miss Scott?" I turned my head for I did not want to indict Mr. Keanne. Surely, I thought, a small lie could not be wrong.

"I do not remember, Sir. Perhaps it was just a dream of mine."

Mr. Moore tapped his silver spoon. "Most probably."

"Then you do not believe that the spirit of Rosamunda visited me?" I pursued the matter.

"No, Ma'am, I do not. Forgive me, Miss Scott, but you did not know my cousin. You have never see her. Her beauty . . ."

"I have seen her portrait."

Mr. Moore seemed startled at my words. "How? Where?" He looked at the other paintings on the walls. "I do not understand."

I explained that Rosamunda's picture was still hanging in her chambers and that I viewed it when I went into the room with Mr. Keanne. But I did not tell him of the children's forays into their mother's apartment for I had made them a promise and could not betray their trust. "I believe Mr. Grayson had the portrait removed from downstairs and hung in his late wife's room."

"Poor Oliver." Mr. Moore shook his head slowly. "He has not gotten over the shock. I wonder if he ever will."

I did not want to dwell on Mr. Moore's interpretation of his cousin's grief for I wanted to clear up the mysteries I personally had encountered.

"Mr. Moore, what I am about to say may seem foolish but, Sir, I believe I have seen . . . or felt Rosamunda's presence."

Mr. Moore turned toward me and watched me as he spoke. "I cannot accept that summation, Miss Scott. What I do accept is that you tell me that you *believe* you have witnessed these things. But in my own life I have found that the impossible has always been just that . . . the impossible. You have heard too many stories about Rosamunda from Mr. Keanne and the servants and no doubt they have told you of the dread night of her death. I fear that all the strange coincidental occurrences here at Ganymede, as you yourself have pointed them out, have influenced your beliefs." He squinted his eyes briefly but it was not in an unkindly fashion—rather it was one that meant that I was to heed his words. "There are no ghosts or apparitions, Ma'am. My cousin, Rosamunda, is dead and buried and neither her memory nor spirit haunts this house. Of that I am quite sure."

I did not want to discuss the matter further and I turned the conversation back to my original fear. "About the doll, Sir. How can we explain that?"

"That is more difficult. Yes, we could go along with the theory that it was Euripides—the dog has been known to attack small animals." He stroked his chin. "but there, of course, could be another reason, Ma'am. Forgive me, Miss Scott, but I think you also suspect that someone is trying to frighten you. In fact, my initial instinct could be all wrong and there may be what you call evil lurking here." He shook his head. "But I do not suspect some spirit. No, I would suspect a human form but I do not know who . . ." He paused and I could tell that he was thinking and that a name had been brought to his mind. But he chose not to reveal it. "No, Ma'am, I could not think unjustly of anyone in this house. But for the sake of argument, let us pursue the matter further. If all these acts were done intentionally—the scent and the doll's destruction—then we are dealing with someone who has made deliberate and calculating assaults. And then, of course, the only conclusion would be that someone is trying to frighten you, Ma'am, and my young cousins." He frowned as though he were thinking and then shook his head vigorously. "But to what end? No, Ma'am, to say that these were deliberate acts is to speak too harshly." He set his palm flat on the table. "I am not willing to accept that premise yet, Miss Scott."

Mr. Moore's voice grew gentle. "But I do believe, Ma'am, the considerable stress and strain beginning with your coming here to Ganymede upon the deaths of your parents and all the events—whether intentional or not— that have lately happened to you have taken a measure of your strength." He looked at me and I could see the care in his eyes. "You look peaked, Ma'am. Is there anything else bothering you, for you should retire soon and have a long restful sleep."

"I cannot conceal another matter, Sir. There is something more." I sat back. "I have something else to tell you," I said and thereby spoke of Mr. Grayson's proposal to me and when I finished Mr. Moore seemed both agitated and alarmed, but he did not speak.

"I will not question you at this moment, Miss Scott, as to your intentions. I would like time to peruse it before I make known my thoughts for it is indeed a shock. I did not suspect Oliver's design. May we speak of this tomorrow?"

"Yes, gladly, Sir. And you are quite right." I stood up—for what we had spoken of this evening had dulled my senses and I was quite numbed. "I would like to go to sleep now." I touched the good man's arm. "No matter whether my mind raced and I formed wrong conclusions about these things that have happened I do want you to know that I welcome your assistance, Sir. In fact, I am most grateful for it."

"Then," Mr. Moore said, taking my hand. "I am glad I have decided to visit Ganymede this evening. There are details I have to attend to—estate matters in the vicinity for the next two days, Ma'am—but I will return once they are settled and extend my stay here for a few more weeks over the holidays. If that would suit you and Oliver."

"I can only speak for myself, Mr. Moore, and that is to tell you I would welcome your presence." I smiled at him. How good it was to hear him say that he will be with us, for at least, I thought, I would have someone to confide in and, in truth, someone who will help me safeguard the children. "Mr. Moore, I cannot tell you how much I shall welcome your stay here. I am afraid I have let my fears inhabit too much of my mind."

"Nay, Lady," he said patting my arm. "I am glad to be of assistance. You know that I shall not let anything hurt you or the children." He took up my hand again and pressed it to his lips. I felt a mixture of fright, confusion, and joy. I should have pulled back my hand, and I did not do so quickly enough for just at that moment Mr. Grayson passed next to the open doorway and saw his cousin and me together. Although I had nothing to answer for, I was most embarrassed. Mr. Grayson pretended not to notice that his relation and I were still sitting alone together at the table and moved away from our sight.

Mr. Moore lowered his voice and spoke in almost a whisper. "We must be careful, Miss Scott," he said, "that we do nothing to appear as a betrayal to my cousin" and when I stiffened for I knew not what he meant, he explained. "Have you forgotten, Ma'am, that my Cousin has asked you to be his wife?"

"Yes, I had," I said and felt the throbbing in my temples. "If you will excuse me, Mr. Moore, I feel I must retire immediately."

Mr. Moore escorted me to the staircase and stayed below as I went to my room. My head was now pounding and all manner of thoughts passed through my mind. Although I had planned that I would adjust to my life at Ganymede when first I came here I now seemed not to be in control of my fate and I wondered, as I fell asleep amidst moments of self-doubt, what was plotted for me in this strange house.

Chapter 29

"I have puzzled over some things since last we were together, Miss Scott." Mr. Moore stopped me in the corridor the next day as I made my way from the schoolroom. "I have thought on it and even though it pains me I must speak now." He looked around the passageway. "Will you join me in the morning room so that we may speak frankly and privately before I leave?"

Mr. Moore sat near the middle of the room in the path of a stream of sunshine and even though I felt some feelings of apprehension I was still fascinated to watch minute particles of dust dancing lazily in the sun's rays. I had settled myself near a window and marveled that the bright sun-filled room seemed to be in sharp contrast to Mr. Moore's dark words. It was a juxtaposition that I would remember always. "I hesitate to speak of this, Miss Scott, but I believe that you should be aware that while I am gone you must be vigilant." I frowned and the gentleman saw my look and continued. "I must confess that I did not believe you when you first told me of all the happenings at Ganymede, but now . . ." Poor Mr. Moore turned his head and I could see the anxiousness in his eyes. I must confess that it was a pleasant feeling—knowing that someone has pain for you and worries for you. I did not know what to say to him for any words might possibly lead him to feel rebuked for disbelieving me.

"The doll—I shudder to think of it. No, something is not right here at Ganymede and I fear it is a recent occurrence, Ma'am, which did not exist when my dear cousin Rosamunda was alive." Mr. Moore looked at me in full earnest and his face became stern. "I do give you my solemn pledge, Ma'am, that I will find out the reasons for these happenings." He moved closer to me and nodded his head in much solemnity. "I shall not let anything hurt you . . . neither you nor the children." His speech caught for one moment before he continued. "Not even if it means I must point to . . ." Mr. Moore's voice choked and he left the sentence unfinished yet I knew wherein his thoughts lie.

"I have reviewed certain events in my mind, Miss Scott." He moved his head slightly so that the sunlight no longer fell upon his head. "Surely, Ma'am, you must have wondered about the day of Virgil's accident."

I started and put my hand to my heart. "What of that day, Sir?" I asked, for I also had had many moments of turmoil about the boating mishap. It was one of the first clues that I should have suspected regarding the terrorizing of the house.

"Did you not wonder why there were no life jackets in the boat on that particular day, Ma'am? Especially when Virgil and I had made known our intention to use it that afternoon?" he questioned and the dread that I thought I had put away from my mind came once more to me so that I held my breath. "I see in your eyes, Ma'am, that you, too, have questioned that fateful day."

"I did, Sir, and still do. I tremble to think what would have happened if you were not there to rescue Virgil." I shuddered and Mr. Moore seeing me shake leaned forward and put a protective hand on my arm. I confess I welcomed not only the warmth of it on my chilled skin but also the connotation that I was not alone in my fear. "Surely, Mr. Moore, we can not accuse anyone of causing that accident?" I asked the question hoping that he would allay all my fears and unspoken accusations.

"No, dear lady," he said patting my arm. "The name of a culprit, that is not for us to even consider. For how could anyone have caused the boat to rock? But . . . I must confess that at one time I wondered if my cousin. . . ."

"Mr. Moore," I protested, "I cannot allow you to place Mr. Grayson's name in this context."

The gentleman moved back in his chair and the sunshine once more alighted on his head and shoulders and formed a halo upon his dark blond hair. "My Dear Miss Scott, yes, I know you are shocked, but I have spoken my Cousin's name, for in truth, could you not say that you, too, have questioned whether he . . . ?" He left the rest unspoken yet I knew what road he was taking.

"We cannot . . ." I said for I did not want to think of the possibilities Mr. Moore was suggesting. "Surely, despite his aloofness and his solitude, he would wish no harm to come to his children. Indeed, I do think him to be incapable of bringing harm to them."

"You are a loyal and devoted person, Ma'am." Mr. Moore moved his chair slightly so that he was now bathed in full sunshine. "Think, Ma'am. Were there not times that you . . . ?" I shook my head, denying his words before they were spoken, but even as I did so, more and more episodes that seemed harmless at first breath now took on more meaning and the Italian word *sinistro*—evil—kept intruding upon my thoughts. It was too forbidding to imagine. Could any father not love his children . . . especially these dear sweet children? Could any father wish evil on his own family? These were puzzling questions and had not Mr. Moore introduced these doubts I would have submerged them deep inside my being and not considered them. I had once toyed with such suppositions—especially when Mr. Keanne told me of Mr. Grayson's suspicions about Virgil's paternity. But the gentleman's manner these past days belied my misgivings and though Mr. Moore spoke of them it was difficult to believe that his cousin would be of such dark moods. Was it to be true? Could my employer be suspect? I could not know the answers.

"I did not mean to frighten you, Miss Scott." Mr. Moore intruded into my thoughts.

"I am frightened, Sir, and I know not why."

"Is it my fault, Ma'am? I merely wished to warn you . . ."

"No, Mr. Moore. I have had these troubling imaginings weighing on my mind for several weeks. I think of the implications every day."

"May I venture to ask, Ma'am, have they intensified since my cousin proposed marriage?" I did not answer quickly enough and Mr. Moore gave a negative meaning to my silence. "I am sorry, Ma'am. The question was of much too personal a nature."

"No," I assured him. "I was trying to formulate the time sequence in my own mind, to clarify it. You are right, Mr. Moore, it has been since Mr. Grayson made his proposal. Yet other strange things have happened, also" and because he was such a caring person I told him about the mysterious light in the tower and how I had learned of Mr. Grayson's doubts about Virgil and Rosamunda.

Mr. Moore became angered. "Did my cousin tell you these things, Ma'am? And did he suggest a name of an accomplice?"

I shook my head once more. "No, Mr. Moore, I do not speak of these things to Mr. Grayson. I have learned of them from the servants. And, perhaps what they say is only conjecture or gossip."

"I think not, Ma'am, for my cousin's thoughts in that instance would explain much. Why he has been so estranged from his children. Why there is no laughter. You, yourself, have mentioned these things to me."

"I suspect his unhappiness is now entrenched in his nature, Mr. Moore. Your cousin's sadness dominates him, although I have learned it was not always so. Mr. Keanne has told me of other times—he has spoken of the love that was once in this house."

"When the Lady Rusamunda was alive." Mr. Moore said her name reverently . . . lovingly.

"I am glad that you speak so fondly of your late cousin. I know Mr. Grayson would prefer to leave her name unsaid but I know the children . . ."

Mr. Moore narrowed his eyes. "What about the children, Ma'am? Do they speak of their mother? Does Antonia . . . ?"

"I know what you ask, Sir. Does Antonia remember that night that her mother died in the accident? I think she does, but her recollection has become blurred. She was much too young and too frightened for any of us to place much weight on her words."

Mr. Moore calmed. "I wondered about the child," he said and my heart went out to him for he had such a true concern for the children's welfare.

I smiled in sadness. "Someday I hope that we will all be able to remember their mother." Again I did not want to betray the children's trust by telling Mr. Moore about how Virgil and Antonia steal into their mother's room.

"I would hope that to be so, but I fear that will never happen. I am afraid, Miss Scott, that there may be other episodes . . . other instances where . . ."

"Mr. Moore! What is it that you say? Have you proof?"

"No, dear lady, nothing of the kind. It is only my feeling." He stared into my eyes. "I pray you will be careful until I return." I looked down at my hands and saw them tremble and I clasped them together both in contemplation and stillness. Mr. Moore watched me. "I am afraid I have upset you again."

"No. You have only made me face my fears, Sir."

"Then I am glad I have asked you to wait for a few weeks before tendering your answer to my cousin. Perhaps," he said, "we will be able to reckon this out. Perhaps you will allow me to assist you, Ma'am, to solve this puzzle."

I heard the chiming of the clock and rose to take my leave—the second part of the schoolday was to begin. I extended my hand. "Farewell, Mr. Moore . . . until you return." I did not want the gentleman to ride away this day but I knew that it was necessary. "I will await your next visit."

Mr. Moore put his hand on mine and stopped my path. "Miss Scott, please . . . one moment. Before I go I have

286

something else to discuss with you." I sat down once again. I could see that some idea disturbed the good gentleman for he drummed on the side table in quick motions, as though a problem were pulling at his thoughts. He began to pace the room—eventually stopping by the window. There was an air of agitation about him but I knew it would benefit neither of us if I compelled him to talk before he was ready.

When he had paced the room several times he came and stood opposite me and looked at me with earnest eyes. Gone was the light in them, gone was the conviviality that I had noticed when we were first introduced. Instead I saw that his face was somber, his mouth set. I knew not what else disturbed him.

Mr. Moore coughed gently into his hand and then looked at me. "If you please, Ma'am . . . I hope you will hear me out and neither accept or reject what I have to say until I have said it all."

I grew fearful—never had I seen Mr. Moore so sober and pensive and in a quick involuntary movement I clenched my fist. Surely he had already warned me . . . had already put me on my guard. What else was there for him to tell me? "Mr. Moore, I am frightened of what you are about to say. Does it concern the children?"

Mr. Moore nodded his head. "Yes, Ma'am . . . the children and you." The silence in the room seemed to be eternal, not even the flames crackled in the fireplace and this lack of noise or household sound served to alarm me even more. Mr. Moore continued to look down at his hands, placing them first together and then apart . . . and finally placing them so that they seemed to be closed in prayer.

"Please Mr. Moore, speak! My dear friend, for you are

surely that, we have confided much to each other. You have been a good companion. How may I help you?"

Mr. Moore's head jerked up and he spoke the words loudly. "It is you whom I want to help, Ma'am, for to do nothing . . ." He shook his head and upon his face there was a grimace and I leaned forward in my chair obeying his words and saying nothing more until he had finished his phrases.

He stood up and paced the room again and my eyes followed him as he stopped to pause at a sculpture, picking it up and then replacing it on top of the credenza.

"To do nothing, Miss Scott," he said, "would be unconscionable. Pray, listen to me, Ma'am." He crossed toward me and stood before me so that I had to look up into his face. "Ma'am, you know how much I admire you and so I pray you will take this in the spirit I tender it." He bowed formally. "Miss Scott, I would be most privileged if you would do me the honour to consider my proposal of marriage."

I gasped. "Mr. Moore!"

"Please, Ma'am, I know you are confused and that you have had no hint of my intentions. I confess, for we must speak truthfully, neither did I when I came here to Ganymede House yesterday. But please be so good as to hear me out. I do offer for you for several reasons. The first," and here I saw his face relax briefly, "because I respect you. Never have I found anyone to be so kind as evidenced by your concern for Antonia and Virgil. Surely, were my cousin Rosamunda alive she would be forever indebted to you for your service to her children."

"I do love the youngsters, Sir. My heart goes out to them."

Mr. Moore smiled for the first time this morning. "I do

288

know that, Ma'am, and for that alone I am grateful, although it is my cousin's place to show his gratitude."

I put my hand to my lips. "We will not speak of Mr. Grayson at this moment," I said. Surely we must talk of other things for Mr. Moore's proposal of marriage baffled me and stunned me so that my mind became muddled. I had had no inkling that the gentleman was thinking along the lines of matrimony, especially not now when I had confided that his own cousin, Mr. Grayson, had already offered for me.

Mr. Moore paced once more. "I'm afraid, Miss Scott, we must speak of Oliver for it is one of my prime reasons for addressing you." His face clouded over once more. "I do not wish to frighten you, Ma'am, but as I told you—I fear for you. Greatly. And if truth be told I also fear for my young relations." He touched the poker in its stand. "I do not mean to cause you overconcern but I have seen my cousin grow blacker in mood these past few months and, like you, I find that there are coincidences that endanger the children." His hand tightened around the poker and he used it to prod the burning logs—stirring them so that they flash-fired and gave off more heat. "Antonia's doll . . ." he said and let his words end while I nodded. "And the matter of not having life preservers in the boat." He replaced the poker. "There are far too many dangerous coincidences, Miss Scott. Far too many."

I agreed with the gentleman. Indeed I had recognized that there were strange happenings in the house— happenings that pointed to a hostile atmosphere.

"It is no foolish whim, Miss Scott, to ask for your hand. I have thought this past night about it . . . ever since, I confess, you told me about my cousin's offer. I felt I had to do something and I do understand your circumstances, Ma'am. A young woman alone in the world needs protection. And that I offer you, Miss Scott, protection from the world and my. . . ." Again he left the sentence unfinished yet I knew what he implied. "If you choose not to accept me, Ma'am, for whatever reason, I will understand and will say no more about my suit. However, I must tell you I have the deepest respect for you and would consider it an honour if you would consent to be my wife." He sat down in his chair once more. "We do suit each other, Miss Scott. Surely you cannot deny that. Our times together . . ."

I nodded and looked at the dear gentleman and was much taken with his words and expressions. To have found so noble a person was much more than I could have dreamt to happen to me since I came to Ganymede. Mr. Moore continued to speak to me telling me of his small home in Surrey, of his diminished income, of the fact that I would not live in such a grand manner as here at Ganymede House.

"I would like the opportunity to be your protector, Ma'am," he said and his green eyes grew darker. "I do press my suit on those terms."

Mr. Moore saw my confusion and understanding and spoke gently. "I do not expect an answer immediately, Miss Scott. I realize it will be rather trying for you to decide between my cousin and myself." He came and knelt at my feet. "But, dear lady, I do implore you to consider me. The two of us would then be in a position to help Antonia and Virgil should they need us."

At the mention of the children I shuddered and Mr. Moore saw my motion and spoke even more gently to me. "I entreat you, dear Miss Scott, to think, if not of yourself, then of the children. I fear they will need us soon."

"I certainly hope you are wrong, Sir." I looked down at my hands. "You have given me much to think about and I am quite befuddled. I do thank you for your suit, Mr. Moore, and I ask you to give me time so that I can sort out my feelings and thoughts."

I stood up and Mr. Moore took my arm and led me to the steps leading upstairs for it was necessary that I return to the schoolroom and my teaching.

"Of course, dear lady. I am afraid that I have given you many shocks. I do apologize for that, Miss Scott." He bowed to me. "I will take my leave now. I promise that I will return in two days and then perhaps you will have come to some decision. Until then, Ma'am, I implore you to be careful."

I made my way upstairs holding onto the bannister lest I stumble for surely I had other things on my mind this afternoon than to watch carefully my steps.

Chapter 30

This was indeed a strange day. I did not feel sleepy this evening and instead worked my stitches far later into the night than usual. My fear had abated and now, in the glow of the fireplace, I was able to think more rationally and more fully. Mr. Moore's words had frightened me but I was alert to anyone's erratic behavior and I knew that I could contend at least until he returned to Ganymede.

Mr. Grayson excused himself, much as he did every evening, and I remained alone except for the time that Mr. Keanne came into the room on his nightly rounds before closing the house. When he had visited the room a second time I told the old gentleman to leave me and not to worry. I would see to the fire and the candles myself and that he should not wait upon me until I retired.

He seemed skeptical at first—not wanting to leave me alone downstairs—but I prevailed on him and finally, either in deference to my obstinacy or to my rumored future position in the household, he left me after extracting a promise that should I need him or any help that I was to call him.

It was pleasant sitting there by the light of the fire, for although I was alone I had much thinking to do and this quiet time afforded me the luxury of not having to compose my thoughts in order to teach and entertain the children or to wait upon Mr. Grayson's remarks. I took up my needlework again for the mere repetition of stitchery—of plunging the needle through the linen, front to back, back to front—allowed me to form and consider my own personal thoughts and opinions. The precision of the stitches—necessarily small for the design and the neatness needed to make it attractive— translated into my mind the exact way I wanted to view the two proposals recently tendered me.

I had much to think upon for I was now completely bound into the weave of Ganymede House and although there were many things I could have wished for—to be back in London with my friends and have the prospect of settling with someone who cared for me—there were many more compensations to be had here in Yorkshire. These, of course, were to be important considerations if I were to accept Mr. Grayson's proposal.

As I had been told in our first conversation when I had newly met my employer all the basic provisions given to those who resided at Ganymede House were to be accorded to me and I neither lacked, nor wanted more, in the way of plain food and comfortable lodging. These primary needs were more than adequately provided to me and although I did not ask for special favors from any of the staff I knew that they did give me the deference that should be shown to one who was responsible for the upbringing and education of the children of their master.

When he had offered for me Mr. Grayson had promised even increased bounty should I consent to be his wife but there were other needs which were of importance to me also. Companionship, entertainment, and yes, even the sound of carefree laughter were deficient in this house. I knew Mr. Grayson's offer to marry me was solely to provide a mother to his children, yet I did so yearn for something more than the confined existence I would be accepting.

I continued stitching on the pillowcase—crossing and recrossing the green silky threads on the leaves of the flowers in my needlework pattern while I thought of the marriage that had taken place between Mr. Grayson and Rosamunda. I now knew enough of the stories about the previous life here and the joy that had resounded at Ganymede House. Theirs—Mr. Grayson and Rosamunda's union—was indeed a love story that had endured for many years and although I did not expect ever to kindle that kind of spirit in an alliance, I had hoped that whoever offered for me would have more consideration for my feelings than just as that of a governess and overseer of the interior of the manor.

I broke off my thread and substituted the red for the flower—a rose as it happened—and thought more of the relationship that had been proposed. While not perfect it would indeed afford me the permanence I sought, and I would no longer have to worry about my future or my position in society. As I contemplated it it was far better than I, an impoverished young orphan woman, could possibly expect to negotiate.

My mind shifted and I thought of Mr. Grayson and of the times I had spoken to him in earnest these past weeks. Although he had exchanged confidences with me and told me some of the details of his marriage to his late wife, it was still a rather cold and insensible interchange. Mr.

Grayson presented all the information he thought I needed to know about the marraige, yet his flat exposition concerning the circumstances surrounding his wife's death seemed more a collection of facts that had been set down in a textbook rather than that of the heartfelt pain and anguish he surely must have experienced. Certainly the pauses and the hesitations in his recitation led me to conclude his feelings but I would have much more appreciated . . . nay, expected . . . that he would have spoken to mé about this personal side of Rosamunda's death had he really intended for me to be a sympathetic and lifelong partner.

But, of course, that is not what he intended my role to be here at Ganymede and he had, in truth, said so. And I, should I accept his troth, must be prepared to accept the limitations set by him on our conjugality. I did not expect him to, but now—thinking back on the conversation—I did feel that it would have been more respectful for him to have asked about me or about my wants and desires for our proposed union but, of course, these were neither discussed nor mentioned. I sighed. Mr. Grayson had even neglected to ask me of my feelings about the life and future he suggested for me. And, in fact, his unbending and straightforward manner conveyed to me that there were some things I would never be privileged to learn about him and should I accept him as a husband I knew I would have to be content with that direction.

I was grateful to know about Rosamunda for although Mr. Grayson told me the plain facts and did not embroider upon them I was not insensitive to the pain that he had endured nor the hurt that he had overcome. No man's heart should be burdened for the rest of his life with a secret as tragic as the one he carried about with him but even so, I could not help but hold an animosity against him for his dealings with his children. To not love his own flesh and blood, to reject them so off-handedly was a trait I could not comprehend nor accept, but then there were so many traits and mannerisms I did not understand in him.

There were times when I believed the gentleman to be a fair, compassionate man for I saw him deal with the staff and his animals, but there were other times—much more frequent—when he lapsed into morose and brooding moods. He seemed not to be able to overcome these dejections and at times I feared that there were deeper, darker thoughts than normal that invaded and dwelled in his mind.

I noticed a pattern of these moods—they came upon him when he had been contemplating and talking too much about his marriage to the children's mother, when he spoke of her to me and when I was lulled into the false feeling that he had recovered from his despondency. There were even times when he retold a story to me and I was able to detect the faintest hint of a pleasure—a lightness in his eye, a relaxing of his countenance. But those have been ephemeral and far too few and while I wait and watch for them—for they make a pleasant change in our otherwise drab nocturnal conversations— I fear that they are just aberrations of the man's generally somber demeanor.

But of the dark moods, the really deep moods that persisted for days, they were the ones that terrified me. It was at those times when I realized how fortunate I was to have Mr. Moore here as a friend and confidant.

I laid my needle and cloth aside for a moment and thought of Mr. Moore who had a way about him as to make life more pleasant for everyone living at Ganymede House—except, of course, for his cousin. What we—the children and I—would have done without him I did not know.

I picked up my needle again and retraced the circlets surrounding the flowers on the linen—reminding myself that it was just not the children's lives that had been made lighter by Mr. Moore's stays. I, too, looked forward to them.

I marveled at the good soul of the man and for his decency in dealing with me and I smiled at his choice of words when I told him of his cousin's offer for me. I knew his marriage proposal was made with much affection, for although there was no love mentioned I perceived the offering to be made in a moment of tenderness and concern for my own well-being. This I did not take lightly for of all the human compassion I have so far encountered here in Ganymede House, his concerns for me were the most genuine.

I appreciated his honesty, the fact that he confessed that he would not ever be in a position to extend many of life's luxuries to me save for those that he received from his small inheritance from his father and whatever tokens that were given him by his cousin. It was a matter of concern much more to him than to me and if I accepted his proposal I must allay his thoughts on the matter.

I re-threaded the needle with brown yarn and began working on the stems of the flowers while I contemplated what would happen if I assented to Mr. Moore's offer. I know that if I accepted him as a husband it would place all of us—Mr. Grayson, Mr. Moore, the children and myself—in a rather awkward position. Would it, I wondered, also serve to create another crack in the already crumbling facade of the Grayson family relationship?

I dwelt on other dissimilarities. Mr. Moore proffered a pleasanter atmosphere and spirit of matrimony although it would be a much leaner and more restricted life; Mr. Grayson, on the other hand, bestowed a regal home, the upkeep to maintain it and the comfort of continuum—although in this marriage there would be no real exchange of confidences or feelings. Would I be able to endure the loneliness?

It was not a happy thought, but, on second sight, most of the marriages I had known from my days in London were based not on love but on both monetary and compensatory factors. Indeed, most of the matches in my own circle of family and friends were originally founded on these terms. Even my own dear late mother and father proceeded into the matrimonial state without ever having uttered a word of love between them and, as I grew, I watched their union flower into a most precious and amiable joining. Perhaps that would happen in my case because I knew that eventually I would most probably accept Mr. Grayson's offer—not because he had the most to promise, but because dear Mr. Moore, I knew, only proposed to me in order to save me from what he surmised would be an unhappy and fearful existence. Would it be so, I wondered? I knew not. Had Mr. Moore even vaguely hinted at an affection toward me I might have more seriously considered his offer.

Mr. Grayson's practical proposal, on the other hand, was much more complex and much more demanding. I would be my own mistress, as he made clear in his overture, but even with that assurance I was confused about the way my life was turning. It was much too much to think about at that late moment of the day.

I turned toward the fire and watched as the flames in the fireplace leaped up and about. It was a comforting sight; the golden colours of the blaze fascinated and mesmerized me and I grew heavy-lidded as I continued to follow the dancing flames. Soon it seemed to be much too difficult to keep my eyelids open and I found that it was far easier to sit quietly and enjoy the last few moments of the evening.

I knew not how long I slept, only that I was awakened by the chill in the room. I saw that the fire in the grate was reduced to embers that sputtered and spread their little exploding points of light before extinguishing themselves. I sniffed once or twice as the acrid odor of the burnt wood caused my eyes to tear and I dabbed at them with my handkerchief.

The candle on the table next to me had burned low until there was but a stub small enough to last only another hour or so. I roused myself, putting the embroidery work into my satchel before I made my way upstairs. I stood up and then began to stoke the embers in the fireplace, remembering my promise to Mr. Keanne to make sure that all was safe and dampered before I left the room. Thus I was busy stoking the ashes and did not realize that someone had entered the room until I heard a heavy footfall and I turned to see Mr. Grayson approaching me.

My employer's eyes were wild and in his hands he held a crystal decanter and glass. I knew the cause of his frenzied look—the brandy that he obviously consumed. He looked the worse for drink—his hair was unkempt and his boots muddied and I knew that had he realized his disorderly appearance he would never have presented himself to me.

He mumbled something I took to be "Good evening."
This was the second time that Mr. Grayson had come
upon me in such a sorry state and I wondered if I
accepted his proposal if these evenings would continue
and become a pattern. It was not something I looked
forward to and not the type of life I imagined for myself.

I remained still lest any of my words or actions enrage
him and he continued to stare at me, saying nothing. I
waited, hoping that the fury in his eyes would abate and I
could excuse myself and retire. I glanced at the bell pull
on the wall that would summon Mr. Keanne but Mr.
Grayson saw my look and only shook his head.

"You are afraid of me, Ma'am?" he asked.

"No, Sir, not afraid. Concerned, perhaps."

He looked at me and then took another swallow from
his glass. "Did you think on my proposal, Miss Scott?"

I nodded my head. "Yes."

He moved his head slightly and advanced another step.
"Good." He moved most unsteadily toward the chair
near the fire and sat down. "Good," he said again and I
saw that as he sat there the rage in his eyes diminished
and I stood at the fireplace, still clasping the poker in
hand, holding it not for protection from Mr. Grayson, but
simply because I had not replaced it in its rightful
container.

I remained thus for but a few moments and could see
Mr. Grayson, by the light of the waning candle, sink
down into the comfort of the plush sofa. I saw that his
decanter and glass were dangling precariously close to
the floor, slipping more and more from his grasp and I
reached out for them before they spilled upon the wood.
Mr. Grayson momentarily opened his eyes wide as I

loosened his fingers and took the set from him and placed them on the table. Then, thinking that he was asleep, I began walking out of the room.

"Miss Scott." Mr. Grayson's speech was slurred both from the excess of the drink and from the lateness of the hour. "Miss Scott . . . Ma'am."

"Yes, Sir."

"Do not go." It was not a command yet I knew I had to remain. His head drooped slightly and his frenzied eyes focused on me.

"The room is chilly . . ." I began. "The fire . . ." but before I had a chance to answer fully Mr. Grayson had fallen asleep, rousing himself only one or two times more to call out indistinguishable words. He rearranged himself on the sofa and I debated as to whether I should leave my employer alone in the cold room. I thought perhaps to call Mr. Keanne but I immediately rejected the idea because it was late and I did not want to summon the old servant from his own warm bed. And so I sat down, across from him, and watched as Mr. Grayson sometimes flailed out from his restless sleep.

So this is what Mr. Grayson did when he took leave of me in the evening! I had always envisioned that he attended to his books and accounts, but seeing him in this unkempt state I realized that the poor gentleman turned to drink at the end of the day rather than to his journals.

I sat there for a few minutes, feeling the chill on my arms and pulled my shawl around me for warmth, hearing the last sparkings of the fireplace, and contemplated Mr. Grayson. Surely if I were to consider his marriage proposal, his nocturnal behaviour would have to be discussed and I wondered what form of questions I should put to him to explain his comportment.

302

Mr. Grayson continued to sleep—no longer calling out—and I had an opportunity to observe the man. How fine a countenance he had—and yet, how sad it was. If I agreed to his marriage proposition, for indeed it was just that and not a marriage proposal, would the worry lines even now furrowing his brow lessen? Would I be able to attend to his household needs so that he would notice and accept me? Or would I forever remain, in his eyes, even after the ceremony, only his children's governess?

I wrapped the stole tighter around my shoulders and body for there was now a distinct chill—a different kind than I had been experiencing—that had lately invaded the room and suddenly I realized that the heady aroma of roses now completely masked the odor of charred wood. I looked about me—half-hoping that I would see something or someone—Rosamunda—but as on the other occasions, there was no one in the room with me save the sleeping Mr. Grayson. The sweet scent continued about the room and I saw Mr. Grayson's eyes glimmer briefly.

Presently my employer opened his eyes and sat up and stared at me with steady, yet hooded, eyes. "I wait, Ma'am" he cried out searching all about the room. I was perplexed and Mr. Grayson turned to me once more and yelled, "I wait, Ma'am, because that is what I must do. That is all I can do," he said with a sob and then added, "I wait for Rosamunda . . . my fair Rosamunda," and the sound of his voice, a deep guttural sound, penetrated the air just as the scent of roses became pure and intense and seemed to fill the entire room. I saw Mr. Grayson look around quickly and then just as suddenly fall back upon the pillows and close his eyes. Even the rhythm of his breathing seemed more relaxed as it returned to normal and I saw the lines on his face smooth in peacefulness.

So Mr. Grayson also knew the secret of the rose fragrance. I drew my shawl even tighter around me both to warm me from the cold and to protect me from whatever was now in the room as all around me the incense grew stronger. It was as though something . . . someone . . . Rosamunda? was circling me—demanding that I acknowledge it, demanding that I confront it. I felt another moving chill in the air, this time of something passing me, and I watched spellbound as the flames in the fireplace railed up and then back toward the far stones— away from the room—as though the blaze itself was reacting to an unbidden and unwanted intruder. I shuddered and moved closer to the fireplace although it afforded me little heat. I stood still, letting whatever was in the room envelop me. I held my breath—afraid to make a sound or a false move. My stillness lasted but a few seconds before the aroma of the roses retreated and I smelled only the pungent ashes. I waited a few more minutes until I was sure the sweet scent was gone and I was positive that Mr. Grayson remained fast asleep. I then pulled the bell cord summoning Mr. Keanne and presently the servant appeared in the room.

"Your master has fallen asleep," I said quietly lest I disturb Mr. Grayson. The faithful elderly retainer looked quickly at his sleeping master, then to the half-filled crystal decanter and glass setting on the table, and then finally at me.

"Aye," was all he said and I hurriedly left the room although I do not think that Mr. Keanne would have asked me any questions about what had transpired this evening.

Chapter 31

All morning the sky deepened to a dark grey—the tell-tale sign of a turbulent change in weather and one that caused much consternation to the staff. The half-light that invaded the house gave a sense of gloom to the dwelling until finally, about the noon hour, it began to snow—huge white flakes that floated gracefully to the ground in a never-ending stream from the heavens. It changed the mood of the servants for where before there was malaise there was now a reason to smile as the rapidly changing landscape outside the windows altered not only nature but the general spirit of Ganymede House. The children—when they first saw the first flakes of snow that fell upon and lightly covered the bare branches of trees and shrubs—were enchanted with the sight and I promised them that after our lessons we would go out and walk the grounds.

The early snowfall brought an unusual amount of activity within the house for it soon became the topic of gossip and discussion whenever the housemaids or servants met on their rounds of duty. It was a change of scene for all of us and even Mr. Keanne would peer out of the window and speak of the other heavy snows that had fallen here in the north of England. It was a welcome turn—an air of frivolity—and one that changed the bleak scene within the house to one of lightness and gentle murmurings and I supposed that this was the way the house was when the Lady Rosamunda was alive. It was a new Ganymede House that I saw on this afternoon.

Later, as I had promised, the children and I donned warm clothing and boots and—despite Mrs. Keanne's dour looks and mumblings about "coughs" and "sickness" as we departed—we went outside to walk in the cold air. The gaiety had infected the children and it warmed my heart that they would cavort and play in the already gathering soft white banks forming along the walks. I watched as they behaved much like other children I had known in London—making footprints and long trailing footlines in newly-fallen snow . . . catching snowflakes as they fell from the sky onto their shoulders . . . and even balling snow and throwing it at treetrunks. It was a sight I enjoyed and I could not but feel happy that all my ministrations and work had finally gotten Virgil and Antonia to smile and when I heard the delighted laughter of the children I knew that, if only for today, they were indeed acting their age.

I joined in their game of snowflake catching and as I did so I looked up and saw Mr. Grayson standing at an upper window, a curtain pulled back so that he could view us better and yet, when I stared at him, he immediately let the curtain fall back to its usual position and his image quickly disappeared. I learned not to puzzle such things and to accept them as they were. Whatever Mr. Grayson saw and thought this day was of no concern to me now, I had time enough this evening to think on it, and I turned my attention back to the children.

Virgil and Antonia had begun shaping large balls of snow, rolling them down and around. I suggested that we continue with the game and fashion a snowman for all to see. The idea was quickly agreed upon and we spent the better part of a half-hour packing and sculpturing the soft dry flakes into a reasonable semblance of a short squat man. We found two partially covered stones for eyes and a broken twig for a somewhat elongated nose and when we were through fussing and decorating the three of us stepped back and admired our rotund creation. It was a figure that pleased the children and one that would welcome guests to Ganymede for the snowman stood sentinel quite close to the front portals of the house.

After one last glance at their artistic endeavor and because we were now becoming quite chilled, we returned to the house and even Mrs. Keanne had to smile and make a fuss when the children implored her to look at what they had created. She praised the children, shooed them upstairs to change to warm clothing, and promised them some hot milk-tea and a slice of cake "for all your hard work." To me she offered a slight smile, a begrudging courtesy to the children's happiness, yet still muttered words like "chills" and "inclement weather" as she made for her kitchen. How much happier we all would be if the lady would only recognize that she and I were on the same side. We both wanted only the best for the children. I sighed, then hurried to my own room to change into drier clothes.

The snows continued through the afternoon and into the evening hours and by the time the children had been dispatched to their beds there still seemed to be no let-up in the fierceness of the storm. The house was warm yet I felt a sense of restlessness and when Mr. Grayson excused himself early from the table—again pleading an excess of work—I wandered the halls not content to stitch and yet not really wanting to take to my room. I had thought Mr. Grayson would refer to last evening's encounter, but again, as his way, he neither explained nor apologized for the evening and it was as though the event had never happened.

I paused once or twice to watch the swirling flakes as they clustered in the corners of the leaded windows that had not yet been shuttered against the night winds. It was a sight I had not remembered for some months and it brought back kinder and gentler moments of my life and my days in London. Would this have been the city I would surely have been joined by friends and we would have spent happy moments outdoors laughing and telling stories as we walked in the city streets near our home. It was a sight that I longed for momentarily and one that I thought I could duplicate if I could but stroll close to the house here at Ganymede.

I told Mr. Keanne of my intentions and though he suggested that someone from the house—Tillie, Old Martin, or even himself—accompany me I resisted. It was a feeling—a reminiscence—that I wanted to recapture and having anyone with me would dilute the pleasure. I did promise Mr. Keanne, as he insisted, that I would stay close to the house and not venture too far and that I would return as soon as I felt chilled. This seemed to assuage the good gentleman's peace of mind and I set out determined that my walk would be no longer than a few moments yet just enough time to retrieve memories of my lost life.

I had not gone far when the doors of Ganymede swung open and Mr. Grayson stood silhouetted in golden light. "Miss Scott . . . if you please." I heard his voice through the soft sounds of the snow hitting the ground and I stopped, waiting while my employer caught up with me. "I should tell you, Ma'am, that I do not like your strolling the grounds alone in this weather. It is not a fit evening for anyone to be out."

I was glad that it was cold for the heat that was rising to my face turned chilly. "I will not chance wandering too far, Sir. It was only that this weather reminded me of my former days." I looked at him. "Please do not trouble yourself, Sir. I will be careful. I only intend to walk as far as the end of the house and back. Only enough to breathe the crisp air."

Mr. Grayson extended his already snow-flecked arm to me. "If it does not displease you, Ma'am, I would prefer for you to have an escort. I will not interfere with your remembrances."

I took his arm. "Certainly," I said for I knew that I could not refuse his offer and together we strolled in the frosty air not saying anything for a few minutes and thinking our own thoughts. Mr. Grayson did not tell me how he came to know that I was walking alone outside and I could only suspect that Mr. Keanne, in his worry, happened to mention it when his master spoke to him.

The landscape of the estate was bathed in a reflected white from the snows and the full pale moon and everywhere I looked I could see, through the ever-falling snowflakes, the sparkling rime as it crusted and formed on the icy drifts against the bushes and trees. It was a tranquil scene and one which belied the tone of the estate and I shuddered as I involuntarily recalled all the sinister happenings of late.

Mr. Grayson saw me shiver and suggested that we return to the house but I begged him to allow me one more turn around the gardens and without commenting on my request, he directed me past the house, toward the side near the Greek maze. In this light the entrance to the garden seemed even more forbidding and I was glad when we turned and silently began our walk back to the main house.

"Have you thought of my proposal, Ma'am?" It was such a direct question to be issued at this moment . . . in this quiet.

"I am considering it, yes."

"Good. Then we will not discuss it further." We resumed our silence until we passed the snowman and he nodded to it. "That is the sculpture that Virgil and Antonia spoke of at dinner?"

"Yes. Although I dare say some of it seems to be sinking to one side. Perhaps tomorrow we will correct it."

We continued walking. "My wife, the children's mother," he amended quickly, "enjoyed playing with the children, too. Although she much preferred the summer weather." He looked back toward the maze. "It was her favorite time of the year."

"I enjoy the winter time, Sir. I think I like it best, when the cold comes for then I enjoy . . . I did enjoy . . . ," I corrected myself in deference to my new position and home here, "the snugness of our home with my family and friends. It seemed comfortable to be surrounded by such love on those days . . ." I sighed for the memory of times past filled me with a sudden flooding of sadness. I pretended that the wetness on my cheeks was from the melting falling flakes. "I do beg your pardon, Sir . . ." I said for Mr. Grayson stopped suddenly in his steps and looked at me.

"I am sorry," he said gently, "for the pain of your remembrances." I saw that under his hat his features had softened. "I, too—" He spoke the words mutely and then shook his head and continued soundlessly walking in small steps with me and we approached Ganymede.

"So, you prefer the cold." Mr. Grayson's voice was low and I knew not whether he spoke to me or to his own mind. "Then you will be my winter wife," he said spontaneously and without thinking. I shivered as I heard the words. Surely Mr. Grayson knew that his statement would cause me pain but I said nothing and I thanked him for his attendance on me and went swiftly to my room.

I lay awake a long time thinking of Mr. Grayson's words, wondering about his intent and his plans for me. How strange it is that he should have, instead of a sunshine wife—Rosamunda—who preferred the warm weather, another lady—I— who would prefer the cold. "You will be my winter wife," he had said and the phrase made me again shudder in trepidation.

The next morning, after breakfast, the children persuaded me to postpone our classes for a short while— cajoling me into a few moments outdoors. The snowfall had finally begun to cease—leaving barely a trickle of small flakes tumbling from the sky—and the entire accumulation was of such depth that only the most hearty hands were up and about their outside chores. Willie had already brought in a huge supply of wood to the house and the fireplaces had been set by the undermaids so that no fire would suffer from lack of replenishment. There was talk from Tillie and the other servants that traveling would be difficult for the next few days, perhaps as much as a week, and I was dismayed that our visit from Mr. Moore would have to be deferred.

Virgil and Antonia and I once more took up our heavy coats and boots and made our way past Mrs. Keanne who stood in the Great Hall and who once again stared at us with small eyes and a frown upon her face trying to intimidate me into changing our course. I ignored her and instead wished her a good morning as I went through the door and the children ahead of me ran toward the snowman.

I heard Antonia's shriek first. "Miss Scott! Miss Scott!" I ran toward her and saw that she stood before a pile of overturned snow—our snowman. No matter what I could say, I knew that the storms had not caused this damange. The main bulk of the rounded body was broken into small clumps and the head—or rather what was once the head—must have been trampled into the buildup of snow. Nothing remained of it and had we not known where the snowman had stood the day before we would not have found it. Although there were no large footprints in the vicinity because of the continuing storm, in my heart of hearts I knew that someone once again had wreaked something vicious and ugly upon us and was warning me . . . us . . . of danger.

I offered an excuse—that the snow had caused the slippage—to the children and suggested that we build another snowman later on. Mercifully, the suggestion was accepted without too much explanation. We even decided to ask Mrs. Keanne for some vegetables for the facial features and thus I was able to divert the children's attention away from the devastation of the first sculpture. Better to let them think that nature again proved her dominance over us human beings, but I knew that I would have to be more vigilant, especially now that I knew that whoever was responsible for this form of terrorism was snowlocked with us for the next few days.

Chapter 32

Tillie brought up the luncheon tray and put it on the set table. "Children will be glad to see their cousin, I suspect," she said as she buttered the bread.

"If and when he can get here." I glanced quickly at the quiet snow scene outside the schoolroom window.

Tillie seemed surprised. "But he's here, Ma'am. Came a little while ago. He's already been settled into his chambers and his horse has been stabled and I suspect he'll be staying until well after the holidays. I heard him speaking to Mr. Keanne—not that I was listening, mind you—that that is his intention." She busied herself with the serving tray. "The children will be happy for that."

"But the snows," I protested to the maid. "The roads are impassable."

"That may be, Ma'am, for I have no way of knowing, but he is here with his luggage." Tillie excused herself and when I sat down to offer grace before the meal my mind could not help but feel lighter. I could not wait to tell Mr. Moore about the destruction of the snowman and to let him know that I was relieved that he should be spending some time with us. I suspect my pleasure was such that on the last words of the prayer I spoke the word "Amen" a bit too loudly and forcefully and both the children looked at me and smiled. Thank Goodness, I offered another silent prayer, that they did not know why I was so relieved; Mr. Moore's visit again eased my mind slightly because, at least for the next weeks, I would be joined in my vigilance for the children's safety.

Mr. Moore and I spent just a few moments together that evening—the long day's journey that he endured had tired him and I thought it best not to speak of my discovery of the destroyed snowman. Tomorrow would be time enough, I reasoned, and when Mr. Moore excused himself early, fearing that the frigid cold combined with his difficult trip might lead to a cough and chills, I sat alone late into the evening. Mr. Grayson again was absent, and because I had nothing to occupy my mind and did not want to work with my hands I went into the library hoping to find a book or journal to amuse me.

The room was dark save for the glow from the fireplace and all the windows were shuttered, but fortunately I carried a candle. I proceeded to the shelves of books lining the wall. The light from the candle was sufficient to read by when I held it close to the books, but it could only cast large shadows upon the rest of the room.

"Good evening, Ma'am." I turned for Mr. Grayson's voice came from a darkened corner of the room.

"Good evening, Ma'am," he said again. I thought I saw his blurred shadow across the room and I curtsied slightly.

"Good evening, Sir. I do beg your pardon. I did not mean to disturb you. I was searching for something to read."

"Something to read, yes. Something to read . . ." I realized my employer's words—though not slurred—were heavier than usual and I could only surmise that he had again been too long at the decanter. "Read . . . read . . . read," he repeated to himself and I turned to go for I did not want a repetition of the other evening. "Don't go, Ma'am." Mr. Grayson's words were sharp and disjointed. I realized that my original assumption about his wine-taking was correct; that my employer had certainly been too long at the spirits. "Don't go, Ma'am," he said again and I pulled my shawl closer and set my candle down upon a table.

"Rosamunda always read, too . . ." he said and I understood that his invoking his late wife's name on so many occasions these past days surely tended to remind him of his pain and sorrow. "But she always used to read to the children . . . and to me. Lovely stories . . . lovely stories." He fell silent and then spoke in too loud a voice. "but the last . . . what I read for myself. That was the cruelest . . . the cruelest."

I hoped to placate my employer. "Do not trouble yourself now, Sir. Perhaps after the morning . . ."

Mr. Grayson stood up and I could see his dark-clothed figure emerge from the shadow and move toward me. I stepped back.

"You do not believe me, do you, Ma'am? You do not believe that my Rosamunda could betray me," His voice cracked. "That such a lovely creature could betray her husband." He stumbled forward and then stood upright as the light from the candle seemed to blind him momentarily. He held up his hands to his eyes. "Wait, Ma'am, I will show you," he cried out. "I will show you," he said and moved haltingly from the room. "Wait for me, Miss Scott. Do not leave." I heard his heavy footfall on the parquetry of the Great Hall and then no more and I knew that he had ascended the stairs.

I did not know what to do. If I chose to go to my room I did not know whether that would anger Mr. Grayson or if he would forget his purpose when he left me and fall asleep in his chambers. I sat a few more moments hoping that Mr. Keanne would appear but instead Mr. Grayson returned with a document in his hands.

"I have returned, Ma'am with the substantiation of my charges. Here is the proof, Miss Scott," he said and held out a piece of ledger paper. "I told you I had evidence of her faithlessness. We found this in the Greek maze on the day after she died. After the storms . . . after we took her body from the sea." He pressed the letter into my hands. "Here is the proof, Ma'am, of my wife's infidelity . . . of her treachery. You can not refute this." I saw that the gentleman had been driven to the brink of despair. "I had so wanted to believe that she was pure and good, but," he cried out to me, motioning toward the paper, "that is the proof. Can you not deny it? Can you not see my hurt . . . my wretchedness . . . my dishonour?" He wrapped his hands around the handle of the fireplace poker and pushed it across the bottom of the grate so that it screeched as it moved the bottom layer of ashes. "It is all gone, Ma'am. My love for Rosamunda is but ashes," he said and I heard a sob catch in his throat. "Do not tell me, Ma'am, that she was my faithful bride." He flung the poker down and it rested against the burning logs and became part of the flames so that retrieval was now impossible. "She is gone. Gone to her reward."

I did not answer for even as he spoke the scent of roses suddenly appeared in the room, flooding it with the perfume, and yet Mr. Grayson did not respond to it. It was as if he did not smell the incense and with each new outburst against his wife's memory the fragrance became more prominent.

"The maze," he suddenly said. "It must be destroyed. It was the scene of her assignation. Of her betrayal." I glanced down at the evidence Mr. Grayson had offered and even by the dim light I could see water-smeared curlicued writing on the lined paper. "Read it and then we shall say no more about the falseness of my accusations." He sat down and stared at the fire and I saw that his shoulders seemed to be hunched over the arm of his chair and even in my confusion and, yes, anger I knew the gentleman wanted very much for me to read the missile.

I tried once more to take the lady's position. "Whatever happened between you and your wife is not my concern, Sir." I stretched out my hand and offered him the letter but he shook his head.

"Read it, Ma'am," he goaded me. "I give you permission to read it."

The note was brief and simple:

"My beloved, Once more I cannot find the words to tell you . . . to remind you . . . that you have given me so much happiness. What has passed between us for these many years can only be a preface to what will always come. You have been the sole source of my joy, my happiness. I shall love you for all the days of my life . . . for all the days of eternity." The signature was a huge flourished "R".

"This does not prove anything, Sir. It could be an early attempt at a poem," I said though I hardly believed the excuse myself. Mr. Grayson looked down at his folded

319

hands and said nothing while I puzzled over the strange note.

I heard Mr. Grayson sigh. "Miss Scott," he then said in a more rational tone, "no doubt you wondered why I have proposed to you." He placed one hand over the other and rubbed his knuckles and continued with this new line. "Miss Scott, I must confess, Ma'am," he carried through and his words sent a sharp chill through my body. "I am afraid that I do things without benefit of restraint or thinking. There are unexplained . . ." I sucked in my breath and held it—afraid to make a sound and disturb this new train of confidences from my employer. "I don't know if . . . The doll, Josephine . . ." he said. "Antonia and Virgil . . ." He looked at me and the tumble of words came pouring out in straight sentences but incoherent meaning. "I need your help, Ma'am, not for myself but for my children."

I sunk back against the cushions of the armchair. Surely I had not heard correctly. Surely Mr. Grayson was not saying these things to me—divulging his most personal secrets. My hands trembled so that I could not re-read the note and I suddenly noticed that the scent of roses was suddenly enveloping us—strong and vivid and pungent.

Mr. Grayson turned and looked past me and cried out. "I am afraid I am going mad, Ma'am. There are so many things . . . the sounds . . . the odor . . . I cannot understand . . . I cannot understand." He lifted his head to me. "That is why I need you, Ma'am, not for me but for the children. To see that they are cared for . . . that they are loved and protected. To be sure that if something should happen to me that they are not disenfranchised. That Ganymede House remains with the Graysons." He

320

rubbed his knuckles once again. "I do not mean to harm them, Miss Scott. I truly love them, but I am afraid I am not responsible in some of my darker moments."

"Please, Mr. Grayson. Surely you are incorrect. Surely your pain can be resolved. Please let me help you . . . and the children."

"You cannot," he said harshly and the dark eyes flashed not unlike the first time I had seen temper in young Virgil's eyes when I challenged the boy. Mr. Grayson turned toward me and I could see the torment now etched across his face. "I am doomed, Ma'am . . . I am doomed." He stood up and paced the room and now thought after thought became entangled as he spoke. "I trusted Edward—I told him about Rosamunda and at first he did not want to hear. Edward disagreed with me but he is not a good falsifier, Ma'am, for then he told me everything. That Rosamunda was with someone . . . he could not identify the man. That he had overseen them in the maze." He looked at me and his eyes were wild. "I have never forgiven him for not informing me, for not telling me. It only made the agony worse, to know that I was betrayed by my wife and that my boyhood friend and beloved relation concealed it from me."

So that was the reason Mr. Grayson treated Mr. Moore so harshly. Why he refused to offer nothing more than the essentials of a good host and relative. Poor Mr. Moore. I could see his hesitation in speaking the truth to an enamored grief-stricken husband. Pity Mr. Moore for having discovered the deed and not knowing what was to be the right course.

"It must have been a difficult moment for Mr. Moore, Sir. I am sure he only wanted to protect you."

"No. No." He came before me and took one of my

321

hands. "Promise me, Miss Scott, that when we marry you will be faithful. That you will not . . ."

My heart ached for the gentleman. "When . . . and if . . . I make my decision to wed you, Sir, I promise that I will never play false with you. You have my pledge."

"And my children? You will love and protect them?"

I smiled at him. "That you may never worry about, Sir, for I love the children as my own."

"Good. Good. I will leave you now, Ma'am. I am tired. Thank you for your promise of fealty." He seemed revitalized. Bowing slightly, he said, "I wish you a good night." He left the room. With him, I noticed, went the fragrance of the flowers.

I had forgotten to give back the sheet of paper with Rosamunda's handwriting and I carried it to my room for I wished to be alone while I reflected on its meaning. I wanted to try and understand why Rosamunda had written the note.

I thought long into the early morning hours and finally, just as sleep was about to come, I realized that the alleged letter of betrayal may have been misinterpreted— that there must be some sort of a clue, an argument against Mr. Grayson's version. I struck a match and lit the tiny stub of the candle next to my bed and looked carefully at the writing. Yes, there was another answer. I took up the note and held it close to my eyes to be sure. The paper was from a journal, surely the lines on it indicated this, and therefore it now all seemed so simple. The letter was not a dispatch to an unknown lover but something Rosamunda must have written in her own private diary.

I put the paper on a table and snuffed out the candle. Tomorrow I would visit Rosamunda's room and search for a diary of her most intimate and personal thoughts. I had no doubt that I would discover that a page had been torn out.

The next morning, before breakfast, Mr. Moore came to the classroom as a surprise to his two cousins and this afforded me the chance to speak to him about my plan. I told him that I wanted to explore Rosamunda's room and although the gentleman made a small fuss about the safety and the propriety of my contrivance, he finally agreed and suggested that he accompany me.

Gaining entrance presented us with no problem. "I shall secure the key when I visit with the Keannes later this afternoon," Mr. Moore told me. "The keys to all the rooms are always kept on a circle on a hook in the kitchen. I shall merely retrieve them for a few moments and no one shall be the wiser. Although I must tell you, Ma'am, I certainly do not approve of what we are about to do."

"But if only to restore peace and harmony between father and children?" I asked and the good gentleman smiled.

"You are too kind, Miss Scott, too caring. Of course I will help you. Of course I will be your willing accomplice." Mr. Moore and I planned to meet in the corridor next to Rosamunda's chambers, after dinner, for now I knew not to expect Mr. Grayson to stay with us in the evening.

When the meal was concluded and Mr. Grayson left us—"Please excuse me, Ma'am, for I have pressing business"—I retired early myself and waited in my room for a few moments before I met Mr. Moore in the hall. The good gentleman had the circlet of keys in his hand and soon found the one that unlocked the door to the late

323

Mistress' room.

"Hurry, Miss Scott. We do not want anyone to see us," he said as we heard footsteps below us. "Mr. Keanne . . ." We both stepped quickly into the room and shut the door—being careful not to light our candles until it was closed tightly. "Now, Ma'am, where shall we look?"

I pointed to the escritoire near the window. "In there, Sir. I am sure she must have kept it there." I moved at once to the desk and pulled at the drawers, opening them and seeing that they revealed odd little silver and gold trinkets such as kept by ladies. One drawer contained dried rose petals—an addition I suspected put there by Mr. and Mrs. Keanne—and the faint aroma recalled me to the many times lately that the scent had descended upon and round me.

I pulled at the last drawer but it did not give way. "It is locked, Mr. Moore. I feel certain that it contains what we are searching for—that the journal has been put away from prying eyes." I tugged at the drawer pull. "Can you help me, Sir? I feel we must open it . . . must investigate it."

Mr. Moore tried once to move it. "I think we have been blocked, Ma'am, for surely it does not give way."

"Your keys, Sir. Perhaps . . ." I held my candle near to the keyhole to determine the size of the key needed to unlock the drawer. "Look for a small key, Sir, in wrought iron," I said pointing to the bunch of keys he held in his hand.

We used a haphazard standard of trial and error and shortly were rewarded, for the lock clicked and turned and when I pulled at it the drawer slid noiselessly forward and there, lying alone on the bare pine-scented wood, was a small daily journal.

I picked up the book. "Here, this is it, Mr. Moore. I believe that this will be the proof to show to Mr. Grayson." I leafed through the pages, turning them carefully, looking for the remnants of a sheet of paper that had been torn away. I did not read any of the entries for I vowed whatever the dead woman had written in secret should remain unread except for that one questionable page.

"Mr. Moore. Look. This is it." I extended the open journal to him. "Here is a half-page. It is a letter to Mr. Grayson but it has been torn away." I looked to where I knew the portrait of Rosamunda hung in the dark room and it seemed that for the briefest moment a ray of candlelight shone on the face of the lady and I could see the beckoning promise in her remarkable eyes.

Mr. Moore seemed stunned beyond words. "My dear lady," he said and I felt my cheeks warm at his salutation, "you have done it. My cousin will be appreciative beyond his wildest dreams." He moved closer to me and reached for the daybook.

"No, Sir. My sense of honour dictates that only Mr. Grayson inspect the diary. We cannot disturb Rosamunda's stilled voice."

Mr. Moore moved closer. "But we must compare, Miss Scott," he said. "Or else how shall we really know."

"I am certain, Sir. I am certain," I said and then lowered my voice as we heard the muffled footsteps of someone passing the room. I replaced the journal into its drawer. "Come, Mr. Moore, we must leave quickly before someone sees us." I blew out my candle and stepped to the door and opened it quietly and examined the empty hall. "Come, Sir. No one is about."

I could not wait for the following morning to share my discovery with Mr. Grayson and unlike any other day—and much to his surprise—I confronted my employer in the morning room where he was standing watching the still-frozen landscape of Ganymede.

"Mr. Grayson, if you please. I have something to tell you—to show you." Mr. Grayson seemed startled yet tolerant and I began my recital in a rush, not pausing for breath, hoping that he would listen to me and accompany me to Rosamunda's room for the proof of my story.

"I do apologize, Sir, for my boldness. I had no legitimate right to be in your late wife's room searching for what I thought would be proof. It is only . . . I know I should not interfere, Sir, but this is of such importance to you and your children. Please listen so that some of the wrongs can be righted." Mr. Grayson tried once or twice to interfere with my words but I begged him to heed me and hold his questions until I had finished.

When all was said I looked at my employer. "When your wife entered the maze on that fateful afternoon to sit for a while—when she sent Antonia back to the house—she most probably had the journal with her. That is probably where she wrote these words. Quietly . . . happily . . . on a late summer's afternoon in the warm sunshine. It was her own special moments of peace and quiet and the times when she could spend alone with her thoughts. Did you yourself not tell me that she loved the Greek maze and that she spent many moments there in private reflection and contemplation?"

I proffered the letter to him. "This was no love letter to an unknown lover. This was no act of betrayal. I beg to differ with you, Mr. Grayson, but this is not the letter of a woman about to betray herself or her family. Indeed, if

326

you read it rightly, you will see that this is a hidden love letter to a husband. See here, where Rosamunda refers to 'these many years,' she is speaking of you and your marriage." I rustled the paper. "I pray you read this note in another light, Sir. This is an affirmation of tranquility and happiness—a testimony to a wife's beloved husband. It is the most private of all thoughts of a woman who has set them down in her journal . . . to say things that she feels with her heart. They were for no one's eyes save hers. Surely you can see that—that the easy writing speaks not of betrayal but of eternal happiness and exultation with the one she has chosen and married. Here—she speaks of enchantments yet to come. You misinterpret, Sir. You have judged your late wife wrongly and unfairly and I know not why."

Mr. Grayson's eyes were closed in contemplation and he did not remonstrate with me, instead seriously considering the truth of everything I spoke. "If you have proof, then I have done a great disservice to Rosamunda," he said simply and I nodded.

"To that I must agree, Sir. But, pray, tell me how come you came upon this interpretation when it is so plain."

"Edward," he said.

I was puzzled. "But what of your cousin, Sir?"

"I was told . . . an unknown gentleman . . . in the maze."

I remembered Mr. Grayson's conversation to me when he first confided what he thought was Rosamunda's betrayal, how he had made his cousin tell him the truth. "Understand me, Miss Scott, although it is no excuse. I was in a melancholy state, Ma'am. My heart was broken. My beloved was dead. And when they brought the note in her handwriting to me, I . . ."

327

"I know you must have been mad. The pain—"

"I was berserk, Ma'am. It was the second of two devastating blows in as many days."

"Perhaps you misunderstood your cousin?"

"No." His word sounded like a shot.

"I concede—you were distraught—but what caused you to think that the good lady would betray you?" I began and then grew silent for I had no right to question him so. Mr. Grayson stared beyond me and I knew not whether I had convinced him of his wife's faithfulness or not and presently, after he had grown quiet and was deep in his own musings, he acknowledged me for the moment. "If you would leave me, Miss Scott, I would be grateful." He looked away. "I will search my wife's desk later."

My heart was heavy, for I realized that Mr. Grayson had not been truly convinced of my words, thinking me only a troublesome woman, and that he still held tightly to the memory of Rosamunda as an adulteress. I hoped he would find the diary for I knew not how to convice him by any other means.

Later, when I had had an opportunity to go over the morning's events, I thought it best to enlist Mr. Moore in trying to change his cousin's mind. I know not how the two of us could accomplish this, but I knew, for the children's sake, I should at least try. Perhaps Mr. Moore would have a way.

Chapter 33

ı

"Mrs. Keanne's in an ever so fitful mood this morning." Tillie put my tea tray down on my bedtable. "She's misplaced the ring of keys to the household and just discovered the loss. She found out about it when she went to the larder and couldn't open the door to it. She's had all of us looking for the circlet but it's nowhere in the kitchen, Miss. She even accused Mr. Keanne—imagine accusing Mr. Keanne—of taking it but everyone's denied it." Tillie prattled on as she drew the curtains wide open. "Of course, she could have mislaid them although that's not one of her faults. Sharp-eyed, she is, and very careful. Still . . ."

I kept my eyes to the teapot for fear that I would show by frown or speech that Mr. Moore and I had taken the set of keys. Yet I wondered why the gentleman had not replaced them sooner and thereby not called attention to the fact that they were used.

"I suspect they'll turn up, Tillie."

The maid curtsied. "Yes'm. That's what we all said——they're probably under a pot or put away by error with

329

the silver. Still, Mrs. Keanne is angry and has been calling out everyone."The maid shook her head. "It's a good thing I'll be in the nursery this morning for I won't have to hear her wrath."

We would have to be more careful and I vowed that when I met with Mr. Moore I would remind him to return the keys to their proper place although when we spoke last night after dinner I was quite positive he had assured me that the keys had been replaced. Perhaps he had restored them to another area. In any event I would speak to him this evening.

Tillie caught my eye later in the morning when I had set the children to copying a test. "Mr. Keanne said that Master would like to see you after the first half of lessons. He would be in the study all morning, Ma'am." I was surprised at this summons for never had the children's father interrupted their school day. When I went to him he sat in his den, a frown on his face, and after the briefest of salutations he spoke directly to the subject.

"I did not find the journal, Ma'am." His voice was flat and I stared at him in disbelief.

"I do not understand, Sir, for I replaced it myself. Perhaps you have looked in the wrong site."

"I searched the entire room."

"Even the locked drawer?"

Mr. Grayson seemed astonished. "There was no locked drawer, Ma'am. All opened easily."

I sat down in the nearest chair. Surely something had gone dreadfully awry. I distinctly remembered replacing the diary in the drawer and turning the lock, listening to its click, and then handing back the ring of keys to Mr. Moore.

"I do not understand, Sir. There must be some mistake." I stood up. "Please excuse me, Sir. I would like to check it again myself."

Mr. Grayson stepped close to me. "We shall go there together, Ma'am," he said and I saw a mixture of anger and confusion and even a glimpse of hope in his countenance.

But it was of no avail. It was as Mr. Grayson said. The drawers were all easily opened and the diary was nowhere to be found in the chambers. Someone obviously had seen Mr. Moore and me steal into the room and knew what we were searching for and removed it when we had both left. It was a sinister thought which I cared not to think about, for it meant that whoever was responsible for all the terror and catastrophe that had happened these past weeks was still at their evil purpose, still wreaking havoc on the family and the household.

"I do not understand, Sir. It was here. I saw it. Mr. Moore was with me, Sir. He saw it . . . although," I hastily added, "he did not read any of the entries. Perhaps if we find him he will tell you, also, and you will believe."

Mr. Grayson opened the door to the hall and waited for me to leave. "I think not, Ma'am." His voice was abrupt and disappointed. "We shall forget all this."

I looked at Mr. Grayson. "Tell me, Sir, is it that you disbelieve me? That you think I make up these tales?" I knew that my voice was much too dissonant yet I had to defend my words. "For I speak only the truth."

Mr. Grayson did not answer me. He closed the door to Rosamunda's room and stood there while I went angrily back to my pupils—waiting for the time when I could find Mr. Moore and tell him what had transpired between my employer and myself and implore him to also speak of our discovery to his cousin.

The afternoon passed slowly and when the lessons were concluded and I had free time I searched for Mr. Moore but could not find him in the house. Mr. Keanne told me that he was in the stables, with the horses, checking on a young foal, and I hurried there, cloaked in only a thin cape, despite the cold damp winds and blowing snow.

"Miss Scott, ye be catching your death coming out in this weather." Old Martin was patting the horse, Sabre, while Willie mucked out the stall.

"Is Mr. Moore here? I must speak to him."

The gardener inclined his head toward the outside. "He be up at my house, Miss Scott. Said he forgot something the night he stayed with me in my cottage. He'll be a-coming back soon, though." He looked at my wet cape. "Ye be going back and getting warm now. I'll see that he speaks to you in the house." Old Martin stroked the horse's flanks.

"When was he at your cottage, Martin?"

The old man took the unlit pipe from his mouth and held it by the bowl. "One . . . no . . . two nights ago, Miss. The night of the snowstorm." He sucked on the stem. "It was late—sometime about midnight—and he and his horse could barely make it to the house. Got as far as my cottage. I had been up for a little time—was roused from my bed by sounds I could have sworn were coming from Ganymede but when I went to the door I saw that it was Mr. Moore. Said he had just come off the main roads and couldn't go no further. Said he was worried about his horse. Its mane had been iced and matted with heavy pellets of frozen snow, and so we bedded the poor animal into the small shed with some warm straw. It was breathing hard, Ma'am, and I saw that Mr. Moore was in none too good a state either. He was too fatigued to travel anymore. I told him he was welcome to share my room and the gentleman made a wise choice for it must have been below freezing, not fit for anyone or any animal. He stayed over that night with me. Was tired, he was, and when I started off to attend to my chores the next morning he was still asleep. I left him some porridge on the stove just in case he was hungry when he arose and I just thought he would get here to the house on his own." He stepped aside to make room for Willie who was now sweeping close to us and listening to our conversation.

"Did he play a game with you, too?" Willie asked and when Martin just shook his head, the half-witted boy started speaking in his sing-song voice. "I seen him . . . I seen him . . . I seen him . . ." he repeated over and over again and then stopped and leaned on the broom handle. "He were playing a game . . . in the maze." Willie looked at Old Martin and continued sweeping. "Mr. Moore's a nice gentleman . . . a nice gentleman . . . played a game with me."

Martin made a nodding motion indicating that Willie was off again in his half-imbecilic world. "Aye," he said to the boy, "Mr. Moore's a right good gentleman. Now, you go on, Willie, you go on and do your job. Best we get to it now—I suspect another snowstorm'll be falling by tomorrow evening by the look of those clouds out there." Old Martin did not notice but his words about Mr. Moore froze me for never had the gentleman spoken about arriving at the estate grounds by night. Surely I must have heard him declare it, but then, I remembered, my mind was still preoccupied with Rosamunda's letter and Mr. Grayson's interpretation of it. No doubt anything told to me at that time would not have impressed me.

I heeded the gardener's advice and went back to the house for a change of clothing. I would speak to Mr. Moore later when I had the chance.

That evening the children stayed with us longer than usual for Mr. Moore began telling us stories of his recent travels. In a surprising and expansive mood, Mr. Grayson gave permission for Antonia and Virgil to remain at the dinner table. It was even more astonishing that he continued to sit with us and although he did not join in the conversation it was a most agreeable time. And while Mr. Moore spoke and regaled us with his tales and humour it was even possible for all of us to forget the ominous incidents at the estate.

Mr. Moore was a natural storyteller and at various points in the narration he would even mimic the voices and speech patterns of his characters. The children were enchanted and when the meal was finished and they finally were to be taken off to their beds Antonia turned and made a curtsy to her cousin prompting him to jump from his chair, doff an imaginary hat and make an over-elaborate and sweeping bow to the girl. It was a delightful act and the children imitated the gesture, bowing low to each other and laughing as they made their way up the stairs.

I thought that perhaps Mr. Grayson would heed my suggestion and speak to his cousin about the lost diary now but when Mr. Keanne brought in the silver teapot and tray of wines he waved the elderly retainer away. "I believe Mr. Moore and Miss Scott would prefer to sit in the parlor, Mr. Keanne." He turned to us. "I again have to absent myself. With your permission, Ma'am . . ."

So once more Mr. Moore and I retired to the privacy of

the room where we spoke of many things; the missing diary, the loss of the keys, and of proposals of marriage.

"Has Oliver been pressing you for an answer, Ma'am?"

I turned my head to the fire and nodded.

"And have you made up your mind?" I did not answer and I suspect Mr. Moore knew where my inclination lie. He grew silent. "Perhaps," he said after Mr. Keanne had come and stoked the fires, "you will still delay and think on mine, also." The sentence was formed in the fashion of a question and I could not help but agree to it although I knew that eventually I would have to assent to Mr. Grayson's offer. I had no other options for I understood that Mr. Moore's proposal only came from his incredibly kind and generous heart and not from any love or passion in my direction. It was a decent proposal from a decent man but I could not allow him to sacrifice his marriage prospects for me. I changed the subject and finally, after another half-hour of discourse, I retired.

I lay awake for a few moments, my candle already snuffed, staring at the swaying shadows that sifted through the shutters. Murky movement tugged at my brain trying to recall me to something. What was it? What was it? I lay still hoping that the inertia would help me concentrate for something seemed to stab at my memory. Yet I knew not what it was, or why it should prick at my mind.

At last, tired and unable to invoke it, I fell asleep still watching as the gloomy shadows danced capriciously on the ceiling and walls.

Chapter 34

It was another cold winter's day and true to Old Martin's prediction a second huge snowstorm was about to blanket the area. Already the household had settled into its isolated and solitary ways and with the imminent advent of an additional snowfall I knew that our estate would be closed off from all visitors for the next fortnight. It was not a prospect I relished for it meant that we would be cloistered with someone who meant us harm though I still did not know the reason. My only consolation was that Mr. Moore would also be with us in the house and could help to fend off any attacks that might befall us.

The sun had not yet shone that day; instead the ominous dark clouds hung heavy over the already whitened fields. I determined to keep a sharp watch on the children and although there was no need for me to stay with them in their rooms after classes I found petty excuses to be with them while they amused themselves.

Everything was settled and quiet in the schoolroom; Virgil was absorbed in a new book his cousin had brought

337

him and Antonia played with the rag doll Mrs. Keanne had fashioned to replace Josephine. Tillie was still about her household chores and when both children seemed tired and took to their beds for a nap I left them in the care of the maid—cautioning her to stay with them until I returned.

I had been absent no longer than an hour but when I returned to the nursery it was silent and Tillie was not in the room. I suspected that the maid had gone downstairs to bring up the tea tray. Before I could enter the bedchambers to wake the children, Tillie appeared, a frown upon her face.

"Miss Scott, is the young Mistress with you?"

I looked around the silent room. "Is she not here?"

Tillie shook her head. "I was only gone for a moment, Miss, but when I came back she wasn't in her room. She's not here, Ma'am."

I tried to keep the fear from my voice. "I'll check below stairs. Perhaps she is with Mrs. Keanne." I went swiftly to the kitchen and called for the child but she was nowhere about and Mrs. Keanne stopped rolling a pie crust and looked at me disdainfully.

"Miss Antonia's not been here for several days."

"Have you not see her today?" There was a slight rush of panic in my body.

The housekeeper folded her arms in front of her. "Not since this morning in the hall near her room." She looked at me and saw my face. "What is it, Miss Scott? What is it about Miss Antonia?"

I did not answer her and instead rushed upstairs to the nursery again and saw Tillie standing in the middle of the room. The young girl's face was contorted.

"Oh, Ma'am, I don't know what to do. The young

Mistress's cloak is gone. She must have gone outside." The maid made a choking sound, obviously frightened that her charge had slipped out without permission.

I looked out the window at the late afternoon light. "That's impossible. She wouldn't go without telling us, and especially not in this weather. It isn't like her to do something like this." My own hand began to tremble as I looked toward the window once again and saw that deepening grey clouds were rapidly gathering on the horizon. I nodded toward the schoolroom. "Master Virgil?"

"In his room, Miss."

I opened the door and rushed into Virgil's room and awoke the young boy who had fallen asleep reading his book.

"Your sister, Virgil, where is she?"

Virgil rubbed his eyes and then shook his head. "It's a secret, Miss Scott," he said and he started to smile.

"Please, Virgil. Tell me where she has gone." I took hold of the boy's shoulder, much too roughly I think, for I saw the merriment vanish from his eyes and a hint of fear and mistrust replace it.

I dropped my hands. "I'm sorry. Truly I am. But it's of the utmost importance that we find Antonia. Please tell me where she is . . . and with whom?" I tried not to raise my voice although every fiber in my body felt taut and the sounds in my throat wanted to escape as a scream.

Virgil started to smile again for he was sure that I had guessed the prank and I could see him trying to decide whether he should tell me the answers.

"All right," he said and I thanked Heaven for the past weeks of trust that dispelled his suspicions of me.

"Where, Virgil? Where?"

"They went outside, Miss Scott. To the maze, Miss . . . the Greek maze. She wanted to see what the statues would look like in the snow. He said it would be beautiful, Ma'am."

"Who said it, Virgil? Who?" I asked although I already knew it. The low bow . . . and the stranger outside my window. That was what had nagged at my memory last night. The low bow. I swallowed hard and tried to keep my voice and my emotions under restraint so as not to frighten the boy. Yet even as I fought to control my excitement his childish voice confirmed my fears.

"Cousin Edward, Miss. Antonia went with Cousin Edward. He visited with us while Tillie was away and told us about the snow and how he and our father played in it when they were children. Wonderful stories, Miss. And he said he would take us out if we wanted to go but he said not to tell anyone—that sometimes we're too restricted—and this would be our secret, Ma'am, that he would show us the maze." He jumped out of bed and listened as the clock's chimes cut through the room. "If you please, Ma'am, I'm supposed to join them soon. Come with me. Cousin Edward said when the clock struck four he would come for me and I was to meet them by the tower. He knows about our secret passageway, Ma'am, that's how they left without anyone seeing them. It's only a game." He reached for his coat.

"No! Stay here," I said. "It is beginning to snow and I would prefer for you to stay. We'll go another day—all of us—I promise." I touched the boy's cheek. "I'll fetch Antonia home."

"Please, Miss, you won't let her know who told on her, will you? It was to be our secret, just between the three of

340

us." The boy looked at me with wide innocent eyes. "Is something wrong, Ma'am?"

I tried to allay Virgil's concern. "No . . . no," I said. "I only did not know where your sister had gone." I turned to Tillie who had been standing in the background listening and watching as I spoke to Virgil. Her eyes were wide with apprehension and her mouth was slightly open, aghast at what she had heard and—I believe—surmised.

"Please, Tillie, tell Mr. Keanne," I said as I reached for my cloak, "that I have gone to fetch Miss Antonia in the maze." I looked at her directly in the eyes. "The snows . . . and the darkness." Tillie nodded. The servant may have needed extra instructions and reminders for everyday chores but I was eternally grateful to her for having taken my meaning so quickly.

"Very good, Ma'am," she said curtsying and rushing from the room.

"Please, Miss Scott," Virgil was now beside me, "please don't tell Antonia that I spoiled the game. She'll be angry with me."

I touched the boy's arm gently. "I am sure, Virgil, that your sister will not be angry with you ever." How to tell the boy that if what I suspected was true he had probably saved her life. "Stay, Virgil. Stay here. I shall return soon with Antonia."

Downstairs all was quiet and I knew that Tillie's information had probably been first met incredulously and then with horror as the household staff began to understand what might happen if we did not act quickly. No doubt the Keannes had already begun to martial the whole of the staff of Ganymede House.

I did not wait for the men to assemble—instead I went outside, pulling my cloak around me. No time must be wasted, I knew, if we were to trace Antonia and Mr. Moore. Oh how my heart ached as I admitted to myself that Mr. Moore—a favourite of the children and the staff and, in truthfulness, of mine—was the person who had maliciously stalked the children and me. There was no doubt now that he was the source of the trail of evil that afflicted Ganymede.

I shivered as an icy blast of wind swept past me and I pulled my cloak tightly about my body. The air had turned damp and clear. The peculiar smell of fresh snow was all about and already errant flakes had begun to escape from the bountiful clouds. The winds had begun to shift. The tall stately snow-clad elms—the trees that I had admired when I first spied Ganymede House—were bent low in obeisance so that in the deepening dusky light they began to cast shadows on the vast expanse of snow-swept lawn. The vanguard of the storm was rapidly approaching and I felt snowflakes fall upon my uncovered head and face and melt and I shuddered from both the chilling wetness and the thought of what I must do quickly.

I made my way painfully and slowly to the maze while at the same time faintly hearing the shouts of the men who were forming a troop back at the house. I moved as fast as I could although the deep snows of the last week made it almost impossible to advance with certainty and rapidness. The hem of my woolen skirt was now soaked through and I could feel the icy stiffness where the top of my boot and the wet rigid cloth met. Nevertheless I pressed forward—my pulse quickening and my breath coming from my mouth in small spurts. I had but one aim: rescue Antonia.

At last I stood at the entrance of the maze looking at

where a horse's hooves—Mr. Moore's steed?—were imprinted and I saw by the last rays of the December sun that the animal's tracks came from the direction of the tower. It was my only consolation for the deep impressions made it easier to pursue Mr. Moore and Antonia into the darker regions of the puzzle. I hesitated briefly at the entrance of the maze for the terror of my last visit to this scene stopped me, but as I paused a heady scent of summer roses suddenly engulfed me in a strong gust of chilled wind and I knew I was not alone.

"Rosamunda," I said into the frigid air and I understood that Antonia's mother was urging me on . . . urging me to find and save her daughter from her menacing cousin. I had no time to worry about my own fears. I hurried noiselessly through the snow-covered paths and came upon Mr. Grayson's horse, Sabre, standing silently tethered to a bare-branched tree. I knew it was another trick of Mr. Moore's to implicate his cousin. I hastened on—the scent of roses still surrounding me—and when I made a false turn in the ever darkening twilight, catching and tearing my skirts on a low-lying shrub, the odor became even stronger, as if it were forcing me to reverse and correct my pattern.

It was as though Rosamunda had taken control of my body and mind and was leading me into the rapidly darkening interiors of the maze. The snows had covered everything and encapsulated the branches and twigs in solid ice so that they shimmered as though they were made of glass and silver. One especially long branch brushed at my cheek and I felt the icy twinge of it as it scraped close to my eye but I did not stop.

I heard scamperings, but I had no use for the scratchings of the night animals or for the sounds of the trees bending against the snow-driven wind. I paid no attention to the small snow-laden branches snapping and falling with muffled thuds onto the white camouflaged paths. There was no time to falter—no time to panic. I had to get to Antonia.

At last, with the fragrance of the flowers still encircling me, I came upon the bower that led to the statues and as I entered I saw Mr. Moore with the child. They were seated on the snowy marble bench beside the stilled fountain. He was speaking to her and did not see me. I hung back, pressing myself against a snow-shrouded sculpture, trying to determine my next move. All about me the statues appeared like frozen sentries. The winds blew through the maze with piercing whistles. High above the maze the trees parted so that the last glimmerings of dusk descended on the smooth chiseled ice-clad faces and naked sculpted arms and caused hundreds of pinpoints of reflected silvery light.

Antonia turned at that moment and saw me. "Miss Scott, here," she yelled out in her innocent and unsuspecting voice. "Cousin Edward is showing me the maze in the snow."

Edward reached down and instinctively held fast to Antonia's arm, the child questioning nothing. Mr. Moore looked at me with slitlike eyes and all pretense finally was gone. I took one step toward them but he jumped up and moved backwards, shaking his head, looking threateningly at Antonia and warning me. I knew I could not dissuade him from his intent to harm the child, yet I knew that if I could occupy him with speaking he might relax his grasp on her.

Mr. Moore looked about the garden searching for the exit. He moved back one more step, close to the statue of the goddess, and its ever-extended arm touched his back so that he instantly turned. It was as though he noticed the resemblance to Rosamunda only now as the half-light glazed the chiseled creation, sending soft shafts of radiance to shine on the face of the goddess.

Mr. Moore's lips moved as though he were speaking silently. The quarter moon passed between the clouds and the trees and then in the punctuated light of the darkness the glowing face of the statue seemed at first pleading, then censuring . . . and then finally accusing. Mr. Moore, in confusion, released Antonia's hand.

In that moment I screamed to the child to run . . . run and hide and the girl, used to obeying my commands, ran off. I smelled the heady scent of the roses as it seemed to leave me briefly and for an instant, both Mr. Moore and I stood, transfixed.

"Why, Mr. Moore? Why?" I cried out and it seemed as if my voice echoed and re-echoed against the stones.

"You dare to ask, Miss Scott? Don't you know? I am the son of a poor gentleman. I have no prospects. My London debts, my gambling chits, are rising and my creditors are issuing summons. My reputation is fast dissipating and my life is in ruins." Mr. Moore advanced slowly toward me. "What was I to do? I had no other way. Oliver was my last hope but I could not approach him, not even when Rosamunda was alive."

He touched the statue. "She was beautiful and I loved her, Ma'am. I worshipped her. Yet she only knew Oliver from the time we were children. Damn Oliver!"

"The letter?" I asked.

"From her diary. I came upon her sitting here just as you suspected. I told her I loved her . . . that I always had . . . and I pleaded with her to come away with me but

345

she only smiled and told me that she could never betray her husband. She loved him."

I shivered as he laid bare his plans and I thought that allowing him to speak might force him to break his concentration so that I could escape.

"Surely there is some other way, Mr. Moore. Some way that does not include death" and then I looked at the statue and remembered Rosamunda and her fall into the sea. Mr. Moore was advancing toward me all the while.

"She became frightened and ran from me but I caught her and pulled her toward the cliffs." He looked at me pleadingly. "I had to, Miss Scott, for she would have told Oliver and then all help for me would have ceased." He moved around the maze, getting closer to me. "I did not mean to harm her . . . I did not! I loved her. I loved her."

I had to keep him talking as I tried to discern an escape route. "The doll Josephine?" I asked.

"I sneaked into the room that evening. The doll had fallen to the floor. I tried to warn all of you, but you did not heed me."

I looked around and saw a break in the shrubs and I edged toward it slowly so that in the blowing snow and deepening shadows Mr. Moore could not see my movements.

"It was to be so simple, Miss Scott. I had only planned to make people think that Oliver was mad. He had been brooding about Rosamunda's death and the letter and it would have been easy. I hadn't planned to hurt anyone else. I would have taken control of the Grayson fortune as the last adult in the family and I would have protected the children. I did not want to harm them." I could not see Mr. Moore too clearly now but I could hear his voice coming closer . . . stalking me. "But then he proposed to

346

you and I grew desperate, Ma'am . . . desperate. I knew I had to act quickly. I tried to alert you, but you did not heed the warning—much to my own regret, Ma'am. I swear that I did regret it, Ma'am, but I had no more time. I had no choice. I would have to kill Antonia and Virgil. And when they found Sabre in the maze they would have suspected Oliver . . . implicated him and . . ."

"And you would have had everything," I spoke more to myself than to Mr. Moore. Obviously, the man was quite mad!

"If you hadn't told me that you were seriously considering his proposal, Ma'am, I would not have been pushed into this contrivance." Mr. Moore's frenzied voice was very close now and I began to run.

I do not know how I found my way out of the maze. I only knew that suddenly ahead of me were the cliffs and behind me, Mr. Moore. I knew that I had to do something if I were to save myself. But what? I was tiring quickly for the snow was now being driven from fast-blowing winds. I knew I was retracing the steps that Rosamunda had taken that fateful summer's day, yet I could not turn any other way for Mr. Moore was fast approaching behind me. It was then my foot slipped in the snow and I fell. He quickly rushed toward me and grabbed hold of me.

I tried to stand fast to my position but I could feel my feet slipping beneath me in the ice-crusted snow. Mr. Moore's arms tightened about me, half-pulling and half-pushing me toward the edge of the cliffs. I could hear the pounding of the furious and cold waves as they broke over the sharp rocks below. I pushed at him but to no avail.

"Mr. Moore, please . . . please think of what you are about to do. You have surely lost your senses." He did not answer me and I knew that he had gone past the boundary of reason. Yet I still hoped to distract him. "Why, Mr. Moore? Why?"

"I am sorry, Miss Scott, but I have no choice. No choice at all," he said and suddenly the scent of roses swirled over and around the two of us so that even Mr. Moore turned—wild-eyed and frightened—to look for the origin. It was then we both saw the torches from the household staff advancing upon us and I could make out the figure of Mr. Grayson progressing toward the two of us.

"Edward," his cousin yelled. "Let Miss Scott alone. Release her, Edward . . . let her go!"

But Mr. Moore was far too crazed to heed anyone. "Stay," he yelled to the men as he put his arm around my shoulders and pulled me to the brink of the cliffs. "Do not come any farther," he shouted as his cousin continued to advance toward us. I was terrified that one or both of us would slip and plunge into the ocean below.

I heard the growling of the dog, Euripides, and could hear Old Martin telling him to be silent. And then it all happened so swiftly. The smell of the roses intensified. The falling snow whirled around us and Mr. Moore released me and began flailing at the air as though fighting off an unseen presence. The scent was more concentrated now and Mr. Moore, in his attempt to thwart something that was about him, paid no more heed to me and I ran from the cliff to the safety of Mr. Grayson's arms.

Mr. Moore balanced precariously on the edge of the cliff, and at one point I heard him cry out, "No, no!" The whole of the night clouds descended and the sky darkened to its deepest grey. The moon was hidden behind the clouds, only briefly showing through them, so that it intermittently cast a cold sparkle on the cliffs and I could make out in the curve of the land the unrelenting sea splashing high over the rocks below. It was a foreboding sight, one that I had never seen before nor wish to see again: the black skies, the streaming white snow, the dark sparkles of the limestone cliffs, and the frothy silver-white ruffles of the crashing waves combining in a majestic but punishing splendor—A time of judgment.

Mr. Moore jabbed once more at the air and took another backward step to the sea, as if he was being forced, and his foot slipped under him on the new-fallen snow and his body arched high. His head wrenched back as though someone had given him a mighty shove and above the deafening din of the waters I heard his last chilling scream—"Rosamunda!"—as he fell to the jagged rocks.

Euripides kept tugging at his leash, snarling and growling, and finally with a great show of strength the dog snapped his restraint and ran toward the edge of the cliff and sniffed at the ground where Mr. Moore had stood moments before. Old Martin walked to where the animal, now quieted, sat, and he stroked its wet fur. The snows continued to swirl more furiously, but even in the dark and half-concealed light I saw the gardener pull something from his jacket pocket and hurl it savagely into the water. I caught but a flicker of it but I could detect from the light of the torches that is was a bit of blue crystal—part of Josephine's eye—and I saw the look of hatred and scorn on the old man's face as he completed his mission. He caught me looking at him and shook his head.

"There be no one ever again to hurt the Grayson family, Miss. No one to ever do harm to Ganymede House. The lovely Rosamunda . . . the lovely Mistress." He glanced back down at the raging sea. "She'll not be restless anymore."

Mr. Grayson now stood scanning the tumultuous waters. I approached the brink of the cliffs very carefully and looked down at the relentless angry sea but saw no signs of Mr. Moore.

"He could not have lived," Mr. Grayson said. "No one has ever survived the fall."

I continued looking at the waters as they rose up and slapped at the huge jagged rocks. "He was pushed."

Mr. Grayson shook his head. "His foot slipped and the earth gave way."

"No," I insisted, "he was pushed. I saw him and I heard him cry out."

Mr. Grayson looked to the far regions of the ocean. "I heard nothing . . . nothing but the sound of the sea," he said taking my hand and guiding me away from the cliffs and all around me, despite the spray of the cold salt water, was the scent of fragrant summer roses.

Epilogue

There are some things that can never be explained, that have to be taken on faith. Like the love of a mother reaching out from her own grave to protect her young.

I know that we will never again smell the mysterious scent of the roses and the thought made me sad. I had become accustomed to it and had found myself forming a bond with someone I never knew.

I had gone to Rosamunda's room after the tragedy and sat for several hours staring up at the picture of the beautiful golden-haired young woman in the white dress. I had hoped to assure her that she need never worry again—that Antonia and Virgil would always be safe and loved. I think that is what she wanted—and that is what she needed to be told—that her children would never be in danger again. She could rest eternally now.

I put my hand to the outstretched hand in the picture—the one offering the rose and touched it very gently.

"Sleep now, Rosamunda. Your children are safe and

your husband at last knows the truth. They will always love you. This I promise you. Go in peace now, Rosamunda." I walked away from the picture and stood by the window and smelled the strong scent of the roses for just a brief moment. "Go in peace," I repeated as the fragrance vanished from the room.

I must go down now and speak to Oliver . . . to tell him that I shall always trust him. Ganymede House will return to its rightful place in the scheme of the countryside; we will go through the seasons and the years in peace and there will be love and happiness here once again. Things will change. We will grow old. But no matter how long I live I will always remember the scent of the roses . . .